This work is dedicated to Debbie

from the twice-returned

The Snowhammer

The First of the Series

By J.F. Leigh

"Any sufficiently advanced technology is indistinguishable from magic."
Arthur C. Clarke

CONTENTS

Postern Gate

Two lines of almost-naked men stood shivering in the thick autumn fog. They waited patiently on the road in utter darkness under the trees. Their thin clothes were bound tightly to their cold bodies. Their faces and clothes were streaked with river mud. Each man carried a bundle on his left shoulder. The first twenty ranks carried bundles of twigs. Each bundle was bound with cords to stop it moving or rustling. At the heart of the bundle was a wooden vessel filled with oil and carefully stopped. The next twenty ranks carried bundles of heavier trimmed branches, also with an oil-filled vessel at the centre. The last dozen men, all big fellows, carried a log apiece. Around the wood-bearers, silent rows of archers crouched in the undergrowth on either side of the road.

At the head of the column stood a handsome man with a scar on his forehead. His name was Colonel Bdescu. He wore dark breeks and a small black satchel slung across his back. The men watched him. He looked at the sky. The darkness was almost absolute, no star showed in the gloom. The fog was at its deepest. He raised his right hand. The two leading men stared at him. The second pair of men raised their right hands and placed them on the shoulder of the man in front. This movement rippled back through the ranks until every man in the column had gripped a shoulder.

Distant sounds broke the silence of the night. From the far side of the walled city came muffled shouts and the clash of arms. As soon as the noise started, Bdescu turned and beckoned to the two men leading the column. They saw the flash of his teeth as he smiled at them. They started to shuffle forward. They watched his feet as he walked carefully in the centre of the road. The column slowly moved forward at a cautious walk. No sound came from the men.

The road sloped down to a small postern gate, which was let into the back wall of the enemy city. As the darkened men neared the high walls they hunched instinctively again the strike of an arrow, a stone or a spear. But the sentries high above them chattered excitedly about the attack happening on the opposite side of the city; on walls that they could not see. They turned their backs on their watch and clustered around their officers, demanding news of the distant battle.

Unseen in the darkness and fog, the column walked down the slope from the trees towards the postern gate. No man was cold now. The heat of fear warmed them. Unarmed and unarmoured, they would be target practice for their enemies on the walls above, if the fog broke and the sentries detected them. Sweating, they fought to hold their fear as they plodded towards the stout wooden gates that seemed never to come closer. Discipline held them in ranks, steadied their pace and kept them moving stolidly onward.

The first two men reached the postern gate. They placed their bundles carefully, forming a mat that spread from the gate out about four paces deep. As each man placed his load, he turned and walked back down the queue of waiting men, keeping his pace and discipline. The kindling was placed first. The heavier branches were carefully stacked on top of them. Time passed with agonising slowness. By now more than half the column was setting off back towards the trees. The scarred Colonel stayed. He pointed where the bundles must go. Finally, the logs were laid and the door was banked with timber to almost head-height. The last but one man set off and still no alarm was raised from above.

Bdescu waited, seemingly oblivious to fear. The column was half way back to the trees when a shout sounded from above, muffled by the fog. A trumpet smartly followed it. Bowstrings snapped high above his head. The escaping men broke into full flight, haring towards the trees. The Colonel could no longer see them. He unslung the satchel and opened it. From inside he took a torch with a wooden shaft, its head soaked in pitch. He took an iron pot from the satchel, packed inside a padded bag. Keeping the pot in the padding, he took off its lid. He blew on the hot coals within and they burned up brightly. Putting the pot on the ground, he placed the head of the torch inside. For one awful moment, nothing happened. Then the torch caught fire with a snap. He walked deliberately along the line of firewood, setting light to its whole length. When he was certain it was alight, he threw the torch on to the blaze, took a deep breath and pelted towards the trees. He heard arrows hum by and strike the ground. He heard the crash of a catapult. Blazing straw was flung into the air so that the archers could see him. But his own archers could now see the battlements. They let fly instantly and he heard some yells from above and behind him. His legs churned. His lungs burned. Something struck his back, high on the shoulder blade. He staggered but stayed on his feet. He reached the trees. He knew that now he was out of range. Men crowded around him, cheering. He looked back and saw that the searing heat of the fire was tearing at the enemy gate. The thick cloud of oil-smoke roiled up the wall, choking the defenders and clearing them from the battlements above the gate. Other defenders still shot their missiles from further along the walls but their range was extreme, the light was poor and the fog thick. They caused no harm to the attacking forces. They heard enemy officers calling for their defenders to stop wasting arrows.

"Cvelthan!" called the injured officer. "Pull this arrow out of my shoulder and tie a bandage over it. And bring my hauberk and gambeson. Lively now!" A hugely-muscled, very tall man leapt into action. "Yes, Colonel Bdescu!" he bellowed.

As the blaze roared, the men stripped off their darkened garments and donned their regular equipment. Underwear first, then tunics and hose. Next they pulled on the padded gambeson. They struggled into mail hauberks, knee boots and leather gloves. In the darkness there was much tripping and cursing. The fear was running free now. The officers had metal helms. The sergeants wore leather caps. All carried round shields and short lances. Swords were strapped across their backs and all carried a long knife clipped to the back of their shield. They tied wetted neckerchiefs across their lower faces to protect against smoke. Their clothing was already dampened, ready for the heat.

A squad of slave-soldiers arrived, hauling a strange vehicle. It had small, wide wheels with iron bands around them. It had a narrow, flat platform and a pent roof of thick timber covered in panels of copper sheeting. It was heavy and hard to control. Iron doors at the front closed it. It was open at the rear. The iron doors had viewing slits and the front wheels were steered by ropes from inside. The slave soldiers aimed it carefully at the blazing gate.

The Colonel, his wound now bound and his armour on his back, stood on the platform at the rear of the contraption. He spoke to the men who clustered around him.

"They can't stand in ranks behind the gate because of the smoke. They'll think we cannot attack until the gate is cool enough for us to break it down. They'll stand back and wait for us to attack. They'll guess we'll come at dawn. They've sent for reinforcements but they won't get many. The all-out attack by our army at the Northern gate will mean that very few reinforcements will come to this side of town. They'll think that the postern's a much smaller gate and a few good men should be able to hold it. The towers that protect the gate are deserted because they're filled with smoke. We have to get through the gate and hold the lane behind it until our main force can follow us in. It will be hard, close fighting. The ones who stand and keep standing will prevail. If you fall, so be it. If you run, you risk the abhorrence of God for you will have condemned your mates to certain death. But none of us will run. All will stand. Many of us will die. Do not worry; you do the work of the Emperor, Holy God's representative on this Earth. God will greet some of us before the day is out. If you see Him before I do, put in a good word for me, lads!" They roared for their Colonel.

He stepped down from the cart and watched the blaze intently. The heat had cleared some of the fog and he could count the helmets on the battlements. When he adjudged the gate weakened enough, he gave the command to board the cart. He sat at the front to steer. His twelve men sat behind him. Each man was hand-picked for steadiness, valour and skill. The two men behind him, Cvelthan and Fenjent, were his Guard captains. He whistled. The slave soldiers pushed and the strange cart rolled down the slope out of the trees towards the burning gate. He heard Fenjent say a prayer. They gathered speed, faster than a man walking now. Behind them the column of spearmen raised their pace to a jog.

The arrows struck the roof of the cart with sharp clacks. Behind, the first cries of pain came from men struck by missiles. He heard the deep thump of a catapulted stone striking the earth and thanked God it had missed the ranks of men.

He had expected more steering to be needed but by good luck the cart tracked neatly in the rutted road and almost aimed itself at the gate. The shouts from above had a note of fear, now. "Faster!" he called. Men pushed at the back of the cart. The speed increased and they began to gather momentum. Now they moved faster than the men could run. He began a prayer of his own. There was a mighty crack from just over his head. He flinched. A heavy stone had struck the roof and a ragged crack rimmed with splinters had opened just by his ear. "Watch out, lads. You don't want a splinter in your eye as you charge out. Pass the word back to the column."

Each man noted the steady calm of the Colonel's voice and took comfort from his confidence.

He corrected a last wobble and the cart struck the gates at speed. He was flung forward, his forehead striking the metal doors. He leaned back and kicked at the doors. They did not move. For one second he thought that the gates had buried his strange battering ram and he was interred in a blazing grave. He gritted his teeth and kicked again. The doors flew open. He could finally see into the city after four months of siege.

"On me, Trusted Men! For Clan, Emperor and God!"

He leaped down from the cart as the defenders ran down the lane towards him. His men clambered out of the cart and formed line across the narrow street. His twelve Trusted Men were the front rank of the shield wall. They moved forward as far as possible and put their shoulders to their shields. Behind them the following troops climbed through the tunnel formed by the cart which was wedged in the still-burning gateway. Men arrived quickly, but not before the defenders crashed into the shield wall.

The line buckled back under the impact. The spears were gripped tightly and in the darkness, fog and smoke the defenders ran straight onto their points. Screams split the foul air as men struggled hand to hand. In that second between the impact and the reinforcements piling out of the tunnel formed by the cart, all was at risk. The Colonel raised his voice. But it stayed calm and inevitable.

"Steady Lads! Keep your line and remember your drill. Shoulders in, keep the shields up. Push from underneath with spears. Go for the legs and belly."

The spears were shortened, their points and edges honed over weeks of preparation. They jabbed out from between the shields with deadly effects. Gutted defenders fell screaming to the cobbles. Yells, grunts and oaths rang out in two languages. The defenders tripped over the bodies of their fallen comrades and lost momentum. The Colonel's troops were well-trained veterans. The line held fast and pushed the enemy back, stepping over the dead, stabbing down to finish the wounded. Fresh men were now packing in behind them. Shouts of encouragement echoed in the narrow street. The gates fell down in a blazing curtain, crashing onto the cart.

Outside the gate, the second wave of soldiers had grasped the ropes trailing from the cart. In lines, they dragged cart and the remains of the gate out of the gap and off to the side. The archers above them had deserted the battlements, called down to the lane to assist the defence. The invading soldiers could work unopposed. They cleared the gateway, stamping on the last few burning spars as they tramped through the narrow gateway and into the salient.

The defenders mounted a second charge. They rushed down the lane, bravest to the front. Some swung long-hafted axes at the fence of shields. They tried to slip between the spear points and hook the axes over the Imperial shields. As they pulled the shield down, the next man would try to get a sword strike in at the face of the exposed invading soldier. For a terrifying moment, it worked. Three or four men went down, screaming. A victorious shout sounded from the defenders.

One shout broke off in a gurgle as the Colonel stabbed the man in the throat. He slashed the edge of his shield across the knees of another then stabbed him in the groin. The spear, wedged between bone and armour, was torn from his grip as the enemy died. He flung his hand over his shoulder, drew his sabre and brought down a third man with a cut to the skull that cleft helmet and head. This ferocity caused a moment of hesitation in the enemy. Nobody wanted to step into the gap in front of this killer. The invaders closed their line around their colonel.

Every soldier heard his calm voice. "Move up lads! Aim at the faces. Stab them! Front rank keeps their shields up! Second rank, stab over and down!" Men obeyed, the line held in the face of his authority. Gradually, disciplined men pushed the defenders back over their own dead and dying. By now, the hidden troops had run the three hundred paces from the forest. Hundreds of Imperial soldiers had come up behind the brave front rank and were hurling javelins over their heads into the closely packed defenders. The press was awful, the smoke overwhelming and the footing treacherous from blood, bodies and the clutter of weapons on the ground. The Colonel knew the outcome – break and you die. The first to yield loses all. "Push! Get your shoulders into those shields! Grit your teeth and send them to hell! Stand and fight! Second rank fill the gaps. Bring more spears. Pass them forward. You on the right, go back a step. Keep the line. That's it lads, just like a drill."

The barbarians broke first. Panic started at the back. The front could not flee because if they turned, they would die, stabbed in the back. The rearmost troops didn't know what was happening, but they began to feel themselves being pushed back. They imagined the slaughter at the front rank and their courage pissed down their legs. They ran, leaving their friends at the front to the Colonel's relentless spearmen. "Charge lads! Kill them. Don't let them regroup. Chase and slaughter!"

The Colonel's men had used flaming arrows to signal their successful entry into the city. The assault on the front gate had been a feint. Seeing the flaming arrows, mounted men left the Northern gate and raced their steeds around the city wall, with foot soldiers chasing after them. When they reached the postern gate they quickly dismounted and followed the Colonel's unit into the breach. All the glory and plunder was here now. Ferocious hand to hand fighting spread through the city streets. As the troops moved outwards from the wall, the streets broadened and more troops could engage. The killing ground expanded and the death toll rocketed. Retreat became rout. Rout became slaughter as the defenders were outnumbered and enfiladed in the wider boulevards of the city centre. The colonel was working his way up a narrow alley. The city troops were brave and fought with guts, but his hard veterans worked methodically, line abreast, stabbing and slashing the defenders.

In the cool light of morning, Baron-General Pdoverin Mnufort laid his large hands on the cold stones of the battlements and watched his slave-soldiers rioting through the streets of the conquered city. From his vantage point on the very top of the Keep, he could see most of the city. It was called Blenv in the local tongue. His army, now a mob, burst into the houses, dragging women and girls out by their hair. He watched keenly as Blenvan men were run down and killed, stabbed with spears or battered with slaver clubs. Blood spilled casually in the heat of victory. Baron-General Mnufort revelled in the screaming.

"Yes, my little wretches, that's it. Stab the men! Rape the women. Put my brand on them. They belong to me now!" Once the men were killed, the rapes began. He saw three soldiers chasing a screaming girl up a cobbled street. One of them tripped her and they were on her like beasts. To his right, the shattered gateway smouldered, still making heavy smoke that obscured his view. To his left, his soldiers were spreading through the streets, the freemen-sergeants keeping them in order. Some of the city's soldiery were fighting a vigorous rear guard action in that quarter. They were few and their morale would soon fail them as they realised there was no escape. No quarter either, if the General had his way.

The General laughed aloud. This was his first siege, his first investment of a city and now he would gain Advancement. He would gain power through this conquest. Slaves, wealth and land were his. He looked at the weighty snow clouds rising over the mountains and realised that winter was upon them. A few more days of siege and his entire army would have starved outside these stout walls. He turned to Dvelt, his bodyguard-captain. "Fetch me Colonel Bdescu." Dvelt ran to comply and the General smiled. Soon the whole Empire would know his name. No Prince would sneer at him now.

Colonel Bdescu arrived and saluted smartly. The General smiled on his protégé. The Colonel was literally coated in dried blood. His sword arm and the whole left side of his mail shirt were black with it. His leather trousers were spattered and even his face was smeared with death's dark juice. Only his shield side was relatively clean. His eyes shone from dark pits. His forehead, already scarred from a previous battle, had acquired a second gash that had dried to a sticky line. The Colonel wondered idly when his killing machine had last slept. It was a day for good humour and the General was expansive. "Bdescu, your stratagem was simply genius. It probably saved the army, not to say my standing in the Rankings. I battered at one gate while you burned the other. It worked exactly as you drew it in the sands last month. You fooled the lot of them. I salute you. You know that the triumph is, and must be, mine. But as I Advance, then I take you with me. Some of what I get comes to you. That is the way of it."

The Colonel bowed. "My Lord is my Bond-Father. What I do, I do for His glory, not my own. My Lord serves the God-Emperor. This is the Law."

The General beamed. Bdescu was always punctilious. No arguments, no legal finessing of the Rules. He kept to his place and carried out his duties. "What is our status, Colonel?"

The Colonel was uncomfortable with praise and looked relieved to be back to business. "The treasury is vested and your personal Guard and Factor have possession. The Prince who holds these lands is captured alive. He is being strapped to an inquisitor's frame in his throne-room two floors below us. His female relatives are split into nubile and non-nubile. The ones of childbearing age are secured in a bedchamber reserved for the General. The others are taken to the slave cages we have set up in the basements. There is no usable dungeon in the place but we are chaining the mobile cages together as an improvisation. All surviving members of his male line are chained up, along with the old women and will be executed at your command. The streets are being made safe and we will eliminate all resistance before nightfall. My Sergeants will keep order and prevent too many fires being set in your new holdings. Men of fighting age are being killed on sight, along with all the aged and infirm, in accordance with Rule. Women, children and babes will be rounded up after the soldiers have completed their pillage. The men are tired, so they will be exhausted in a couple of hours and we will restore Order to my Lord's city. This is my report, may it please my Lord."

The General put his arm around the Colonel's shoulders and hugged him once. Even allowing for the armour, the Colonel's body was as unyielding as wood. "Loyal and brave. These are good traits for liegemen. But not many are also intelligent, diligent and effective. These are the marks of the great captains, celebrated in the tales of old. Go and find some rest. My factor will see that your officers are fed. You've been in armour these four days without respite. I want you in charge again when the night comes. There may be attempts on our lives."

The Colonel looked hesitant. "There is a small matter, my Lord. I have walked the streets and looked from the Keep. There aren't enough people."

The General smiled tolerantly. "What do you mean, 'not enough people'?"

"Sire, there are many houses, large and small. All are in good repair, so there must be resident families. When we tried to escalade the walls last month, many soldiers opposed us. I estimated over two thousand men at arms, if you recall my report. Yet in mopping up the streets we've killed three, maybe four hundred men. Their soldiers are fighting a desperate and well-co-ordinated rear guard action in the Eastern corner of the city. Ltencha's division are meeting strong resistance. I've sent every man I can spare to support him. There are women and children to be sure, but less than I expected. Many of the houses are empty. They are furnished and looked inhabited. They'll yield good plunder. But I think the slave count will be far lower than my Lord would wish."

The General smiled. "I think you worry too much, my boy. There were two gates. You took the one and we had the other covered. Besides, the Northern gate is still boarded up, locked solid. We had the place surrounded. I cannot see how troops, men, women and babes could have slipped away, can you?"

Bdescu looked embarrassed. "No sire, I cannot".

"Then they are hiding in cellars and our scum-boys will find them for us. Be off with you, lad. Try to relax and savour our triumph. Rape a few girls, have some fun, get drunk. Tomorrow will be soon enough to count the winnings."

Bdescu saluted, backed away, turned smartly and marched off. The General's small eyes watched as Bdescu's tall frame swayed slightly. He knew the man was exhausted, running on duty alone. The General smiled. It was time for the women. He was full of energy. He'd rape a couple, while his guards stood outside the door listening enviously. He laughed and left the rooftop, rubbing his hands as he descended to his new bedchamber.

The General decided first to see the Prince. This arrogant man had defied an Imperial army for so long. His soldiers had defended their city with great courage, so the Prince must command the obedience of his people. The General walked into the room that had been the Prince's throne chamber. An iron frame had been erected amongst the wreckage. Four bodies, two of them Imperial Sergeants, were piled carelessly in a corner. Their broken limbs draped over one another in unmistakeable abandon. Four bodyguards manned the chamber and they snapped to attention. The General ignored them and went to look at the tall figure strapped in the frame. He was of middle years. He was upright and spread-eagled, stark naked as a condemned man should be. His genitalia were shrunk into his lower body but he looked reasonably unscathed. Many bruises, to be sure and a few cuts and grazes, but no deep wounds. He looked at the General with utter loathing.

In very passable Imperial he said "there is no level of your Hell deep enough to punish you for what you have done here. This is a peaceful sovereign state. You have no right to be here. I will be avenged and so will all my friends and family. Your dreams of avarice will be your death. You will try to push further on, into the mountains. And there you will meet your nemesis. The Snowhammers are waiting for you and they will turn your dreams to shit."

The General smiled tolerantly. "My friend, you'll die tomorrow and I'll watch you suffer. Why antagonise me? It will only make your death more painful. And please don't try to scare me with tales of mythical beasts. What in God's holy name is a snowhammer, eh? A bird so large it can kill and eat a man! So heavy, it can fly only in the gales and the blizzards? This is a story to frighten children. Have you seen one? Go to your death with dignity, Princeling. Don't demean yourself with childish threats. They are not appropriate for a man of your Rank. Or former Rank I should say. I go now to pleasure myself with your females. If God smiles on you, some of them might live long enough to see you die."

The General walked away, wondering where the Prince learned to speak such good Imperial. It didn't bother him for long, once he started enjoying himself amongst the princesses, his new slaves. Their screams and struggles kept him amused until nightfall. Then he slept.

In the darkest hour of the night came the snow. Silently it landed, first in light flakes and soon in constant, thick draughts. The sentries grumbled and searched the pillaged houses for furs and felt coats. The white merciful blankets covered the uncaring dead. In the Keep, the General slept, smiling like a child amongst weeping women while his envious guards stood watch. In the north-eastern district, the sleepless Colonel walked his beat, kicking sleeping sentries awake. No man would shirk his duty while Bdescu lived. At every corner, a knight or a freeman-sergeant would salute him. Each time, the Colonel would stop. "Fenjent, you young rogue! Still alive, eh? I saw you at the gate. You stood your ground like a man. I saw that big bastard swing at you but I couldn't get at him. I'm glad you made it."

Fenjent stood up straight and smiled at his Colonel. "Thanks, Sir. Cvelthan got him from the other side. We knew you'd get us in, Sir. You'll never fail us." The Colonel waved away the compliment. "I've often wondered, lad, why you've such a strange name?"

Fenjent grinned. "Aye sir. My family are from the Islands. No double consonants in their names. Children born since we were brought into the Empire and getting them now, of course. But I was already named and nobody bothered." The Colonel laughed, thanked him for sharing this confidence and moved on.

This type of encounter was repeated a dozen times as he walked the streets of this alien city. The sergeants and knights loved this taciturn fighting man, his face as scarred than theirs, his sword hand more calloused and his armour more blackened.

Burning the postern gate had cost many lives from Bdescu's foot soldiers. The General and his other Colonels, Ltencha and Vrabelm, had gone to the opposite side of the city to attack the Northern gate with a battering ram. Bdescu's mounted knights had gone with them. It was essential that the city's defenders thought that all Imperial forces were attacking the Northern gate. Casualties at the main gate had been few. His rival Colonels now had more foot soldiers than Bdescu. Now he had another thing to worry about.

Fenjent looked at the Colonel. "Are you all right, my Lord? You seem tired."

Bdescu stirred from his memories. He would never forget those awful moments in the teeth of the gateway. "Yes, I am fine. No sleep for four days. That doesn't help. And I can't sleep until you lazy lot learn to stay awake on guard duty!"

Fenjent smiled. "We'll try, Sir".

"God watch you, Sergeant. Stay alert and keep us safe this night. This is my will and your Duty." Fenjent liked the Colonel's old-fashioned way of speaking. He spoke the High Tongue with clipped royal accents and often used these archaic forms of address. Fenjent found it comforting, as if the Colonel were his father.

Bdescu marched into the snow, his boots crunching in the unfamiliar footing but his steps secure. The Colonel had made a slave cobbler put nails in the soles of his boots in readiness for this place.

He wanted to know where all the people had gone. Some instinct drove his feet eastwards, and he could no longer hear any fighting. As he rounded a corner by a wrecked inn, a Sergeant rushed up, slipping on the unfamiliar snow. He carried a torch and almost burned the Colonel's face. "Sorry, Sir!" Bdescu took hold of the man's arm and turned him into the torch's light. Once he could see his face he relaxed. "Vdurin! What in the name of God are you doing, running around like a fool?"

Vdurin leapt to attention and saluted. "Sire, there's a hole in the wall." Bdescu didn't ask questions. "Show me", was all he said.

In the Easternmost corner of the city there was silence in the deepening snow. Bodies, Imperial soldiers mostly, were scattered thickly on the ground. Officers, sergeants and slave soldiers alike lay together. Some carried obvious battle wounds, others seemed oddly unscathed, but none lived. The blood looked pale, as the snow had started to cover it.

Bdescu stared at the wall. In the Easternmost corner, directly facing towards the mountains, a cylindrical hole had been made in the city wall at ground level. The hole formed a perfect tunnel, slightly taller than Bdescu's head. The wall was faced with stone on the inside and outside. It was five paces thick. In between the stone facings, the wall was filled with rubble and earth. It was made so that if an army tried to tunnel through it, the collapsing rubble would fill their hole as fast as they dug it. Yet this tunnel had not existed half a day ago. Taking the torch from his silent sergeant, Bdescu walked boldly into the breach. The tunnel was perfectly formed. The sides were fused solid, as smooth as polished wood. The surface was so hot he could feel it on his face. He knew better than to touch it. He walked the few paces to the outside and looked down. This side of the walls was protected by a moat because the ground was level. The moat surrounded two sides of the city, fed by a canal from the nearby river.

At the end of the new tunnel stood a wooden bridge over the moat. The dark stagnant water rippled in the light breeze. Yesterday afternoon Bdescu had ridden right around the city walls. No bridge had existed then. After his tour, he had withdrawn his encircling forces to concentrate them at the gates. Often, a few people would escape down the walls on ladders or ropes when a city was attacked this way. It was a trivial matter, few could do it and they were easily rounded up afterwards. And none could escape down a wall with a moat. But this was different. Somebody had built a stout wooden bridge in a single afternoon. He could not imagine how the hole, or the bridge, had been created in so short a period. His was not a temperament for brooding. He'd find out later what had happened. For now, he crossed the moat and knelt in the grass, bringing the torch's light closed to the trampled earth. He saw thousands of footprints leading through the grass. Half or more of the city's population had escaped the sack of the city. "What shitbug let this happen?" Bdescu would find the traitors who had allowed this treachery and gut them in front of his General.

"Sergeant! Get out here!" When the nervous sergeant arrived, Bdescu had already formulated his actions. "We are insecure while this cursed hole exists. Go to Fenjent, he is nearest. Get all his men here. Burn the bridge. Barricade and defend this breach. Nobody comes in or out. Detain any who try. Don't kill them. I want answers, not corpses. Send a runner to me every Bell to report status. Repeat my instructions then run."

Vdurin had relaxed now the Colonel was here: he was no longer responsible for this situation. He repeated his orders clearly. Satisfied, Bdescu set off back to the Keep. His intuition had been correct; the city had been cleverly evacuated. The witchcraft that made the evacuation possible was beyond the ken of a simple soldier. He'd need priests, Imperial Agents and the like to give meaning to this conundrum. He hastened to his General. Halfway across the town he came in sight of the Keep, its bulk rising from its hilltop vantage. He glanced up to see a flash of light from the highest window, just under the battlements. Intuition told him it was from the throne chamber. A heavy concussion thudded against his ears causing a sharp pain. He saw something, a white body, against the wall of the Keep, but it was too dark to see what it was.

Perhaps it was a body falling from the balcony of the throne room. He shook his head and yawned to clear the ringing in his ears. He forced his tired legs to run towards the Keep.

Bdescu ran up the Keep's internal stairwell through a crowd of shouting men. Gentlemen officers barked orders at freeman Sergeants, Sergeant yelled at slave soldiers and men ran up and down without obvious purpose. Bdescu forced his way through, grim and determined. He came at last to the top landing and pushed his way through the crowd and into the throne room. He saw the General sitting on the throne, apparently unharmed but clearly in a rage. The General turned his small bloodshot eyes on his bond-son and barked "Bdescu, at last! I thought the imbeciles would never find you. What do you make of this then, eh?"

Bdescu looked slowly around the room. His mind shut out the noise from the landing. He just looked. The heavy wooden shutters that guarded the window were buckled into the room. One shutter lay on the floor. The other hung drunkenly from broken hinges and moved slightly in the wind. The drapes were wrapped around the shutters in elegant rags. Outside, the balcony was intact. The torture frame was buckled into scrap iron and empty of its prisoner. Four of the General's personal guard lay on the floor. Each had a single wound to the neck. He bent down and looked at their fatal wounds. He wiped away blood with a fragment of drapes. "Axe. They were very sharp but quite small and probably heavy too. All blows to the same spot. Four men, perhaps five broke in here. All were expert assassins." The Imperial troops were all quite dead. Being officers, they carried sabres as befitted the knightly class. Only two had drawn sword. No enemy was in sight, living or dead. The torches in the sconces and in the hands of the assembled soldiers flickered in the draft. The three sconces nearest the windows had been blown out. Bdescu's forensic musing continued.

"Assuming nobody moved the bodies, then judging by where they lie, the attack came from the direction of the windows. Somebody either roped down from the roof or climbed up from a lower window. Either route was hazardous. Brave men and well trained. They broke down the window shutters. Anybody see any heavy hammers?" All shook their heads. "Another puzzle then. Send a squad to search the ground below the window in a hundred-pace radius and bring whatever you find to me here."

Men ran to the exit and clattered down the stairs. He turned to the torture frame. "More heavy work. The bolts were drawn, that was easy. Then they wrenched the frame out of true to spring the padlocks. That took more than five men. Let's say a dozen, then. They somehow carried the Prince to the balcony and roped or rappelled him away. What shape was he in, could he walk?"

The Baron-General confirmed that he could.

"Well, my Lord, all I can say is that if these men had been at the postern gate this morning we would never have got in here. They were amongst the finest warriors ever trained. Silent, disciplined, strong and fearless. Let's hope they've gone somewhere far away. They must've been the Prince's personal Guard. How they got past us I'll leave to others to find out. But we failed here and somebody needs to be given a taste of the whip."

The Baron-General ground his teeth and nodded. Bdescu was right. The air reeked of treachery.

Bdescu turned to the nearest officer. "Whoever took the Prince may try for his family too. Take twenty men to the General's quarters to guard the princesses. Send more men to the basement to guard the other members of the royal family. Kill any strangers. The rest of you, form guard around my Lord General, in case they come back. Do it NOW". Almost as soon as he had finished, the deep concussion came again, shaking the floor under their feet. Cracks as wide as a finger appeared in the stone floor. Dust flooded the room. The sound came from the General's new quarters. Bdescu turned to the General. "My Lord, thanks to God that you were here. Had these sorcerers found you with the women, I fear your fate would have matched that of your guards."

Bdescu charged into the General's new billet, sword in hand. He led a troop of knights in full battle array. The room was empty. Again the window was gone. All the Imperial guards were slain by the same precise cuts to the throat. And five women of the Prince's household were also gone. One remained. She lay on the floor, bleeding freely from a head wound. She was tall and slim with hair the colour of ripe grain and a robe of deep forest green. Her skin was pale.

A knight spurned her with his foot. "Dead." He stated.

"Don't be a fool. The dead don't bleed." Bdescu put his fingers to her throat. "Get a surgeon. Somebody find out what's happened in here before I run completely mad."

The Baron-General strolled into the room. He looked down at the unconscious woman.

"Only one concubine left, my Lord." Bdescu pointed at her.

His bond father looked sour. "That lanky thing? No tits, pale skin, thin hair! Are you joking? I like them short and busty like a temple virgin. I'm not having that skinny bint wrapping its scrawny thighs around me. You can have it. You're not that bothered about the rape bit anyway, are you?" He walked away.

Consolidation

The General and his Colonels, Ltencha, Vrabelm and Bdescu sat in tribunal with their Imperial colleagues. The Rector of God's Chosen was named Flantr and he represented the Church. The Imperial Agent, Commissar Rbunft took his seat at the head of the table. Scribes sat below, their quills sharpened to record the wisdom and judgement of the court. Bdescu's scribe was Byardil. Byardil had grown up with the Colonel and held a position of trust. His intelligence and discretion had earned him the highest post a slave can attain – private secretary. He watched his handsome master enter the room and felt the guilty thrill of a love he could never admit. He had watched his master dress this morning. Bdescu had dictated orders to Byardil while another slave bathed him. Byardil could hardly stand to look at his master. The sight of his lean muscularity gave Byardil a shortness of breath and a strange sliding feeling in his chest. He forced himself to look away. He shook his head to clear away the visions. The proceedings were beginning.

Baron-General Mnufort stood and spoke the archaic High Tongue with the accents of a practised courtier. "Gentlemen. This Tribunal is convened in due solemnity to invoke his Holy Majesty's justice. We are quorate for the administration of said justice. Let all present now agree or not, calling aye or nay as they see fit". Every man called "aye".

"The matter at hand is treachery. The foulest crime known to a man is to betray his brothers to the enemy. Yet we have seen this done and we are dismayed. But let our outrage be not a blindfold over our judgement. I declare myself plaintiff in this case. I seek justice and ask it to be final. My suit is this. Yesterday, at the moment of triumph of our holy war to expand the Empire in His Holiness' name, one amongst us betrayed our trust. He let in our enemies while we sought to consolidate our hard-earned gains. As a result, the Prince and his ghastly brood escaped Imperial justice. Some or many of his former subjects escaped with him, dragging eastwards into the Teeth of God Mountains to seek refuge amongst the savage tribes that cower in the foothills. I name

Guard Captain Qrilgin as defendant in the case and seek reparation from his body, his family and his lands."

The Imperial Agent, Commissar Rbunft, stood. He was an ascetic figure. His lean face housed an aquiline nose, sharp pale brown eyes that missed nothing and a mouth that seemed to taste a sour fruit all the time. His tall body was lean but lacked muscle tone. He was bad tempered and wished himself back at Court. "This Tribunal calls upon its panel to declare their purpose in being here".

Ltencha, Vrabelm and Rector Flantr stood and were sworn as witnesses. Bdescu declared, to the shock of them all, as Qrilgin's defender.

Rbunft opened proceedings by ordering the scribes to write every word then asked the General to tell his story. The General, an accomplished courtier for all his soldierly demeanour, told his tale with wit and convincing detail. Qrilgin, he argued, had been in collusion with the enemy during the siege. He had connived with them to save their Royal Family and some of their citizens, planning to sneak away after the event and live amongst them, free and rewarded. It had been Qrilgin who had told the General that all was well while the Prince was spirited away. Qrilgin had deserted his post in the throne room while the renegades scaled the wall, broke down the shutters and took the Prince down rope ladders to the safety of the street. But most tellingly, it had been Qrilgin who had allowed the guards on the street to desert their posts and come inside the Keep to get warm.

The three witnesses swore on oath that the General spoke truly and they concurred with the suit. Qrilgin was guilty and should be put to the question to remove all doubt. The Tribunal became silent and all eyes turned to Colonel Bdescu to perform the ritual defence. They expected a few words about Qrilgin's previous good character and they could all adjourn for some decent wine and an early night. Then Qrilgin would be tortured to death in the morning. Bdescu rose to his feet. After the fighting he was sore, but his bearing remained as formal as ever.

"My Lords of the Court. I have many questions to ask in this case. I doubt not your judgement as a properly-constituted Tribunal of his Majesty's authority." The members smiled. Bdescu was playing his part perfectly.

"If Qrilgin is guilty, how was this deed done? In the space of six Bells, a man-sized hole was burned through the city wall. May I remind the Court that this was the same wall that had defeated our most vigorous attacks for five long months. Then, a wooden bridge over the moat was built in half a day. Citizens, including women, children and the elderly, walked in an orderly manner through this still-hot breach, over this brand-new bridge and headed for the hills. They were moving fast enough to evade our cavalry patrols, who have still yet to apprehend them. In fact, none of our cavalry has returned. Their mounts have returned without their riders, many covered in blood. This is more than one man's treachery. This is sorcery or worse."

"Secondly, how did the burglars get on to the balcony, break the stout shutters and kill our men before they could draw swords? How, in the time it took us to rush down the stairs, did they break a weakened Prince from stout iron fetters and bear him safely to the ground, along with his five womenfolk? How did they evade our diligent search that followed in hot pursuit? Until we know these answers, I submit that we are all at risk. Let Qrilgin be questioned first. If the Inquisitors are too keen and he dies, then we may never know the form of our enemy. That is a lack we may come to regret."

This line of argument caused a stir. Members started speaking to one another in low voices. The Imperial Agent raised his voice. "Colonel Bdescu raises interesting and valid questions. It is his duty to ensure our protection and we thank him for his kind concerns. The judgement stands. Death by Torture is our will. Say Aye and be finished."

Every member of the Court said aye except for Bdescu, who abstained and Ltencha who had no vote because the culprit was of his clan.

Qrilgin died under Question without changing his sad pleas of innocence. His screams hung like a weight in Bdescu's mind. He knew Qrilgin was a poor soldier. He was the fifth son of a noble family with no prospects. He had joined the Army at the order of his father and had little talent for soldiering. He was lazy. He lacked courage and hung back from a charge or a skirmish. He was little loss. Bdescu was not concerned with his death but with the questions left unresolved. The nobles now accepted the explanation. Try as he might, Bdescu could not see how it had been done. The concussions alone were beyond anything he knew.

A quartermaster sergeant took the extraordinary step of breaking the line of command and coming to see the Colonel in his quarters. The man half expected a flogging. He was delighted to be greeted cordially. The Colonel's reputation seemed more formidable than the man. Bdescu simply asked "What is our status, Freeman Quartermaster Sergeant?"

"Sire, the city has enough food to see us through the winter, if we are careful. The flour is well stored and there are dried meats, fruits and plenty of clean water in the wells. There are stores of beer but no wine or spirits, regrettably. The problem is that there is no seed. No root vegetable sprouts, nothing." There followed a long and detailed discussion of foodstuffs, provisioning needs and water supplies that left the poor quartermaster wondering if Bdescu had been a merchant at some part of his life. Bdescu dismissed the quartermaster and leaned back in his canvas chair to think uncomfortable thoughts.

Bdescu closed his eyes. His unease burned like a pain in his chest. They knew we were coming, he thought. They burned the seeds so that we could not plant a crop. We cannot stay here beyond the spring, that's their plan! We'll crawl back to the Empire or starve here. They'll come back and re-possess their city. It was the strategy of a twisted genius. They planned to hold the Imperial army here until winter made re-supply impossible. They must have drawn lots to decide which of their people would live or die. Leave a skeleton population and a suicide guard to hold the city long enough for the majority to escape, no doubt to a prepared refuge in those cursed mountains. They had planned to fool His Holiness' finest army and perhaps sacrifice one person in ten to death or slavery. His mind baulked at the scale of their planning and the audacity of their actions. These people had courage. He tested his theory against every alternative he could think of, but he knew his instinct was true; they had walked into an elaborate trap. Wearily, he climbed to his feet. Telling the Baron-General would not be an enjoyable experience. But first he must give the order for food rationing. The nobles wouldn't like it but if they ate too much they'd be roasting cavalry mounts before springtime. He headed for the commissary.

They failed in all attempts to pursue the escaped citizens. The weather was against them. The mounts were cavalry chargers, trained to rush into the clamour of a battle. Each time their iron-shod feet slipped on the packed snow they panicked, snorting and biting at the air. After a few minutes of fruitless urging they would simply refuse to move. The heavy wagon drays were no better, although less aggressive and highly-strung, they too hated this uncertain surface. Bdescu waited, fuming.

The General's fury had abated slightly, but he'd killed one slave and wounded three others for minor infringements. Every noble officer had been tongue lashed and every sergeant abused. He stalked around the city, knout in hand, lashing out at anyone who seemed not to be working. The few Blenvan slaves, the survivors of the sacking of the city, were strong and intelligent. They were silent and unsmiling, showed appropriate deference and obeyed orders without demur. They seemed to be the one thing that cheered the Baron General. "Wait while we get the rest of them, lads!" he would say in the nobles' dining hall. "They're strong, healthy and willing. We'll catch the rest in the spring and sell the lot on the blocks at Kcharkinlact." The name of their fair capital, with its sunlit streets and dusty corners, brought a smile to every noble face. The good cheer lasted until they had to walk out into the torch lit darkness and its hard cold bite. Even a short walk to their billets had them swearing.

Bdescu stayed out of the way. After being so utterly gulled by the locals, he trusted them not. To his watchful eye, these people were still hoping. They were biding their time, expecting no doubt to be re-united with their loved ones. They must know that if the Imperial Army did retreat, they'd be taken back to Kcharkinlact as slaves. There was more to this plan yet to be revealed, he was certain of it.

The days were sunny and cold. The snow fell at night but showed no signs of melting. Bdescu knew he must solve the riddle of how to travel in this strange land, or go insane from frustration. At least now he'd solved one riddle – why his enemies had had no cavalry. Just keeping the beasts fed was a struggle, leaving aside the exercise problem. The mounts were out of condition as they put on fur and fat against the cold. The shit was piling up in the stables. Without carts, getting the stuff out of the city and on to the fields was using too many slaves. The slaves needed too much food to keep them working. It dawned on the Colonel that finding a solution to the problem of travel was vital for the survival of the army. They needed game and the local fields and woods were hunted out. The thick forests at the foothills of the mountains would be crawling with life. The other nobles spent their time complaining, gambling and raping the few local women worth the effort. Fights broke out as men became bored, or quarrelled over women. Bdescu thought, worked and planned.

Not every night but often, a guard on duty on the wall or the top of the keep would simply disappear. Gone without a trace. The Baron-General suspected desertion. Bdescu was certain that could not be the case. Only an absolute fool would leave the warmth and safety of the city to freeze to death in the harsh weather. Especially when he knew how many days' march it was to get home. Some of the vanished men were slave soldiers that Bdescu knew personally. No, Bdescu was certain it could not be desertion. It always happened when a man patrolled alone. It never happened if a man was in sight of other men. That suggested guerrilla attack to Bdescu's mind. How it happened was a mystery. No Blenvan locals had been seen on the streets and no outsider could possibly climb the sheer walls, coated in ice, then escape without disturbing the snow under the walls. The General's idea of desertion was actually more credible than Bdescu's. In either case, Bdescu ruled that all patrolling must be done in teams of three. From that moment, not a single man was lost but the mystery remained unsolved. Once Bdescu had stopped the losses, all the other nobles promptly forgot about the matter. Bdescu was deeply worried by anything he could not explain.

Then one morning it rained. Admittedly a cold, dank rain but it cleared the snow in hours. Bdescu had his patrol up, saddled and ready in half a bell, but then they waited a full bell while the General and his sluggish nobles prepared to join the hunt. It was late morning when they finally cantered out in full battle array towards the distant mountains.

They followed the river. It flowed out of a wide valley that led into the wooded foothills of the mountains, which the Imperial troops called the Teeth of God. The grass was easy going and mounts and men revelled in the fresh air. The rain stopped and a dull sunlight broke through. A ragged cheer broke from the men's throats. The mounts were sluggish, though. Bdescu's charger was his finest possession, a huge Jnadviz with belligerent manners and bottomless lungs. He was fearless and Bdescu had mastered him, trained him and loved him for three careful years. In battle and skirmish and tourney, none could match him. But now he laboured under the hair and the fat, sweating up and bad tempered. He patted the beast's neck. "Easy, Warhammer. You'll soon be your old bad self again." After two bells' ride the column stopped dead. Bdescu had been at the back, checking his troops. He rode out of column to the front to join his brother officers. He joined them just to see what they saw.

As they had emerged from a dip, they came upon a road. It started from nothing, a neat line of flagstones in the grass. It ran, straight as an arrow, into the valley ahead of them. It was paved with stone blocks a forearm wide. The surface was bevelled to let the rain run off. There were broad drains on either side to keep it passable in the spring melt. It was wide enough for two wagons to pass side by side.

The decomposing corpses of the pursuit patrol were propped up in sitting poses across the end of the road, their swords braced against their bucklers and the bucklers against their backs. In front of the corpses was a post, driven into the earth. On the post was a board with words painted on its flat surface. The characters were well formed High Imperial and the grammar was that of an educated scribe.

"Welcome to the Republic of Byekvoranp. You are welcome here. We welcome trade, knowledge and friendly visitors. Do, please be advised that our laws forbid warfare, slavery, theft, rape, killing, lying and evangelising. The penalties are strict and strictly enforced. Observe them and enjoy your visit."

An outraged roar broke from the patrol. This was a threat as well as an insult. The General turned to his bond son. "Why did we not find this road during our siege, Colonel?" he asked, with apparent mildness.

"Sire, we never foraged this far. Once we had surrounded the city we settled in for the siege quickly. There was grain in the fields, fruit in the orchards. All the game was in the forests on the other side of the city, and plenty of it. It was too far to drag game back from here so we never came this far. We had no reason to traverse a grassy plain with nothing worth hunting."

The General turned to his officers. "General Counsel. All dismount." Since the patrol was strictly cavalry only noblemen were present. The General looked around his cadre and spoke slowly. "We have suffered a mortal insult and a heavy loss. These men were our brothers and we declare blood feud against this Republic of Byekvoranp, whatever that might mean. We will wash their fields in the blood of their men, thrice-rape their women, sell their children on the block, burn their houses and fire their fields. Is there any man here says otherwise?" He waited for the cheering to die down. The General was not a stupid man, for all his rages and bluffness.

"If we attack now, this winter will starve us. There is no grass for our chargers, nor food for our men. The snow is the only enemy we cannot defeat with a sword. I say we use cunning and fear nothing. We must attack in the spring, when the weather will stand full battle array. Our mounts must be well fed, our bucklers stout and our sabres sharp. We will drill, stay fit and prepare all winter. We will return in the spring and bathe in blood, wallow in women. Bdescu says we have enough food to last until spring. It will be enough. We will take their food as they took ours. We will pillage their towns. I will find the shitbug who painted that sign and personally shove it up his arse then stake him up for sabre practice. Questions?" There were none. They loaded the bodies of their comrades onto saddle pommels, wrapping them in cloaks to avoid the stench that arose as they thawed. It was a quiet group that cantered back to town. Bdescu was worrying again.

In the hard-packed frozen snow outside the walls, the scribe Byardil came to see what his master was doing. He came around the corner of a wall by the stables and watched, enchanted, as his master showed the world his cleverness. The dray walked effortlessly across the slippery surface, lowing contentedly. The cart behind it tracked truly, without sliding at all. The wheels were shod with bands of hammered iron. Set in the bands were hundreds of nails, sprouting outwards. The nails gripped the ice. The thwarts of the cart stopped the heavy beast from toppling and made him feel more secure. Then Byardil realised that the brute was wearing spiked shoes nailed to its hooves. He clapped his hands and cooed delightedly. "Master, you are a genius." Bdescu, who was driving the contraption, smiled and waved. "Hello! What do you think, eh? It works!" Byardil smiled shyly at his hero. "Master, why are you so keen to get carts working?"

"Because we need to go to those hills, kill some game and drag it back here. Because we won't be fit to fight unless we keep up our strength with meat. Because the mounts need exercise. Because the shit needs hauling from the barns. And most of all, because I need something to do! Whoa, boy… there's a good lad, easy now." He jumped down from the cart and turned to a slave-smith standing in the shadow of the stables. "Get every spare slave you can. I will square it with the officers. Fire up every smithy and get to work. Two carts a day until I tell you to stop. My will is your Duty, go!"

Byardil's heart was a leaping fish in his chest. He could hardly breathe around Bdescu when he was in this all-conquering mood. He had never seen his master so happy. "I cannot stand idle, you know."

Trespass

Bdescu and Byardil walked back to the Colonel's billet together, the Colonel pleased with his day's work, the scribe thinking only of his master. They were quartered in a small stone house on the main street, known as Mason's Row. The other Colonels had taken the grander houses, filling them with slaves. They jealously guarded their property and especially the captured women, who had been allocated by the General according to the Rules. This meant that Bdescu, his bond son, had been awarded the tall slim princess as his body slave. He could have had more, but he had demurred. He had his own motley household; so one extra pair of hands was plenty for his monastic life.

The princess' name, translated into Imperial, was Summer. She was blond, tall and very severe. Her body lacked the fullness preferred in the Empire, where a woman was expected to be lush, soft and warm with large breasts and long thick curling hair. Summer was lean with a hunter's walk. Her hair was straight and fine, moving with a life of its own. She moved quickly and silently about the house. She was taciturn. Her steely green eyes were watchful and devoid of emotion. His personal surgeon had stitched her head wound, which was shallow and superficial. She claimed that one of the Imperial guards had struck her with his blade during the melee and she had no knowledge of what happened. She said the Prince did have a crack personal Guard unit but the men who entered the room wore hoods. She had been struck down before seeing the event that followed.

She was guarded in her answers. Over the weeks since the conquest she had relaxed around Bdescu but made no effort to speak to him. Bdescu, in his turn, left her to do the domestic chores. He had not raped her, nor molested her in any way. Byardil absolutely loved her. She spoke to him as an equal. She mended his clothes and washed his hair. She told him long stories when he couldn't sleep, which happened more frequently now, so far from home.

When Bdescu and Byardil entered the house, Summer was waiting in the hall. Her lower lip was split. Blood flowed slowly down her chin onto the plain brown dress she wore. A large contusion despoiled her face, swelling above her right eye, which was almost closed. She silently held up her wrists to show the ligature marks where they had tied her. He looked down at her ankles and saw the tell-tale marks there too. Bdescu raised an eyebrow. She nodded. He stepped up to her and lifted her long skirt. Her thighs were bruised, indented with finger marks and the unmistakable imprint of scale armour. A noble rapist had abused her, then. Having sex with a slave woman was no crime, even if she resisted. But someone had entered Bdescu's home and molested his property. This was a crime against his honour. He asked his first question. "Name?"

"Vrabelm." She was equally terse. Byardil was weeping silently but knew better than to speak. Others might think the Colonel unnaturally calm. Others might mistake this quiet concentration but not Byardil, he'd seen it before. Bdescu asked his second question. "Where?"

She walked back into the kitchens and showed him a smear of blood on the tiled floor. He bent on one knee, his leather riding breeches carefully kept clear of the smear. He studied the ground like a hunter. He reached down and picked something up. He concealed it in his hand as he stood up.

"Come with me, Summer, if you please. You too, Byardil." They set off in grim company for the General's house.

The Baron General heard Bdescu's suit with astonishment. He knew the Rules. He convened a General Counsel within two bells, as required by Rule and Custom. Vrabelm was belligerent and slightly drunk. He hotly denied the charge. "What, that skinny bitch? Look at it! Bones and sinews, not a bit of meat worth chewing! Watch it sneering down its long nose at us. Bdescu ought to be charged for his bad taste, not me for my appetites, even if I did fuck it, which I didn't. Next thing, he'll be asking it to speak! He's a man-fucker! He could've had a pretty little princess, but he picks this dry gorge instead! Why? Because she looks like a boy! He's a sodomite, it's obvious!"

The General frowned, calculating. He could tell Vrabelm was blustering and suspected his guilt. But one noble against another rarely concluded in a decisive result. He also knew how deep Bdescu's pride ran. If the Colonel made an accusation that did not stand, Vrabelm could disgrace Bdescu for wrongful accusation. The word of a slave held no value. She was not permitted to speak. Bdescu spoke slowly. "Do you deny entering my house, uninvited, in my absence, and raping this woman who is my property?"

"I just said so didn't I"? Vrabelm felt that the on looking nobles were favouring him, several smiled at his sarcasm. Few liked the exacting style and harsh methods of Colonel Bdescu, who always wanted a man to work when he should be gaming, drinking or fucking.

Bdescu held up a small object, glinting in the gloomy room. "This is a scale from your armour that I found in my kitchens." He walked over to Vrabelm and held the scale up to the gap in his armour. "Let the Imperial Agent judge if this is the case. I will stand by his rule."

Commissar Rbunft walked ponderously across the floor and looked intently at the scale. It had a distinctive tinning and the hammer marks matched the other scales. Worse, as it had torn loose it left a shred of its metal attached to the stitch that remained behind in the leather jerkin beneath. He matched it and turned to the Counsel. "It matches. But it only proves Vrabelm was in the kitchen, not that he raped the woman."

The general's temper, always uncertain, gave out. He bellowed across the chamber "it still makes him a trespasser and a shitbug who lies to his brothers in Council! And a man who accuses a brother officer of being a homosexual, a mortal sin, without a shred of evidence! Bdescu a sodomite, eh? Somebody will die for that remark, my brothers!"

Bdescu walked over to Vrabelm and spat in his face. He spoke formally, in High Tongue. "I call upon my brothers to witness this act. Pdense Vrabelm, I denounce you as a trespasser, a traducer, and a liar. Name your time, place and weapon."

Vrabelm erupted. "The time is now! The place is here! The weapon is my axe! I'll cut your balls off, you sanctimonious little arse-tickler! You homosexual piece of dung! I'll teach you to spit, but this time with blood!" He was a huge man, a head taller than Bdescu and a confident warrior. But even in his drunken rage he was smart enough to know that Bdescu would best him with a sabre. Every man in the room had seen the Colonel with a blade in his hand. But the heavy axe, more ponderous, demanded a powerful wrist to wield it. Vrabelm's arm was as thick as Bdescu's leg. Surely Bdescu was doomed.

Axes were fetched. Vrabelm sent a slave soldier to his billet to get his favoured weapon. He spent the waiting time limbering up and boasting to his cronies about how he'd always thought Bdescu a shitbug and now he would prove it to them all. His bondsmen cheered him on, waving their tankards aloft and singing snatches of drinking songs. Two thirds of the room seemed to be on the side of Vrabelm. The other third, the General's men, were watchful, neutral. None of Bdescu's housemen was present because they were on guard duty that evening. None cheered for Bdescu. He walked over to a brother officer and politely asked if he might borrow his axe. It was a two-headed axe with a long haft bound with thick wire. He swung it through the air three times as if testing its balance. Then he placed the head carefully on the planked floor and rested his hands on the haft.

Byardil was terrified. Vrabelm would kill his beautiful master. Then Vrabelm would own him, would torture him, rape him and kill him. All the slaves knew Vrabelm's horrible reputation. Byardil was shaking. He felt a warm dry hand take his. The slave woman, Summer, stared fixedly ahead. She gave no signal but her hand was confident. Trust him, the hand said. And he felt better almost at once. "Kill him, my Colonel." He muttered under his breath.

After much shouting and posturing, Vrabelm squared up to Bdescu. "Still time to apologise, Shitbug! Get on your knees and beg me. You know the position, you've taken it up the arse a few times, I bet!" He raised the axe and swung it effortlessly above his head. Bdescu didn't move. Vrabelm moved quickly, deceptive for so large a man. His axe cut straight at Bdescu's head but Bdescu slid his foot back and swayed his head out of reach. The heavy axe sliced past, a finger's width from his face. He felt the cold air as it rushed by. He drove up with his own axe, not with the blade but the haft. The solid wooden haft caught Vrabelm under the chin and everyone in the room heard the clack of his teeth breaking. He reeled back, spitting blood. Bdescu spun the axe and on the fore cut he slashed Vrabelm's knee open. The man screamed as he lurched over onto his good leg, right into the path of Bdescu's backswing. The axe blade entered his head just above the ear. It penetrated his skull, cleft his brain and killed him. He fell, folding dead to the floor without uttering another sound. Bdescu had already released the weapon, still embedded in the corpse's head. The assembled nobles let out a collective gasp at such reckless proficiency. The nobles now knew the power of this half-hated brother officer. Not a man in the room would have believed that the Colonel could best Vrabelm so easily.

The General had seen his warrior-son in many a tighter spot. From the instant the Commissar had pronounced that the scale matched, the General had assumed only one outcome; a clan without a leader. The Rules of single combat were quite clear and gave Bdescu two courses of action. Bdescu could take Vrabelm's place and assume control of his family, lands and holdings. This would involve subjugation of all Vrabelm's people and fighting all comers to retain his place. This would double Bdescu's wealth and his standing in the Rankings. Obviously he risked murder, if any of Vrabelm's bondsmen had the competence and guts to do the deed. This choice would take up the whole winter in conflict and change. Or Bdescu could take a second option and step aside. This would leave the third Colonelcy to Vrabelm's younger brother; Jcluid Vrabelm.

The General could not guess what his bond son might do. He held his breath as Bdescu walked over the floor towards Vrabelm's people. Bdescu gestured to Jcluid to come to meet him. Jcluid was a handsome young man with a growing reputation as a good soldier. His older brother had mocked him in public – and abused him in private, many said. He stood firm in front of Bdescu, who looked straight into his eyes.

Bdescu's voice was quiet but carried to every ear in that silent room. "I have killed your kinsman. I did this because I had cause and right. I did not do it to take over his clan or his bonds. His death discharges my grievance and I am satisfied. The clan is yours and I renounce my claim. I pray you, answer me this. Do you want blood feud between us? Or can we be brothers? I have no grievance with you or yours. Our enemies are in the mountains not the keep. If you give me your hand I will give you mine and all will be at peace. If it is blood feud then show me the fist, that I may know your mind."

With due solemnity Jcluid thought for a moment. Then he stuck out his hand and Bdescu took it warmly. Bdescu leaned in close for a moment and spoke softly, just for his young peer to hear. "I hear good things about you, Jcluid. I am proud to be your brother and I hope we can also be friends. I now owe you a blood honour debt. You must call on me if ever you have need. I swear I will come to your side."

Wild cheering broke out. Tankards clashed together and hats flew into the air. The General called for music, women and more beer. He cleverly asked for the last of his precious wine to be shared out for the celebration, bringing even wilder cheers. The General knew that the tension must be released or more feuding might break out amongst his bored warriors. The Council turned into a feast that turned the day into night and ran on into the morning. Jcluid's new bondsmen and relatives came over to congratulate him, some with genuine feeling, some from duty and others with an evaluating stare. His life would never be the same. Only the General noticed when, half a bell later, Bdescu slipped from the room with his concubine and his little skinny slave. The General sighed. If only Bdescu would realise that his choice of chattels made a mockery of his status.

Bdescu lay in his bath. His one luxury, Byardil reported to Summer with gleeful gossip. "Oh, he's so clean! Hot bath every day. Likes to relax in the hot water, says it helps him think. Oh, thank the God Emperor he is alive! Vrabelm would've buggered me to death. Some say he's killed a hundred male slaves like that! Thank God for my master. He's so gorgeous, isn't he? Have you seen his muscles? They're like solid wood. Well, nearly, except he is supple too. He can bend like a child, practices every day. That's why he's so good at fighting. They can't get him, he's like a serpent!"

Summer listened to his prattle and smiled at his obvious relief. She shared that relief. She held no illusions about her fate at Vrabelm's hands either. But her information about the Colonel's prowess was more comprehensive than Byardil's could ever be. She walked into the bathroom with another pitcher of hot water. The Colonel lay in the tiled bath which was set in the stone floor. She suspected he had chosen the modest house purely because of the bath. He was unselfconscious. He had grown up being tended by slaves and had no physical modesty. He also had no idea what a good-looking specimen he was. She watched him covertly as she poured the water carefully into the bath near his feet. He surprised her when he spoke.

"Summer, I know that a surgeon cannot minister to the hurt you have suffered, so I did not summon one. Physicians are useless, in my judgement. They seem to kill more men than they save, and they know nothing of women. But a hot bath might alleviate your hurts and cramps. If nothing else, it will make you feel cleaner. I am done, thank you. Let us fill the tub for you and I will leave you to relax."

She nodded and found that her eyes were burning. She brushed an angry hand against her face and found it wet. "Thank you, my Lord."

He smiled. "Take a couple of days to rest. I'll get some help to lighten the load and my lazy scribe can help you too. He's a good lad and he's fond of you. We'll all take a little holiday, right here in the house. This is my prescription. You see? I am a rotten doctor."

She fled the room, weeping. She did enjoy the bath, though. Byardil sat in the corner chattering. She didn't mind, she knew he had no interest in her. The other slaves laughed at Byardil's obvious homosexuality. He had no friends outside Bdescu's household yet none dared challenge him openly. Bdescu's reputation enveloped him in a protective cloak. She wondered if Bdescu knew that his slave was guilty of a mortal sin that would get him executed if any noble denounced him. She decided that Bdescu knew, but did not care. Most of his slaves were defective in some way. Jrabney the groom had some kind of criminal past. He had been a freeman-sergeant at some time past, but had been broken down to slave status and sold at auction. He moped around with a sly, calculating look but he kept his master's mounts in superb fettle. Mridka the cook was old and nearly blind. But they all doted on their master in spite of his reputation as a killer. This paradox fascinated her. He was iron hard when with the other nobles, an unbending disciplinarian with the knights, sergeants and slave soldiers. Yet he presided over a household of the feckless and disadvantaged. The atmosphere in the house was tranquil and friendly. She had come to like this collection of strangers. They were kind to her, fearing neither her foreignness nor her royal status. The Colonel was quiet and aloof, moving silently around the house, leaving at odd hours to check on his soldiers and see to his duties. He returned in equal quiet. Sleepy slaves would rouse themselves to go to him, preparing food, cleaning his clothes and running his errands. He asked for nothing, shouted no orders and imposed no discipline. She knew from the other captives that most of the nobles were drunken louts who beat servants, raped females and used whips, clubs and fists as they fancied. She decided to ask Mridka, the old half-blind cook.

The old woman stirred a pot of meal, seasoned with herbs and a little leftover cold meat. The winter's grip was harsh and the food was boring. The old cook made light of it and cooked with imagination. Her food was tasty and nourishing.

"Ah, Lady. That's because they ain't real genklemen, is they? They's shitbugs, doesn't follow Rules, see. Says how ter treat slaves in yer Rules, all clear and writ down, see? Says about treating us fair and equal. Not beat us if we's does us jobs. Feed us regular, feed us proper.

Milord's not same at all. E's proper genkleman, 'e is. His mother was a princess but 'e was second-son, so 'e gets nothing. Eldest gets it all. But 'e ain't bitter. 'E bonds up with General and serves 'im proper, like in't Rules. And 'e's done right well. Faithful. Serves General like a proper bonded man. Don't allow no gossip about General, oh dear me no. Keeps them shitbug officers in line, keeps 'em on toes. There's some might want ter murder't Baron-General and grab 'is Place. But them's scared of milord Colonel, in't they? E'd cut 'em up like sausages, ev'ry one! Them's'd get his whip if they even said a bad word about General! E's a real Prince, see? Not a shit bug. That's why. Easy, really."

Summer smiled at the old lady's rough but loyal words. Her gutter accents were warm with her love of her master. "So being a slave can be all right then, Mridka?"

"God-emperor bless you, Child, you're just an iggorant furriner, eh? We's all borned to our right places, see? God's will. Can't be changed, can't be argued wiv. I's a slave an' youse a slave. Masters are masters, stands to reason. Can't 'ave people running around out of Place, can we now? Anarchy, they'd 'ave, wouldn't it?"

Bdescu returned from guard inspection in the small hours. He had been dismayed by some lax patrolling and had been forced to explain a few men's duties with a short stick. They'd sleep no more. His own men knew their Colonel might appear randomly from the darkness. They never slept on guard. But some of the other nobles appeared to allow such laxities. Bdescu had never relaxed in this lovely city. That hole in the wall never ceased to worry him. He felt watched, all the time. He would turn quickly and at random to try to catch out a stalker. He would stop dead to listen for stealthy footsteps behind him. Nothing was seen or heard. He told himself it was just boredom or idle fancy. The feeling never went away. He watched the skies, feeling something above him. He saw nothing at all.

He opened the front door to make for the kitchen. Somebody would be awake and find him some food. In the kitchen he found Summer alone, stirring a small pot of thick soup. Bread waited by his place at table. There was oil for the bread and beer in his tankard. In spite of his friends' distaste for the local beer, he found it refreshing and preferred its milder alcohol to the heavy Imperial wine. A bowl of water was set on the dresser for his hand washing. The floor was swept clean and the table top had been sanded. Fresh herbs hung from the pot frame, filling the room with a light scent. He realised how tired he was. He sat down as she served him, silent as ever. "Join me, Summer, if you will. Take a seat and have some food. It's late and you must be tired, so thank you for staying up and making my homecoming so pleasant."

She sat beside him. Her looks were troubled, he noticed. "Is there something you want to tell me, Summer? Are you still in pain from the episode last ten-day?"

"No, my Lord, I am fully recovered. To be truthful, his manhood was small and although painful and humiliating, I don't think I am injured. More happily, I do not think I am pregnant. If I am, I will kill myself."

Bdescu surprised her by not offering platitudes or protesting that she should not do such a thing. Suicide is a mortal sin in the Empire, she knew. He just nodded as if he understood. He complimented her on the soup.

"My Lord, will you and your clansmen go to fight the people in the Teeth-of-God Mountains?"

"Of course. It is my General's wish and thus my Duty".

Tears flowed quietly, unnoticed from her eyes. "Please don't go. You do not know what you're taking on. The Byekiy are sorcerers. They know everything. They warned us about you before your army ever appeared on our borders. They knew your numbers, your plans, equipment, everything. They begged us to take refuge with them, they offered to evacuate the entire city and feed us until you were defeated. Then they said that we should leave you to starve in an empty city and then we could come home safely. We refused, we said we could defend our strong walls against any bunch of barbarian invaders."

Bdescu, startled at being thought a barbarian, watched her intently. "Go on" was all he said.

"When the Prince said he would defend his own kingdom, they offered a plan in case it all went wrong. He is proud, my father, but he is not stupid so he agreed. The Byekiy said they could evacuate us if the worst happened. Some of us would have to stay behind to make it look real, to give them enough time to get the weak and wounded onto their fast carts and away to the hills. The Witch herself was here! I met her, I saw her face!" She put her head into her hands and wept bitter tears.

Her shoulders shook with harsh sobs. "Where is my father? Did he escape?"

Bdescu walked around the corner of the table and knelt next to her. He put his arms around her, awkwardly from the side. "Yes, I think he did. How did they do that trick, getting him out of that high tower so fast?"

She turned in his arms. Her face was reddened and streaked from tears. "They are sorcerers, especially the Witch. She can fly. I know that. She says she is not a witch at all. The Byekiy believe in her magic and they try to learn it too. They want it to make them all-powerful like her. I do not know if she is a witch but I know she's really strange. She commands the Snowhammers. They hate slavers. They will not tolerate you on their lands. She said so. She said if one of their people is harmed they would go to war right away. They know all about you, Colonel. They even know your names!"

Bdescu jumped. "They know my name? They actually told you my name, before I even arrived here? This is impossible."

She smiled sadly. "I know it is. I know you think me a stupid slave. But in my world I was a princess and my father's trusted daughter. I was there at the council when the Byekiy came here. They sent their most important officials. They're called simply "the Five". They are sort of councillors. They each represent one of the sections or classes of their people. I forget the order they come in but first there's a man who represents the artisans. There's a woman who represents families and another who represents the priests, teachers and doctors. Another man represents farmers. The Witch represents the army. She doesn't usually say much. The others told us how they'd look after us, along with the escape plan. My father asked about the Imperial invasion forces and then the Witch talked all right. She knew all about you. 'They are nominally led by a General, but he's a coward and a politician, not a real soldier. The one to watch is Bdescu, he's the strategist and tactician. He's the one who will break through your gates. He'll figure it out. Kill him and you'll have a much better chance of survival.' That's what she said."

Bdescu believed her. Her intelligence was without doubt. Her position in the royal family might have given her access to these meetings. Not in the Empire, of course – a woman would never have been invited, unless it was to serve wine or food. In these wild lands anything might be possible. Could a princess know the answer to the riddle?

"How did they make that hole in the city wall, Summer?"

"I didn't see. Witchcraft is what we all believed. The Witch laughs at such words. She says it is 'technostitsch' or some word like that. She says that in many centuries we will be able to do these things too. She says she is from an older kingdom where such miracles are everyday things. We must just be patient and we will learn. She teaches magic to the priests, the doctors and the soldiery. The soldiers call themselves Snowhammers. They have armour. Every single soldier has armour, not just the knights. They have superb weapons. They are organised. They will come at you, Colonel and they will kill you!"

Without warning, she put her lips on his and kissed him. She forced her tongue into his surprised mouth. Her kiss was hot, passionate. It was not the kiss of a slave seeking favours. Her blood was roused, he knew. To his amazement, he discovered a powerful response swelling up in his own body, a swift arousal. She reached down and put her hand on him. He stood up, picked her up in his arms and carried her to his rooms, all without breaking the kiss. When she felt the strength in his arms she moaned and clung on tightly to his neck. He took her to his bed and found a new, wonderful form of lovemaking. He discovered lovemaking where each took their turn, where his head spun from the power of his lust and the completeness of his fulfilment. He knew that she felt the same power. Something changed forever in those moments. His mind opened to the void inside him. For the first time he knew his own loneliness. He recognised that his fierce independence was a shield against the absence of this – this powerful, engaging passion that was now glowing inside him.

She kissed him again. She ran her expert hands over his sweating body and looked at him in the firelight. "You're beautiful", she said.

"What, this scarred old alley-fighter? I've been in continuous action all my life. You are either suffering from blurred vision or…"

"Or what? Or I'm in love with you? Of course I'm in love with you. I've been dreaming about you since I first laid eyes on you. It's stupid. You are my enemy. You killed my people. You're a slaver, a killer, an invader and probably worse. My people will never forgive me. Your people will always treat me as a slave. And all I want is to climb back on top of you and have you love me again."

He was mysteriously aroused again, so they did exactly that.

Bdescu watched her sleeping. He had no idea that he was capable of these feelings. He had never found a woman who caused this depth of sensations. Arousal occasionally. He'd dallied with lovemaking, of a perfunctory kind. Not this, this was new. His reflective character needed to think. Each time he looked at her he felt a hot, sliding sensation inside, somewhere between his heart and his stomach. She turned in her sleep, threw her perfect, pale arm across his chest. She unconsciously nuzzled his armpit. He looked at her bruises and felt a sickening surge of rage. He wanted to hold her, protect her from harm. He wanted to walk in fields with her, drink with her, watch her eat, watch her dress and bathe. He clasped her to his side and whispered to her. "I love you too, golden Summer." He stopped thinking so that sleep could slide over him. Her eyes opened and she smiled.

In the morning he quizzed her about the mysterious people of the mountains, the Byekiy. Every new piece of information gave him further amazement. "They believe all men, women, kids and even mad people are equal but different. I told you they have a government made up of the Five Elders. There's a sort of hierarchy of Elders. Each town has a district and that has its own Five. Each province has Five as well, but more senior. Finally, there's the First Five, they run the whole country and who basically make all the laws. You have to be a certain age to be allowed to stand. Then you get people to vote for you. If you get the most votes, you can be an Elder."

He smiled. "Go on."

"Then there's the Judges. They settle all the disputes and enforce the laws. Judges can't stand as Elders or the other way around. Judges have magistrates working for them. Magistrates work on crimes and disputes. They are supposed to find out the truth about what went on if a crime or a dispute happens. Then there are the constables. They work for the magistrates and keep the peace, arrest criminals and administer punishments. Judges are not elected. They must start as constables, then be promoted to magistrate, and then finally judge. It's all kept separate from the Elders and what they do."

Bdescu must have looked as incredulous as he felt. She laughed. "I know, madness it must seem to you, with your Imperial ways. We have traded with these people for centuries. We are still a monarchy and we loved our Prince, my poor father. When he gets to forty he'll be King, and a good King too. We were proud of him and proud of our land. Even we don't really understand the Byekiy. What I have told you I believe to be true. I have travelled in their lands in the summer on Royal visits. They are prosperous, happy people. Their kids are tall and well behaved. Their animals are fat, the fields and barns are full. They make the finest farming tools ever seen, far better than we can make. Their ploughs are sharp and run straight. Their spades will dig for a lifetime. A Byekiy ploughshare ploughed every field of ours. They might strike you as insane, but their crazy ways work for them. They believe they are right, just as strongly as you do. You think you will round up a few hill tribesmen and carry them home as slaves. The truth is their legions will roll over you like ocean waves, drowning you all. I fear for your life, my love, my forbidden love. I fear you will go and never return. Take me with you. I want every day that God grants us together."

Bdescu smiled fondly at her. "Summer, do these people have cavalry?"

"No, I don't think so."

"Then hear me and believe what I say. We are heavy cavalry. Every noble knight has been trained for war from boyhood until this very day. The weak and the cowardly are ruthlessly eliminated by constant fighting, feuding and duelling. We wear chain mail and scale armour. Our mounts wear heavy padding. We charge at our foes with lance, sabre, mace and flail. Every infantry we have ever met melted away at our charge. No man is insane enough or resolute enough to stand up in the face of a cavalry charge. The beats of our hooves, the noise of our war cries, the sight of our armour and our shining weapons is too much for a common soldier to bear. The very best of them run and skirmish. Most of them just run, and keep running. We ride them down and kill as many as we catch. Never have we failed, in two hundred years, to break an enemy line. Once the cavalry breaks their shield wall, then our slave-soldiers pour in behind their lines, stabbing and causing havoc. I've seen us beat armies three times our size and lose a dozen knights or less. I have met people like the Byekiy before, I'm sure they are brave but they are foolhardy if they try to resist us. We have conquered a whole world with our methods and remained unbeaten. They will be a tough but disorganised rabble, tribesmen who owe allegiance to a lord who is easily killed. We are the owners of the battlefield. Without cavalry, your former allies will be fodder for the carrion-eaters two bells after we join battle with them."

She looked up at him with trusting eyes. "For our sake, my Lord, I hope so. What is your name?"

He smiled. "My family name is Bdescu. You must use that in front of everyone. Lord Bdescu. In private, inside the walls of this house, you may call me Gvant."

"Gvant. What does it mean?"

"It means 'born to rule' and is a very common name in the Empire."

"Then, my Lord Born to Rule, kiss me and stop me worrying. For I fear that even your heavy cavalry will meet its nemesis in the mountains. You call them the Teeth of God. The inhabitants call them 'Slaver Bane'. Only one of you can be right and I pray it is you. I am torn in half. I want you to live but your friends to be defeated. Can my desires be satisfied? If you live, I fear that all those I love will die as slaves. If you die and my friends go free, I will die a lonely spinster. I cannot be happy. I am doomed."

Gvant took her in his arms and rocked her gently. "All will be as God wills it. If I am to die I will do so happy in my service and my devotion. I will meet you in Heaven and all will be forgiven. There is no need to worry. You are mine as I am yours. We will care for one another and be happy as we are allowed."

"Now tell me, what in God's holy truth is a Snowhammer?"

"I do not know. Blenvan people think it's a legend. The Byekiy describe it as a bird so big it can kill a man and carry off his body. A dead man is so heavy that the Snowhammer can only take off in a howling blizzard. It lives right on top of the Teeth of God mountains as you call them. Because it only flies in blizzards, you never actually see one. That's what the Byekiy believe. Everyone else says it's impossible."

Bdescu stroked his beard. For a moment he thought he could see a solution to all these mysteries. But then his logical nature asserted itself. "I can see why. If it's so big it must eat a lot. Flying takes lots of energy. Birds can't get fat, they have to eat little and often. How can it fly for only part of the year? Surely it would starve in the summer? And all animals die eventually, so we'd find corpses even if we never saw a live one. No, I'm thinking that the Blenvan people must be right. I used to train birds of prey to hunt with, so I know a bit about it, and I can't see this one being real."

He spent hours questioning her about the mysterious people of the mountains. What she knew, she told him although it betrayed her loyalties. Her distress was plainly visible.

Invasion

The column marched slowly out of the city gates. The General and his troops went first. Bdescu and his retinue came next. The spring air was fresh and clean. Bdescu's mount was in fighting trim after his winter exercise. He snorted and danced at the newfound freedom of the march. Behind Bdescu came his knights, five hundred and seventy-one mounted fighting cavalry. They were drilled and disciplined, laughing at jests and battle-ready. After them marched his infantry. Two thousand slave-soldiers controlled by fifty sergeants. They too were drilled and ready, marching in neat orderly lines. They sang their marching songs and wagered on the plunder they would draw from the coming raids.

Behind Bdescu came the shambling troops of the two other colonels. Their knights slouched in the saddle, out of condition after a winter spent wenching and gambling. The sergeants grumbled as they marched, whilst the slave-soldiers muttered darkly about incompetent leaders dragging them into a holocaust. Morale in these divisions was low, so far from home and sunshine. The rain drifted in fine draughts, soaking their clothes and their spirits.

And last, behind the lowest slave soldier, came the camp followers. The baggage train was a miniature marching city of whores and tinkers, armourers and smiths, peddlers and gamblers, moneylenders and pot washers. They straggled along on foot, by cart, by wagon and on scrawny mounts. The food wagons were in their care, a fact that never once crossed Bdescu's mind.

The Rector of God's Chosen, Flantr, had blessed the army, handed over to his Senior Chaplain, and left with a strong contingent of bodyguards, headed back to his Palace. The army left behind a garrison of wounded soldiers, camp followers, clerks and factors. Bdescu had insisted that Fenjent, his Guard Captain and one of his Trusted Men, was left in charge. The Treasury was well stocked so the General was reluctant to leave it unattended. In spite of Bdescu's protests, the General left a dozen of his personal Freeman Guard to keep the metal safe. Bdescu, alarmed by Summer's stories, had attempted to interest the General in his knowledge, but his bond-father had laughed off his fears. "It's not like you to show fear, my boy! Get over it. Think of the slaves, the riches, the Advancement! Already we have moved up the Rankings of Court. One day soon I will get my Audience, and then we'll really make it! Have patience, lad. One more campaign and we're made for life. Trust me I've never failed you yet!"

The Imperial column moved slowly across the savannah towards mountains called the Teeth of God. Once they reached the well-made road, progress became swifter. The road was hard and gave good grip even in the rain, taking all the weight of their mounts and carts. The mountains rose before them, first the green foothills, then far further, the great jagged peaks white with snow. Ahead lay a wide, open valley. The road led faithfully into the valley. Cliffs that offered no through route for an army flanked the valley. As they drew nearer, Bdescu's sharp eyes could see that the valley was deeply wooded with mature trees. The trees had caught the avaricious attention of the Baron General and his Imperial colleagues. At the last Council, Commissar Rbunft had explained to him the realities of Imperial wealth. Slightly patronising as usual, the lean Agent had told Bdescu how it would be.

"The foothills are clothed in hardwood trees in a density I have never seen before. The hot summers, cold winters and wet inter-seasons could be designed for the purpose of growing trees. They are taller, thicker and stronger than anything we can grow in the plains. Our rising population has exhausted our forests. We need such woods for a million purposes, from building houses to ships. Many outlying provinces have good forests. But the problem is getting them to market. Here we have a river that flows all the way down to our lands. If our slaves cut a tree down here it will cost next to nothing to roll the tree to the river, rope it to others to form a raft and float it downstream to market. At market, one of these giant hardwoods alone will fetch twelve Imperials." Bdescu whistled appreciatively. He could see how such a venture could make them all rich. "And that's just the wood. Add slaves, gold, furs and any other good stuff we find and we could all be Princes in three years!" Bdescu thanked Rbunft warmly for the explanation and went about his duties. He felt unmoved by his imminent advancement. His mind kept seeing those green eyes. No other Blenvan had green eyes as far as he could tell. Was this a sign of her royal blood?

The river that they followed flowed from a lush valley. There seemed to be no other route into the Teeth of God. Rugged cliffs and thick forests blocked the way to North and South. Due East and into the valley was the only option, a thought that kept Bdescu awake at night. His enemies knew he was coming. They understood his dispositions and his methods. His fellow-Colonels were slack and ill disciplined. Even the usually cautious General was basking in the company of the Imperial Agent rather than tending to his knightly duties.

At first when they camped, parties of slaves would go into the forest to collect timber. They reported nothing untoward. Over time they became more bold and ventured further into the dense, matted undergrowth in search of game and fruit. One afternoon a ragged band of wounded slaves blundered into the camp. The Colonel was summoned by the uproar. Summer walked swiftly beside him.

One of the slaves had been killed outright, another blinded and all the others lightly injured. Their wounds were caused by thorns the length of a man's hand. Each thorn had a feathery growth at its blunt end – a flight. The story emerged of a large tree whose curved branches had whipped towards the foraging party. The branches held hundreds of these thorns which were flung from it, straight at them. Summer called it a "whipthorn" tree and said that she'd heard they were common around here. She also said that there were predators big enough to attack a man or even a party of men, in there.

Most of the fruits the slaves had gathered were bitter and gave people stomach cramps or diarrhoea. Bdescu restricted foraging to the edge of the forest for wood gathering. Men could feed themselves by shooting the fat birds that clustered in the trees at the edge. There were abundant fish to be netted from the river. They would never starve in this land. Bdescu saw no need to risk fighting men to unknown dangers in a forest.

Each night they camped by the river, which provided water, washing and a latrine. The sanitation given by the kindly river made for a happy, healthy camp. There was little dysentery. In fact there was little sickness of any kind. Not for the first time, Bdescu wondered why an army always stayed healthy when it camped by a river, but rapidly became sick when it camped far from fresh water.

They pitched camp at the opening of the valley. Behind them stretched the improbably straight road, its bevelled paving acting as a measure of their progress. Beyond the green rounded hills reared the real mountains, their snowy peaks carving the heavens. Bdescu had seen hills, but nothing like these monsters. The clouds seemed to form around their heads as they scratched at the base of heaven itself. He could see large birds circling around the peaks. He wondered if these were the fabled Snowhammers of legend.

His slaves pitched his tent. Summer directed them. After so few months in his service she led his retinue. Her calm authority and her influence with the master were an unbeatable combination. They begged her to petition him for favours. She adjudicated fairly in their petty squabbles. Only a handful of their issues needed the master's attention and Bdescu knew that she lifted a terrible burden from his shoulders. She now ran the household as his factor. She kept his pocket book and paid his debts. She negotiated with the vendors of the baggage train with relentless arithmetic and unyielding authority. His tent was immaculate. His clothes were clean and smelled fresh. His food was cooked better than any campaign kitchen ought to manage. His old cook looked up to Summer as a mistress and followed her lead without demur. Truly, she acted like a princess. Yet no man resented her. Under his care, her eyes had softened and her smile had warmed. She walked with the athletic grace of a temple dancer. Her sinewy body rippled with youth and vitality. Her looks and her charm won everyone over. A man could hardly bear to look at her without smiling. Even one or two of the nobles had commented favourably on her. "Bdescu, you've worked a miracle with that one. I'd thought her a cold cut of meat, but with your firm hand she's turned into a proper slave. Respectful, obedient – why, she even looks prettier. You've done well there." Bdescu thanked his brother humbly and went about his business. None but Byardil saw the cold light of battle in his master's eyes.

As for Bdescu every time he saw her, his chest constricted in the familiar sliding sensation. And every night in the comfortable intimacy of their tent their lovemaking found new heights. She matched his ardour with equal passion. In this time of order he found a deep peace. He looked forward to his duties and even more so to the end of them. He laughed as he combed his mount's rough coat. He smiled at his best officers, joking with them. He singled out the men who worked hardest, giving them arm-clasps in front of the rest. Where once the men had respected and feared him, now they came to love him. Every soldier in his levee found the new, mellow Bdescu a warmer, more understanding master. He was calmer, less driven and more prone to listen rather than snap to judgement. It was the happiest march his retinue could remember. And every one of them knew it was the tall, green-eyed foreign slave girl that had tamed his temper. The slave soldiers idolised her. They called her 'Lfescung' – blessed one. They left wayside flowers by her tent. The sergeants set up a guard roster so that every free man could have his turn at guarding her about camp. She knew all their names, their familiars and Ranks. She laughed, she sang, she tended wounds when training became too rough. Her skill at stitching wounds became a legend in the camp. Her herbal brews cured diarrhoea in babies and stomach cramps in adults. She lanced boils, laced blisters with astringent spirits and showed the women how to minister to their children. She became Bdescu's wife in all but name. What had been missing from his retinue these long years had now arrived. Every man, woman and child in the camp felt the better for it. Bdescu had been their conscience, and now they had a heart.

Byardil was happy too. He knew his master would never return his love. But Summer had not excluded him. She kept well away from his duties and treated him with care and respect. They still met for a hot drink in the morning when the Master was with his troops. They gossiped and giggled like girls as they sipped the brew. She told him that the Byekiy treated homosexuals like everyone else. He gasped when she said the unsayable words "they let people like you get married. If you love somebody, you go to the priest and declare it. He or she will call the village together and witness your union. If you fall out, the priest will tell you you're a faithless waste of time and the other villagers will tell you to get back together. But if you don't, they won't really mind. They just think that it is better to be a couple than a single. They are an odd lot, but that's the way they are."

Byardil was enchanted by her stories, although he found them a bit far-fetched. "So if I fancy a nice boy, and he fancies me, we can just, you know, do it?"

She shrugged. "Yes."

"What, sex with a man? Proper sex, not just a fumble, but stuff that would get me anal-spiked in the Circus? Seems hard to believe." He stared at the mountains, just visible in the spring moonlight. "And all of us slaves would be free, if we were born there? I'm not sure I'd like to be free."

She looked at him in astonishment. "Why ever not?"

"Well, look at me now. I have everything I need. I have a kind Master, an even kinder Mistress, a job I can do and I love. The other slaves respect me, even if they don't like me. If I were free, I'd need to earn my own money. How would I do that? Would I sell my services? I'd need to find my own home. I'd never learn how to do all that!"

Summer smiled fondly at him. She rubbed his back with her long-fingered hand. "One thing at a time, my friend. First we have to survive this war. Then we'll talk about being free."

Byardil smiled back. "War? This will be a slaver raid, not a war. These people are savages, they won't give my master a single battle, let alone a war."

Summer smiled her pleasant smile and watched the birds circle endlessly on the mountain winds.

After four days' travel into the valley they had not seen a single human being. The road went straight up the centre of the valley floor, while the river meandered along, sometimes near, sometimes a half-bell's walk away. The road was flanked by meadows of well-grazed grasses, yet they saw not one grazing beast. The meadows were always four hundred paces wide and then came the forest. Thick undergrowth beneath heavy mature trees gave an impenetrable cover that caused Bdescu endless worry. Even under Summer's exhausting sexual appetite he could not sleep easily. He felt that every minute of his day was scrutinised. He felt prying eyes on him always. He told Summer that her Witch was watching him. She smiled sadly and just nodded. He petitioned the General in a Council one evening.

"My Lord Baron General. An enemy could conceal an army of skirmishers in these woods. One night we could be attacked and severe damage done if we are not watchful. I humbly request that we increase night watches. I will stand one watch in two as evidence of my concern."

The General could hardly be bothered with this routine matter. He would stand no guard in any case. He looked at his other two colonels. "My lords, I leave this to the majority. If two of three agree with Bdescu, then I authorise it. If two say nay, then I say nay. How say you?"

Ltencha wanted no part of it. "My Lords, a barbarian rabble will not get past our normal picquets. The Colonel is right to be concerned about our safety but I fear he overstates our risks. Let the men sleep in their tents. When we close with the enemy we can worry about their strength." The General was minded to agree.

Jcluid stepped into the Council circle. In a clear voice he called his position. "Sire and Lords here assembled. I am the newest of your company and not fit to grace your halls until I am honoured in battle. I beg your mercy. My levies and I stand beside my brother Bdescu. He is our foremost warrior. I will accept his noble guidance in this matter. My levee will stand second guard so that no man will be discommoded."

The General looked at the young man with a careful eye. He had sided with Bdescu, the man who killed his brother. Yet, by taking the other watch he had allowed Ltencha to walk away without losing face. This was a clever pup. "So ordered. Bdescu shall be allowed to double the guard. He and Jcluid shall man the picquets. Ltencha and I shall enjoy our women, safe in the care of our brothers."

As the General walked away, he noted Jcluid and Bdescu clasp arms in brotherly accord. This bargain had been struck long before this meeting. He knew Bdescu was gaining political skills. He suspected that the green-eyed slave girl was educating his bond son in the dark arts of deal making. Well, that might be no bad thing, so long as Bdescu kept faith with his bond father.

The next day they came upon a large building by the side of the road. It was a handsome structure, built of stone with a tiled roof, steeply pitched. It boasted an upper floor and an attic above that. The doors were snugly fitted and the shutters too. It was floored in hardwood planks that hardly creaked. The staircases were even and strongly made. Bdescu worried even more. This was not the work of savages. The stones were cut evenly and fitted tightly together. Between them was filler that looked like sand but was as hard as stone. He had never seen the like. The planks were cut arrow-straight and sanded perfectly smooth. An Imperial office was built with less craftsmanship than this humble way station. The General was delighted. He ordered his officers to each take one of the large rooms. "We'll stay a few days. We need to hunt, wash our clothes. This is the perfect hunting lodge. Bdescu, you and your princess can have the upper left room. I'll go up top. The others can agree amongst themselves. I'm sick of flapping tents. Tonight we sleep indoors!"

Bdescu awoke. It was the deepest part of the night, when men sleep insensible. Summer had gone back to her quarters with the other captive slaves, as she always did. She said his honour was ill served by people seeing her climb out of his bed. He felt troubled. Always he felt this sensation of being watched. He listened intently but could hear no sign of trouble. He flopped back onto the camp bed, restless and irritable. He got up again and started to dress. As he was awake, he might as well inspect the guard. Just as he finished lacing his shirt, he heard the early sounds of conflict. Shouting and clanging sounded from the far side of the camp. The row sounded like it was coming from the baggage train. "The food!" He shouted as he grabbed sword and buckler and ran for the door.

He burst out of the lodge and kicked a sleepy guard awake. "Ring the alarm bell. Don't stop unless you are killed". The strident tones rang out as he saw flame arrows arc over the camp. Signals. He ran through the sleeping soldiers, slapping men with the flat of his sword, shouting at them as they staggered to their feet. "We are under attack! Grab a weapon and follow me!" He saw fire spurt from a baggage wagon and the clashing and screams of combat. He burst into the wagon compound and saw black figures boiling out of the darkness through the perimeter. They moved fast and in silence. He saw that they clustered into tight groups. They carried shields and short spears. He watched as a piquet slashed overhand at a raider. The barbarian took the blow on his curved shield then stabbed up under the guard's mail shirt. Bdescu knew the wound was fatal even as he ran to the fight. Three of the raiders came at him. He slashed and parried, fighting for his life. The raiders were skilful warriors. They crouched low, bunched together. They covered one another with their shields as they stabbed at his legs, forcing him back. As he started to give ground, Cvelthan rushed to cover his shoulder. The raiders backed away immediately. He risked a look to his left and saw one of the assault teams reach a wagon. The one at the centre of the group was unarmed but carrying a clay pot. He threw it onto the wagon. It smashed and gurgled. A torch tumbled through the air and landed on the wagon. The sweet smell of spirits reached him. "Get away from the wagon, they'll burn it!" And the wagon caught fire with a deep cough. The spirits in the clay pot ran over the wagon's cargo, spreading fire. Mounts screamed and hauled at their ropes. Men shouted and fought like animals in the flickering light. Whistles shrilled in the darkness. Bdescu looked around and the raiders were gone. Every one of them had reacted to the whistles instantly, slipping away into the darkness towards the forest. Carrying their wounded, they ran quietly like beasts of the night. Their wounded did not scream or cry out. Bdescu had never seen such discipline. Its implications made him shiver. A hush fell on the dazed soldiers. Then the screams of the wounded and the rising flames called them back to the scene.

Bdescu shook off his frustration and called his orders. "Nobody follow them. There might be an army of them under those trees. Cvelthan, take the second section and form a piquet line. First section gets the fires out. Third section sweeps the camp. Count our losses. Bring me enemy wounded – alive if possible. Corpses if you find them. Move!"

Eleven wagons had been burned. All were grain wagons. Pots and pans, shoes and cloaks, all these wagons were unscathed. But all the grain was ruined. In the smoking dawn, the General held Council upwind of his ruined wagons.

Bdescu threw an enemy corpse on to the ground at the General's feet. The Commissar and the High Priest were standing on either side of the General. They recoiled from the gory remnants of a human being. The General jerked his chin at Bdescu. The Colonel knelt by the body and stared at it. Speaking in a low voice he told them what he saw.

"A well-fed man in his late twenties. Very good muscle tone. Calloused on both hands. The calluses are aligned with the weapons he carries, so he is a highly trained skirmisher. He wears a linen tunic in black. His skin has been blackened with plant dye so that his fair skin does not betray him in the darkness. His boots are short, tight laced to his feet and nailed for grip on soft grass. His hair is very short, cut with sharp instruments. His spear has a haft of lathe-turned hardwood with a rough rope grip. The blade is forged, very sharp and well formed. A deadly weapon, used well. The shield is boiled leather formed over hardwood, four layers then lacquered. Superior design, light but effective."

Bdescu stood up and stared down at the corpse. "If this is how they fight, we'll slaughter them in a pitched battle."

The General smiled. Bdescu was cheering up the men. They trusted him and soon his word would be all over the camp. The General spoke loudly so that they could all hear. "Hear that? We'll make them pay for this outrage. And I'm sick of bread anyway. Let's slaughter some beasts and have a proper feast!"

A ragged cheer went up from the men. Then a runner arrived, one of the General's aides. The General motioned for him to speak. "Sire, the slaves we took from the city…"

"What about them?" said the General, impatiently.

"Sire, they're gone. Run off during the attack."

The General's voice rose to a bellow. "What? How the shit did all those people walk out of a guarded camp in the middle of an attack? Get after them, now!"

Bdescu raised his eyes to heaven. Their plan was now revealed in all its glory. The first attack was a feint to rescue the Blenvan people. He knew that Summer and her fellow slaves had held a 'prayer meeting' last evening. That's when they had made the arrangements. How the raiders had got word to the Blenvan group he knew not. He suspected that his fine princess was the ringleader at this end of the plot. He smiled wryly and walked back to his billet. He felt no anger at being duped, only sadness at her leaving. Tears filled his eyes. He wiped them away with the base of his hand and muttered 'smoke' in case anyone had seen. A patrol rode by, their swords drawn. There was no point in hunting for the slaves. These people left nothing to chance. They were long gone. He guessed that the raiders had crossed the river by boat and overrun the picquets at the edge of the trees. The former slaves would now be safely on the far bank. He walked into his billet and sat on the cot. A crackle came from under him. He stood and reached under the rough soldier's blanket. He found a letter. It was a single piece of parchment, excellent quality. He walked to the window and opened the shutter. A slim gold chain slipped out of the folded paper. By the dawn light he read her words.

"My darling Gvant. I hope that by the time you read this, my people and I will be gone. I wanted to stay with you but your General would have had me killed slowly. I decline this honour. We both have our duty and you will understand why I did what I had to do. When you come against the Snowhammer, bring a large shield and leave your buckler behind. Stay alive and perhaps we will meet again. The chain is my gift of remembrance. Forgive me, but do not forget me. I love you. Summer."

He looked at the chain. It shone in the cool dawn light. He put it over his head and settled it under the shirt against his skin. For an instance, it felt warm against him. Then he felt nothing. He now knew that she had led the escape. He smiled heavenwards. "What a woman!"

They wasted a day repacking wagons, cremating their dead and treating wounded. The General chafed and argued, angry at the delay and at last night's outrage. He shouted threats to the wind. Men kept clear of his knout as it twitched in his hand. Bdescu looked at his buckler. It was formed of stout hardwood with a bronze boss and edging. It was painted with his house colours of purple and silver quarters. It was designed to deflect the heavy cuts from an enemy sabre in a cavalry melee. Why did she advise him to take a bigger shield? Was it another trick, a way to slow him down in battle? Dare he trust her? He decided that God would decide his fate and that her love was real. He discarded the buckler and took a heavy infantry shield. He had practised many times with shield and spear, so it was familiar. It would be heavier, but Bdescu did not lack strength.

As he was adjusting his mount's harness, a slave messenger summoned him once more to Council. He found the General back in a foul temper. Jcluid and Ltencha were just arriving as the General's scribe read aloud from a parchment identical to the one left by Summer. The parchment was written in High Tongue in the most formal and archaic style.

"Slavers. Leave our lands. If you leave now, no one will be harmed. You have arrived in battle array with dreams of wealth. Your wealth is based on slavery and we find it abhorrent. We will fight you if you keep coming forward. If you elect to come on we will meet you on the morning of the third day. Make camp on the hill with the white cairn and arm yourselves. Make peace with your God, for Hell awaits you there."

The scribe was ashen. "It is signed Fifth of Five, whatever that means."

Bdescu knew what it meant. "They are ruled by a council of five elders. The fifth one is their military commander. Apparently a woman leads their armies. And a witch, no less. She must have written this letter."

Ltencha and Jcluid looked incredulous and the General snorted with derision. "Well, I've never lost a battle and I've fucked plenty of women, so I think we'll be OK, eh lads? I suppose your fine Princess told you all this, Bdescu?"

The Colonel nodded. "You're right my Father. If they're all girls it might be pretty good fun."

The General laughed aloud. Battle and spoils. No more waiting. At last they had closed with their elusive enemy. "Come to my tent fellows. I have the last four flasks of wine, all the way from home. A proper drink is what we want." He threw his arm around Ltencha and young Vrabelm. Bdescu walked beside and all the camp saw the confidence of their leaders.

Battle

They camped by a white cairn of stacked rocks on a low hill overlooking a wide, shallow valley. On the opposite side of the valley they plainly saw the enemy. The enemy troops had picked an excellent place to make a stand. They were also on a hill, but no more than a rise, nothing to slow a determined charge. Their right flank was protected by the river, the hill falling onto the riverbank in a series of steep bluffs. The valley narrowed here. Their left flank was anchored by a marsh. The General's scouts had reached the marsh unchallenged. It was deep, wet and treacherous for infantry; hopeless for cavalry. A smooth green meadow, close cropped by grazing animals, lined the shallow valley. The centre of the enemy's hill was clear of obstacles. Sharpened wooden stakes, driven into the ground at an angle, protected the right and left flanks of the hill. Clearly they were supposed to deter a charge. But they had miscalculated. The unprotected centre was easily wide enough for a full cavalry attack. In fact, the whole arena could have been purpose built for the General's army. There was ample space for cavalry in good order to charge. There was enough depth in the field for the slave-soldiers to amass behind the nobles. Battle order could be maintained until the moment of breakthrough when the slaughter could begin.

To Bdescu's eye, the whole site was an invitation to a frontal attack. This was the favoured Imperial tactic. So why, after showing such intelligence, was the enemy being so stupid? It worried him more than he could say. And the sensation of being watched grew ever stronger. He looked up at the cliffs rising on either side of the valley but could see no watchers.

Bdescu stood at the edge of the camp and stared at his enemies in a bright, sunny dawn. They were deploying into battle lines. They moved with a slick precision just as their skirmishers had. Their strangeness bothered him. Firstly their uniforms were odd. Every man wore an identical costume. Boots, a tunic and an odd sort of cuirass that seemed formed of iron bands. The bands wrapped around the chest, then shorter bands over the shoulders. Each man carried a huge shield that covered one side of his body completely. Every shield carried an identical house marking, some sort of animal face, sketched in white paint on a dark background. They wore heavy helmets. The men in ranks wore plain helmets. Those standing front and centre of the ranks had crests of stiff bristle attached to the top of their helmets. These crests were dyed in different colours. These must be officers or sergeants, he surmised.

All of them carried spears. These were not the long spears that could defend against cavalry; they were more like heavy javelins. Strangest of all was their formation. They stood in blocks, four ranks deep and seventy men wide. The blocks were laid out like bricks, with gaps in between. There were four blocks of men at the front, then a space and five blocks in a second rank. The second rank overlapped the gaps in the first. Another space then came four blocks in a third row, again overlapping the gaps. It looked like a game board. He was at a loss to decipher their battle array. But counting them was easy. "Four thousand men." He nodded at Byardil's words. "Yes, old friend. Just four thousand against our twelve thousand. This will be a slaughter."

Behind the soldiers, atop the hill, were a row of catapults or similar. They looked like oversized crossbows.

At the sides of the infantry, amongst the sharpened stakes, were archers. Byardil counted roughly a thousand on each flank. Counting all, the enemy army was half the size of its Imperial antagonist. Not even a decent skirmish, thought the General.

Bdescu spoke, as he always did, to his household. "I think this will be a short battle. I am confident that we shall prevail. If I fall, you will become the property of my bond father, the General. Byardil is in charge, as ever. Obey him as you would me. If it comes to it, serve my bond father faithfully. If I have the luck of the day, have my bath ready for mid-afternoon!"

They cheered. They had no fear or doubt. Byardil had plaited his hair and beard to keep them from catching in his hauberk. The scribe now helped him on with his helm. He noticed that his master had a large shield. He realised that the enemy had archers and realised that Bdescu knew this business better than anyone. He relaxed. "Put the scabbard on the saddle grip. I'll use a flail today. They have armour and I'm not breaking my lovely blade on them." Waving to his house slaves, Bdescu walked slowly towards the field. Byardil led the giant mount Warhammer by his halter. He knew better than to speak because his master was putting himself into his battle mind. He was calm. His breathing was slow and even. Other knights joked, swore and mocked the enemy. As they gathered in their four Houses, Bdescu was a silent presence amongst them. Then he turned to Byardil and gripped his wrist. "God bless you, my old friend. I'll see you later."

Bdescu's sergeants had set up a high-sided wagon in the midst of the Bdescu levies. His knights stood at the front, clustered tightly around the wagon in accordance with the Rules. Behind them stood the freemen sergeants and the larger crowd of slave soldiers stood at the rear. But all could see their tall colonel as he stood, armoured but bareheaded on the high wagon seat. Silence fell. The colonel began to speak in his sonorous patrician voice, the High Tongue spoken clearly and without hesitation.

"A man is not judged by his birth. A man does not build his reputation on his looks or his garments. A man is known by his deeds and the outcomes of his actions. The lawyer is famed for his advocacy, the priest for his services and the sword smith for his blades. I am a noble born son of Empire and today I will be judged either by men of this Earth or by God in the world above. I do not know my fate. I do not know if I will live or die or suffer a maiming wound. In battle all is at risk and life is cheap. But there are things that are certain. To these things I hold fast. I am certain that I will fight for my God, His Holiness the Emperor and my Bond Father the General. I know that I will lead the charge and you will see me at your head. I know that you will follow me and that you will stand at my shoulder and fight as my clan brothers. And I know this: that when this night comes if I am dead, I will stand in heaven and say I did my duty. My men did their duty. Some of them are here with me, my Lord God. Look upon us brothers and smile. So I fear nothing, not even God on this day. I might be disappointed not to meet Him, since I command the finest fighters in the whole Empire!"

He looked down at the sea of faces. Many were smiling. He judged their mood as he could read the winds on his native plains.

"But we will not die. We will cut them down like mown grass. We will take their women and children as our slaves. We will harvest their crops, from grain to trees and we will prosper. Those of you who charge the line at my side will share in the glory and the spoils. Those who hesitate, wait for a hero to take your place, you will get nothing from me. Dead men cause gaps in the Order so that heroes might win Advancement. Slaves will be freemen after today. Freemen will become knights and knights, nobles. Any man who breaks through the enemy line will kneel before my sword and be a knight by nightfall."

A gasp ran through the crowd. Murmurs and whispers rippled around the wagon. He raised his hand for silence.

"It's in the Rules. Do you think that I would make a promise I could not keep?"

"Never!" brayed a huge voice from the middle of the crowd, sparking a laugh from the soldiery.

"Thanks Cvelthan, you're excused Guard for a fortnight!" The laughter spread and the men around burly Cvelthan started joshing him.

He commanded them to kneel and blessed them by their Order, first the knights, then the sergeants and the slaves. He raised them up and led them in cheering the Emperor and the General. He leaped nimbly down from the wagon. As he walked through the crowd a corridor formed as the men fell back. Each man touched his knuckles to his chin in salute as the Colonel walked by. He smiled. He stopped to touch a man on the shoulder or rap his breastplate. He reached his mount. Byardil helped him to put on his helm and sealed the buckles firmly. He grinned at the worried scribe.

"Time to earn the Rank, eh? See you at teatime. And try to find us some decent grub!"

They mounted. The knights, two thousand of them, led the army forward. The silver and purple of House Bdescu were to the right hand of the red and black of the General's levees. Right of Bdescu walked Vrabelm in gold and green. Ltencha's yellow and blue colours took station on the left. Pennants fluttered on bright lances. Caparisons newly washed and bright, gave splendid colour to their array.

Behind them marched the infantry. Ten thousand foot soldiers wore jerkins in their House colours. All were kept in order by their rugged sergeants who called the time and the dressing as they fell in behind the cavalry. Each man wore a brass helmet and a plate across his chest to cover the heart and lungs. The plate hung on leather straps over a padded gambeson of leather. The coat would absorb shocks and the plate prevented most mortal wounds. The house colours were worn on top. The slave soldiers were comfortable in their gear because the weather was much cooler than their normal hot summers.

Every troop had three drummer boys who beat the times. Trumpets gave the signals and the drummers changed the tempo as the trumpets commanded. In the warm sun and clear light it was a gorgeous sight. Byardil stood on the hilltop and watched the army march towards its next victory. He could just see his master's form at the front of House Bdescu's levies. "Please survive, my Lord and my love." This was his prayer at every battle.

Bdescu looked across at Jcluid. His forces were in some disarray, reflecting the young man's lack of experience and his struggle to exert his authority in the power void left by his brutal brother's death. Bdescu grinned at him and waved. Jcluid wondered why the grim Colonel looked so happy. He realised that this was an act to keep up the men's spirits and give them confidence. He turned in the saddle and smiled broadly at his own knights. "More slaves, lads! Roll over the little shitbugs and we'll be up their women by nightfall!" He saw them grin, leaning across saddles to punch one another's arm. He gave silent thanks to Bdescu for that piece of leadership training. How Bdescu could think of him at this moment was beyond him. His sureness about the Colonel's prowess grew every day.

Bdescu was mindful of the fact that the most important factor in a cavalry attack is the timing. If the catafalques got too far ahead of the infantry then the break in the enemy line would not be fully exploited. The heavily weighted cavalry chargers would tire very quickly if asked to run too far, too fast. A slow build up of speed was needed before the fatal charge could be driven home. Bdescu was the expert in this dark art. His trumpeters sounded the walk, the canter and the gallop according to his instincts, which were famously accurate. A charge called by Bdescu always crashed into the luckless enemy at just the right moment of maximum speed and aggression. The General always gave Bdescu this responsibility and was glad to be rid of it. Safe amongst his personal Guard, the General made a show of charging but rarely engaged the strongest opponents amongst the enemies.

They walked towards the enemy lines, confident. Safely out of arrow shot there was nothing to fear. Clearly, from across the field came a barrage of harsh metallic clacking sounds. Bdescu's quick mind knew it came from the distant ballistae, their wire strings crashing forward as they flung their bolts. The dark missiles moved at deceptive speeds from the contraptions mounted high behind the enemy ranks. Every single one was aimed at the cavalry and they arrived in deadly volumes. The General was hit first. One moment the burly General was riding his mount surrounded by his personal Guard. The next, a dark wooden shaft punched into the centre of the General's body. The impact threw the General's body back onto the haunches of his mount. Dvelt, the Baron-General's personal Guard captain, leaned over across the neck of his own mount and seized the General's arm in a vain attempt to stop the General from falling to the ground. The action saved Dvelt's life. A bolt went over him and struck another knight behind him. In spite of Dvelt's efforts, the General fell lifeless to the ground and the entire troupe stopped dead.

Bdescu ducked as a missile came straight at him. It struck a knight and screaming started. With a flickering, hissing sound the bolts flew into the close-packed ranks. Men were hit all around him. The entire advance stalled as men tried to seek cover from the terrible shafts. "We stay here, we die! Sound the Charge!" Bdescu kept his voice under control. His well-trained signallers sounded the order to advance at a canter and the army shook itself from its halt and began to move again. The enemy archers bent their bows. Bdescu looked at their strange long bows, which they seemed to draw not to the chin, so they could sight by eye, but to the ear. Surely they did not think they could cause any damage at this distance? Nor even aim straight, with the arrow crossing their line of sight?

Shrill whistles sounded. The archers loosed every shaft in the same instant and two thousand arrows crossed the sky in two swarms, one from the left and the other right. The ballista shafts kept coming too. Men fell all around him. Then the arrow-strike hit. A strike perfectly judged even at this extreme range. Two thousand arrows landed virtually at the same instant. Mounts screamed as the stinging arrows wounded them. They flinched, ran sideways, bucked, reared and panicked. Men were thrown and trampled, with no chance of getting up amongst the swerving beasts. As the arrows landed, a second flight was already aloft. They wasted no shots on the slave soldiers. Every shaft was aimed at the cavalry. Bdescu's big shield saved his life twice in six heartbeats. The heavy shafts protruded from his stout shield but he kept it high.

Then the enemy unleashed a third projectile strike. With a distant clash, long arms of catapults sprang up into the vertical. From the baskets at the ends of the arms, dark masses sprang into the air, spreading as they rose. Bdescu stared intently and realised they were darts of some kind.

"Shields aloft!" he bellowed.

The dark masses reached their zenith and fell with sickening speed onto the dense-packed Imperial troops. With a harmless-sounding rattle they struck. Bdescu saw one strike a nearby knight on the shoulder. An iron spike as long as a man's arm and weighted to fly truly, pierced the knight's chainmail. It went through unchecked. The knight fell screaming from his mount. Bdescu looked up. The catapult shafts were already pulling back towards the horizontal and he knew a second dart fall was instants away.

"Sound the gallop! Let's get amongst them!"

The trumpets sounded and every knight put spurs into his mount's sides. They surged away from the levies, rapidly opening a wide gap between the two arms of their forces. As the cumbersome mounts started to gain speed, there was still time for two more flights of arrows, each as deadly as the last. Mounts stumbled, collided and fell. Riders all around him tumbled to the earth. At this speed, an armoured knight hit the ground with enough force to snap his bones. As they gathered speed, Bdescu gained confidence. Although they had suffered worse losses than he had ever seen before, there was still a formidable force of armoured cavalry bearing down on a few thin lines of men. Soon the enemy would turn and flee. Their tall shields might be useful against a sword, but a heavy horseman would ride over them, they would soon start to quail. Once the panic broke out, they were prey. "God Be With Us!" bellowed Bdescu and the cry broke from a hundred throats around him. In a few short beats they would be amongst the enemy and all his worries would dissolve.

As they reached a point less than a spear cast from the enemy line, a single trumpet started to sound from the enemy lines. In one smooth practised movement the enemy stepped forward. The front rank grounded shields. The second rank raised their shields above the front rank's and formed a wall, two shields high. The third rank did the same and from nothing a wall of shields higher than a man appeared. Bdescu's mount Warhammer saw what looked like a solid wall, too high to jump, appear right in front of him. He, and every other mount, dug in his heels and braked to a dead stop. As the cavalry charge deteriorated into a shambles of turning, stopping mounts and cursing men, the enemy threw their heavy javelins. The first ranks of men brought down their shields and flung the projectiles in one motion. The arrows had been bad, but these missiles were terrifying. It was carnage as men were skewered in their saddles. The hard steel points, driven behind a long thin shaft mounted on a heavy hardwood pole, punched through mail as if it were not there. They caused deep mortal wounds. The screaming of wounded men and animals merged into a cacophony of pain.

A spear struck Bdescu's trusted shield, drove cleanly through it and sliced into his bicep. Letting his flail fall and dangle from its lanyard, he reached over and yanked the spear out of his arm, screeching with the pain. He flung the now useless shield to the ground. The enemy were marching smartly and in good order towards him. Their second rank was drawing back their spear arms for another javelin cast. As the spears landed in a second sickening fall of death, the enemy troops ran the last few paces and smashed into Bdescu's struggling cavalry. He tried to get Warhammer to move, but the beast was confused by the melee. Enemy soldiers swarmed amongst the stalled cavalry. They held shields high. Their short swords stabbed in short murderous thrusts. Mounts or men, they did not discriminate. Their methods were simple; push and stab. Bdescu waited, his blood now cool. He raised the iron flail to half port, leaned a few degrees to his right and swung a timed blow. The enemy soldier turned and saw the ball coming but he was much too slow. The flail's ball caught him squarely in the neck, snapping his head across. He was dead before the hit the ground. Bdescu felt a deep shudder from inside Warhammer and he knew that the beast had sustained a mortal wound. Before the great creature could fall on him, Bdescu swung his leg over onto his right side and slipped to the ground. The enemy line was upon him. He pulled a short sword from his saddle and watched for his opening. The big shields loomed, the short enemy swords jabbing through the gaps. His knights, many now dismounted, were forced back into the melee of struggling men and mounts. The enemy tactics did not allow a man to fight. They closed the spaces so that a sabre had no room to swing. It was like being forced onto the teeth of a macabre saw. Their heads and shoulders were clad entirely in iron, so a sabre cut to the head rarely had any effect. But their short, stiff, sharp-pointed blades slipped through the gaps and killed. Bdescu used the flail to drag down the shield of an enemy, as the man's surprised face came into view he stabbed him through the cheek and he went down. Using the flail in precise arcs through the gap he had created, Bdescu grimly struck one soldier on his exposed elbow. He fell, screaming with a broken arm. On the backswing, Bdescu struck the other soldier across the kilt that covered his thigh. He yelled but stayed on his feet. The second rank stepped forward and closed the gap Bdescu had created and his chance of breaking through was cut off. Blood poured down his injured arm and sweat ran into his eyes. He swung and stabbed, pushed and danced but he made no headway. All around him knights were falling. He could not look around, the short blades threatened at every side. He had to move like an eel just to stay alive. He knew with calm certainty that today he would meet his God. Then as he parried an enemy thrust with a raised sword, he felt a shocking blow under his armpit and knew he was hit badly. The enemy dragged the sword out of Bdescu's body. He turned and backhanded the man with the flail's handle and saw the blow break the man's jaw. The strength began to drain out of him. The wound was like an anvil in his chest. He fell to his knees. A soldier raised his sword and brought the hilt down smartly on his head. His vision went black and he fell under the feet of the combatants.

Byardil saw the awful battle from his vantage point on the low hill. All around him, camp followers screamed with fear. The cavalry charge broke without even reaching the enemy lines. The slave soldiers had become separated from the cavalry because of the premature charge. By the time they caught up, they could not form lines and reach the enemy because of the confusion before them. They pushed forward driven on by their sergeants. They bunched up behind the cavalry but they merely pushed the knights onto the enemy line and reduced their space to fight. Their arrival just made the whole thing worse. The enemy archers fired scores of arrows at the slave soldiers, whom they could hit without risk to their own lines. The arrow falls made the slave soldiers bunch all the more as they tried to get forward and into the battle line.

Byardil saw the enemy break through the defeated knights. The enemy formed a wedge of shields, locked together. They pushed the wedge into the knights' ground. Their soldiers followed in behind the wedge, forming a salient. The salient grew as they met the lightly armed slave soldiers, who were no match for their heavier armour and weaponry. The battle became a slaughter because the Imperial soldiers were helpless against this adversary. The sergeants yelled and shoved, but they were losing ground, and men, at an accelerating rate. Then the Imperial forces broke. Men at the rear panicked and started to back away from the carnage. This released the pressure on the men in the middle and they began to turn away. The mood changed in an instant to panic and the entire army broke. Men threw down their shields and spears and ran back towards their own camp.

Byardil saw them come streaming back. He turned away, eyes flooded with tears and thinking only of his master. He ran swiftly towards the tents and wagons. His legs lost all speed when he saw the enemy archers haring down the road. They out ran the tired Imperial forces and formed line between the fleeing slave soldiers and the imagined safety of the camp. With one movement they nocked and drew. Not one man had the courage to face those arrows and the Imperial flight became a milling rabble of confused, shouting men. The archers started to chant. To Byardil's amazement they spoke Imperial in an accented but understandable form.

"We're not freemen, we're not lords.

We're the fighting legions.

Sit right down and drop your swords.

We don't kill our prisoners."

They chanted this three times. The Imperial troops began to sit down. The few still armed threw away their weapons and sat down too. Soon thousands of men were sitting quietly in a field in this foreign land. Men started talking in low fearful voices. Perhaps the barbarians are cannibals. Perhaps they will torture us. For the slaves it was bad enough. For the freemen, and the few knights with them, it was worse for they had never been slaves before.

Byardil

Byardil walked towards the battlefield to find his one love. His tears were dry now and he just wanted to find Bdescu's body and hold him in his arms. All around him that pleasant field was churned and bloodied. Dead and dying mounts writhed or lay as they had died. Men crawled dragging pierced limbs and broken bones. Men cried out pitifully for help. Byardil kept moving. He looked around and saw the strangest things. The enemy soldiers were loading wounded men, friend and foe alike, into strange carts. The carts were softly sprung with iron torsion bars. The cart's bed was a frame with notches. The soldiers would bring a contraption of canvas and two poles. They rolled the wounded onto these stretchers and lifted them gently onto the carts, locking the stretchers' hafts into the frames. A dozen wounded men went into each cart and it moved slowly from the battlefield, onto the road and over the hill out of sight. A line of these carts rolled in procession along the road. A second line flowed back down the hill to empty the battlefield of men. A group of men and women in blue tunics were moving around the battlefield with papers, recording where the dead had fallen, apparently. Yet more men walked in lines across the field collecting weapons, discarded armour and other junk. Groups worked on the dead mounts, methodically butchering the beasts and starting smoking pits. Over the pits they assembled neat frames to dry and preserve the meat.

Byardil wandered amongst this purposeful activity feeling lost and numb. Nobody seemed to want to harm him. But he walked amongst the dead of Clan Bdescu and did not find his Lord. A blue-tunic walked past him and smiled. "Do you speak my language?" asked the lost scribe.

"Yes, of course. Everyone here has to learn Imperial in school. Most people here speak three or four languages. Who have you lost, my boy?"

Byardil wept without noticing. "My master. Earl-Colonel Bdescu Gvant."

The Byekiy gasped. "Are you Byardil?"

"Yes," said Byardil completely confounded by a stranger knowing him by name out here in the midst of an alien battlefield.

"Follow me, please. You've a friend in high places."

The stranger led the slave over the hill past the former positions of the enemy army. The ballistae were gone. As they crested the hill he saw a camp laid out before him with the precision and planning of a small city. Tents were set out in accurate lines at set distances. Roads of pounded earth were reinforced with stout planking. Flags flew on trimmed poles at corners. And all the while, the carts carried the moaning wounded into a cluster of tents in the middle of the camp. The Byekiy led him to a small clear space between tents. There, incongruously, stood the Bdescu clan's best wagon with all the Colonel's personal gear, the tents and cooking equipment. Standing around it was Bdescu's retinue. Mridka tottered over to Byardil and threw her ancient arms around him, weeping. She handed him a paper and a red bandanna. "They fetched us from camp and gave us these."

He opened the letter. 'Dear Byardil. I hope that you have survived the conflict and that my friends have treated you well. You are now in charge of the family until I tell you different. Wear the bandanna and people will help you. Set up camp. Feed everyone with the food we placed in the wagon. Wait for me. I have no news of Gvant he is lost for now and we will search for him. I will see you soon. Summer'.

"What does we do, Chief Scribe?" asked the old cook.

"Cook some lunch, put up our tents and wait, I suppose". He walked to the wagon and set them to unloading.

After a meal the others sat around worrying but Byardil was too restless. He walked over to the tents where they were still bringing wounded. He found an extraordinary scene. Men were checked over by the blue tunics people first. Some men were too badly wounded and were given a drink that made them fall asleep. Probably forever, he guessed. The lightly wounded were treated in their stretchers then carried back to a cart and loaded for transfer. The badly wounded were taken into a tent. As a flap was thrown back he saw surgeons in white uniforms and blood stained aprons. He drew back in fear from the carnage. Then he noticed the lack of screaming. There were moans, even whimpers. But every surgery he had ever seen had involved the full throated screams of agony caused by bone saws and sharp knives cutting flesh. This place was too calm. Then he saw a familiar face. Jcluid Vrabelm was carried out of a tent on the now-familiar stretcher. His pale face was pinched and grey. His left arm was off at the elbow and a neat bandage covered the stump. So he had suffered an amputation in silence – how? Byardil walked over to him and walked alongside. "Sire, have you seen my master?"

The tired eyes looked up at him with the squint of a drunken man. Slurring his words, he chilled Byardil's heart. "I saw him fall. He took a sword blade under the arm and a bad blow to the head, then he went underfoot. He fought like a prince. I was pinned under my dead charger with a broken arm. I never struck a single blow." He started to cry as they reached the ambulance wagon. He was loaded aboard and taken away. Byardil stood helplessly as the smoothly sprung cart moved smartly away.

For three ten-days Bdescu's retinue camped peacefully in the midst of an enemy army. Carts brought food to each tent. In each tent a dozen men were billeted. The enemy rested after the conflict but kept busy with repairs to their equipment. They sharpened swords, hammered straight their armour and sewed uniforms. They marched with precision and bellowed orders in their rolling tongue. They ate together, worked together and laughed. There were constant exercises and contests: throwing, carrying boulders, jumping, running and even full-scale team sports. Byardil watched as two teams of twelve men ran around with sticks and balls, crashing into one another, knocking men bloody and scoring goals in a square net. The watching troops cheered and made wagers. It looked like pretty good training for combat, thought Byardil. He stood at the edge of their sports field watching the fit young men run around. His feelings were deep and guilty. An officer came to watch and stood beside Byardil. "Greetings. You must be the Imperial man that Summer told us to look after, eh?"

Byardil, unused to being addressed as an equal, was unsure how to react. The man spoke imperial, but in the peer-to-peer syntax. Not the downhill manner of master to slave. Clearly this was a man of rank. His tunic was smartly pressed and coloured a deep green. His boots were polished leather and his hair cut short in the local manner. He was good-looking, as so many of these mountain people seemed to be.

"Ah, yes, my name is Byardil. I have the honour of being Scribe and Body Slave to Lord Bdescu."

The officer gave him an appraising stare. "Look, my friend. I know that being a homosexual is a capital offense where you come from. But here nobody gives a damn. Some of these men are like you. Most are not. But nobody cares either way. It is, however, considered rude to stare at people's legs! If you want to make contact, I'll introduce you to some guys like yourself. That way, you'll make some friends and you won't offend anyone. What do you say?"

Byardil blushed to the roots of his hair. He hardly had the strength to nod. The officer offered his hand. "Rinshant, Centurion, First Spear." Byardil shook the firm dry hand and followed the officer deep into the enemy camp.

At a stout wooden hut Rinshant opened the door into a bar. Men were sitting at tables drinking the ever-present beer. Some played games on boards or with cards. Women sat amongst them, shockingly immoral to Byardil's eyes. Then he looked across at a table with five men. He felt a tightening in his chest as one of them looked him in the eye and smiled. The young man waved him over, patting the bench by his side. Rinshant touched his arm. "You're among friends here. They will show you back to your billet. The charming centurion grinned briefly and walked away, leaving Byardil to do the hardest thing he had ever attempted: he sat down openly with men like himself.

They spoke rough but understandable Imperial. Their bawdy jokes made his face burn. Their tales of sex, battle and home life revealed a world that existed only in his dreams. A world where a man might live a natural life as a homosexual, without fear. Fat tears formed unnoticed in his eyes. His new friends decided to try to cheer him up. "Come on, Byardil! Have a drink! Tell us your story."

He took a deep breath, a long pull of the sharp, cool beer and started to tell someone, for the first time ever, of his secret love for Bdescu Gvant. Nobody laughed but everything changed.

Byardil walked back to their billet with light steps. He felt odd, as if his legs had no weight. He even felt more positive about Bdescu. Surely his master was alive – he could feel it! When he arrived back at the tents he saw nobody. The fire was out and Mridka was nowhere to be seen. The flap of Bdescu's personal tent was thrown back and Jrabney the groom walked out. He stopped and stared at the scribe in an insolent manner. "So, my little catamite, you're back are you? Been at somebody's arse, no doubt. Well, things are a bit different here now. I've taken charge in the Master's absence. And as the new master, I'm making a few changes. No more arsemen. On your way, or I'll slit your throat." To make his point he drew a long skinning knife from behind his back and held it towards Byardil. Byardil was terrified. His teeth wanted to chatter so he clenched his jaw. His bladder and bowel felt weakened and his voice trembled as he spoke.

"Jrabney, I am the senior slave here. The master wanted me in charge. I am sure you feel his loss as much as we all do, but this is not helpful. P-put the knife down and let's talk about this, can we?"

Jrabney laughed a short barking sound. He took a swift pace forward and lunged at Byardil's stomach with the point of his knife. Byardil leaped backward, the knife falling short by a finger's width. The groom laughed again, with even less humour. "Come on, you little pervert, I'll drop your guts on the ground and dance on your entrails. I've skinned animals worth more than you!"

Byardil heard a calm voice in his head. It was the master. "Grab one of the iron legs of the cauldron tripod." He reached across and clutched the iron bar. He found the strength to wrench it out of the ground, the cauldron falling into the ashes with a loud clank. Jrabney sneered at him and held the knife low.

"Do not hesitate, run at him with the point aimed at his belly." The reassuring presence of his master gave Byardil enormous courage. He took three fast steps toward the groom, holding the iron leg like a spear aimed at Jrabney's navel. The point struck Jrabney in the chest and knocked him off his feet. Byardil's momentum carried him forward and he fell on top of his opponent. Jrabney stabbed at him with the knife and he felt a tearing sensation in his side. Face to face with the snarling slave, Byardil realised that he was still holding the makeshift spear. "Stand up. Use the iron as a crutch and force it further into him" said the cool voice in his head. He brought up his knees and climbed hand over hand up the shaft of the iron bar. Every movement forced the shaft deeper in to his enemy's body. Jrabney screamed. His body convulsed around the bar that was killing him. Byardil ground his teeth and gave the bar one last shove – and stood up. He looked down at a corpse. The voice spoke again. "Thank you Byardil. You are my trusted man. Wait for me and have faith."

The presence left him. Byardil looked down at the gore oozing from his wound and staggered away from the death he had wrought. Timidly, the other members of the Bdescu household emerged from behind the wagons. Mridka had a contusion over her left eye. She grinned at the others. "Told yez. 'E looks like a pansy boy but he's a more better man than youse lot. And the Boss left 'im in charge. So you'd better shape yerselfs unless yer wants ter end up like that dung down there." She spurned the dead man with her foot. "Come on, Master Byardil, let's sort yez wound out, eh!" She managed to help him into the tent before he fainted. She smiled down on his face. "Master's left us in good hands, young man." She started to bathe the wound.

When Byardil awoke he saw a familiar face gazing down at his own. A cool dry hand smoothed the sweaty hair from his eyes. "Summer! He grabbed her hand and kissed it. "My princess. Thank you for looking out for a humble slave and his master's retinue. You are indeed an angel."

She no longer wore a slave's tunic. She wore a kilt of woven wool of complex green and blue plaid with a shirt of plain white linen. Her shoes were flat and practical, brown leather with laces. Even in this outlandish garb she was lithe and feminine. Her hair shone as it moved around her face. Her fair skin glowed with vitality. Her teeth were clean and white. She was unearthly. She squeezed his hand.

"Byardil! I'm glad you made it. The Snowhammer Legions are staying here but you are not. All of you are to spend one year as prisoners of war. You have broken their laws and they want reparation. You will be billeted in a village and asked to work on a farm for a year. After that you can choose to stay here as a free man. Or you may leave, go back to the Empire and be a slave again. You decide. Tomorrow a guide will come and take you to a convoy. It will lead you to the village where you will live for the next year. You will be settled in time to help with the harvest and over winter with the villagers. I'll come by and see you sometimes but not very often."

"Thank you, my lady. Is there any news of my lord?"

"None yet. Pray for him, if you will. Goodbye."

She hugged him, briefly and was gone. His heart was alive and his first prayer sent heavenwards. All he needed was hope.

They packed up the next day. A smiling girl, not yet twenty years of age, came to see them and gave them instructions for the road. She had the Byekiy look about her. Large framed and quite tall, with long limbs and strong flat muscles that stood out on her calves and upper arms. She had white teeth, as they all seemed to. Her hair was dark brown and her eyes amber. She helped them load up and watched as they harnessed the drays. Then she led them out of the camp via the far gate. They walked slowly out of the camp, on to the bevelled road and on into the foothills, into the alien, alpine landscape of the Republic.

Cvelthan

On the morning of the battle Master Sergeant Cvelthan awoke early and knelt at prayer. He roused his sergeants and led their prayers. He then dismissed them to wake the men and make sure they said their morning rituals properly. On this day a man could have need of his devotions. After a poor breakfast of cold game he inspected kit with his habitual rigour. God protect any slave soldier whose spear lacked an edge or whose shield straps were loose. Once the men were lined up in formation he marched them to the muster point to hear Bdescu's words. His involuntary cry of loyalty to his master earned him a barracking from the other lads. But not one man doubted that he meant it. He formed his troops up behind the cavalry and waited for the order to advance.

At first it went so perfectly. Bdescu's trumpeters called the pace and they moved smoothly because the ground was even and the footing firm. Cvelthan was confident. He was a blooded veteran of seven battles. He had risen from slave soldier through sergeant to First Sergeant. His broad body was a fighting platform, honed by marching and drill. He called to his sergeants to dress the lines and smiled. Then the bolts started striking the cavalry and noblemen began to fall. The arrow strikes began to flail the army as the catapults flung their deadly payload into the melee. Shouts and screams broke out all around him and the trumpets did not sound. In those vital moments he kept his head and his men in hand. The cavalry charge sounded. It was clear what must be done.

"Advance at the double!" And he led his men at a soldier's best battlefield trot towards the enemy lines.

As they neared the struggle he could see that the whole charge had failed. Under the bolts, arrows and now the terrible spears of the enemy the cavalry had stalled. A knight stuck fast is vulnerable. The enemy were already in amongst the struggling horsemen. Cvelthan rushed into the gap where he thought his lord should be and saw straight away the familiar form of Warhammer. The beast was on his side and clearly dying. Cvelthan saw the unmistakeable stance of his master. He saw Bdescu's artful strikes with sword and flail. He saw his lord fall. Pushing through the press he squeezed past the fallen mounts and stood over Bdescu's body. Hunching behind his shield he grasped his heavy spear and roared his challenge.

"Come on you scum suckers! Come and get some Imperial steel!"

The line of foreign troops advanced at him. Cvelthan raised his shield and stabbed out low, a wicked thrust that caught one of them in the thigh. He went down and Cvelthan blocked a thrust from the side that caught and stuck in his shield. He dragged the shield back to pull the stabber off balance but the man just let go of the sword. Cvelthan stumbled slightly and they stepped forward, crowding him with their enormous shields. He dropped the spear and drew his knife from its hiding place inside the curve of his shield. He saw a small gap in their shield wall and thrust through. His knife glanced harmlessly against iron armour. Something smashed into his outstretched forearm. The pain rocketed up his forearm and he heard the bone break, a liquid crunching sound. The blade dropped from his useless hand. As he tried to turn a raised shield struck him with its iron boss. His nose broke. Tears streamed into his eyes. He heard a hard bang inside his head. His last thought was to wonder if it was the sound of his death. He fell to the wet earth, the shield trapped under him. The line of enemy soldiers stepped over him, thinking him dead. With one arm pinned between body and shield and the other arm broken, he might as well be. He tried to shield his arm with his body but however he moved the pain exploded and he could do no more than try to keep his eyes open. The enemy wore stout boots of leather with nailed soles. They were ankle-high and tightly laced with thongs. Above the boots they wore steel greaves, enamelled a uniformly green colour. The tears in his eyes stopped him from making out any further details and he fainted for a while.

When Cvelthan came to, a man was leaning over him speaking accented Imperial. He wore a leather skirt that came to his knees where it met his long blue socks. On his torso was a short sleeved blue shirt of fine fabric and he sported a kerchief of black. He was about forty with dark brown hair tinted grey at the temples. His upper arms bulged with muscle. "Sergeant. Sergeant. Can you hear me?"

Cvelthan nodded. "Yes. My arm is broken." He was surprised how steady his voice sounded.

"I can see that. It's not a bad fracture. I will immobilise the arm and we'll get you to a doctor. The battle is over. I need your word that you understand that fact and that you will cease hostilities. If you do not promise this I will get some soldiers over here and they'll be a lot less gentle than I am. Clear?" Cvelthan nodded. "Yes, I give my word."

The man smiled. "Let go of the shield and try to roll onto your back. I'll support the arm."

The man was as gentle as a maiden. He had a leather bag with him and took out a sling. He bound the arm so that it could not move. He gave Cvelthan a drink of water, then a clear fluid with a strong aromatic smell. It made him feel slightly woozy but eased the pain considerably. He took Cvelthan's good arm and hauled him to his feet.

For the first time Cvelthan saw an Imperial army in heavy defeat. All around him was the detritus of battle. Corpses littered the ground, which was stuck with arrows and the iron spikes from their catapults. Discarded weapons were strewn around amongst dead and dying beasts. Men and women moved amongst the wounded. Wounded were being carried on litters and loaded into carts, which moved cautiously across the churned and bloody ground. As he looked around he could see large groups of prisoners, guarded by the armoured Byekiy soldiers, being herded up the road and deeper into Byekvoranp. Looking back, he could see that the camp was taken and all its occupants were taking down tents and packing up the baggage train. The sense of tranquil order was more shocking than the defeat. They had not only beaten an Imperial army but expected to do so.

"Do you want to ride in the cart or can you walk?" asked the solicitous doctor.

"I'll walk." Cvelthan bent down and picked up a broken spear shaft. He used his good hand with the shaft as a walking stick. His legs were weak and he felt faint but he would never show frailty to an enemy. The doctor pointed up the hill where the Byekiy forces had made their stand. "Go over the hill to the white tents. Just find anybody in a blue shirt and they'll get you treated. I hope you make a good recovery, Master Sergeant." They even understood his badges of rank. How in God's holy name did they acquire this intelligence about the Imperial army? He set off slowly for the tents. The doctor was already bending over a fallen slave soldier.

Cvelthan arrived at the bustling tented area and a blue-shirted woman walked straight up to him. She carried a wooden board with a scroll of paper drawn over it. "Hello Master Sergeant. May I have your name and clan, please?" She smiled.

"Cvelthan of House Bdescu."

Her eyes widened. "You are on my list. Come with me please."

She led him to a tent. She pulled back the flap and announced him by name. A tall thin man in a long white coat ushered him inside. He was sat up in a wooden chair. The man unstrapped the arm and looked at it carefully. It was blackening and swelling. The man looked into Cvelthan's eyes.

"You have a radial fracture of the upper arm bone. It has not broken the skin, which is great because it won't get infected. But it will take some straightening before I can set it. I will need to give you some herbal medicine to relieve the pain. It's administered in a strong drink and it tastes horrible. But we are not trying to poison you. If we meant you any harm we'd have killed you on the ground where you lay, wouldn't we?" The doctor grinned. "Then we will stretch the arm using a padded wrist cuff and ropes. Even with the herbs it will hurt like Hell. Scream if you want but try not to throw up all over us both, OK?"

Cvelthan was past caring and just nodded. He drank the vile potion that the woman brought him. They buckled him to the chair with broad leather straps. The doctor set up a contraption with a crank, a winder and ropes. The ropes attached to his wrist with a very tight cuff and the doctor hauled on the crank handle. Cvelthan felt the arm being torn from its socket. He clenched his teeth and wheezed. Sweat burst from his forehead. He heard a sucking, grating sound. "Excellent!" cried the cheery doctor. "Straight as an arrow!"

The doctor and nurse then placed splints around the arm and bound them in place. Already the pain had subsided and he could open his eyes. He looked at the arm, straight as the doctor had promised. He realised that an Imperial doctor would have left it to heal or go rotten, then cut it off if recovery had failed. These people knew so much. He thanked them and fainted.

When he came to he was lying in a bed, propped up against some kind of frame so that he did not bend his arm. He was in a tent but the sides were rolled up and a fresh breeze blew over him. His clothes were stiff with blood and dried mud but his hands and face had been washed. His boots had been removed and flopped at the side of the bed. He looked around. Vdurin lay in the next bed. His torso was covered in bandages and blood seeped gently through them. His face was pale and his lips almost white. "Hey, soldier!" called Cvelthan. Vdurin opened his eyes and smiled a little.

"Master Sergeant! We thought you'd fallen. Praise God you're alive. Vdurin looked at him intently. "And not too badly injured, by the looks of it."

"Any news of the Master? I saw him fall. I stood over his body but when I looked down he had gone. He seemed badly injured but he must have crawled away. I know he was not dead. Have you heard anything?" asked Cvelthan.

Vdurin shook his head. "They won't say. I've seen Fenjent and he knows nothing. Most of the sergeants made it, you know. The arrows and bolts were aimed at the nobles. There are hardly any knights left alive. The new Vrabelm master, Jcluid is one of the few and he's lost an arm. With Bdescu gone and no knights, who the Hell will lead us now?"

Cvelthan shook his head. "Who says they'll let us stay together? We don't know what they've got in store for us. But get used to one fact – you're a slave now, my old friend."

Cvelthan and Vdurin healed quickly and after three days the two of them were moved to a camp where they were re-united with the other survivors of House Bdescu. The camp was in a pleasant meadow by the river. Tents had been erected for their shelter. Wooden huts provided cooking facilities and communal meeting areas. There were benches to sit on, folding cots for sleeping and blankets to cover themselves. One of the huts was fitted out with shelves and on the shelves were all the possessions that had been recovered from their baggage train and camp. It all seemed perfectly intact. The Byekiy had not looted any of their money or possessions. The camp was surrounded by a wooden palisade with four watch towers and stout gates. The latrines were against the rearmost wall. They were deep pits with plank seats over them. Leaning against the wall were a dozen shovels to throw dirt onto the spoil. The whole situation was typical of the Byekiy: carefully planned and well thought-through. The afternoon of the day they arrived, a delegation of Byekiy civilians arrived. One of them, a woman of advanced years, climbed the steps of a watch tower.

"Men and women of the Empire. Gather around, please. I am Zildern, I speak for the families of the Republic. I am a member of the Council so you can think of me as a person of authority. I want to tell you some important information. We, the Byekiy people are angry that Imperial forces have invaded our lands after being warned not to do it. We want reparation for the death and damage you have caused. All survivors of your army are therefore required to stay here for one year and work to repay the debt of honour you owe to us. All will be treated well. You will be housed, fed, clothed and shod. You will be taught to speak Byekiy. You will be released at the end of one year and will be free to return to the Empire or stay here as citizens of the Republic. It will be a free choice. While here you must obey our laws. Copies of our laws will be posted in your huts. Anyone of you that break the law will not be permitted to stay on at the end of the year. Any violation of our laws will be subject to our justice and I warn you, it is fair but we can be harsh on evildoers."

"You will be separated into single persons or small groups. We will keep families together so please let us know if you are a couple and who your children are. We now have a list of your names so we will start allocating placements to you tomorrow. Wagons will come and take you to staging points within the Republic and from these you will travel on foot to your final destinations. When you arrive you will be asked what job you want to do for your year of service, so be thinking about that. We will do our best to give you honest work that you are capable of doing. You will be billeted with a community or a large family. Most of our citizens are farmers so farm labour is our major employment here. But there are many other jobs if you have skills."

"After one year you will all return to this very spot. Each of you will be asked to decide whether to return to the Empire or stay in the Republic. No person will be permitted to influence the decision of another. Those who stay will be offered a home and work. Citizenship may be earned, in ways that we will explain later. Those of you who elect to return home to your Empire will be given food for the journey and transport as far as the Blenvan border. From there you must make your way home and face whatever consequences your Emperor decides to mete out to you."

Zildern paused to let the words be absorbed. The crowd was silent. A man passed her a glass of water. She took a long drink and spoke once more.

"Our society is ruled in a different way from yours. Each community elects five Elders. Each region chooses its best Five from the communities in its area. Then the regions pick the First Five to run the country as a whole. Elders represent their interest groups. The five groups are artisans, families, professions, farmers and soldiers. I represent families and my title is First of Five. It is my duty to tell you these things and to ask for your patience over the next hours and days. You'll see people around the camp wearing black neck scarves. These people are professionals. They might be scientists, doctors or herbalists but ask any one of them a question and they will help you."

"There are many things that you must learn. Respect for one another is the first lesson. Here there are no Ranks. All men and women are equal under the law. So are children, babies, old or sick people, wounded and mentally disturbed people. I am a leader but it is just my profession not a Rank in your terms. I earned the right to lead and I was elected by my people to do it. From this day forward, no so-called freeman may tell a former slave what to do. No man is allowed to strike a woman or take her without her consent. Murder is a capital offense no matter whom you kill. Our laws forbid warfare, slavery, theft, rape, killing, lying and evangelising. So keep quiet about your religion, keep your hands off other people's property and do not be violent."

"Our judiciary is more complicated than yours. If you are the victim of a crime you ask anyone to contact a Constable. Constables keep the peace and arrest suspects. The constables work for the magistrates. Magistrates investigate crimes and try to discover the truth. Judges then convene a trial and oversee the process of justice, punishment and reparation. Just as you are subject to our laws, so you will be protected by them."

"Now I know that was a lot to understand. But do any of you have any questions?"

The crowd started murmuring but nobody spoke. Cvelthan stepped forward.

"Where are all our Noble Born?"

She looked at him carefully. "Master Sergeant, I am sorry to tell you that almost all of knightly class of your clan has been killed or severely injured in battle. Those who recover will be placed, just as you will be, and given exactly the same treatment."

There were no other questions.

As the woman and her two associates left through the gates, a stream of wagons arrived. They were loaded with food. There was bread, loose grains, fruit both fresh and dried, several different root vegetables and plenty of dried meats. There was a well in the centre of the compound so water was freely available. A screen of skirmishers, the same tough soldiers who had raided the camp, protected the Byekiy drivers. Cvelthan looked at them. They were equipped with leather jerkins sewn with overlapping steel discs. A leather kilt covered their lower bodies. They wore light versions of the infantry's boot. Their arms were free and held the lacquered shield and the short stabbing spear. Their upper body muscles were as large as Cvelthan's, the strongest man in clan Bdescu. Their hair was cropped short. This deceived him for a moment. Then he realised that the one nearest to him was a woman. She had long curving eyelashes. Her mouth was full, her lips plump and soft. Her arms were slim and her muscles were flatter than the men's. She caught his look and tossed her head challengingly. He smiled. That seemed to catch her off guard and she turned away.

"Fuck my old soldier's arse" he said to Vdurin. "Wenches in the army. These people are as barmy as shitbugs".

Vdurin turned wryly towards him. "Shut up, Master Sergeant. Don't tell anybody we got fucked by a bunch of lasses or we'll never live it down. Now come and get some chow before our new equals scoff the shitting lot."

Cvelthan travelled in a wagon with a load of vegetables for almost a week. The driver spoke no Imperial or didn't own to any. Cvelthan sat beside him watching the endless fields, farms and occasional village trundle by. Above the valleys loomed the endless forest. It boomed with bird and insect calls. Between the trunks grew riotous undergrowth. Most of the trees at the edge of the forest were coppiced or pollarded. The many branches were harvested for everything from firewood to spear hafts. He saw many wagons rolling down gravel tracks from the forest, loaded with cut staves, nuts, fruit and fallen wood.

Each night they stayed at an inn. He saw no money change hands. They fed him at the inns. His meal was a bowl of the local stew with a chunk of bread. Sometimes he tasted different meats, other times just vegetables with grains and usually nuts. Sometimes it was savoury or perhaps spicy. Once it was even slightly sweet, with fruits in it. He ate like a soldier, mopping the bowl with his bread then licking both sides of the spoon. The food was delicious. The mug of beer was even better and he rapidly developed a liking for the clean astringent taste. The locals came to the inn too, playing games on boards, drinking beer or spirits and chatting. Kids ran around the tables and pet animals lay in corners. The inns were sociable, friendly places. People looked at him a little but he saw no hostility. One or two bolder children spoke halting Imperial to him and he was patient with them. The locals relaxed when they saw this.

In the morning he and the driver would breakfast on grain porridge sweetened with tree syrup and dried fruits. The driver would get bread from the inn for their midday meal. Then they would harness the beasts to the cart. He had previously thought that he knew all about beasts, but these were larger and better trained than any he'd worked with before. This was lucky because with one arm still very painful, a restive animal could have injured him. He came to like their massive gentle nature. The driver called instructions in Byekiy and Cvelthan started to pick up a few words. The man was friendly enough, just a quiet sort of bloke.

On the sixth day they travelled until dusk. They came to a large town and trundled through streets packed with market stalls, shoppers and revellers. It seemed to be some kind of festival. The driver spoke at length. Cvelthan shook his head. The man pointed to a large building and waved Cvelthan towards it. The Master Sergeant grabbed his sack of clothes from the footboard of the cart with his good hand and climbed carefully down, favouring his arm. The driver pointed to the large building and then waved. Cvelthan, his good hand occupied, simply nodded and smiled. The cart groaned as it headed off through the throng.

Cvelthan walked through handsome hardwood doors into a wide atrium with a ceiling six times his height. It was lit by oil lamps made of some yellow metal. They seemed to burn quite cleanly and had a mildly alcoholic smell. The floor was made of square ceramic tiles as wide as his arm was long. It was a palace, obviously. A small dapper man in the Byekiy clothing, shirt, kilt and boots, came through a side door and over to him. He wore a complex plaid and Cvelthan fancied that the plaids were tribal symbols, like his own facial tattoos. The neckerchiefs definitely meant something although the big sergeant had not worked them out yet.

"Cvelthan of House Bdescu?" He enquired politely.

"Aye. Who are you?"

"My name is not relevant as I won't be handling your induction. Come with me please and I will introduce you to your Board."

He followed the short fellow at a brisk pace through a door and down a corridor. Every surface was polished. Every wall was panelled in wood and painted white. The floor gleamed. The place smelled of wax and lamp oil. It was the most immaculate building Cvelthan had ever seen. When he had accompanied Bdescu to the palaces of other nobles he had seen opulence. Never had he seen anything like this austere wealth. As he pondered, the small man opened a door and ushered him through. He found himself in another large, well-lit room. It contained a single upright chair again made of polished hardwood. The chair faced a table and seated at the table were four women and four men. The small man showed Cvelthan to his seat. He pressed his uninjured arm and smiled. "Don't be nervous. We won't hurt you." He left as briskly as he had arrived.

One of the women spoke to Cvelthan. "Master Sergeant, is it true that you are Cvelthan of Bdescu and the Freeman Guard Commander to Colonel Bdescu Gvant, leader of that clan?"

He nodded. "Yes. Who wants to know?"

"We are a group of local officials. Our job is to help you. Now, you are a special case. We have clear instructions that any member of Bdescu's direct retinue can be assigned to his household, who are billeted together. Bdescu himself is missing in action and as each day goes by we become less sure that he might have survived. However, that is not our duty today. You will stay in the Republic for one year. You may either re-join Bdescu's former retinue or you may apply to have a job and be independent. How do you choose?"

He did not hesitate. "Without my lord colonel there's no point in my hanging around his old slaves. I'll take a job."

"What job will you choose?" asked one of the men.

"I apply to become a legionnaire." Cvelthan sat back and folded his arms. He knew this would shock them. They started a fierce whispered debate. Then the oldest of the women, a grandmother with pale blonde hair, banged on the table with the flat of her hand.

"Colleagues, please! I cannot say we're being polite to the Sergeant. I have read the standing orders and they do not say that the military is an excluded profession. Just state your fears in front of Cvelthan of Bdescu and he can join in the argument! But let's have some decent behaviour at least."

"His only purpose in joining the military is to gain intelligence about our forces! He will run straight back to that child-molesting monster and spill his guts! We'll be at a tactical disadvantage!" This came from a well-muscled man with short hair and a military bearing. He obviously knew what Cvelthan had in mind. Cvelthan smiled at him. To his surprise, the military man smiled back. These people were hard to fathom.

The old woman looked at Cvelthan. "Is that true, Master Sergeant?"

He shrugged. It was obvious, let alone true.

The old woman addressed her remarks to the whole group by leaning forward and looking at each in turn. "Friends, we know this is true. Our esteemed captain gives you sound guidance. But the Fifth of Five has given us a different view. She says the Emperor will not hear what Cvelthan and others have to say. He will not even meet them because they are too low-caste for his presence. Officials will torture the information out of them. Thus only distorted stories will be sent up the line through many layers of the bureaucracy. No military man will see the reports before the Emperor has had them read to him. Only then will the Generals be briefed and they won't get much from it. She further says that even if they do understand our weapons and tactics their rigid society will not find it easy to adapt their methods. Chivalry is after all a matter of birth not training. She and I believe that the risk is low. You are well able to decide the case on its merits."

Cvelthan heard what she said about torture and realised that it might well happen. But he knew his duty and he was convinced the God Emperor, infinitely wise, would hear him and be warned. This was the mission of a lifetime and with his master dead it fell to him, big stupid Cvelthan, to do the noble work. He waited breathlessly for the verdict.

The old woman asked for a vote. Five yes, three voted against. To his amazement the Captain said aye.

The old woman smiled fondly at him. "So, Master Sergeant, you're as brave as you look. From now on you are Volunteer Kelthan Descu. Do you accept this name?"

He grinned. "Close enough. I mean, I do."

They all stood up and he did the same. "Then I pass you over to the good Captain who will escort you to your unit. There is a fresh intake of volunteers at Yellow Crescent base. You will be working with a group of young volunteers. You will be treated as one of them. You will find our army very different from yours. If you fail the assessment you will be returned to the Bdescu clan with no dishonour. May your God smile on you."

The Captain stood, walked around the desk and jerked his head. Cvelthan followed him to a waiting pair of mounts. They rode off into the almost darkness. Cvelthan was a foot soldier and felt uneasy on a mount. He found the beast well-schooled and biddable in spite of its massive size, but the jolting hurt his injured arm. He followed the Captain along the paved road to the outskirts of town where he had his first sight of a permanent Byekiy military establishment. Twin gate towers, five stories high, towered up over a wall. Massive gates that seemed entirely of iron stood open and guarded. They rode unchallenged through the gap. He heard the gates grind shut behind them and Cvelthan was more alone than he had ever been.

Bdescu

When Bdescu awoke he wondered if he was alive. His eyes were glued shut or he was blind. Slowly, as his wits gathered, he realised that he could perceive bright light through his eyelids. He lifted his hand to assist in opening his eyelids. His arms were weak and heavy. Slowly he placed his fingers above and below his eyelids and tugged. With a distinct tearing sensation his eyes opened. Then the tears flooded his view as the full light of a summer's morning washed over his face. At first he could see nothing but the light. By closing then cautiously opening them, he realised that he could see. A vast relief rippled through his being. I am alive was all he could think. He remembered a strange dream. In the dream he had killed his groom, Jrabney. It was so vivid, as if it had actually happened.

With his vision returning to normal, he looked around his room. He lay in a comfortable bed alongside a white painted wall. The other walls were white too. The ceiling was high above him but sloped lower as it crossed the room toward a window. The window was made of well-cut timber and glazed. One of the casements was open. Plain white curtains hung heavily beside the window, suspended from a wooden pole by wooden rings. This must be a rich man's home, then. The floor was smooth planks, oiled or varnished. A patterned rug covered the centre of the floor, reaching the side of his bed. The door was varnished wood like the floor. On a bench under the window were his mail hauberk, his clothing and his riding boots. His weapons were absent. By the bed was a low table. It supported a ceramic jug of fine quality and a beaker of the same stuff. The jug contained water. He hesitated to pour and drink it. Then he realised he had been helpless in these people's care for some time. Had they wished him harm he'd be dead already. He drank the entire jug and wished for more.

He wore a strange undergarment. It was a pair of short pants tied with fabric tape around his middle. Around his neck he still wore the gold chain Summer had given him. His family seal ring of solid gold was on his finger. His capturers had not looted him, then. He tried to stand. His legs had lost all strength and he sprawled on the rug, undignified in his odd attire. The noise attracted attention. He heard the door open but was too feeble to turn his body. He heard a woman's voice speaking accented but clear Imperial.

"Hey, hey, steady now. You'll hurt yourself! You're too weak for walking yet. Give yourself time and all will be well. Now, let me help you back onto the bed." She strode into his view, a tall, buxom creature with sandy hair that hung thickly to her jaw. She bent down, put her hand on his wrist and lifted his arm over her shoulder. She put her other arm around his waist and stood smoothly up. She lifted him easily. She walked him carefully back to the bed and sat down carefully beside him. Then she stood again. She bent to the floor and lifted his legs, swung them onto the bed and settled him. She pulled extra pillows from under the bed and lifted his torso. She placed the pillows in a stack behind his back and shoulders so that he was sitting up and could see out of the window.

He looked up at her. "Thank you, lady. I am indebted to you."

She laughed a loud and joyful sound. "You're welcome, soldier. But I'm no lady!"

She checked the empty jug. "Good, you've had a drink. Any needs at the other end, as it were?" He shook his head.

"You must be hungry, though?" She had a habit of tossing her head, to move her hair out of her eyes. He guessed her age at about thirty-five. He had never met a stronger woman. Except perhaps Summer. The thought made him feel hungry. He nodded.

"Good! I'll go and get you some food. Then we'll get you a bath, some clean clothes and a shave. We'll sort your hair out and clean your teeth. You'll feel a lot better. Oh, my name is Jarleh, by the way."

"Bdescu, given name Gvant."

"Oh, I know who you are, love. We've been expecting you for over a year. Never expected to meet you in person, did I? You're famous, you are. Quite a news item for a small hospital like ours."

She left the room. He noticed for the first time that she smelled nice. He looked at his wounds. Under his arm was a livid red mark. It was sore but appeared to be completely healed. His arm had a deep score where the spear had gored him. The wound showed as a neat line, also healed. His head had a dent, a shallow impression on his skull. It was tender to the touch but hardly painful. He had been healed by a miracle of God's love. Or witchcraft. He was weak. Clearly he had been recovering, unconscious, for some time. Judging by the heat it was high summer. He had fallen in early spring. Where had he been?

Jarleh fed him delicious soup, rich in meats and vegetables. There was crusty bread, gritty with seeds and husks. She gave him some sweet fruit juice that was equally tasty. She walked him down a corridor, all painted white, to a large bathing room. A huge tub was filled with steaming water, apparently just for him. She bathed him, shaved him, cut his hair and rubbed his unfeeling legs with an ointment that burned slightly. But it pushed back the numbness in his limbs. She sat him on a commode and let him relieve himself, then cleaned up with a smile. Then she put her arm around him again and walked him back to his room. She dressed him in a light robe of pale brown then sat him up in bed so that he could see out of the window. He looked across a rich valley. Small fields surrounded farmhouses. The houses were stone, with steep pent roofs of slate. To his astonishment, every house had glazed windows. In the empire glass was a luxury product. The fields were bounded by either a raised bank with a hedge on top, or a dry stone wall. Each field looked to have a different crop or a small herd of animals in it. It was so alien to his eyes. He was used to vast sweeping fields of grain. In his experience, a farm grew either one crop or husbanded one sort of animal. This randomness seemed inefficient and foolish to Bdescu.

All around the valley rose hills covered in dense forests of mighty trees. The hills rolled away into blue distance. Always behind the hills reared the jagged crags of the Teeth of God mountain range. This view of the mountains was completely unfamiliar. He realised that he had no idea in the world where he was. Once his strength returned he'd have no trouble escaping. But without knowing his location, he might walk in exactly the wrong direction. A man might travel easily up or down these valleys. Crossing the densely forested cols would be entirely another matter. Navigation was only one problem. Wild beasts, lack of water and avoiding pursuit were other matters to be considered. He knew it was his duty to return to the Emperor and report what had happened here. His Holiness needed to understand the threat that lurked on His borders.

From the hospital a gravel track ran downhill to the cluster of houses that seemed to be the local village. The village stood on a paved road that ran arrow-straight up and down the valley. Carts laden with produce trekked to and fro, pulled by drays like the ones he had known all his life; except half as tall again as any he had ever seen. They were gigantic shaggy beasts with three polished black horns, heavy fringes of hair flopping in their eyes and heavy, leathery tails. They hauled the heavy carts with a slow, steady gait and seemed to steer themselves; the drivers strolled amiably beside them.

Then he saw a large animal come racing up valley towards the village. His eyes widened. It was a hlant, a savage predator as tall as a man's shoulder. Its lower tusks curved up from an under-slung jaw. Its high haunches and thick back limbs propelled it forward in rapid bounds. Its shorter front legs with their terrible talons seemed to tear the stones as it charged. He could see its clear amber eyes and the long fringes that hung from its ears. Its long, thick tail was held out behind it, giving the beast exquisite balance as it hurtled along. Its killing tusks were folded flat against its lower jaw, its mouth open as it gasped for breath. Its brindled fur was slick with dark patches of sweat. Bdescu had not seen a hlant in ten years. All had been hunted to extinction years ago across the empire. But here was the largest specimen he had ever seen, running like a pet along a public street. Farmers went about their business without sparing the brute a glance. To add to his confusion, it seemed to have a set of leather panniers strapped to its sides like a pack mount. The hlant swung off the road and skirled to a halt in the yard of the largest building in the village. He could see its barrel chest heaving with its gasping breath. A small stocky man walked out to the beast carrying a pail of water and set it down respectfully in front of the animal. As the beast lapped, he unbuckled its satchels and carried them into the building. The hlant finished the bucketful. Another, taller man came out with a shank of meat. He placed it in a stone trough by the hlant. The creature gave a bellow, a deep bass drum roll. It took the meat in its jaws, wandered out of the yard and settled under a tree by the roadside. Once comfortable in the shade it started to tear lumps of bloody meat from the bone.

Bdescu saw the portly man walking up the gravel track towards the hospital, with one satchel slung over his shoulder. The other satchel had another destination, apparently. As he neared the building he disappeared from Bdescu's view.

He heard Jarleh's firm step running upstairs and onto the landing. She knocked at his door. "Please come in, Jarleh," he called. She walked in grinning. She waved a package at him.

"More excitement! That was a special delivery for my honoured prisoner-of-war! Somebody just used up a lot of favours. They must really want you to have this so I better stop talking and hand it over."

She passed him the package. It was a bag made of a waxed fabric and tied up carefully with fabric tapes. Each tape had been sealed with a complex impression.

"Snowhammer seal. Legion business, eh?" He was learning that his country nurse was desperately curious about him. He wished he had some way of satisfying her inquisitive nature, but he was at a loss to understand how he had survived, let alone made his way here. Wherever 'here' actually was. He opened the package. Inside were a letter and a red bandanna. He opened the letter out and began to read.

My darling Gvant

Please forgive me for not coming to you. I have been watching over you and I know you are recovered. Jarleh is a dear girl and she will look after you. Don't worry about escaping, I'll send you back to the Empire by and bye. Build up your strength and we'll get you re-united with your people. Byardil and the others are alive. Many of your knightly brotherhood were killed in battle and you are now the senior surviving person of rank. You need to know your situation.

The Byekiy people are angry that Imperial forces invaded their lands after being warned not to do it. They will seek reparation for the death and damage you have caused. All survivors of your army are therefore required to stay here for one year and work to repay the debt of honour you owe them. That includes you. All will be treated well. You will be housed, fed, clothed and shod. You will be taught to speak Byekiy. You will be released at the end of one year and will be free to return to the Empire or stay here as citizens of the Republic. It is a free choice. Anyone of you that break the law will be punished under the Byekiy legal code. If you want to gather intelligence to take back and warn the Emperor, that's fine. My advice would be to wait until I join you in a few days before you decide what to do. Wear my red bandanna and anyone you meet will help you. It symbolises something to the Byekiy that is similar to money in the Empire.

I know you think I betrayed you. By your standards I did. Just as you have duty, so do I. I have tried to make amends to you. I have broken the laws of my people to save your life. I did it because I love you. I am yours if you'll have me.

Summer.

He wiped a tear from his eye. He put the letter down and watched the hlant sleeping under the tree. It had rolled on its back with its thick limbs in the air, as relaxed as a baby. He shook his head. Perhaps he had died after all, and this was some strange vision of Heaven. The effort had tired him. He fell asleep sitting up and failed to notice Jarleh putting him to bed. She tied the bandanna to the bedhead and stroked the hair back from his face. "Handsome for a savage," she murmured.

Training

After five weeks of recuperation at a rehabilitation centre, Cvelthan's arm was healed, if tender. He had presented himself immediately back at the local garrison for recruit training, which appeared to be just starting with an intake of new recruits. He'd arrived late, been shown to a small bed in a billet full of sleeping men and fallen instantly asleep.

"Wake up you dozy bastards! Get yer hands out yer pants! Roll and bounce, roll and bounce! Bath time for girls!" The drillmaster ran along the cots whacking the recruits with a cane.

Cvelthan leaped out of his cot. He pulled on his grey underpants and laced them. He stood rigidly at attention at the foot of his bed as others were doing. He was determined to be the best. Quite a few of the squad sat up rubbing their eyes and moaning. The drillmaster tipped their cots over onto the floor and then screamed at them to clean up their mess.

Cvelthan looked at the drillmaster. He was in his late thirties with the characteristic massive upper body muscles of the legionary. He wore no beard or tattoos. He wore only his pants and his badge of rank was a short black cane made of twisted hide. It was only slightly flexible but delivered a very painful swipe.

When all the recruits were in pants the drillmaster led them at a fast trot out of the gate and down to the river. At the side of the camp wall an eddy in the river created a deep pool. Each recruit had to leap into the near-freezing water, dunk his head and rub himself down vigorously. Only when the drillmaster was satisfied were they allowed out of the water. They ran at full speed back to the barrack hut where the twelve recruits lived. They dressed, still dripping, in full kit. In spite of the complexity of the kit, Cvelthan mastered it quickly. In fact as a professional soldier he was impressed by the kit and could see how well designed it was.

He dressed from ground up as instructed. Wool socks of a light brown natural fibre. Thick leather boots laced criss-cross and tightened fully, then a double knot in the thongs. Above them he fitted greaves, leather shin guards with metal plates riveted to the front and sides. His pants were dry by now. He wrapped the heavy leather kilt around his midriff and buckled it inside then outside. He hung a thick leather belt from his waist, with jointed metal strips to protect his genitals and lower abdomen. In front he hung a stiffened leather pouch for his personal items. The pouch was called a sporran. Next he pulled the heavy linen shirt over his head and laced it at his throat. Over the shirt went a padded waistcoat, fabric inside and leather outside. This layer was obviously to absorb the shock of blows. He lifted the armour over his head and slid it down over his arms. The armour fascinated him. It was made of soft iron bands, lacquered green to prevent rust. Circular bands encircled his torso, joined together at the sides with steel clips that were adjustable. The bands were joined to one another by leather straps inside. The bands overlapped and slid across each other to provide flexibility. Semi-circular bands were fastened over the shoulders, overlapping again in a kind of fan shape.

Finally he pulled on his helmet. This was a complex iron cap with a shock-absorbing layer of crossed strapping inside. Welded to the front was a peak to protect the face. Steel flaps covered the sides of the face and laced under the chin, but kept the ears free to hear commands. A neck guard projected outward and down at the back.

Cvelthan was dressed first. The others struggled and swore in Byekiy. Cvelthan now knew that Byekiy had many dialects and that all recruits were expected to learn Imperial. He had no idea why. The drillmaster walked up to Cvelthan. "Name?"

"Volunteer Cvelthan Bdescu, Drillmaster!"

The drillmaster looked at him with contempt. "So, a slaver with an unpronounceable name, eh? Well I'm not bothering to learn your stupid name. And you'll have an army name from now on, anyhow. From today, you are called Beast. What's your name?"

"Beast, Drillmaster!"

"Right. If I hear you using that stupid Imperial name again I'll make your life hell, got it?"

"Yes, Drillmaster!"

The Byekiy officer turned to the troop, some of who were half dressed. "At ease a minute you fuckshy bunch. Now hear this. The rules of this army are very simple. You fight as a unit. You die as a unit. So you succeed or fail basic training – as a unit. So that means if one member of this troop fails the course you all fail. If a man can't run you carry him or you fail. If a man can't learn then you sit up all night and coach him or you fail. The Beast here has to learn Byekiy and if he doesn't – guess what? You all fail. Plus you need to learn his language so learn to trade with him."

He strolled down the beds touching each recruit on the shoulder with his cane. The fat boy with the floppy dark hair was first. As the cane landed on the lad's shoulder the drillmaster called "Podge."

He walked the line: "Spotty. Whitey. Joker. Squint. Lame. Blondie. Nervous. Lazy. Twitch. Talker." These sad titles are your recruit names. I will personally award you a man's name worthy of real a soldier if you show me that you have earned it. Now take it all off, down to yer bare arses, and do it again. That's if you actually want to eat breakfast!"

Breakfast was typical Byekiy food. Hot porridge with syrup and fruit, the favoured hot drink, a brownish fluid made from steeped herbs. Called chasser, it was slightly bitter but it was all right once you got used to it. The refectory was crowded with recruits. Most legionaries were men. Women were trained as skirmishers but it usually took male muscles to become heavy infantry, so relatively few women were big enough. The recruits were all volunteers, a word that Cvelthan had never heard in Imperial so he used the Byekiy word. There was plenty of food but nobody was putting on any weight.

After breakfast the drillmaster took them at a fast jog, in full armour, out of the camp and into the forest. Cvelthan had never run in his adult life. Although strong he was unfit. Soon he and Podge were labouring in the heat in their sweltering clothes and armour. The others had disappeared into the woods on the well-churned gravel track.

When he and Podge arrived at the clearing the others were all flopped on the ground, panting. "No rest for you two fat fuckers. Get on with the exercises."

They were issued with wooden swords. They formed two lines of six. On Cvelthan's side were all the smaller or weaker boys: Podge, Joker, Twitch, Spotty and Lame. Soon they were shield to shield with the other six, pushing and shoving and trying to stab each other. Cvelthan 'killed' his opponent easily but his side lost. Podge fell down and Joker was pushed over. Twitch was so skinny that his opponent could literally walk him backwards. Cvelthan found himself exposed on both sides. Wooden swords poked the back of his armour and the drillmaster declared his squad vanquished six to one. "Losing team, run back to barracks. Winning team, march back. Come on, girls, let's move."

When they returned to barracks, Cvelthan turned to his gasping team. "Listen men. They want me out. This is not your fault but we have to stand together. I am a soldier. I can teach you to be soldiers. But you must teach me Byekiy or I fail. Today was shit. I don't want to be a loser, do you?"

They shook their heads. Podge looked up, his face purple. "I speak the best Imperial. So I'll teach you Byekiy, Beast. My dad and granddad were soldiers. I don't want to fail. I can't help being fat."

Joker spoke. "Fuck you, you fat fool! If you could run we wouldn't be in the shit! Why don't we just chuck you out and get Blondie or one of the other lads to join our side? It would be fair! And you can fuck off..."

His voice was cut off as Cvelthan's fist struck him in the upper abdomen. His armour clanked, his breath shot out and he dropped to the floor, wheezing. Cvelthan leaned over and spat on him.

"A fighting line has three key positions. Centre man calls the moves. Anchor men stabilise the ends. Line breaks, we die, all of us. One man falls, we die, all of us. So anybody want to insult my friend Podge? He's my language teacher so if you fuck with him, you fuck with me. Anybody want to fuck with me?" Cvelthan looked around. No response. He bent down, grabbed Joker by the arm and hauled him to his feet. He grinned at the lanky kid. "You OK?"

"I think so." Joker looked nervously at the older man.

"Stand to. Drillmaster approaching. Gobs shut, ears open, form on me and do as I tell you."

The drillmaster smiled grimly around the room. "Girls. Nice of you to dress up. Now we've all had a nice rest, let's go back to the woods. AT THE FUCKING DOUBLE THIS TIME."

He hared off towards the wood. Cvelthan started at a trot. He grabbed Podge's left arm. "Spotty, other arm. Twitch, grab my left arm. All together, at the double". With linked arms they trotted all together towards the wood. Cvelthan gasped out his instructions.

"We must protect each other. I take centre with Podge on my right. Twitch on my left anchored on me as well. Joker next to Podge. Spotty and Lame take the ends as anchor men. There are only two moves, forward and back. We will trick them. We push in. When they start to push I will call 'step' and we all take a smart pace backward. If one of them falls over, kill him and step over him. Then we've won."

The enemy fell perfectly for the trick. Three of them just stumbled over in the mud and were despatched. The others were surrounded and 'killed'. Six nil. The drillmaster chased the losers back to base. As they trooped back, Cvelthan laid it out for them.

"It's obvious that they want us to fail. They have put us together because they think we are losers. So we prove them wrong or we let them fail us. It is not fair but life isn't fair. I can teach you to soldier. You can teach me the rest. I will now prove to you I am serious. Come on, Podge. You and me, son, we have to learn to run." He set off at a stumbling jog towards the barracks. With a groan, Podge fell in behind him. The others stood looking at each other. Joker shrugged and set off in pursuit. The others followed.

As the summer went on the tasks became ever harder. Lessons in the morning, drill after lunch and household duties in the evening. Inspections were frequent and detailed. Every garment must be folded, every corner swept and every training weapon gleaming. Cvelthan and Podge sat up late at night getting Cvelthan through his Byekiy exams. Joker taught him mathematics and Spotty taught him military history and strategy. Cvelthan and Podge sweated and laboured with their running but gradually began to speed up. Podge lost some of his puppy fat and started to build muscle. Cvelthan made him centre man to develop his confidence. After every practice session Cvelthan would run extra drills and his team started winning. Soon they were reunited with the other six members of their squad and started to train as twelve. Blondie now had a Problem.

"Look Beast," he said one morning at breakfast, "I'm the centre of our line and I'm obviously much better than that fat fucker that you've given it to. So get him out of the way. He's a weak spot in the line, he'll get us all killed."

Cvelthan smiled. "No. You don't understand. We have to get through this together. That means all of us. You can't leave him behind and win by yourself. If he fails, you fail and I fail. So I build the team around him, like a wall. Every day he tries harder, gets stronger. He teaches me and I teach him. Now he can run and I can speak some Byekiy. We will be OK. Unless some cocky fuckshy like you comes along and tries to wank up the plan."

Blondie hawked deep in his throat and spat on the side of Cvelthan's face. The Imperial warrior smiled. "Meet me on the practice field after evening meal. We see who can spit the furthest." Without wiping the spittle off his face, he continued eating his porridge. The rest of the troop looked on, aghast.

They spent the day learning to service armour. They field stripped the corselets and rebuilt them. They did this three times then once blindfolded. Once every man could do it, they were released. Cvelthan and his five team members met the other six in a corner behind the storage hut. Blondie was stripped to the waist, his torso densely packed with muscle. He was taller than Cvelthan. His friends were slapping him on the back and encouraging him. Cvelthan's team were nervous. The veteran sergeant gave no sign of fear or any other emotion. Slowly and methodically he removed his shirt and handed it to Twitch. Podge, Joker, Spotty and Lame formed a semicircle as Blondie's team had already done. When the circle was complete the lads could see Blondie's clear skin sharply contrasted with Cvelthan's dark, scarred chest.

Blondie moved in fast. He feinted left and swung his right fist into Cvelthan's face. It made a sound like a fruit dropped on a tiled floor. Cvelthan did not flinch. Blondie swung again, thumping a hard left into Cvelthan's stomach. This hardly made any sound at all. Blondie hit him the face again, his strong right cross opening a small cut on the older man's eyebrow. Still the Imperial warrior made no sound or movement. "What's the matter with you?" demanded Blondie. "Fight me, you slave monger!"

Cvelthan smiled. One of his front teeth was chipped. Twitch, Podge, Joker, Spotty and Lame started to clap, slowly and rhythmically. "Kel–than, Kel–than" they chanted. Blondie rushed in again, hitting Cvelthan in the head, the chest and stomach. But the man was like a tree. The blows struck him and showed no effect. His smile never wavered. Blood poured from his eyebrow, from his nose and from a cut on his right ear.

"Enough! Stop it Blondie. Can't you see, he'll die rather than give in? If he gets injured, the drillmaster will find out and we'll all fail. You can't beat him... you can't even take the grin off his face. Face it, he's harder than you are. Harder than any of us. We're just recruits. He's a fucking warrior." Whitey stopped and looked around the others. Blondie stood still, fists raised, his face suffused with angry blood.

Whitey walked across to Cvelthan. His pale young face looked up at the bloodied countenance of the sergeant. He extended his right hand, offering the soldier's grip, forearm to forearm. "Beast, I am sorry. I'm not your enemy. You've got guts and you know what to do. You should be our leader. This is just wrong and we shouldn't be fighting each other. I don't want to fail just because Blondie needs attention all the time."

Cvelthan took the lad's grip, his smile deepening in his smashed face. Whitey stepped back and very deliberately walked into Cvelthan's team.

Squint, Nervous, Lazy, and Talker followed. Now ten lads stood behind Cvelthan. Blondie looked sullen. Cvelthan walked over to him and held out his hand. In truly appalling Byekiy he spoke clearly: "Podge holds the centre. I'll anchor the right, it's my usual position. You're left handed so we need you on the left flank. We three hold the line. All in?"

Before Blondie could reply a familiar voice screamed from the trees behind them. "Get back to your hut you bunch of fuckshy shitters! At the trot!" The drillmaster hounded them back to the hut. As they charged in though the door, the drillmaster grabbed Cvelthan's arm. "You stay outside, I want a word."

They sat on the visitor's bench by the parade ground. The drillmaster was quiet for a moment. Then he started to speak slowly and clearly in Byekiy.

"First of all, I object to you telling them that I am trying to fail you. You get the same treatment as everyone else in this army. We don't play games here. These are young men and some of them won't make it as soldiers, but we'll give them a good try out. Clear?"

Cvelthan nodded. His lips were split and painful.

"I watched the fight. You took the squad over without Blondie realising he was being outflanked. Good tactics. You showed desire, intelligence and courage. We reward these qualities. Beast I'm promoting you to acting Decanus. You're now responsible for this unit and it is called, from now on, the Seventh Contubernium (Provisional). Is that what you wanted?"

"Yes Sir! Thank you Sir!" His lip split and blood flowed down his chin. Cvelthan didn't notice.

The drillmaster took a small cloth patch from his sporran and handed it to Cvelthan. "Here. Sew it onto the right breast of your shirt. Then tell your armourer to paint a replica of this emblem, the size of your spread hand, onto your armour." He stood up. He took Cvelthan's salute and walked away.

When Cvelthan got back to barracks he found that a crate of strong ale had been delivered. The men were ecstatic. They cheered him and slapped him on the back. Blondie hung back. Cvelthan opened the first flask of ale, took a small swig and handed it to Blondie with a grin. "You've broken my tooth, you might as well drink my fucking beer!"

Blondie laughed and Cvelthan put his arm around the lad. He put his free arm around Podge. "Welcome, ladies, to the seventh contubernium! All in?"

"All in!" They cheered some more and drank the ales. Cvelthan reached into the crate for another flask and his hand brushed a paper. He pulled out a folded packet. It was sealed with wax and stamped with the Legion's official seal. The boys became quiet, staring at him. He opened the packet. Inside were a letter and twelve slips of paper. He read the letter aloud:

"Men of the Seventh Contubernium (Provisional). After due consideration, my drillmasters have decided that you are the unit that has tried hardest at soldiering. You have achieved the highest level of improvement. We respect your efforts and those of your new Decanus. We reward you with a weekend pass and twelve tickets to an entertainment in the town. Congratulations.

Colonel Janthro, Commanding Officer, Fifth Snowhammer Legion whose oath is "Shoulder to Shoulder".

Joker grabbed the tickets. "It's Pelva! She's on at the Five Hall this weekend! And the Bright Lights Band! We're all going to see Pelva!"

In the hilarity that followed, Cvelthan cheered aloud. He had no idea who Pelva was. But the spirit was high and that was good enough for the big man. His mouth still hurt though.

Byardil's First Day

Byardil stood nervously in front of a class full of young children. The children were fresh faced and eager looking. They seem to behave well although he was still terrified. The head teacher stood behind him; he could not see her face. Her voice was strong and confident as it came from behind him. "Now class, this is our new teacher of the Imperial language. His name is Byardil. Please treat him with respect and you will find he is the best teacher of Imperial that you could possibly have. In his own country he is a well-respected scribe. That means he writes documents for people in their own Imperial dialect. That means he can speak low, middle, high and court languages. So he is well able to teach you all he knows. Now, you are his very first class. That means that he's going to judge every class of our schoolchildren by your behaviour. So it better be good."

The head teacher patted Byardil on the back. She smiled encouragingly and walked out of the room. Byardil turned to look at children. He felt breathless and his knees were slightly weak. He took a deep shuddering breath. Hoping his voice wouldn't break, he began to speak. "Well children, it's really great to meet you. My name is Byardil and I'm going to be here for the full year. The head teacher has asked me to teach you Imperial. She also told me that you are all very clever children. I've never taught a class before. And I'm a bit nervous. Let's start by finding out how much Imperial you know so that each of you to tell me your name where you come from and how long you've been in school.

The children's Imperial was surprisingly good. They had all been taught the high tongue. Byardil, as a scribe to nobles, spoke mostly high or court. Because of his rank as a slave and the necessity of dealing with other slaves, he was also fluent in low and middle. As the family scribe he was expected to write letters for all members of the household from highest to lowest. This facility with all the dialects of the Imperial language gave Byardil a unique appeal to the educators in this country. When he had gone to the interview at his local town hall, they had offered in jobs in farming but he had showed them his soft pale hands which had never done a day's manual labour, the rough old farmer on the panel smiled at him and said "farming would probably do you some good young lad, but it'll destroy those lovely hands"

They had discussed a range of opportunities for Byardil. And then one of them, the head teacher of the school where he was now teaching, had suggested that he try his hand at this. He had jumped at the chance because he knew he would never be an agriculturalist. Byardil had spent a few days in various classes at the school, watching the teachers and pupils. Because he had taught many other slaves to read and write, he had a good understanding of how to teach. His problem was, he had never tried it on so young an audience. He had to endure an hour of this, his first class. At the end of the hour the bell rang very loudly in the corridor. Byardil realised he hadn't noticed the time pass. The kids were charming. They were keen to answer, bright, cheery and very well-behaved. He began to really like them. The children sat neatly at four rows of desks. Each row held five children for a class of 20 in all. Each child had their own shelf underneath the desk. On the shelf the children kept all their equipment. They had paper made from fibrous plants. They had steel pens that they dipped in a small inkwell embedded at the front edge of the desk. They had a rag to clean the pen which they kept in a pouch hanging on the side desk from a hook. Like everything he had seen in this strange land, the school seemed ordered, bright and airy and filled with laughter and good temper. He began to relax and tried a few funny stories. They were just anecdotes about mistakes people made with the Imperial tongue. In High Imperial if you have had enough to eat you say, "I am full". In Low Tongue slang it means "I'm pregnant." The kids seem to like it. They chuckled and tried the phrases on one another.

Byardil walked down the corridor. He had conquered his fear of the children. His next challenge was the staff room. He had learned his way around the school - it was a small enough establishment. He turned left at the bottom of the corridor past the big windows which opened onto the playing field. On the field the children played rough-and-tumble sports. There was much emphasis placed on these sports. Some were designed to favour bigger, stronger children and the boys did better at these. Other games were more about cunning and agility and girls were the champions. This was all strange to Byardil. In the caste system of the Empire you played sports only if born into the gladiator caste.

There were children out there now playing the curious game which he had seen in so many places. The game was called Bagataway. It was played with a curious bent stick. The stick had a shaft which was straight for two-thirds of its length. Towards the end, the stick bent over to one side and then back across itself to form two sides of a triangle. The open side of the triangle was then bridged with sinews woven into a strong fibrous 'wall'. The triangle was then filled with a mesh of woven cords. This mesh formed a pocket into which a ball could be thrown and caught. The ball, made of leather, was small and hard. It was flung with tremendous speed through the air. If the ball struck you it must be quite painful, thought Byardil. But the kids charged around the field screaming excitedly and slinging the ball from person to person with great accuracy and verve. They changed hands, playing left and right handed. They threw the ball with the stick vertical or at any angle. Some could even shoot from ankle height. They'd obviously played all their lives. Byardil had heard that the big matches played by adult men and women drew huge crowds. He also heard to his amazement that men and women competed on an equal footing in such games, although he found it very difficult to believe.

He opened the door of the staff room.

The other teachers were men and women varying from their early 20s through to one gentleman who was obviously of great age. His hair was long and white and in the local style, spotlessly clean and marvellously plaited in long braids around the back of his shoulders. Despite his obvious age his hair was full, his face ruddy and his smile welcoming. He walked over to Byardil and took his hand. "Welcome to the school Byardil, it's great to meet you."

Byardil return the pressure in his hand and smiled back "I'm a little bit nervous my first morning. But thanks for making me feel welcome." Somebody put a hot drink into his right hand. Somebody else put a fragrant cake into his other hand. They ushered him into a seat and continued their discussion on who would win the inter schools championship. Byardil had no idea whether the subject was academic, sporting or some other category of which he knew nothing. Their energy and obvious enthusiasm for their profession were highly infectious. After a while Byardil's blushes subsided. He didn't feel confident enough to join in the discussion. He just relaxed, drank the slightly bitter hot drink in his cup, munched the delicious fruit scented cake and wondered if he would enjoy a year of this. "So far so good" he thought to himself.

Byardil sweated his way through a day of intense experiences. Then the bell rang in a different pattern; a double note struck quickly then another double note struck slowly. The children leapt to their feet. They began to cram their working utensils into their desk. One of them, a tall boy walked up to Byardil. He smiled shyly and said "thank you very much Mr Byardil. We are very pleased to have you here. My mother says I'm lucky to have somebody who speaks really good Imperial. If I get really good at speaking Imperial perhaps I can get into a high kudos profession."

Byardil was slightly overcome. He blushed again. "You're very welcome," he smiled. The other children smiled shyly and waved as they left the room. One boy was left behind. He had sat in the far corner of the room and had not once made eye contact with the new teacher. He was a large child, broad in the body and tough looking. He walked slowly up to Byardil's desk. Byardil looked up at him and smiled. The boy hawked up a gob of phlegm and spat it in Byardil's face.

"My Dad died in the White Cliff salient fighting your shitting cavalry. He was a hero, a fighter, not a queer like you. But you slaver bastards killed him. Why don't you fuck off back to your kiddy-fiddling Emperor, eh? Just watch yourself, slaver man. I know people that are gonna get you."

Byardil took a slow breath to control his voice. "Let me just say two things. One, I'm a slave, not a slaver. So you're blaming me for the actions of other men. Two, I was at the recent battle, and took no part in the fighting. As you say, I'm a queer not a warrior. So I'm sure it wasn't me who killed your Dad."

The child looked at him scornfully. "Not that battle, you fuckshy arse puller! The White Cliff salient was at the battle of Two Rivers, six years ago!" With that triumphant finish, the boy walked out of the classroom and slammed the door behind him. Byardil took a long breath and shook his head.

Byardil gathered up his possessions and put them in a small leather satchel that he had been given by the head teacher. He slung the satchel over his shoulder and walked out of the school into the bright afternoon sunshine. He paused by the playing field to watch some of the older children playing this strange game, Bagataway. They were big brawny kids. They rushed around the pitch flinging the ball at high speed and catching it with great deftness. They crashed into each other with bone jarring tackles. They grunted and shouted. On the sidelines, some younger children watched the game, cheering on their champions. The games seem to require a large number of officials. There was a referee in each half plus a line judge on each side line. The goals were about the height and width of a tall man and perfectly square. They were painted white and had a net on the back to catch the ball as it flew into the goal. The pitch extended behind the goal and the children ran behind the goal and passed the ball over the goal towards their onrushing team mates. Although Byardil never watched a sporting contest in his entire life, he became interested, put down his satchel and watched for a while. The elderly teacher walked slowly along the touchline towards him. Byardil smiled and the old man stopped and grinned at him. "Well Byardil" said the old man "I hear good things about your first day. The kids seem very positive, the teachers seem happy enough, and the head teacher speaks very highly of you, young fellow. I expect you'll make a pretty good teacher."

"Thank you sir. I have a question for you, if you have a moment? As the old fellow nodded, he plunged on, "how long exactly have the Byekiy been fighting the Empire?"

The old man smiled grimly. "Off and on, about twenty years. It started with slave raids, stealing crops and burning villages. Our militias had been fine in dealing with savages, but we'd never met anything like Imperial cavalry and they murdered us. Our Council was called the Four back then. The Four asked our allies for help. They sent us the Star Witch. She joined the Council as their fifth member and became Fifth of Five. She trained the Snowhammer Legions and the other specialist units. Since then we've won every encounter. She's a genius and we're lucky to have her. Without her, we'd all be slaves by now."

Byardil walked home slowly, buying time to think. His walk took him through the village from the Southern end to the Northern side. It was an Alpine village deep in a wooded valley. The village was bisected by a fast-flowing river. There was a handsome stone bridge across the river, joining the two halves of the town. The town hall and community centre were the largest buildings, clearly visible across the bright water. The school stood on the Eastern side, as did Byardil's new home. He walked through the town streets in the bright afternoon sunshine. The bars were open, several of them flourished along the riverside and people were sitting on tables and benches in the fresh air, drinking the inevitable flagons of ale. He was struck by how cheerful and friendly these people were, in this country that seemed to have no money. He had yet to work out what kudos meant. The red bandanna seemed to give him endless credit wherever he went. He could walk into a bar right now and order a huge dinner with endless beer and they would just provide, without question and with a smile. He kept walking through the sunny streets. The houses were large and built of cut stone which had a buttery colour. Many of the walls were covered in vine-like plants which flowered in deep pinks and violets. The roofs were tiled with thin wide stones of a greenish black. The doors and the glazed windows were painted in bright colours, all different. Each house had a small patch of land at the front, planted with flowers or sometimes vegetables. The gardens were bounded by low picket fences of painted wooden palings. He emerged from the streets onto a sloping meadow of dense grass and thousands of wild flowers. In the far corner of the meadow, in the lee of a wood, stood the large house where he and the remnants of house Bdescu were billeted.

Byardil walked through the front door, which was always unlocked. He hung his satchel from a peg on the wall. Mridka the elderly cook waddled out to greet him. He walked through the timbered hallway, arm in arm with the old woman. She prattled in her low

Imperial about the minutiae of her day. Years earlier the old, snobbish Byardil would have found her patter irritating. He tolerated it out of compassion. But now as master of the house, he felt it his duty to pay attention to her. He had found that her conversation actually had a worth of its own. Buried in the details of the day were small items of news that he often found helpful. For her part, the old lady found this newfound attention very rewarding. She had always loved Byardil, her "strange sad boy". Before being taken up by Bdescu she had belonged to another kind of master. His depredations had left her barren and terrified of men. She had no living children, she said.

When Byardil arrived at the dining room the entire retinue, 14 people, were sitting around the big scrubbed timber table. The glass doors at the back of the room were flung wide open. The scent of the garden drifted into the room and mingled with the cooking smells of roasting meat. Byardil sniffed appreciatively. "Well gang," he said "I've survived!" The rest of the household smiled.

Byardil was always nervous, sitting at the head of the table. But he had promised the master he would look after the others. If that meant being the boss, he'd find a way to do it. He had much to tell Bdescu, if only the master would return.

Rehabilitation

Jarleh and Bdescu ran down the hill. The broad sandy path ran through thick forest. The air under the trees was cool and moist. Shafts of sunlight penetrated the leaf canopy and illuminated the dust motes that hung in the still air of the glades. Bdescu pushed his pace up a notch and gained a few strides on the fleet woman. She was dressed in a short kilt of light fabric with a matching shirt. Her feet wore light sandals with thick soles that made little sound on the track. Her long legs were hard muscled and she ran with a smooth rhythm that Bdescu had struggled to equal. Before this he had prided himself on his ability to run, but this woman had beaten him every morning for eleven consecutive days.

As they emerged from the trees the track hardened into a paved road. The hospital was in plain view, just moments away. Bdescu took a few extra gasps of the humid air and pounded past her. She was slow to react and had little acceleration left. He charged through the gates into the hospital grounds just a stride in front of her. They fell on the lawn, gasping. She rolled over and slapped his upper arm.

"Well done, Colonel! I now pronounce you cured. As usual, my timing is perfect. Someone will come and collect you this afternoon. This will be our last day together." She gave him a long look. All traces of his wounds seemed gone. His colour was deep and healthy, his body lean and fit once more. His eyes were clear as he stared at her.

Jarleh lay on her belly with her chin on her cupped hands. "I'll miss you. You're a rare one. Good listener and very polite. Handsome too, in a dark and mysterious way. But I get the feeling you're someone else's man. Shame really."

"Who will come and when?"

"I'm not permitted to tell you who. But for sure, today's your last day. You'll be leaving tomorrow."

He looked away, thoughtful in this quiet moment. She watched him. His hair was almost black with a few stray strands of silver. He wore it long and plaited in the Imperial style. He wore a clipped beard and moustache around his mouth and chin, the sides of his face clean-shaven. His skin was a light tan, darkening further as he spent more time outside. His face carried dramatic scars from a life of war and tourney. His eyes were a strange shade of amber brown. His looks were utterly foreign to her, accustomed as she was to the lighter skins and fairer hair of the mountain folk.

"Jarleh, you are a great doctor. I do not know how I cheated death's grip, but I felt it on me. I know I would have died if not for you. There are no words for such thanks as I owe to you. And my duty lies elsewhere, so this is a burden of debt I must bear forever."

"Me? I didn't cure you, you fool! I just nursed you and got you back to fighting fitness. I'm no doctor. I'm a battlefield nurse on a special mission for the Army. I was in barracks and got a command from Very High Up that I should come here and nurse a prisoner. They even went back to my home village and brought all my clothes here so I wouldn't have to be in uniform all day. I had no idea who you were. To be honest, I still don't know why you were singled out for such special treatment."

"Have you any idea how I was saved? I was stabbed high in the chest. I felt the blow pierce my lung. I was drowning in my own blood. In my whole career I've never seen a man survive such a wound."

"Oh, that's easy. The Witch saved you. The Fifth of Five her very own self. She walked straight across the battlefield to the exact spot where you fell, four Trusted Men with her. They wrapped you in clean sheets and put you in her personal carriage. She galloped off at top speed with you, leaving the men behind in the road. She took you to her castle on the mountain. I think she needs to be there to do her sorcery. When she had cured your wounds, she brought you here to me. I guess you were well enough to be left in the care of a mere mortal."

"How do you know this?"

"Her sister told me. She, the sister that is, arrived here in the small hours one night. She and you were in a carriage. There was a detachment of skirmishers with her. You were unconscious on a stretcher. We carried you upstairs and put you to bed. She spent a few beats alone with you. Then she came down and told me to let you sleep, no matter how long it was. You slept for about six hours. Then you woke, we met and you remember everything else."

He rolled onto his back and put his arm over his face. "Who is she, this Witch?"

"Nobody knows for sure. Some say she's just that, a sorceress. Others say she's from a far country that's far in advance of ours. It's great to speculate but the truth is that nobody knows. She refuses to answer the question. Generally we Byekiy don't believe in religion, magic or any stuff like that. We're a pragmatic lot. But I'm telling you, I've seen her do things that'd make you disbelieve your own eyes!"

"Like what?"

Jarleh smiled. "One day we were building a road. One of the lads had cut his hand and I was sewing it up. There was a massive tree, right in the path of the road. As you know, we build our roads straight. So the poor old tree had to come down. The stump had to come out too. Huge job, would have cost us a couple of days. I finishes patching up this fellow and as I'm telling him how to look after the dressing, she rides up. You can't miss her. She rides a tall slim mount, really fast. She's a brilliant rider. She wears all black. She's got black hair cut in a fringe at the front and the rest hanging level to her shoulders. She jumps off the mount and lands light as a rain drop. She sees all the troops preparing to cut this tree down and she says, "stand everybody back thirty paces from the tree."

"So we all backs up and watches. She stands near the tree and raises her arms. She starts shouting in this weird language. There's a deafening noise, cracking and tearing. The tree starts to shake. Then slowly it starts to wrench itself out of the ground. A little at first, then faster. The roots start to show. Dirt sprays out all around. More cracking as the roots rip out of the ground. Some break, most are hauled out like in the worst storm you ever saw. We were amazed at how many roots there were. I swear there's more of a tree under the ground than there is above it. Now the tree is high in the air, the last few roots clear of the ground. The dirt pours off it and back into the hole. It shakes like a wet animal and more dirt clears off the roots. She moves her arms in a throwing gesture. The whole tree is flung sixty paces to one side, where we can cut it up and use the wood. It falls so silent you could hear the blood in your own ears. Then she dashes back to her mount, takes a running jump onto its back and grabs the reins. She's gone without another word. Two thousand soldiers saw that trick. There's not one of them – or me – that doubts she can do magic."

Bdescu stared at her. "Jarleh, in my country people routinely believe in devination, augury, truthsayers, fakirs and a whole load of other tricks. I've seen dozens and I can't say I believe any of it. But I have also seen something I cannot explain."

He described the smooth, burned tunnel in the wall of Blenvan's walled city. She smiled. "Yes, she can do that. There are a dozen canal tunnels that she made. She never lets us watch that trick. We don't know how she does it. There's no waste, not a grain of sand or a speck of dust, after she's finished. Where does she put hundreds of cartloads of rock? If it ain't magic, it might as well be. Tell you something else. One of the tunnels is six hundred strides long. The walls are perfectly flat, completely smooth and the ceiling is level. I mean absolutely level at every single point. Baffling."

Bdescu described the night of the Prince's escape from the Blenvan keep. He told Jarleh of the loud concussion and the movement he'd seen high on the wall.

"Her, for a certainty. Many of us believe she can fly. She's been known to turn up in a place, then forty megastrides away a few beats later. She does more things in a day than any normal person. She'll be in a council meeting with the other Four in the morning, then supervising a building project half a country away at lunchtime, then be at a University seminar by mid-afternoon somewhere else."

"Then she sends a message out that she's off for a while. She'll disappear and nobody knows where she is. We all know she has some kind of hide away. What's the point of trying to find her if she can fly? That's why the Imperial assassins will never get her. Dirty slavers, murdering shitbugs."

"And did you say she had a sister? There are two of these mythical beings?"

"Yep. No idea what her sister does. She's no soldier. Seems more of a secret, really."

Bdescu stared up at the sky. From the corner of his eye he caught a glimpse of movement. The hlant wandered into the hospital courtyard. His hair stood on end. The brute towered over them as they lay in the sun. Jarleh rolled over. "Ganborje. Here boy."

The predator stalked over to her and flopped on the ground. She scratched its huge head, behind the ears. Its eyes closed and it emitted a deep vibrant purr. Bdescu's surprise must have been visible. Jarleh giggled.

"You hunt these, don't you? The smartest beast in the forest. The surest way to make sure that nothing eats your flocks or robs your house. The truest friend. The happiest, sunniest personality in the animal kingdom. And you people kill them for sport. That's why, handsome enemy, we'd better win and you'd better lose. The world will be a better off in our hands than yours."

"Talking of losing" Bdescu changed the subject, "what do you think will happen after our year is up?"

"We suspect that most of your countrymen will stay here. All the slaves will, unless they're completely insane. Most of the freemen will too. We need them, too. Our lands are tough to farm, we need more people. But you nobles have the most to lose by staying so most of you will go home – the few left alive that is. And every single one of them is making a calculation. Will the Emperor kill them for failing, or will all the blame fall on you? They'll gamble that you'll go back and take the blame for all of them. But you? You're different. Knowing that you're certain to die, you'll still go back. You'll make your report and swing from a gibbet.

Your sense of duty is so obvious to me I can see it on your face. I've told you too much already, you charmer. Any further intelligence you want you won't get from me. I'm a soldier and I should keep my own council."

Bdescu raised an arm in salute then reclined back on the grass.

"Let me ask a less ah... tactically sensitive question. Apart from saving her enemies from certain death, making roads and teaching school, what's she here for, this so-called Witch?"

Jarleh looked for mockery in his face and saw none. "She came to save us from you lot. When the raids started, oh, about twenty years ago, it was your cavalry against our farmers. You slaughtered us. Then we organised a militia and you slaughtered us even faster. The Four were helpless, they didn't know how to organise for military action. We begged the people of Blenvan for advice. Then one winter day a tall woman walked into Council and told them exactly what they had to do. They were smart enough to listen. They gave her what she asked, which was five hundred men and five hundred women. They had to be under forty and not child-bonded. These were the only conditions. She trained the thousand in secret over the winter."

"That spring Imperial slavers came back after more slaves. The Witch led our first successful defence. Everyone knew that we needed to make the Witch part of our government, it was the only way we'd survive. So we held a vote and it came up near-unanimous. The Four who led us became Five, and the former Witch became the Fifth of Five, which is her official title. In your language she'd be Minister of War. What are you staring at?"

"Twenty years ago? You've been in contact with the Empire for twenty years?"

"At least. They sent emissaries at first. They wanted trade and treaties. They've cut down all their own forests and at first they only wanted timber, and we were very happy to help them with that. But they wanted us to give them slaves to handle the timber. Imagine. Free men and women traded like beasts. We refused, of course. Then they started raiding along our Southern border. That's their shortest route to our lands. Your lot came the long way around, along the river from the South West. We expected it, of course, because the Witch used her magic to watch you."

She looked up at the sun. "I must go. I have a hot date tonight. He's gorgeous and if I'm in a good mood he might get lucky. Don't wait up."

She climbed to her feet and walked by him. She dropped her hand to his head as she passed, ruffling his hair. This had become her gesture of affection towards him. She had no idea of the turmoil inside that head. The hlant rolled smoothly to its huge feet, yawned prodigiously and wandered off on business of its own.

He was awake when Jarleh came back. She was obviously a little drunk. It took her three attempts to open her bedroom door. She was singing a popular song with scurrilous lyrics. He thought about going to her and asking more questions while her guard was down. Instead he lay thinking until exhaustion conquered thought.

Pelva

The men of the Seventh Contubernium (Provisional) arrived at the concert hall in good time. Their leader, known as Beast, had never been to a musical entertainment in his life. In fact, Cvelthan had barely heard any music. The slave-soldier barracks might have a couple of talented musicians but few could obtain or play instruments. Only the household slaves got the benefits of their masters' cultural activities.

The boys all wore their best clothes. Podge wore brand new clothes because his old attire no longer fit his massive upper body and leaner hips. Cvelthan had also traded kudos for clothes, as he owned none. It felt good to own his own stuff and he wore his plaid kilt with a manly swagger. His new sporran was of good leather, if plain. His shirt was smooth fine cloth and felt wonderful against his skin. His hair, now cropped short in a Byekiy soldier's cut, was washed. He smelled clean and fresh and felt just fine. The early evening air was warm, the sun still high. They showed their tickets at the door and a uniformed woman smiled at the lads and handed each of them a numbered ceramic tankard. She waved them to their seats – centre front row. "Remember your numbers, please," she called in a sing song voice.

"Fuck me with a bent spade, Beast. We've got the best seats in the house!" Even Blondie was impressed.

Several lads and lasses walked around the auditorium with large jugs of beer. The audience passed their tankards to the end where the teenagers filled them. Then people carefully passed them back. Cvelthan watched this strange ritual with his customary respect for Byekiy logic. Everyone gets a tankard full, everyone likes beer. Everyone gets served, quickly and without queuing at a bar or arguing over who is next. He shook his head. No wonder they made good soldiers, even the kids were well organised. He watched the kids dashing back through the doors at side of stage, where he could just make out the bar area. The jugs were filled as fast as they were emptied. It was like watching a military parade.

They chatted as the hall filled. It was a curved space with rows of seats banked so that every seat had a clear view. The seats were wooden but well shaped and comfortable enough. In front of the seats was a picket fence protecting a pit. In the pit sat about twenty musicians, handling instruments that were strange to his eyes. Some seemed for plucking or strumming. Some were obviously drums and others pipes or horns made of wood or metal. The musicians practiced a few notes each, getting ready. It made an odd dissonance that was not unpleasant. Beyond the band's pit the stage rose, slightly higher than his seat. But if he relaxed back in his chair he could see perfectly.

A man stood up in front of the band and all their noise stopped instantly. He raised his arms and they all came ready, instruments poised. He dropped an arm and music rose all around the hall. The shape of the auditorium made for a wonderful sound. After a short tune, the standing man brought his hands together and the music ceased. He turned to the audience. "Fellows. Tonight a rare treat. From Five Rivers, the sweetest voice in the entire republic. The justly celebrated artist, Pelva!"

The place was lit by high windows. A strong shaft of light from a window at the back was in direct line with the setting sun. The shaft of light fell centre stage and into its brightness stepped a woman. Cvelthan looked at her and stopped breathing. She was of short stature, for a Byekiy woman. Her hair was deep auburn and fell in dense waves half way down her back. She was dressed in a formal gown precisely the colour of her hair. Her figure was womanly, curving in spectacular form under the fitted gown. She smiled at the audience and spoke in a loud, clear contralto. "Hello folks. Nice of you to come. Tonight, we'll start in mellow mood with some soppy love songs. Then we'll bend the walls with some louder, more upbeat stuff. Then I've got some really sad numbers to get you all emotional. We'll end with a couple of classics. You ready?"

A roar of assent went up from the crowd. Cvelthan was not expecting it and jumped. He looked around but every eye was on the woman, nobody had noticed his gaucheness. The standing man started moving his arms again. The music swelled and Miss Pelva began to sing.

Cvelthan spent an hour of complete enchantment. His eyes never left her face. His attention was focused completely on every word from her lips. He strained to understand the Byekiy but he could not fail to understand the emotions. After an hour, Pelva changed to Imperial. She sang a song about a handsome young slave boy. In the song, the boy was pulled from his mother's arms to be sold at the great auction hall in Kcharkinlact. The weeping mother's cries upset her master's children, who felt sorry for her plight. The master beat her for this annoyance. The boy, unsold, wept in the slave crib, surrounded by older slaves who look with hot eyes at his young body. Tears rolling down his face, Cvelthan was transported. The song ended with the boy hunching defensively against the wall of his cell, crying for his mother. Cvelthan stood up.

"It's true! It's all true! That's what happens, I know it's true!" He looked around, face afire. He sat down heavily. A roar of approval went up from the crowd and people started clapping their hands and stamping their feet. Someone patted him on the shoulder from the row behind. "She gets to you like that, mate. I cried half the way home last time she sang that." Cvelthan nodded gratefully.

Pelva came to the edge of the stage and looked down at the legion's newest decanus.

"Soldier, I'm so glad my song is authentic. And glad you enjoyed it too. Now here's one to cheer you up a bit. What's your name? Not your legionary name, your real name?"

"Cvelthan, miss."

She returned to her centre stage position. By now all light had gone from the window and the lamps had been lit by silent helpers. "OK, folks, this one's for my newest and bestest fan, Kelthan!"

She mispronounced his name, as all Byekiy did. The double consonant eluded their ears. She sang a song of riotous, bawdy lovemaking that made Cvelthan's face burn once again. But he never once stopped smiling.

When the show had finished, the crowd applauded and cheered themselves hoarse. She bowed, curtsied and blew kisses as she left the stage. All around the lads, people started talking about this marvellous performance. The audience started to rise and file out of the seats. At the right of the stage was a bar, most people seemed to be headed there so the seventh Contubernium went with the flow. Every one of the squad wanted to buy Cvelthan a beer. With his numbered flagon in hand, he endured their joshing about his outburst. Surprisingly, none mentioned the tears and looking closely he saw that they all had reddened eyes. He realised that crying in public was not a sign of weakness here. Then he noticed that the boys had stopped talking and were staring past him. A light hand touched his shoulder. He turned and looked down into Miss Pelva's eyes. She smiled. Off stage and without make up she was a little older than she had seemed, but still heartbreakingly lovely. He guessed her age as a little younger than himself. Like most slaves, he was not exactly sure of his date of birth and had no birthday to celebrate.

She took a freshly-poured beer tankard off the bar and drank it down without taking a breath. "Thanks lads. I needed that." The boys had become star struck, blushing and silent. Cvelthan had more courage.

"Miss Pelva. I really enjoyed your singing. It was the first I ever heard and I still hear it inside me. Thank you."

She cocked her head on one side. She looked up at Cvelthan to see his eyes. "Are you serious? You've never heard singing before?" He shook his head. "Never" he said simply.

"Where in the world have you come from then?"

"From that slave crib in Kcharkinlact." Her eyes widened. She looked up at the tattoos on his forehead, which were slightly obscured by his deep tan and the roughening of his skin from the helmet's lining.

"You're a slave soldier?" he nodded. "Was. I'm a Freeman now." She was too close to him; he could smell her breath and feel the heat of her body. His skin tingled. He felt helplessly oversensitive. The sporran was a dead weight on his arousal, luckily.

She seemed fascinated by him. As they talked, the boys took the hint and faded away. The bar emptied. Pelva and Cvelthan told one another their stories. Hers was a simple tale of a happy family, a musical talent then music school. She had worked hard. She was a singer and songwriter, famous in a small way as she described herself. Her story was light, amusing and full of anecdotes.

She paled as he told her of life as a slave. How he had endured the beatings, being bought and sold, having no home. He described himself as surly, aggressive and difficult. He had often been whipped. Then he recounted how he had met Bdescu for the first time. In his late teens, Cvelthan was owned by a farmer, a minor noble. One day, Cvelthan was once again on a punishment duty for some minor transgression. His master and his overseer both hated him. The overseer had harnessed him to a plough and set him to furrow a field of heavy soil. The overseer was using liberal amounts of whip to force Cvelthan onwards. In the burning noon sun Cvelthan was dying of sunstroke and dehydration. Blood dripped from his back. Out of Cvelthan's line of vision a tall stranger stopped his horse and watched the proceedings for a few moments. The stranger called to the overseer to tell him where the master was to be found. The surly overseer pointed with his whip to the manor house then set about Cvelthan's shoulders again.

A short while later Cvelthan's master had ridden up in company with the stranger. The master ordered the overseer to cut Cvelthan out of the yoke and hand him over to the stranger. "This gentleman has just paid a handsome sum for him. The slave is his now. Back to the house and let the Lord take his new slave away."

Cvelthan could barely walk. The scarred stranger helped him to a nearby tree and sat him down propped against the trunk. He took the stopper from a water gourd and gave Cvelthan a drink. They waited a while until Cvelthan felt stronger. The stranger said little. He seemed lost in his own thoughts. Eventually he helped the huge slave onto his own mount and led the animal along. They walked for the rest of the day. The stranger seemed never to tire. They arrived at his ancient castle after dark. There Cvelthan was washed, fed and his wounds dressed. There seemed to be no overseers, just Mridka the cook and a handful of kitchen slaves. The kitchens smelled of good food and herbs. Cvelthan was given a bed in a room with four other slaves, all of whom introduced themselves and bid him welcome.

Cvelthan, back in the present, raised his tankard in a toast. Pelva raised hers too. "Best day of my life, the day I met Gvant Bdescu. No more whips. Suddenly I had a proper job as a slave-soldier. In one day I got myself a home and a name of my own - in House Bdescu. Bdescu taught me soldiering and I made sure I learned. I stood in the shield wall and fought like a mad beast. First he promoted me to Trusted Man. I fought, I marched, I never complained. One day I held the line against four barbarians, killed three of the shitbugs and wounded the other. The line held. Bdescu comes up to me after and he says, "Cvelthan of Bdescu, are you ready to Advance to Freeman and take your oath to my House? You've earned it soldier." He Advances me in front of all the men, sword in hand, properly traditional. Then he hands me my papers, all signed before and full legal. Tattooist already arranged so I had my Freeman tattoo done right away. He's a stickler for correct action is Colonel Bdescu. So in a single year I went from being a field slave, the lowest Rank in the whole Empire, to a Freeman. All because of Lord Bdescu. He's not one for smiling and joking but he's the best man I ever met and I'd die or him."

Pelva was aghast. "Are you serious? You never had a name until you met Descu?"

"Yes. Field slave are usually numbered. All the lowest Ranks are. Miners, sewage clearers, field slaves, all the same. You get your master's family name and a number."

Pelva seemed shaken but she gestured for him to go on.

By this time they were alone in the empty bar. They'd been talking most of a night and dawn was showing at the windows. She stood up. "Come with me." She led him across the street to a small, neat inn. He followed her up the stairs into a large bedroom with a wide bed. It was the largest bed he'd ever seen. She undressed him. She looked down and smiled. "What a compliment! Have you been in that state all evening?" He nodded, crimson.

She led him to the bed. "I'm taking you to bed, handsome man. I'm not ready to sign a baby bond with you, so no funny stuff, OK?"

"You're safe with me, Pelva."

"I know I am. Now do as you're told and we'll see how we get on."

She used her hands and breasts to release his ardour. She showed him how to please her with gentle touch. When it was over, he lay on his back with her on top of him. She marvelled at the solidness of his body. "Was that your first time?" she asked shyly.

"Pelva, you have no idea. On this wonderful day I spent my first pay on my first own clothes. I went to my first concert, heard my first songs and cried in public for the first time. When I thought the day was as perfect as a day can be, I met you. Then I kissed you. Then we touched each other. I'm so happy I'll never forget a single instant of this day."

She gave him a cheeky look. "I know! We'll make this your birthday. You told me you don't know when you were born and slaves don't get a birthday. But you're a freeman now – in more ways than you know. So why don't you adopt this date as your birthday and that will help you remember your happy day. Plus you'll never forget me, which is flattering."

He nodded, eyes shining. She kissed him and rolled off to lie beside him. "Make spoons, big man. We need to go to sleep before it gets any lighter". He fell asleep with a beautiful woman in his arms and the sweetest dreams in his mind.

Two glorious days later, Cvelthan was seated on the edge of his bunk in the barracks hut. His uniform felt harsh and scratchy but his spirits were soaring. The lads hung on his every word.

"Then she had to move on to her next show, three days' travel from here. So I kissed her goodbye and set her off on the coach."

"Wow!" Podge was a little stuck for words. "Imagine. Beast's been to bed with Pelva! Did you actually, you know, do the deed?"

"Mind your own business, kid." Cvelthan stretched his arms above his head and decided to try this new terminology. "Put it this way, I'm not ready to sign a baby bond just yet!"

The lads looked at each other, nodding wisely. Joker spoke first. "I bet there was plenty of rude stuff though. She was looking at him like she fancied him, I bet."

Cvelthan let them speculate. His stock had never been higher. He was happy to be back with his mates, he loved the banter and camaraderie of the bunkroom. The only cloud in Cvelthan's personal sky was the deep longing in his stomach for a curvy woman with white skin and copper hair.

Darker Bearings

Byardil walked home through a bright evening. The gardens smelled of flowers and it was a warm, mellow end to a tough day. The kids were restless and bored. They had played up all day and Byardil was exhausted. His bag of books was heavy and he was sick of trying to speak Byekiy without a heavy Imperial accent. His tread was slow as he walked down a narrow passageway between two rows of houses. A group of three men blocked his path. They were young, probably late teens. They were dressed alike in dark trousers and leather jackets. Byardil waited for them to move aside, smiling in a polite manner. One of them pushed him, hard in the shoulder.

"So you're the slave-monger, eh? Fuckshy shitbug child-molester! You're a nonce!"

Byardil reeled backwards. "I'm not a slave-monger. I'm a slave."

This seemed to anger them all the more. They jeered at him. One spat in his face. Byardil knew he was in deep trouble. On impulse, he threw the satchel of books at them, turned and fled. They were too fast. One of them tripped him from behind before he'd gone more than a few paces. Heavy shoes thumped into his ribs and the kicking began. Byardil hunched into a foetal position. He wrapped his arms around his head, pulled up his knees and tried to protect his face and crotch. Slaves, even pampered household scribes, have seen enough beatings to know the best way to survive them.

He screamed with pain as a boot hit him in the spine. The pain opened him up like a split shellfish. Another kick landed in his stomach, driving all the air out of him along with most of his lunch. "Sorry," he gasped absurdly.

The blows stopped. He dimly heard sounds, like ripe fruits being thrown against a stone wall. He heard shouts, then shrieks, then whimpers. A strong hand gripped his upper arm and a clear male voice asked him; "are you badly injured, Mr? Shall I summon a medic or can you sit up?"

"My belly and back hurt. I think I can sit up." The strong man lifted him bodily from the floor, carried him a few strides out of the alleyway and set him down in a sunny corner on the grass.

He looked around. The youths were lying on the ground in the alley in various contorted positions. Two groaned, one was unconscious. Standing over them were two men and a woman. The standing people wore dark blue jackets and matching kilts. Their sporrans were black as were their boots. Long blue socks were pulled up to their knees. Each leaned on a staff of some dark wood, smoothly turned and tipped with a metal ferrule. The woman spoke to a youth who was groaning on the ground.

"Listen to me, Dancle Shelp. This isn't the first time your gang's attacked somebody is it? I warned you there would be consequences if you racked up again. What was it this time, eh? Thought the Imperial guy was fair game? Thought nobody would bother if you bashed an enemy? Well let me tell you, I'm the shitting law around here. And nobody gets assaulted on my beat. You're in shit, laddie and I'm going to shovel some more on you. Now get off your lazy arse and help your so-called mates. You got them into this and you can shitting well sort them out. Do it now, before I lose my temper, you little turd."

Groaning, the youth climbed to his feet and rubbed his shoulder.

The man who had lifted Byardil now smiled down at him. "You OK? Must hurt quite a lot. We can drop you at a doctor if you like. You can come to the Constabulary House tomorrow, or whenever you like to press charges against these young thugs."

Byardil shook his head. "I'll not press charges, I do not want to get involved. I'll just go home, if that's OK."

The man frowned. "Sorry, Mr. That is not how it works. These young shites need to face a court and a conviction. The Republic has a grievance against them under the law. It's not your place to decide whether they get done or not. That's up to a magistrate then a court. You're a key witness and you'll testify truthfully. If you don't, that will be called perverting the course of justice, then you'll be in trouble too. So get ready. All you have to do is tell the truth."

Byardil nodded weakly and said he would comply tomorrow on his way home from school.

"Good man. Remember, we protect you. That's our duty. You help us to convict these men – that's your duty. They get punished and with luck they stop being a drain on the public kudos. I live in hope. When you come to the Constabulary, ask for Renketh. That's me. This time of day I'm usually there. OK?" Byardil nodded. The constables had raised the hooligans to their feet. They were bruised but not seriously hurt; the constables had wielded their staffs with skill and restraint. They bound the hands of the guilty men with buckled straps and led them away. The constables grinned at Byardil as they walked away. Sighing, the scribe limped off home.

Muster

A quiet evening ended abruptly with a harsh trumpet sounding the call to muster. The Seventh Contubernium (provisional) rushed to their armours and weapons, expecting another drill. Then they heard the whistles of the centurions. "It's a march!" They piled out of the hut, dressed but unarmed. The heavy wooden practice swords would be no use on a march. As they looked around, a cart appeared, loaded with real weapons. They rushed up, grabbing swords and peelums. Then they hauled down the heavy packs that were also on the wagon. The whole camp was mustering in the gloom of late evening. The recruits formed ranks with the veteran troops, dust rising around their heavy boots. They lined up in front of the Commander's dais, where Janthro and a female Colonel in full Skirmisher kit stood at attention. Janthro's voice could be heard by every soldier.

"Men of the Fifth Snowhammer Legion, this is Colonel Jarleh of the First Corps of Skirmishers. She's the most experienced officer in the whole army and has served as personal guard to the Fifth of Five. It is my privilege to introduce her to you. My original plan was that she would take over integration training, getting the recruits used to working with archers and skirmishers, cavalry and artillery. The recruits needed practice in our mixed-forces battle order. This will be postponed. We are on full alert. We need every man. Imperial raiders are attacking villages all along our Southern border. Seven villages have already suffered raids. The Imperials are taking slaves and murdering innocents. So far the body count is over eighty dead, almost two hundred wounded and seventy six taken into slavery, including more than thirty children."

He paused as an angry roar rose from the ranks.

"The Empire has broken the truce. I am instructed to use military force against them. Here is my order from the Council." He held up a single sheet of white parchment.

"By this authority the Five command you to defend the republic. You are authorised to use deadly force against all and any Imperial personnel who break our laws. Kill, wound or capture the invaders and stop their predations. The time for kudos is upon you. Put your bodies between our children and the enemy's spears. Some of you will die. Many will be wounded. Every one shall have their name recorded in the Regimental Hall of the Fallen and their name will be chanted on the Rolls of Honour."

Janthro put down the scroll. He raised his voice again. "Be proud to fight alongside your mates, as I am proud to stand with you. And be even prouder to stand beside Colonel Jarleh. We will split into small, fast-response units. We will move quickly, strike hard and send some slavers to the torment that they call hell." He paused.

"Not one man, woman or child will be taken as a slave. This is your oath. Repeat it on my count of three. One, two, three..."

The sentence was bellowed across the parade ground. The din hurt Cvelthan's ears. Four thousand eight hundred men spoke as one. It gave him a strange hot sensation in the chest. Janthro stepped forward again.

"You will split into cohorts. The First Spear centurion of each cohort will command. You will march to your area of action and rendezvous with skirmisher, archer and cavalry units on the way. Each cohort will take its own field artillery and a minimum baggage train of marching rations, field repair kits and ammunition. Local villagers will provide other foodstuffs when you reach your areas.

Shoulder to shoulder!" Again the men roared and this time Cvelthan with them.

Centurions bellowed the orders to dismiss and reform by cohort. There was much motion until the units were formed into their marching orders. The 7th Contubernium, 9th cohort, 5th Legion stood in ranks amongst seasoned veterans. The smell of sweat, iron and leather overwhelmed the summer breeze as the men waited patiently on the main camp road for their command to move. So long was the delay that they weren't ready when it came and had to jump to move in step with the more experienced men. Cvelthan had moved smoothly on command, so they followed his step. He smiled. Training was over. Now he would learn how these damned legions worked.

Escape

In the darkest hour of a short summer night, Bdescu walked carefully down the stairs. On his back was a pack fashioned from a sheet. It contained food stolen from the kitchen and a water jar. He wore dark clothes and his old boots were folded under his arm. No doors were locked and he was soon outside. The streets were deserted but he went out of the back of the village, wary of Hlants and other guard creatures. He walked around the village until he reached the river. He thought that the river must be a tributary of the Great River that flowed all the way home to the Empire.

On the edge of town was the boathouse he'd seen from the hillside when he'd been running with Jarleh. Like most Byekiy property, it was unlocked. He found a small, fast skiff. He untied the beautiful craft. He climbed aboard, unshipped the oar and eased the craft out into the swift current. In moments he was out of the village. There was enough starlight to see by. Provided he didn't strike a hidden rock or sandbank he should be a long way away by dawn.

The night passed slowly. He steered with the single, rear-mounted sculling oar and kept to the centre of the stream. He'd lived by a river as a boy and was handy with boats. This one was light and manoeuvrable. His was such a simple escape plan. The best plans were always simple, he reminded himself. He smiled in the darkness and kept to the far bank as he passed a row of houses. No challenge came.

By dawn, Bdescu was deep inside the forest. Giant blue-green trees hung over the edges of the river, their drooping fronds obscuring the banks. Birds, animals and insects called incessantly, a deluge of hooting, barking and grunting; and sounds for which he had no names. The river ran slowly with a deep smooth progress that delighted him. The trees hid the sun, but he began to suspect that the river was not heading South-East, towards the Empire, but North-Eastwards, deeper into Byekiy territory. He sculled for the bank and hauled the skiff through the branches, finding a safe mooring in a sheltered pool under the trees. He climbed out and set off to find a clearing where he might get sight of the sun and a bearing for his direction. A short distance from the bank he came upon a Byekiy road. The smooth slabs, constant camber and rain gutters were unmistakeable. So he knew he was still inside the Republic. He heard a distant sound that was not of the forest; a deep regular hammering, metal on wood perhaps. He dithered for a moment. Should he run back to the boat and keep going, or should he take the risk of staying here and finding out where he was headed? Curiosity won over fear, and he headed boldly for the sound.

After a few beats, he emerged from the ancient woodlands into a broad riverside meadow. Here the river rushed down through rapids. A channel had been cut, lined with smooth stones. Part of the river rushed down the smooth channel and drove a mighty waterwheel. Bdescu had seen many waterside mills but this was on a scale like no other. The wheel was four times a man's height and attached to a three-storey stone building of huge scale – a small palace or medium-sized temple. From inside the building came the hammering. As usual for Byeki buildings, it was well-endowed with windows. He walked casually up to one of them and peered inside.

He saw a manufactory. Dozens of Byekiy worked inside, all tending machines. The water-wheel turned a mighty shaft that spanned the hall within. The shaft was supported on tall brick columns, twice the height of a man. Each column had a curved brass bearing on top, through which ran the shaft. He saw a boy on a ladder pouring oil onto the top of one of the bearings, obviously to keep the shaft turning smoothly. The main shaft drove wide belts that descended to various contraptions that Bdescu had never seen before. Some of these machines were for turning timber poles, and he realised that they were lathes. Not the lathes of an imperial carpenter, turned by a lad and a handle. These powerful machines were all for producing wooden pole-shaped objects. With a start, he realised that they were spear shafts, the very spears that had pierced his shield just a few weeks before. He walked further along the building. The next section was a forge. Here the mighty shaft continued, but the belts drove bellows, and trip-hammers. In his imagination he saw men forging the long iron shanks and sharp steel tips for the spears. Finally, at the end of the building, he came to a despatch area. There were carts, each loaded with hundreds of finished spears. He counted the carts. Over thirty. He worked out how many spears this one facility could make and his blood cooled. His determination to warn the Empire was redoubled. With a deep foreboding he looked up and finally caught sight of the sun. His fears were confirmed. He was headed North-East, ever-deeper into the Republic and away from home.

Bdescu turned away from the building to head back to his boat. Blocking his way were five men. They wore leather clothes, much-worn and faded. One carried a bundle of snares. One carried a mesh bag full of dead animals. All of them carried stout sticks.

"What's this then, eh? said the one with the snares. "An imperial spy! Get him!"

They threw aside their bundles and rushed at him. Bdescu kept his hands low until the very last instant then flung a punch straight into the face of the nearest man. It struck fairly on the man's nose and he yelped. Bdescu stepped under a swinging cudgel and pushed another man over. He tried to run through the gap he had made. One of them stuck out a foot and Bdescu tripped. He fell heavily, unable to get his outstretched arms underneath him to break the fall. Boots and sticks thudded into his body as his vengeful attackers swarmed around. All of the blows hurt, but one kick landed exactly on the wound under his arm. Bdescu screamed and threw up.

"Kill the shitlicker! Go on lads, let's do him!" Bdescu knew he could take little more punishment. One rib was badly hurt, he could feel the stabbing pain when he breathed. The kicks to his legs and backside were bad enough, and he used his arms to shield his head, but sooner or later they would splinter a rib, puncture a lung and he was dead. Bdescu started to say the Prayer for the Dying as he felt his life slipping away. He closed his eyes.

Through his clenched eyelids he perceived a brilliant flash of light. He felt a heavy jolt and he heard a screaming sound. Not a human scream, this was unearthly. Convinced he was passing into God's Realm he tried to say his prayers aloud.

Criminals

The next morning a bruised and sore Byardil walked into the Constables' building. It was a modest four-roomed single storey place. The front door led into a corridor. He turned right, into an office with a desk surrounded by chairs. Through a door in the back of the room he could see a small gaol with two separate cells. Both were empty.

Sitting at the desk was the smiling Constable who had lifted him off the ground. "Take a seat. Would you like a cup of chasser?"

Byardil shook his head. The Byekiy favoured this strong herbal brew made with leaves steeped in boiling water. He found that he liked its clean, astringent smell but the slightly bitter taste did not appeal.

"Is it too bitter? You can try it with some sap in it, that'll sweeten it?" The smiling Constable poured some from a jug into a ceramic beaker. He took a smaller flask and poured some of the brown tree-sap that they used as a sweetener into the beaker and stirred it with a spoon. He offered it to Byardil. "If you don't like it, I can always drink it myself!"

Byardil sipped the hot drink and found it very palatable. He smiled through cracked lips. "Thank you, Constable Renketh."

The female officer in charge strode in from the street door. "Ah, Mr Bdescu. Thanks for coming in to do your civic duty. Constable Renketh will take your statement and I will witness it, so just let him do all the work, eh?" She smiled and sat down in the corner chair.

Renketh took out a piece of paper. It was fine-quality parchment made of some good smooth material and bleached almost white. He took a metal pen and opened a ceramic vessel of ink. He wrote slowly and carefully his own name, that of his superior, and then Byardil's. He added the date and the name of their village. It was silent in the office. The chair was comfortable and Byardil started to relax.

"Now, Mr Bdescu. I've written down the names of the accused men and the time, date and location of the attack. I now need a simple statement in your own words, of what happened."

Byardil recounted his memory of the event. He did not know the names of his assailants but gave neat, accurate descriptions of their faces, heights and builds, including a facial scar on one particular youth. Renketh wrote it down, carefully. He made no errors and when he read it back to Byardil it seemed to contain all of his words. He was impressed.

The senior Constable had something to add. "Mr Bdescu, those lads that attacked you have a long sad history. They take things without giving kudos. They bully and threaten people. We've had a string of complaints about thievery, assault and even an attempted arson. They never do any work. But this last one was more serious, they'd have killed you if we had not come along."

Byardil was sceptical. "I don't think you just came along. I think you were following them."

She smiled. "Smart man. Yes, we were. They'd been in a barn looking for hung meat to steal. It was a granary so they came out empty handed. That made them angry so they set about you. I confess, we were expecting a more low-level crime, more thieving perhaps. If we'd known they were out for assault we'd have been closer to them and you wouldn't have taken so bad a beating. I am sorry for that."

"Please don't be. I've been beaten by professionals. That was nothing. I've never been so glad to see anyone in my life. So what happens now?"

"Well, they've been up before judges before so the magistrate will have to send them up for trial. You'll be a witness, as will Renketh and I. If convicted, they'll face serious penalties. If lucky they'll get a whipping and if they are very lucky that will be that."

"And if they are unlucky?" Byardil wanted to understand.

"Ostracised." Her voice had a stark quality to it. She obviously thought ostracism to be serious. She saw the blank look on the scribe's face.

"You need to understand something, Mr Bdescu. Right now in high summer this place is a paradise. There are fruits on the trees, crops in the fields and animals as fat as pillows. Six months from now, you'll get frostbite on your uncovered nose in the time it takes you to walk to the school. Drifts of snow will block roads, close the passes and isolate villages for three months. When this happens you need a stout roof, thick walls, a decent stove with plenty of firewood, a cellar full of well-stored food and above all, kudos. You need the help of friends, family and neighbours to survive. If you get sick, break a limb or just have a domestic accident, you'll need lots of help. We work all summer to help one another. When the harvest needs reaping we pitch in and help. When a barn needs building, we're there. All summer we work hard so that we have enough kudos to survive the winter."

Byardil had seen a little of these Northern winters. But not like up here in the mountains, the very Teeth of God.

"So if people break our laws we beat them. If they still don't change their ways, then we ostracise them. Mostly the ostracised ones die. A few of them band together and survive up in the forest but it isn't much of a life. Some come crawling back and say they've learned. Sometimes a judge will rescind their banning order, sometimes not."

"Why not lock them up?" asked Byardil.

"Because it's too expensive in food, housing, attention... why should people who have made zero contribution to the life of their fellows, then be looked after over the winter? We'd all starve if we acted like that!"

Byardil was getting an insight into the realities of life in the Republic. The Byekiy had seemed a tolerant, friendly people. Now he realised that they just had different priorities. They were far more forbearing with foreign invaders than with domestic criminals. The real enemy was not the Imperium. It was not Imperial soldiers. The real enemy was starvation. That's what occupied their minds, that's where their fears came from. He began to worry about his own modest household.

"I've never lived through a Byekiy winter. I've not got lots of firewood, nor a cellar that well stocked. Perhaps my people and I will starve too."

Renketh laughed in his deep bass voice. "You're under the protection of the Fifth of Five! Someone will come with ten cords of firewood. Someone else will bring your food. I expect somebody will even show you how to dress for winter. You'll come to no harm, my lad!"

Byardil was baffled. "But why? I've not even met the Fifth of Five, whoever he might be. Why is he protecting me and my house?"

The woman spoke. "First off, the Fifth is not a man, she's a woman. Second, she's always got a really good reason for everything she does. Third, whoever gave you that red bandanna has a direct connection to the Fifth. I've never even seen a red bandanna until I saw you in the street. They are rare things. The bandanna means every citizen must help you in any way they can because senior members of our government have decided you're important. I don't know any more than that. Somebody has plans for you, that's all. And all kudos gifts must be repaid in full – before winter's end!" She smiled encouragingly as she pronounced the proverb.

Byardil finished his chasser. Renketh asked him to sign the statement after reading it carefully. He did so, finding the metal pen a wonderful writing instrument and the paper a joy to write on. The woman clapped him on the shoulder, hefted her baton and strode off into the street for her patrol. Byardil got up to leave.

Renketh looked up at him. "Any chance you might be going to the inn later?"

Byardil smiled. "Yes. When later?"

The jolly policeman smiled his broad beam. "Straight after school, the inn's on your way. You could call in for an ale. Then perhaps I'd better walk you home. You know, make sure you don't get duffed up this time?"

Byardil grinned. "Yes, I'd feel a lot safer. See you at the inn, then?"

Renketh nodded and waved as Byardil left the office. He walked to the schoolhouse. He felt as if his feet were not quite reaching the ground. He'd forgotten his bruises.

Skirmish

They marched as if the world would end. Nothing in training had prepared the 7th for the relentless pace of the fighting legion. On hard paved roads there was little dust and plenty of grip for their nailed boots. The pace was unrelenting. Cvelthan had insisted on full water bottles, "every belt, every alert", so at least they had water. They noticed that the veterans did not drink. They just marched, chatting as they went. All night they kept moving, guided by weak moonlight and the pale stones of the marvellous Byekiy road. Cvelthan estimated a pace of around seven Imperial miles to the hundred beats[1] and was hugely impressed. This was more than double the speed Imperial soldiers moved, hampered by baggage trains, priests and lazy officers. In the republic of Byekvoranp, the officers had risen from the ranks and marched with the soldiers. The wagons were light carts, easily keeping up.

As the sun rose, the cohort stopped by the roadside under the shade of high trees. The command came to fall out. A rill ran beside the road and there was a broad grass bank for the soldiers to rest. They drained the bottles and refilled them. They munched on the marching rations which Cvelthan now preferred to the dry biscuit and biltong of his Imperial days. The Byekiy rations were more varied. Today they ate chunks of cooked cereal, studded with dried fruits, held together by a sweet and rather sticky substance. Each chunk was the same, weighted and fair. Each chunk was wrapped in a small cloth which the troops wetted in the stream then used to wash their hands and faces. Food was carried in belt pouches and could be easily discarded in an alert. Too soon they were falling in and moving off. Cvelthan's legs ached and his back was sore from the heavy pack but there was no respite from the relentless legion's pace.

---

[1] An Imperial mile is a thousand paces of the current Emperor's stride. The current incumbent is a short man so a Mile is only round 2,000 feet or around 0.6 kilometres. A beat is the Imperial measure of time and is supposed to be the heartbeat of God. The marching speed equates to about 4 mph.

In mid-afternoon they acquired a skirmisher unit and a corps of archers. The light troops were standing in marching array in a field beside the road, waving as the legionaries marched by. A veteran beside Blondie told them how it worked. He spoke in a broad East Byekiy accent.

"Skirmishers'll fall in front of us in case we come on to th'enemy. Archers'll fall in be'ind. Then thes'll come past us and deploy to sides. Then yous'll know we're near th'action. Cavalry will depend on where we's working. Narrow valley or hillside we might get none. Depends. Yous'll hear 'em comin' anyways." Blondie passed the information around the 7th.

They camped beside the road that night. In spite of being dead-beat, Cvelthan decided to go and meet some skirmishers. Their camp was in the next field so he found the gate. In Byekiy fashion the gate was a stout wooden affair made of riven timber and locked with an iron clasp. He opened it and made sure to close it behind him. For some reason, Byekiy were very sensitive about gates and doors being left open. The etiquette baffled him so he just left them as he found them.

He saw some skirmishers relaxing around a small fire so he wandered over.

"Hello lads. Any idea where we're going?"

They all looked up, surprised. He saw that they were all women. The youngest looked to be around eighteen, like his lads. The eldest was around forty. All were tough looking and fit.

"Who're you calling lads, you fat shitbug?" asked their decanus, the older woman.

Cvelthan took a breath. "Sorry. New guy. Ignorant, obviously."

The woman looked at him properly. "You're an Imperial, aren't you? I heard some of you had joined up. You an experienced soldier?"

"Yes. I've served twelve years. Fought six pitched battles and a dozen skirmishes."

His frankness seemed to relax them. Their hostility evaporated and somebody patted an empty space on the ground. He sat down and joined them. Someone passed him a ceramic jug. He took a swig of the alcohol thinking it was water. Tears streamed from his eyes and he coughed. The woman slapped his shoulder. "Vudeck fruit brandy. Clears your tubes, eh!" They howled. Cvelthan grinned. Women or not, these were soldiers. Same jokes, same manners.

The decanus leaned back on her pack. "Latest news. Your former masters have decided that if us Byekiy won't trade slaves, they will just come and take some. The truce has been torn up, again. We're headed for Seven Falls district, the worst-hit area. We're pursuing a particularly obnoxious group who have caused mayhem in the lower valleys. They've filled sixty wagons with women and kids, could be as many as four hundred people captured. Now they're heading home, having made a fortune. The plan is to cut off the retreat then bring them to battle. They have a troop of proper heavy cavalry and the action could be pretty warm. They'll be moving slowly on account of the prisoners, but they move slowly anyway, it's the Imperial style to bring your girlfriends and shoemakers on a hunting trip, eh?" She aimed the last question at Cvelthan, who simply nodded. The female decanus looked at Cvelthan directly. "What's your name, big man?"

"Beast."

She smiled. "Well Beast, day after tomorrow we'll meet some of your old mates. Us girls will put a few darts in their arses and you fat boys can knock 'em down. It might be the greatest test of loyalty you ever face. Will you fight for us?"

Cvelthan climbed stiffly to his feet and looked around the faces. "Yes. Watch out for flails, they'll come over your shield and split you head open, helmet or no. Lift your shields up and tilt the tops towards yourselves so they cover your heads. Then stab under the lower edges. Go for their balls." He walked away.

At dawn they formed up in parade order. Janthro stood atop a wagon and shouted his last briefing to the men before they met the enemy.

"Men of the Ninth Cohort, Fifth Snowhammer Legion. Today we meet Imperial troops. We are marching in a valley of the Seven Falls district. From this point we are in silent order. No cheering, shouting or singing until contact with enemy forces. We cross a few more fields to the village of White Bridge. The village is bisected by a fast-flowing river. There is no ford. There is a stone bridge, which is white, surprisingly. This side of the bridge is clear, according to Colonel Jarleh's scouts. The Imperial forces have invaded the village across the river and are searching houses, looking for children. Thanks to their ignorance, they do not realise that nearly all the kids are in school, on this side of the stream. We must not allow them to cross the bridge. That is our first objective."

"We march fast to the bridge. We will cross the bridge if we can, that's our second objective. Jarleh's troops will follow us and seek to enfilade the Imperial troops in the streets or riverside. They will hold the bridge behind us. My best guess is that we are slightly outnumbered. They will be encumbered by prisoners which slows them down. Our third objective is obvious: we must win a quick victory so that no prisoners can be used as hostages. Marching calls will be passed down the line. Best of luck. Shoulder to shoulder!"

They marched in silence. The stamp of 500 boots made plenty of noise but not a single man spoke. They marched through wooded glades then emerged into clear farm fields. To right and left were pleasant Byekiy houses, built of stone with roofs of stout slate. They could see the school house across the fields to their northern side. The road sloped down to the river, so tall Cvelthan could see the river and the bridge over the heads of the column. He could also see smoke rising from several houses.

They reached the bridge unopposed. It was wide enough for the column, four abreast, to march straight over without breaking formation. Cvelthan could almost hear his master's sarcastic voice, speaking in his ear. "No scouts? No pickets? Fucking amateurs, Freeman Sergeant!" Cvelthan felt more confident. Whoever these troops were, they were not prepared for a proper fight. They reached a crossroads and deployed in cohort order.

Gulbradge their Optio gave them an update. "Enemy approaching. Heavy cavalry and spear men. They sacked another village further up the valley. They are headed home with a load of prisoners. They thought they'd delay here and pick up a few more slaves. Bad decision, slavers! The legion will hold them here while skirmishers attack from the flank and the rear. Hold fast. Our success depends on you."

Cvelthan stood in the centre of the second line, his lads at his sides. The cohort was a shade under 500 men, arrayed in the Byekiy way. Blocks of troops nine men deep and ten men wide arranged themselves to bar the way. There was a gap between each block of troops. With 500 men in the cohort that meant five blocks of 90 men, plus officers.

The Imperial column came into view. The Imperial commanders shouted warnings. Cvelthan realised that his intuition had been right, the Imperial force had not sent scouts ahead of them. Idiocy or overconfidence, he knew not which. The Imperial troops scrambled to get into battle order. Cvelthan heard the familiar trumpets sound as they deployed the heavy cavalry in front of the slave-soldiers. Behind the troop, Cvelthan could plainly see the iron cages of the slave carts and the people inside them. He could hear cursing from every Byekiy throat. He found a strange anger welling up inside him. "Come and get some steel, you robbing shitbugs!" shouted Lame. Others joined in, yelling insults in Imperial. The cavalry was almost in line and Cvelthan's hackles rose. He was about to face what everyone feared; an Imperial cavalry charge. He looked at the faces of the lads beside him; they were ashen.

Cvelthan opened his mouth and began to sing one of Pelva's more colourful numbers:

"You came to her house and climbed the walls,

She opened the window when you called,

But she fell over backwards and her bended knee,

Landed plumb centre in your hairy balls..."

By the second line his contubernium were joining in. By the third, the whole cohort was roaring out the bawdy lyrics. Every face was grinning and Cvelthan knew they'd stand.

From the houses close to the Imperial troop a tight group of soldiers emerged. They were Byekiy skirmishers, running flat out. They closed with the Imperial slave soldiers at the left side of the Imperial force. A heartbeat later Cvelthan heard the muted sounds of a fight. The clash of weapons and screams of wounded sounded far away, muffled by distance and the Imperial cavalry that stood between him and the fighting. The cavalry turned, hesitating. As they argued over whether to attack the skirmishers, the first flight of arrows rose swiftly from the other side of the Imperial column and fell on the knights. Again Cvelthan heard the terrible sound of mounts hit by war arrows. The squealing grated on his nerves. Several knights fell and the riderless mounts ran around in confusion. More arrows fell. Some of the knights broke ranks and rode around the flank to try and rout the skirmishers. A dozen or so rode at the trees, obviously to attack the archers. Some slave soldiers followed their lords and the formation began to fragment.

The lead centurion blew his whistle. "Advance at rank pace!"

With measured strides, the cohort marched towards the fray. The bulk of the cavalry were still in good battle order and they charged at once. The slave soldiers followed at a clumsy run.

"Front rank, deploy pikes!" called the calm centurion. The first rank soldiers were somehow concealing very long spears, almost three times a man's height. They grounded their shields. They dug the spear butts into the earth and men from the second rank put their feet on the butts to hold them firm. The front-rank men put shoulders behind their shields and held the spears steady.

The Imperial cavalry arrived just as the wall of pikes became firm. The Imperial knights tried to force their mounts past, or onto, the glittering steel points. The mounts reared into the air, screaming. Several knights were thrown to the ground but the beasts would not move forward.

"Peelums!" came the calm voice of the centurion. The deadly spears fell on the Imperial troop and the battle was joined. Knights jumped off their mounts and tried to close with the front ranks of Byekiy legionaries. The unarmoured slave soldiers were faster on their feet and crashed into the front ranks. Heavy fighting broke out. Cvelthan grasped his peelum and waited for the call.

"Peelums! Aim high, over your men, release!"

Cvelthan saw a dismounted Imperial knight, a tall man, raise a heavy falchion to crush a Byekiy helmet. Cvelthan flung his arm forward and launched the heavy shaft. He saw it strike the knight in the very centre of his chest. He folded, killed instantly. The outnumbered front centuries were taking a heavy beating. Cvelthan could see them starting to thin as men went down. "Come on, give the order!" he muttered.

The peelums had caused a brief check in the Imperial onslaught and the centurion timed his call perfectly. "Front rank, retire in order... go!" And the front ranks broke contact with the enemy and dragged their wounded back through the gaps between the centuries of the second rank. As they did, the second rank moved smoothly forward and closed with the enemy. They spread out slightly, closing the gaps in their line and stepped carefully over the dead and injured. Cvelthan was now only one line of men away from the Imperial soldiers. The Imperial forces, catching their breath, charged again. The man in front of Cvelthan stopped as if he had walked into a wall. Cvelthan saw a spear point emerge from the back of the man's neck and knew he was dead. Cvelthan shoved the dead man over with his shield. The dead man's weight pulled the spear down and the slave soldier holding the spear was too slow to let it go. Cvelthan stepped around the dead man and stabbed the slave soldier in the face. Careful to hold his place in the formation, he did not move forward. A knight stepped into the breach left by the dead slave soldier. He wore a long coat of excellent chain mail. He had a high, crested helmet and a curved elegant sword. He swung the sword, hard and fast at Cvelthan's head. Cvelthan yanked his shield up and the blade bit deeply into the side of the shield – and stuck fast. Cvelthan pulled the shield down again, hauling the knight off balance. He stabbed low, below the man's buckler. His strike found the inside of the thigh and the knight grunted. The knight tried to swing the edge of his buckler at Cvelthan's face. The big decanus slashed his short sword across the knight's forearm, cutting deep. Pulling back smoothly, he stabbed the tall knight in the throat. The knight fell to the ground, gargling. Something smashed into Cvelthan's armour but he didn't see what it was. He looked up to see a mounted knight coming at him from his right. The enormous charger pushed its way through the slave soldiers. Its rider wielded a heavy war club with shocking effect. The mounted man struck downwards at Blondie, who was on Cvelthan's right side. Blondie went over, blood gushing from under his helmet. Cvelthan swallowed. Raising his shield over his head he took two quick steps toward the knight's mount. It was a huge grey beast. The knight pulled hard on the bridle and his mount rose up, its heavy feet flailing at Cvelthan's head. Cvelthan raised his shield and braced himself. The four-toed feet smashed down onto the curved shield's face. Cvelthan's muscles, honed from training, swelled and almost tore under the impact. He felt a strong hand on his back. A legionary in the rank behind had seen his move and braced him. As the animal's feet slid along the shield's surface, Cvelthan held his sword out, locked rigid and pointing up. The mount's neck landed on the sword point and the beast's own weight drove the weapon deep into its windpipe. The sword was torn from his grip as the mount fell. The knight was unseated and hit the ground hard. Podge stepped in, bent over and stabbed him as he writhed. The young recruit's considerable weight drove the sword clean through the chain mail and into the knight's heart.

Cvelthan staggered back a pace and looked up. Again there was a lull in the fighting. He heard the command to withdraw, the whistles sounding all around him. He and Podge grabbed Blondie by his harness and dragged him through the gaps in the third line. The third line marched forward and closed with the slave-soldiers who were all that was left of the Imperial troop. Cvelthan and Podge dragged Blondie to the rear. Two medics raced over with a stretcher and began to load

Blondie, but one of them put his fingers to Blondie's throat and shook his head. Cvelthan and Podge rushed back into position as the second line, now at the rear, started to reform. The trumpets sounded stand down. The centurion shouted that the fight was over. Cvelthan could clearly hear a freeman-sergeant calling for mercy. The Imperial force had thrown down its arms.

Cvelthan felt the rush that came to him after he had survived a battle. It was a combination of relief, nausea and exhilaration, a contradictory whirl in his body. Then Podge tapped him on the forearm. "Blondie's dead." Tears rolled down the young man's cheeks, unnoticed and unashamed. Cvelthan gripped his protégé's shoulder and looked fiercely into his eyes.

"Yes. He died doing what we do. Fighting for our mates, our legion and our honour. That's why his name will live on. His family will revere his sacrifice when they cry for his loss. And one day, when this is over, we will chant his name and many others, in the Hall of Remembering. Now we are brothers, Podge. We fought, we killed and we won the day. We have survived, shoulder to shoulder like they told us. We shed blood together and lost a friend." Cvelthan's eyes were wet too. "We are all warriors now."

Podge raised a weak grin. He gripped Cvelthan's forearm and nodded. "Yeah, ok but I killed a man who was lying on the ground. He was nearly dead anyway! You killed two outright and wounded one – not to mention the mount as well. From today I am a soldier. There's only one warrior in this troop, Beast, and that's you mate."

Cvelthan busied himself checking his men. Apart from a few flesh wounds and a deal of cuts and bruises they seemed to be alright. All were a little dazed and he knew it was battle shock. He slapped backs, shook hands and tried to bring them around. He knew it would take them time to calm down.

After a while, the Centurion's clear baritone rose clearly above the background chatter of relieved soldiers. "Beast? Where the fuck is he?" Cvelthan stepped out of formation.

"Here. Sir."

The Centurion grinned at his foreign recruit.

"Well, Mr Beast. You've earned some kudos today. I admit we were wrong about you. We never thought you'd fight for us. I said you'd back out, freeze up or just run away. I was wrong and I apologise. You fought like a rutting hlant today. You held the line when the enemy had a clear breach. You killed their champion and his fucking mount as well. Down on your knees, son."

Cvelthan knelt. There was a murmur from the lads that spread out through the ranks. It became quiet. The Centurion took out his sword and raised it above his head.

"By the power delegated to me by the Fifth of Five may all hear this. As Centurion of this Century and officer of this Legion I make a field promotion. Bear witness and be part of this truth."

He brought the flat side of the sword down onto Cvelthan's left shoulder. It made a dull clank against the iron armour.

"The Recruit known as Beast is hereby promoted full Decanus with all kudos, status, obligations and duties due to that rank."

He raised the sword again and repeated the touch, this time on Cvelthan's right shoulder.

"As Decanus he will lose his recruit name. From this day he will revert to his own name to be used with his new rank. Arise, Kelthan Descu, Decanus. Stand with honour and lead your Contubernium."

He stepped back and saluted, his sword hilt raised to his forehead in the legionnaire's gesture of respect. Cvelthan had lost his own blade in the throat of an Imperial charger. He drew his knife with a hand still sticky with blood and returned salute. The Centurion smiled and offered his right hand. Cvelthan gripped his wrist in the Legion's handshake. The Centurion leaned forward and spoke into Cvelthan's ear.

"I nearly lost a whole troop today. If you hadn't blocked that breach, we might have been slaughtered. I've seen what happens when cavalry break a line. I hope I never see it again. I owe you, soldier. By my Lodge I swear blood debt to you. From now and forever I am your trusted man. Call on me on your day of need."

He hugged Cvelthan, chest to chest. He stepped away, smiled and left.

The lads clustered around Cvelthan, pounding him on the back and cheering wildly. He noticed with amazement that he was weeping again.

The inevitable order to fall in came too soon.

"We need to clear all Imperial elements out of the village. Form into centuries and work street by street upriver. Check every house. Kill or detain every Imperial person whether combatant or civilian. Take control of the area."

Haven

Bdescu opened his eyes and saw clear blue sky. There were no trees. His entire body ached as he struggled to sit up. He found himself lying in a patch of loose dirt, small stones and clumps of grass. The debris was itself scattered over a pristine grey footpath. He looked to his left and saw an immaculately trimmed lawn with flower borders in full and well-tended bloom. Beyond the borders, a sheer cliff of smooth rock, rising as high as his stiff neck would allow him to see. He turned his head, carefully. On the path next to him was a Byekiy boot, complete with part of a leg, neatly amputated halfway up the shin. He stared at it for a moment. He raised his head. To his right were a set of low stone walls, made of the neatly cut Byekiy stone, beyond them another cliff, rising hundreds of heights[2] above him, soaring aloft towards the jagged mountains that he had so often seen from afar. He sat up. To his front and only ten paces away, a waist-high wall. Beyond the wall, nothing but sky. He climbed to his feet. The low stone walls revealed themselves as raised beds. But they bore no flowers, just row upon row of vegetables. Each rectangular bed was ten paces long by five wide, the walls around waist high. The beds had stone paths between them. The beds were laid out in a checkerboard pattern of five by three. Together they held enough vegetables to feed an entire troop.

He limped slowly towards the wall. He leaned over cautiously and instantly recoiled from the void. More slowly still and gripping the edge of the wall, he looked out over the most astonishing view he'd ever seen. Below, hundreds of heights below sprawled a vast valley. Its sides were peaks like the one above him. Its further reaches faded into distant blue and what looked like lower, but still considerable, hills. Its wide floor was dominated by a vast lake. A river flowed from the base of the mountain on which he stood, gushing into the nearest edge of the lake. In the middle of the lake stood a steep-sided island, which seemed utterly covered by buildings. Tall, towered and galleried buildings swept up its sides from water level to over a hundred heights. Narrow streets wound around the island and he fancied he could see movement in the

---

[2] An Imperial measure, a Height is approximately five feet or 1.5 meters.

streets. He traced the lake to its far side, where the river flowed out again.

He turned to look behind him. At the back of the meadow were more crags, sharp jagged rocks rising up into the mountain above. And nestled at the very base of the cliff was a house. It was of conventional Byekiy design. Thick stone walls and a pitched roof with tight-fitted slates, sharply angled to shed snow. A stone chimney stack protruded from the middle of the roof. A stout hardwood porch stood dead-centre of the ground floor. There were seven windows in the front of the house, all filled with the remarkable Byekiy clear glass. The frames were painted white. The house looked substantial, comfortable and utterly incongruous. How in God's name had they dragged the materials up here? The porch door was open. He limped through the porch up to the front door. He turned the stout latch and walked inside.

The house was pleasantly cool, very bright and smelled of fresh bread. Bdescu salivated at the scent of food. The hallway was whitewashed. The floor was polished wooden planks which bore his weight without a single creak. He followed it to the end and turned left into a kitchen. Also painted white, the room was equally bright and dominated by a large wood-burning stove which seemed to have been made from a single casting of iron, then enamelled black. Four large plain iron rings were on top of it, obviously for cooking. He opened the door and put a careful hand into the ashes. Stone cold.

On the back wall was a door to a pantry. The pantry had shelves that were attached to solid rock. There he found a jar of biscuits that were perfectly fresh, and ate all seven of them. He found a large lidded jug of water and drank all of it. Best of all, he found a stoppered flask of fruit brandy, and took a generous slug. It did not take away his pain, but it cheered his spirits immensely.

Flask in hand, he wandered around the mysterious house. There was a sitting room at the front. It had a woodstove too, but smaller and not designed for cooking. A black iron chimney sprouted out of the stove and fed smoothly into the wall up near the ceiling. The part of the wall where the chimney went through had a black iron plate to protect the plaster. He couldn't fault the design of the house. The floor was timber, but mostly covered by a deep luxurious carpet in a plain sea-green colour. There were two large couches in plain off-white fabric with matching cushions. Four armchairs matched the couches. All were slightly worn and well-used but clean and serviceable. There were windows on two sides, two with the infinite view forward over the path and lawn, and one facing the flower beds and then the cliff to the side. There was a sideboard, well-stocked with flasks of beverages and flagons and small glasses for drinking. Whoever lived here liked their alcohol. He touched a few of the vessels. Dusty. So either they liked an occasional drink or they weren't here very often. He hoped it was the latter, at least until he recovered from the beating.

The opposite room was a dining room with a large table and twelve chairs. There was no stove, just a small fireplace. The firedog was stocked with shavings, kindling and small logs. A strike of tinder would light it. Someone well-prepared then. Plates were stood up on a dresser, along with cutlery in its drawers. So far, all he'd found was a family home. He noticed that the windows had heavy drapes pulled well back. He looked behind one and found timber shutters pinned back against the wall. The wall was as thick as his arm was long. This house could stand fierce weather.

Bdescu walked back outside and along the path. The dirt, stones and clumps of grass were gone. The amputated leg was also gone. Not just blown away, for there was no wind, but utterly vanished, as if they had never been there. The sensation of being watched came over him again. He scanned the skies. The deep metallic blue hurt his eyes. He was certain there was something up there, high above him, almost beyond vision, a suggestion of movement. Unconsciously, he fingered the slim gold chain that Summer had given him.

He took another generous slug of the brandy and went back indoors. Whatever happened, whoever arrived, he was stuck here. The cliffs were too steep to climb. He had found no ropes. He was injured and bone-weary. So he walked up the un-creaking staircase, found a room with a large bed, stripped off his dusty clothes and climbed into the soft, fragrant sheets. For some strange reason he felt no fear; he felt oddly safe and at home. His head touched the pillow and he fell instantly asleep.

Bdescu awoke at dawn, as ever. He was hungry. The vegetable beds meant that he could never starve, but it would be a miserable diet. He walked into the kitchen. On the work table he saw a flitch of bravelle meat, an iron skillet, a saucer of fat and a loaf. There was a small pot, which he opened to find oil for the bread, Imperial style. There were six discs of blood pudding and a large platter. At the edge was his tinder box, freshly loaded with dry wood shavings. He looked around hastily then ran around the house, searching frantically for someone, anyone, who could have brought his favourite breakfast to a mountaintop in the middle of God knew where. The house was still empty. In the living room, in the exact centre of the floor where he was bound to find it was a large canvas bag. He opened its roll top and tipped it upside down. Out clattered his scabbard and sword, his knife and flail, his mail coat, helmet with arming-cap inside, his boots and all his clothes. Even his purse was there, with every coin still inside. The clothes were patched, washed and pressed. The weapons and armour were cleaned, burnished to a glitter. Bdescu had never in his life believed in sorcery, but he was starting to doubt even his own sanity right now. He dressed quickly, feeling better for being properly dressed and armed. He wondered if being armed was any defence against sorcery.

He lit the woodstove and as soon as the stovetop was hot enough, he fried his breakfast and ate it with relish, even scooping the fat from the skillet with the last of the bread. He closed the damper on the stove as he had seen Jarleh do it in the hospital kitchen, marvelling at the efficiency of this innovation. The fire, starved of air, quickly died. He sat in the sun for a while until his food had settled, then he set to work with the flail. He worked his stiff muscles, hurling the heavy flail through the air in complex arcs, twisting the ball harder and harder until he sweated. The stiffness had eased, although he still hurt from the beating. He swigged a shot of brandy and settled down to await the return of the sorcerer.

After a while he dozed. The place felt so empty, so secure, that he could not see how anyone could reach it. He knew the feeling was irrational: someone had brought the food he had just eaten. Still he relaxed and fell to daydreaming, then to a light sleep.

He awoke as a shadow fell across his face. He looked up at a tall figure standing over him. He rolled aside and bounced up onto his feet. He whipped the knife from his belt and dropped into a crouch. The stranger did not flinch. Bdescu saw a tall slim fellow of young appearance. His hair was blond and short in the Byekiy style. His face was broad across the forehead and narrowed into a sharp chin. His nose was aquiline. It was a clever face, full of life. He wore a kilt, a sporran and a loose shirt with laces at the neck. His socks were rolled down over unlaced boots. His fair skinned face was red and sweaty. He smiled and held out a hand.

"Hello there. Sorry to make you jump. I just got here and wondered if the boss was around?"

Bdescu shook his head, wary. "Nobody here but me until you arrived."

The blond grinned. "Yeah, I know what you mean. Still, you're pretty fast coming up with that blade. Warrior, no doubt?"

Bdescu stood upright and took a pace back. When correct distance was in place he sheathed the blade. "Yes. And you?"

"Oh, I'm just a back room guy. Nothing so glamorous as a warrior. I do fetching and carrying, messages, diplomacy, a few long trips to meet people, find stuff out, you know."

They had been speaking Imperial. The Imperial word for diplomacy implied espionage. Bdescu assumed the charming young man was a spy. The man was looking at Bdescu without embarrassment.

"You're Bdescu, Gvant of Clan Bdescu, aren't you?" The address was perfect, as was the young man's accent. Yet another mystery for Bdescu's battered head to ponder. He nodded.

"Well, I better take care of you then. First off, manners. I am Lundy Brench. I am instructed to assist anyone claiming allegiance to Clan Bdescu with all power at my disposal, which ain't much, to be truthful. Not sure why your clan, albeit of impeccable heritage, reputation and breeding, should attract such an order, but there it is. In addition, my lord since your Baron General is dead, has no living male children and made you his legal bondson, I must now address you as Brevet-Baron-General Bdescu of Clan Mnufort, subject to Imperial ratification, which surely is a formality?"

In all the events of the past weeks, Bdescu had never once considered this. It was technically true. He was the Baron-General's legal heir. Technically he was now responsible for all of the Baron's people as well as his own clan. With his people scattered and him facing the ultimate disgrace of losing an entire Imperial army, he had had other matters on his mind. He wondered who of his clan lived, and who had fallen. He thought of his scribe, Byardil, the elderly cook Mridka and his servants, freemen and slave soldiers. He knew nothing at all of his peers amongst the noble knights, even if any had survived the battle. He stared at Lundy Brench.

"Where are we, Lundy Brench? This eyrie seems inaccessible to normal men. Are you people able to fly?"

Lundy chuckled. "No my Lord Baron. There is a way to climb up here. It is arduous and secret, but a healthy man with good fitness can climb up here in half a day. Impassable in winter, though."

"So what is this place?"

"Think of it as a staging place. Certain people need to get away for a while. To rest, to heal or to receive instructions. Sometimes we need to re-equip, to sharpen our weapons, as it were. We have conferences here. We store equipment up here. But mostly we come here when we need to be out of the eyes of others. Imperial spies, for example."

Bdescu grinned. "There are no Imperial spies in Byekvoranp! We only discovered the place a few months ago! My Baron and his forces were the first Imperial expedition to come this far. The Imperial Commissar told me so himself."

"Then he lied. Imperial emissaries first arrived here over a decade ago. They demanded slaves, timber, furs and precious metals. They offered no payment for these riches, only Imperial protection from what they called criminal elements. They claimed that the Imperium had rights over our resources, including the bodies of our people. Stupidly, we did not take them seriously. We assumed that they were braggarts and fools. We told them to get lost, in so many words. They responded with immediate violence. First came the slave raids. Gangs of slavers would raid farms all along our borders, out in the foothills. We had no soldiers to defend us. Farmers fought with the bow and knife - and were slaughtered. Then came the probing invasions, like yours. A strong Imperial force would come up a valley and settle there. People would be enslaved, trees cut down and farms devastated. We were lost."

Bdescu thought for a moment. "You're not lost now. You have an army. From what I've seen, a damned strong one too. How did you get from no military to a powerful force in less than ten years? It doesn't seem possible to me."

Lundy shook his head. "Quite simply, the Fifth of Five happened. We were ruled by four elders. Along came a Fifth and took charge of our military development. Call her a witch, call her a warlord, no word can actually describe what she does here. We wanted her to be called Minister of War but she forbade it. She calls herself 'Fifth of Five' to stress that she's part of the Elder community. That's all I am allowed to tell you. This narrative is known to all citizens and we are all permitted to tell it. The rest is secret. I will not tell you."

"Alright then. Keep your precious secret. Can you perhaps tell me how long I am to be stranded here?"

"Until the Boss calls for you, I imagine." Lundy's good humour seemed to have returned. "Meanwhile, it's time for lunch and a flask of beer. You'll be glad to see what I have brought up with me."

His words were true. The luncheon of cold cuts, salads and fresh cool ale was superb. They carried a table and chairs from the kitchen and ate on the lawn. Lundy entertained him with jokes in both languages, all of which were either improbable or obscene. Bdescu found himself liking the young fellow more and more. It was the way of these Byekiy, they all seemed relaxed and affable. Bdescu was also worried that the fellow was lulling him, wasting time while other events were set in motion. Under his laughter he seethed with impatience. There was a whole play going on and he was not in it, not in the audience and not even near the theatre. Once again he must escape and try to reach the Empire. Somehow, all of these mysteries must make sense.

After lunch Lundy lit the stove and heated water. He washed the dishes and Bdescu dried them with a cloth. Then he took a large basin and a pot of hot water and went outside. Standing stark naked on the lawn he washed himself all over in the hot water. He shaved with a straight razor. He walked around in the sun until dry then dressed himself. Bdescu waited until the younger man had gone upstairs, then tried it himself. He felt better. The bruises from the beating were livid and sore but he was moving more freely. The hot water helped. Rather than shaving, he rinsed off by tipping the basin of water all over himself, it was soothing.

Walking into the kitchen to rinse and replace the basin and pan, he noticed a draft. The door to the pantry was open and moving gently as if by a breeze. He walked over and opened it. Instead of the shelves that had been there yesterday, and the bare rock behind them, now he saw an opening. Now there was a doorway, a tunnel leading into the cliff face. It was perfectly dark but fresh air flowed out of it so it was not a dead end. He grabbed his tinderbox and struck a light. The tunnel had that now-familiar smoothness. The tunnel led away into the dark. He opened the stove, took out a half-burnt branch and blew the burnt end into a small flame. With the small light ahead of him, Bdescu stepped forward into darkness.

New Flame

The school building was filled with pupils. Lessons were in full swing and Byardil was deep in Imperial grammar when the assistant Head Teacher put her handsome head around the door. "Byardil. A word, please."

He motioned relax to his class and walked into the corridor. The Assistant Head's face was creased with worry. "Imperial slaver raid. Just entered the Northern end of the village. Thanks to Mother Nature they are on the opposite side of the river from us. A scout messenger just arrived. Our troops are almost here so hopefully we'll be rescued. We must protect the children. Shutter the windows, lock the classroom door and do not open it unless you hear the word "Snowhammer". Clear?"

Byardil nodded, wide-eyed and walked swiftly back into classroom. Once he told the children what to do, they seemed well-rehearsed in the procedure. Stout wooded panels were fetched from a cupboard and handed up to him. They showed him how to fix the shutters into place with strong steel locking bars, five across each shutter. Then he barricaded the door the same way. The children looked excited but not too afraid. He started to tell them a favourite story, amazed by their disciplined equanimity.

After a couple of hours he heard a voice at the door giving the code word. He unbarred the door and the Head Teacher herself was there.

"Byardil it's good and bad, I am afraid. They took over about a quarter of the village and some people were killed. The Imperial troops were beaten in the open conflict and our soldiers are clearing house to house. Some of the kids will be orphans and as yet we don't know what to tell anyone. We'll keep them here until their families collect them. Are you OK to stay and do that?"

Byardil nodded. "Thank God it wasn't worse!"

She nodded. "Aye. We were lucky this time." She headed off to brief another teacher and Byardil went to tell his boys and girls that there was still danger, but not to them. It was almost dark when the last child had been collected, some by ecstatic parents and others by grief-stricken relatives. To his immense relief, all his class seemed to leave with mum and dad. He walked home in deep relief.

Byardil arrived home to find the living room full of young women, all of whom seemed to be pregnant. Mridka was standing by the fireplace. There was something strange about her face. He stared. She was wearing a strange contraption of fine metal holding twin glass lenses over her eyes. Through the lenses her eyes looked larger. She stood more upright and spoke with confidence.

"When baby get to be ready then it'll turn ready for out, see? Problems come when baby don't turn."

A woman asked a question and Mridka answered instantly, confidently.

"Now Lasses, there's a man in't room so I's got ter talk to 'im. Eat yer cakes and I'sll be back in a few beats."

Byardil noticed that the table was full of cakes, Mridka's special skill. The women picked out cakes and chattered happily amongst themselves.

Byardil pulled Mridka to one side. "What's going on?"

"You ain't t'ony one to ave isself a job yer know. I's got one too. I delivered more slave babies than you ever 'eard of. Plus I delivered 'is Lordship's babies. 'Undreds, probly"

"What is that strange thing on your face?"

She grinned. "S'a new Byekiy invention I just got. They sez a midwife got to see proper. So they made me look at stuff and tell how much I can see – or not see. Then they gets these for me. Called spettaculls. Brilliant, they is. I's seein' better than in twenty years! Like being born anew, it is!"

Byardil was still puzzled. "But what in the name of God Emperor is going on here?"

"I's a midwife now, see? An 'igh koodos job it is too. I went to't school fer midwives and they loved me. I done the training in 'ygiene, which was all news ter me, but it all makes sense ones yer knows why. They's brilliant at midwifin' 'ere. I's learned a lot. But they really likes a lass like me, wiv experience, see? They says I's ter tell the young mums 'ow it will go, what's ter do and any problems they's may be 'aving. I's 'elping with local births, part of the commune elfcare team. Never bin in a team afore and I loves it! Lotsa older women like meself, all good lasses an' a right laugh they are too."

Byardil smiled at the old lady's enthusiasm. "How did you get started into that?"

"Well, see the lass next door was 'aving a baby. I talked to 'er over garden wall. She's a nice lass, like most o' these Byekiy women. She took me along to 'er midwifing class, which is a proper good idea in my 'pinion. But the teacher was wrong on a couple things, so I put 'er right. Next thing, they's round our 'ouse asking me to join school. I was worried they'd be mad at me, criticisin' 'em. But no. Never take offence, these. Just bring yer in and use yer skills. Teach yer what they know, ask yer fer what yer know. Swapses, sorta thing. Clever really. Plus they's workin on me Byekiy and I's getting proper good at it. I thinks I talks better in Byekiy than I do in Imperial. Never got taught to talk proper at 'ome. Learnin's free ere."

"The best bit's next though. We don't just do midwife job, oh no. We keeps lookin' after Mum an' baby after birth. Makes sure it grows up proper an' strong. 'Elp ter look after it, give 'er a break. Give Dad some advice. Find wet nurses if she ain't got enough milk. Call fer 'elp from't Midwife School if there's any problems. Tell 'em about 'ygiene, nootrition and 'ow to be good parents. Best job in't world, if yer likes kids as much as I does."

"Anyways, got me own koodos book. Got me own friends. Some 'o the older midwifes is a great crowd. We goes to't inn and 'as drinks after lessons. I can stand me own round and we 'as a proper laugh."

Her kindly wizened face had lost ten years. The old slave was animated beyond anything Byardil had seen before. He kissed her cheek impulsively. He was shocked to see tears in her eyes.

"Yer knows that I's always loved you, don't yer? My babies was all took away. All of my lovely kids, took away and sold. You and the other slave kids, 'is Lordship's kids, you was all my family, all I ever 'ad." She pressed his hand in her surprising grip.

He smiled. "I know, love. I love you too. Are you happy here?"

She looked at the chattering mums-to-be. Their bright, glowing faces seemed to illuminate the room.

"God aye. Look at them young women! Lovely, they is. Every one as smart as a lordling. Can all read and write, do numberin', draw, talk languages and I don't know what else. I ain't no slave 'ere and neither is these lasses. These don't talk down ter me. They respect me. Call me 'Nana Ridka'. Can't say me name, any of 'em. But still me friends though."

"I's'll bring these babies inter the world and then I'sll be a gramma as well as Nana, eh! 'Undreds of grankids. We've a big 'ouse 'ere, I's'll let 'em all come 'round fer cakes. An 'ouse full of kids coming round, screamin' and laughin'. Can't wait, mate! Now, clear off and let me get on. There's food in kitchen for yers. I'sll see yer later, eh?"

She turned away. "Now ladies, 'as anyone left a cake fer poor old Mrıdka?"

Byardil heard them laughing as he closed the door. They seemed unaware of the Imperial invasion. He envied them that. He walked through to the kitchen and ate the pie she'd made for him. He felt oddly jealous of those happy women. They were taking away one of the last people in his life that he loved. He hated the idea that Mridka would leave the house and find her own way in the world. But all the other members of his household had left. One by one they'd made friends or found work in the vibrant Byekiy society. He had always lived in a sprawling household and he felt alone, friendless here. He dismissed his feelings as ridiculous, and went to the study to do his preparation for tomorrow's lessons.

The next day after class, a shy and red-faced scribe walked nervously into the White Cloud Inn. He walked up to the bar and asked for a small ale. He picked up his ale pot and turned around to see a large figure grinning at him. "Where's mine, then?" Renketh, seen close up was even bigger than Byardil remembered. His shoulders were wide, his upper arms massively developed and his hands like shovels. His broad face was weather-beaten, his teeth wide, flat and white. He wore a fabric shirt of forest green, with the usual laces at the throat. It had short sleeves to show off those arm muscles. His kilt was soft suede, a pale tan colour. His sporran was old, worn smooth and stamped with a trifoliate flower. His boots were tan leather, worn unlaced and without socks.

The barman handed Renketh a large ale, without asking. "Let's sit in the garden, it's lovely and warm outside." Byardil followed, tongue-tied.

Two hours later he was no longer speechless. He had never talked so much or so frankly. Renketh's friendly face showed empathy, horror, grief and amusement as Byardil told him most of his life story. Byardil was drinking large ales now. Renketh warned of the effects of too much ale on an empty belly, so ordered janneries from the barman. The jannery was the Byekiy snack of choice. Thin flat bread was spread with sliced meats and rolled into a tube. The tubes were served with a bowl of gaolutch, a paste made from ground beans, milled grain and oil. You dipped the bread rolls into the gaolutch. It was nourishing, filling and easy to eat. Byardil ate heartily.

At sunset the two men walked unsteadily back to Byardil's home. Renketh was laughing helplessly at one of Byardil's stories. When they got to the door, Renketh kissed him gently on the lips. "See you tomorrow?" asked the big man.

Byardil nodded helplessly, smiling.

Renketh walked away, waving. Byardil almost fell through the door. He was still smiling when he fell asleep.

Street Fighter

The century moved quickly through the streets of the village. The lovely limestone buildings were arranged in typical Byekiy fashion, with flowers gardens at front and vegetables to the rear, on broad paved streets with drains along the edges. Every few yards was a mature tree. The broad leaves shaded the street from the sun. Yet smoke blew from burning houses, screams tore at the very air, and people walked, limped or ran down the street with tear streaked faces. Cvelthan marched swiftly in the front rank with his lads. They double-timed up the paved street in tight formation, shields up and swords drawn. All those hours of drill paid off in effortless line discipline. They rounded a corner right into a charge of slave-soldiers.

Cvelthan called the command. "Brace and present" as the slave-soldiers closed on his thin line. The slave soldiers had short spears and round shields and as they reached his line they tried to either thrust past the Byekiy shields or push soldiers over with their shields. For every trick there is a counter. The one coming at Cvelthan held back until the last instant, then stabbed at Cvelthan's face. It was an expert thrust, controlled and well-aimed. For all that, Cvelthan simply jabbed up his shield, slid the shaft of the spear up over his head, then stabbed the enemy in the belly. He smashed the shield forward, knocking his opponent to the ground.

"Death's Head! On me! On me!" bellowed Cvelthan and charged forward into the breach he had made. Stepping over the gutted slave soldier, he pushed hard into the enemy line. Podge on his left yelled assent and stepped in with him. Lame on his right pushed in too and the men behind filled the gap.

The men formed a wedge, called in Byekiy tactics the Death's Head. Cvelthan, Podge and Lame on point took the brunt of the enemy blows. Cvelthan's mind was eerily calm, his psyche overtaken by the battle mind. Sounds seemed slower and deeper. His enemies appeared to move in a dull torpor and he could see their moves almost before they made them. His shield turned spears aside without conscious effort and his sword slid home through every gap, finding flesh. He never swiped, slashed or cut. He stabbed. Short, hard thrusts. Blood spurted from his enemies onto his face, his right arm and shoulder. His face ran with blood and sweat. He grunted with every move, but he kept going, stepping over the fallen and leaving his followers to finish the wounded beneath his feet. He broke through the back of the Imperial line and found himself behind his enemies. He turned to Podge. "Attack left." He turned to Lame. "Attack right." His men attacked the enemy line from behind. They instantly panicked, broke and ran.

"Hold! No pursuit!" called Cvelthan.

The slave-soldiers tried to retreat the bridge. But as they raced down the slope a century of archers poured arrows into them from the river bank and another century of skirmishers presented a thicket of spears across the bridge. While Cvelthan's troops had held the slave soldiers, the skirmishers had held the bridge. The Imperial soldiers were cut off and surrounded.

Cvelthan's century of heavy troops marched down towards the bridge, trapping the Imperial soldiers between the legionaries and the light troops holding the bridge. Cvelthan had agreed the next move with his centurion before the skirmish. Now he called to the hapless slaves.

"Cease fighting. Cease fighting and you will live. I an Cvelthan of House Bdescu. You know my House. You know my master. I give you my word that you will be spared and not ill-treated if you throw down your arms now."

Most of them did. The rest, realising that they were finished, reluctantly followed suit.

The skirmishers took charge of the prisoners. The centurion had a few words with the archer and skirmisher leaders. Then he called to his troops.

"Leave these. We keep to the plan and sweep the town for stragglers. Clear every house. Don't forget outbuildings, sheds and stores. Split into conturbatia. Each decanus has a row to clear. Go, and earn your kudos. At the double!"

The thirteenth were to cover the furthest street, so they deployed last. This far from the river the houses were all intact, although there was thick smoke in the street. Cvelthan sent five men under Podge to clear houses on the left side of the street. He led the other five to check the other side. They had a method. Taking turns to go first they would burst through the door. They would run in, shields high in case of ambush. They checked rooms, two men to each room.

The first house was empty.

The second held a terrified family with two young children. "It's alright folks", said Lame. They had agreed that Cvelthan's appearance and Imperial accent might terrify them, so he let the Byekiy lads do all the talking. The family were unharmed. They said that the Imperial soldiers had warned them that the children would be taken today. The man was hugging Lame, the woman sobbing in the arms of Joker and the kids, who were below school age, were crying on the couch.

The third house was empty.

At the fourth house, Lazy was first through the door. He checked the latch and found it locked. He charged the door, shoulder behind shield. The latch tore out of the frame and the door broke open. As it opened a long Imperial cavalry sword took Lazy straight through the neck. The point of the blade came out of the back of his neck a hand's breadth from Cvelthan's face. Lazy jerked, trying to scream as he bubbled out his dying breaths. Blood spurted from the death wound as he spasmed and twitched.

For an instant, Lazy was jammed in the door way. Cvelthan booted the door open. Lazy's heavily-armoured body fell forward. As Lazy's body tumbled, Cvelthan stabbed into the breach with Twitch tight on his side in the narrow entrance. They kept shields high and moved inside, where they fought for their lives in a narrow hallway. The Imperial knight who had killed Lazy had blood pouring from a facial wound, Cvelthan's work. There were three others behind him and for a few moments nobody could land a blow in the confined space. The Imperial swords were for slashing, hard to turn and use in the press. The

Byekiy short weapons held a tremendous advantage at close quarters. Cvelthan and Twitch blocked their enemies with the big shields and pushed them back against the walls. The other lads piled in behind and stabbed the Imperial knights through any gap they could see. The small space was filled with screams, grunts and the wet sucking sound of blades in flesh. Blood washed the floor and they slipped on the slick timber. And then there was no more movement. There was no sound but the panting of his men. All the Imperial fighters were downed and killed.

The men seemed a little dazed. "Search the house. Heads up, shields up, shoulder to shoulder," called Cvelthan, trying to get them back on task.

They found a couple dead in the kitchen. The woman had obviously been pretty. She had been raped and her throat cut. The man had been bound, probably forced to watch them rape his wife. Then he'd been killed with multiple knife cuts. The angry Byekiy slipped in the blood and cursed.

"Find the children". Cvelthan was sure there must have been valuables here. That meant slaves, and to an Imperial mind the best slaves would always be children. Probably hidden, hence the abuse of the parents.

They found the kids under a pile of dead leaves at the bottom of the garden. He left Twitch, who had sustained a flesh wound in the thigh, to guard the children and keep them away from the kitchen. He proceeded with a depleted group of very angry young men.

In the fifth house they found an elderly couple hiding in an underground vegetable store. The Byekiy lads found it immediately because they knew where to look. Cvelthan would have walked past the subtle trapdoor in the shed floor without seeing it. Luckily for the old couple, the Imperial troops had been just as blind. The old gentleman came up to Cvelthan. He was tall and upright, very well kept for all his wrinkles and obvious years. He grabbed Cvelthan's hand.

"Thank you, Decanus. And thanks to all your men. Have you saved my son and his wife up the street?" Cvelthan had to tell the old man the awful news, then hold him as he sobbed.

He sent Nervous back with the old couple so that Twitch could re-unite the grandparents with their surviving relations. When Nervous returned, they cleared the last six houses. All were empty.

At last the town was cleared of Imperial troops. The prisoners were being held in a makeshift prison, a large grain barn in the centre of the village. They were receiving the same messages, and the same treatment that Cvelthan had. The weeping villagers had gathered on the village green, by the pond, to thank their rescuers. Seven Byekiy soldiers had died in the skirmish and nine were injured. Eight villagers had been killed, all for hiding children.

Colonel Janthro had arrived with a small party of staff officers to ensure that the bridge was secure. Two conturbatia, lads who had not seen any fighting, had dug the graves. Janthro then presided over the burial of the dead in the leafy village cemetery. Cvelthan and Podge lined their troops up to say a last farewell to Lazy, a good comrade. Birds sang in the trees and the shared loss felt by the soldiers and villagers was a bond between them. Janthro told the centurion that he should billet his troops here to rest and recuperate. "Officers will gather on the village green mid morning on my trumpet, three blasts. Any changes to your orders will come through then. Muster and brief your troops afterwards. Dismissed!"

As the troops saluted and dismissed, the old man who had talked to Cvelthan earlier sidled up to the big soldier.

"We are told that you lads are staying here for a few days, is that right?"

Cvelthan nodded and smiled.

"My name is Prelvo. I've lived in this village all my life and it's been a happy life until this bloody day. We are afraid, my wife and I. Please come and stay with us, Decanus. We have plenty of room, my wife is a good cook and my daughter is on her way home, so she'd probably love to meet you."

Cvelthan liked the old man and agreed with thanks. He first went off to see to the accommodation of his men. He needn't have worried, all were soon billeted amongst the grateful villagers. He made a note of where each man was staying and made sure that they understood the whistle calls for immediate muster: two blasts for muster/march, three blasts for muster/deploy for attack. He arranged to meet them under the trees in the village square at midday in case orders came in.

He found a trough in a side street and washed the blood off his body. He retrieved his pack from the muster point and set off for his host's lovely old house on the village green. As he walked, he realised that he hadn't a single scratch on him. He looked up at the sky and smiled. He'd made good decisions and still lost men. But they'd been fighting the cream of Imperial soldiers and they'd won. It was hard to imagine how, in those tightly packed hallways, they could have done better.

Killing Floor

Bdescu stalked along the tunnel. Its perfectly smooth walls were a tube, so the bottom was not flat but arced upward. He had to walk with his feet on the sloping sides. Luckily it was not slippery. It seemed dead straight. There were no turns, nor branches, just this eerie hole in the side of a mountain. The torch gave a poor light as it blew left and right in the strong draft. After about 200 paces he came to a dead end. He looked up, feeling the air moving that way. He saw a pinprick of light. Seemingly out of the rock came a voice.

"Are you Bdescu?" He flinched. The voice spoke pure High Tongue, with a courtier's accent. He had not heard his own language spoken so perfectly since he'd left home. He looked all around but saw nobody.

"I am he. Who asks?"

"Do you wish to ascend?"

The Voice ignored his question and Bdescu had no idea how to respond. But he could go no further and his curiosity was stronger than his fear, especially now that he was fully armed.

"Yes, I wish to ascend."

"Put down the torch. Arms by your sides." Bdescu threw the torch a few paces back down the tunnel. He stood up straight and put his arms flat to his sides.

"Move half a pace to your left." Bdescu did so.

In an instant, Bdescu felt a heavy pressure coming at him from all sides. His arms were pinned against his ribs. He felt another pressure against the soles of his feet and a cold draft rushed into his face, making his eyes water. He rocketed up the smooth sides of a vertical shaft, utterly unable to move. For a few heartbeats he accelerated up the shaft, then felt the pressure easing and the draught slackening. As he blinked, light flooded into his eyes and he found himself standing in a white room.

He looked down. The floor was covered in a mosaic of tiny white tiles. He could see no join where the strange lifting device might have come up into the room. He had no water to test for gaps between the tiles, and his eyes could detect none. The tiles seemed perfectly uniform. He knew that if he took a single step he would never find this spot again. So he took out his tinder box, sucked his finger and then pressed his fingertip into the black ash at the bottom of the firebox. Crouching, he drew a careful circle around himself with the ash. It took several spits and dips before the was satisfied that he could find the way back to the exact spot; if the Voice ever offered him a way down.

He looked around. The room was large, twenty paces across at least. It was high too, three times his height. It was domed, like a ball cut in half. At each cardinal point was a door. Above him, a circular opening let in bright daylight from a sky of very pale blue. As he stared up, he saw a flurry of snow blow across the ceiling and realised with a shock that the ceiling was not open to the air, but was formed of perfectly clear glass. An impossible, circular piece of glass ten paces in diameter. He blew through his teeth, drew his sword and walked over to the door directly in front of him. It was white. It had neither latch not lock. He pushed it but it did not yield. The door to his left was the same. The door to his right also.

The door that had been behind him was completely different. It was made of a beautifully figured wood, polished to a waxy shine and apparently made of a single piece. In the centre was a large iron knob. In the centre of the knob was a keyhole. The door had no other features. He grabbed the knob and twisted it. It turned. He raised his sword to waist height and pushed the door open. Inside was a corridor, panelled in the same wood. The floor was of the white mosaic tiles and the ceiling of white-painted plaster. There were no windows, just a soft pervasive light that seemed to come from everywhere and nowhere. Half way down the corridor was a coat stand with garments neatly hung from its pegs. Boots and shoes were lined up underneath. This domestic normality made the surrounding strangeness all the more unnerving. He checked that the door would open from the inside. The latch seemed simple enough, so he stepped inside and made his cautious way along the corridor. Just past the coat stand he came to a door. He stood outside it, undecided.

"Come in, Bdescu." A clear voice, deep but obviously female, came from inside. He clicked open the latch, a perfectly normal Byekiy door opening in this outlandish place. He stepped into a beautiful room and into the presence of the Witch.

The room was large, thirty paces long by fifteen wide. The floor was flat and carpeted but the walls curved up and across the ceiling in a single sweep, like half a barrel. Painted a creamy white, the walls were flawless and, smooth. At the far end, strong pale white light shone through large windows. A rich carpet of a deep blue covered the floor. It was like walking on a well-kept lawn. The furniture was of light wood and some fabric that looked like leather, but was far too smooth to be such. He took in that much before he saw the woman sat at the blond-wood desk halfway along the room. She stood up and walked around the desk towards him.

She stood as tall as Bdescu. She wore a single garment, black as night that hugged her figure. Her hair was a dark brown, with a couple of streaks of pure silver running through it. She wore a fringe halfway up her brow, the rest of her hair cut in a straight line to just touch her shoulders. Her shoulders were broad for a woman, her hands pale and fine with long slender fingers. Her bosom was neither large nor small but well proportioned like the rest of her. He looked at her face and for an instant thought her a very young woman. Then he saw the experience and wisdom in those deep near-black eyes. He noticed the fine wrinkles at the corners of her eyes and finer lines on her forehead. He revised his estimate up a couple of decades.

She smiled and held out her left hand for the soldier's arm clasp. "Bdescu, Gvant of Clan Bdescu. I am the Fifth of Five."

He took her arm. It was as firm as any soldier's. He debated whether to kill her at once, or whether he could gain any useful intelligence from her first. She smiled and stepped back.

"Obviously you're considering whether to kill me now, or get information from me first, either by conversation or by some more forceful means. I understand that you are acting on the orders of your God-Emperor. I also know that you're a man who is not easily deflected from his mission." She raised an eyebrow to invite his response.

Bdescu blew out his cheeks. "You speak the truth. You are my enemy and I am bound to try to work for the advantage of my people."

She nodded. "OK, please follow me." She walked briskly down the room. Half way along the wall was a door, perfectly curved to fit the vaulted shape of the room. She pushed it open and walked into an adjoining room. He followed.

This room was identical in form but very different in purpose. It was stark white. The floor was timber, smoothed but not slippery or polished. Along the opposite wall was a rack of objects. She selected one, a black rod about the size of a sword. She walked calmly into the middle of the floor and stood at low guard, the rod held upwards from waist height and pointing at his chest. Bdescu drew his sword.

"Miss Fifth of Five, are you seriously going to fight me? My sword against a stick?"

She bared her teeth. "Come and kill me, hard man. We'll see who's better armed."

Without a sound, Bdescu drew sword and attacked.

He struck from the draw, a perfect practice-floor move that had caught out dozens of opponents over the years. His hand flashed to the hilt of the sheathed sword, grasped the hilt and drew in a fast arc across his body. But instead of moving the blade into a guard, he swept it at his opponent in a diagonal cross-body cut, going in over her low guard, whilst taking a fast step forward to bring the blade to bear. She stood perfectly still and at the last instant turned her black rod under his blade, pushing it upwards. She stepped inside and struck him in the face with the heel of her left hand. He twisted his head to soften the force of the blow and drew back quickly to disengage.

He faked a cut and lunged with the point. She parried. The rod seemed weightless, she could move it with appalling speed, yet when his blade struck the rod it seemed as heavy and solid as a broadsword. For the next few minutes he probed with cuts, thrusts and feints. She blocked every move. They moved faster. Bdescu's strong wrist was uninjured and his eye as sharp as it had ever been. He began to produce his finest swordsmanship, his legs flickering across the floor, his arm moving so fast it could barely be seen. Yet nothing got past her guard. Then out of a hopelessly defensive position, she attacked.

She dodged to the left twice, flicked his blade aside and the rod came up across his body and struck him in the bicep of his left arm. He danced away and felt the sharp pain of a wound. She did not follow but put up the rod and took three paces backward. He looked down at his arm and saw a runnel of blood soaking into his sleeve.

"First blood, Bdescu, Gvant of House Bdescu. I claim right of parley". He panted, teeth gritted, then without warning, not even looking at her, he stabbed her in the chest. It was a perfect strike, coming up under the ribcage and into the chest cavity for a heart or lung wound. Invariably fatal, powerfully struck.

As the blade touched her black garment it stopped dead. It felt like he had stabbed a stone wall. The blade did not slide off, as it might with plate armour. It did not push in, as with mail. It just stopped. She had not so much as flinched. Her clear black eyes never left his. She whipped the black rod up and across her body. As it moved there was a faint hum. It sheared clean through his heavy cavalry sword with the smallest tinkling sound. The blade clanged on the floor. She stepped back four quick paces and saluted.

"Well struck. I offered parley and you didn't accept. You were well within bounds to take the strike. Remind me to stop under estimating you."

"You are wearing armour under that black garment?"

She smiled and nodded agreement. "Sort of. The garment itself is armour. It's a different principle from yours but it does the same job. Like the stick. It's a rod when I parry and a blade in the cut, then a needle point in the stab. Any other time you can use it as a curtain rod if you like." She dropped her rod carelessly onto the floor. It made almost no sound and did not bounce, he noticed.

He threw the ruined sword aside in disgust. "Do you have anything to drink?"

The witch gestured towards the door and followed him back into the study. On a shelf on the study wall stood a ceramic jug and two cups. She poured water for them both and handed him a cup. She drank hers off and smiled. He followed suit.

She pointed to his arm. "Does it hurt?"

"Yes, a little."

"Allow me to dress the wound. Then you can decide if you want to try another assassination – or whether you'd like to know more about us." He nodded.

She indicated a comfortable chair. He sat while she fetched a spotlessly clean white bandage and a jar of some salve. The salve, spread liberally over the wound site, seemed to make his skin pucker and wrinkle. The bleeding stopped at once. The dressing, which was round, affixed itself over the wound without winding or knotting. The stinging pain abated immediately. More sorcery, he imagined. While he was thinking, she handed him another cup, this time of the fragrant fruit brandy favoured by the Byekiy.

She raised her cup. "This is the good stuff. Makes your hair curl. Cheers." She smiled as she drank.

"Do you know how you came to be here, Bdescu?"

Bdescu looked around the room, in no hurry to answer. He opened the laces that secured the neck of his shirt and lifted the gold chain around his neck. He spoke slowly.

"I think that "my Princess" is actually your agent. She gave me this gold chain. It is the only thing I have on me from when I last saw her. So, assuming you are a sorceress and that she works for you, and the only talisman I have of her is this, then it follows that the chain must the instrument of your sorcery. Through this trinket, you – or she - must be able to follow my movements and set off the sorcery that carried me here. The sorcery, whatever it is, operates on a limited space, a kind of bubble. For the proof of this I saw that when it snatched me, it cleanly amputated the leg of one of my attackers. Then, later when I was at your mountainside eyrie, the sorcery finished its work by removing all traces of itself, including the severed limb. Thus, I cannot prove anything and I start to doubt the evidence of my own eyes. Or think myself insane. But you can rely on this. I do not doubt myself." He drained the brandy and sat back in the chair. It really was indecently comfortable.

She had looked intently at him without interrupting. She did not speak until she was sure he would say no more.

"You don't say much but you see a hell of a lot, don't you, my Lord? And you know when to keep silent too? Summer said you were a smart one, but I would never have guessed at this level of sheer intelligence. You are that rare thing, a man who exceeds his reputation. Truly a prince among men."

He smiled grimly and held out his empty cup. "I take your answer as confirmation. But I am no prince. Just a second-son, making his way in the world."

She laughed, loudly. It surprised Bdescu. "Yes, well said my Lord. Although you may soon be hearing news that might affect all that.

Anyway, ask me your questions. Like you, I work to a higher power. I am sure you understand that I will give you no intelligence that will damage my people's interests. So ask." She walked to the dresser, poured two more cups of brandy and handed him one before she sat down.

"Who are you, warrior witch?"

"I am like you, in a way. I too am bonded. In your case, to a man. In mine, to a mission."

"And what is your mission?"

She smiled thinly. "To make sure that the Empire does not prevail over the Republic of Byekvoranp."

Bdescu blinked. He gave no other sign of surprise. "Why in the nine levels of Hell would you want to do that?"

She settled back in her chair and took a sip of the fiery brandy. "Where can I start? Oh, to make sure that civilisation evolves in the right way. To prevent the dominance of the patriarchy. To avoid the subjugation of women, children, homosexuals, mental ill-health sufferers, cripples and the poor. To stop the insidious spread of monotheistic religion and the wars, famines and plagues that will naturally follow it. To end slavery. To halt the spread of monetarism, usury and the misery of indebtedness. To prevent a million deaths in future wars. Enough of the negatives."

She took a deep breath. "To bring about a society that relates to and protects the natural world. To promote slow development over rapid exploitation. To sustain equality, fairness, happiness and peace. And finally, to protect our allies from your lot. I trust those are sufficient reasons for you."

Bdescu's eyes were wide. "You make this little mountain realm a paradise, eh? Because they farm? Because they have no God? Because women do not know their place? Because catamites and sodomites walk freely in the streets? These are not blessings! These are curses!"

"Why, sir are they curses?" She seemed genuinely curious. There was no trace of rancour in her voice.

Bdescu struggled to control himself. He took a few breaths, then launched into the speech of his life.

"The Byekiy are a nice people. Their lands are fruitful. But they make nothing of any of it. They do not apply themselves. They do not work hard. They have no aspiration, either in personal growth or in God's favour. A society needs order. A man knows his place, be he Emperor or the humblest slave. A man can strive for Advancement within the order, that brings hard work and discipline. A woman knows her place too, she works beside her man. She supports him, cares for him, raises his children and they in turn know their place. If you do not have these things, you have anarchy. A leaderless mob, a rabble. Where are the Byekiy temples? Where are their great works of architecture, their palaces, their bridges and their monasteries? I see none such."

"These things are nothing though, compared to their godlessness. How can there be merit, or morality, or blessedness, without a kind and merciful God? These people are ignorant of the Creator! Once they have been incorporated into the Empire, God's Chosen will send missions, converting them all to the Truth. Thousands of souls will be saved, Order will come and you will see, a happier, more contented Byekvoranp will naturally follow."

The witch looked pensive. "So, why haven't you punished your slave, Byardil, for being what you call a "catamite"? I believe the penalty is death by anal spike, is it not?"

Bdescu looked flustered. "Byardil is no catamite. In fact, God's Word says that a man that resists temptation is a blessed man for he shows strength in the will of God and turns not from the path of righteousness."

"Nonsense. You know damned well that you could spike him tonight and no law of your land could prevent it. If you'd lost the fight with that fat fuck Vrabelm, he'd have buggered Byardil to death, raped

Summer and killed the pair of them, and none of his actions would have caused so much as a raised eyebrow amongst the other nobles."

"God did not allow that though, did he, Mistress Witch? I prevailed and my people were safe. That was my duty. That was their fate. God saw it through as I knew He would."

The Witch smiled again. "So if you hadn't been the most lethal soldier in the western Empire, they'd both have died? Lucky for them. What if Vrabelm had cheated and killed you before you even got to the challenge?"

Bdescu shook his head. "You can't speculate like that. It did not happen. If God had decided my fate, and theirs, in a different way, then that would have happened."

She leaned forward. "Hear me, Gvant Bdescu. I do not believe in Gods. Yours or any others. I do not believe that a man should buy or sell another man. I do not accept a world where a man can be slaughtered for loving another man. Or a woman another woman either. I do not allow children to be molested, fathers to rape daughters or any other of the countless crimes against the people that your bloody handed Emperor sanctions every day he lives. Crimes which your precious church aids and blesses daily. You do not understand me. I am not here to defend Byekvoranp."

Bdescu was genuinely baffled. "Then why are you here?"

"To wipe your Empire from the face of the Earth."

Bdescu began to laugh. She smiled too. "You think I am joking?"

"No. I do not. I can see you're serious. But you do not know the Empire as I do. His Imperial Majesty the God Emperor commands close to three hundred thousand troops. He could flood these sparsely-populated valleys with armies that would wipe every man, woman and child out in six weeks."

"And we will defeat them as easily as we did you."

"Mistress, that was unworthy of you. We were unprepared, both for your tactics and your weapons. Once we are masters of the battlefield again, we will rout your troops."

She started to speak, halted and looked at her wrist. "Are you hungry?" He nodded.

"We're eating at my sister's place. She's expecting us and I've made us a bit late, sorry. Follow me." She jumped to her feet, put down her empty cup and headed towards the door. He noticed that night had fallen outside the windows. He followed. He could not think of anything else to do.

She walked out into the circular room that he now thought of as a lobby. Night had darkened the circular roof-window, but he could still make out flurries of snow whisked across it by a silent wind. The Witch walked to the door to her left, touched it and waited. The door swung silently inwards. A tall woman walked out of the door, smiled sweetly at him and put her long arms around his neck.

"Summer!"

Dilemma

Byardil looked around the court room. He had been placed in a comfortable chair on the left-hand side of a large square room. Behind him were large windows, allowing a bright light into the room. He sat with his back to the windows. To his right, at the far end of the room were a pair of doors made of carved wood. The doors sat at the centre of a white-painted wall. The ceiling was high, at least three Heights. Between Byardil and the doors were five rows of chairs, neatly arranged. People were filing in through the open doors, murmuring as they took their seats. He breathed a sigh as Renketh bustled in at the front, taking a seat where Byardil could see him clearly. Opposite Byardil was a raised dais, running most of the length of the wall facing him. In the middle of the dais stood three chairs, identical to his own. To his left was another dais, this time with five chairs. In the centre of the room were more chairs, he counted fifteen, facing towards the doors.

As he sat silently worrying, various people filled the chairs. The fifteen chairs were filled by eight women and seven men of various ages, none younger than around twenty years. The room was buzzing with low conversation. A tall imposing woman walked in. She raised her clear voice and called: "please stand for their honours, the Five!" Everyone stood up.

The five chairs were filled by four women and a man, all elderly. Once they had walked in and taken their seats, the loud woman spoke up again. "Be seated!"

Byardil sat. The court became hushed. Through the open doors came three police officers leading the three youths who had beaten up Byardil. He felt a shiver of fear as they were led to the three seats opposite him. They were staring around the room, full of bravado. Byardil knew that it was false courage, he could see the fear in their faces.

One of the Five judges spoke. She was a very old woman. To Byardil's eyes she seemed ancient, decrepit. But to his surprise she spoke in a commanding tone, in a loud ringing voice.

"I am the elected member for this Land. I represent Families and am the First of Five. These young men appear before this jury of fifteen to face charges of assault on the Victim." She pointed at Byardil. "Are you Byardil of House Bdescu, who was assaulted by these men?"

Byardil had been instructed by Renketh to answer simply: "I am".

The old lady spoke to each of the fifteen members of the jury in turn. "Do you know any of these three men, by family, by tribe, by nation, by association or by acquaintance?"

One by one, the jurors replied in the negative.

The First of Five addressed the court. "I am satisfied that the jurors are not prejudicial by association. Are there any objections from the floor?" Nobody spoke.

"Very well. I call the examining magistrate to describe the case."

A rather handsome woman of middling years arose from the public seats. She stood in the narrow space between the public seats and the jury. She spoke clearly. "I examined the victim, Byardil of House Bdescu." She pointed at Byardil. "I found contusions, cuts, grazes and bruising consistent with an attack by multiple assailants. I interviewed the victim and he indicated that his injuries had been sustained when the three defendants attacked him on his way home from school."

She asked Byardil to describe the attack. With a low voice, he told the court what had happened, from his pleasant walk home from the school, to the sudden and overwhelming moment of the attack and the timely intervention of the constables.

Then the magistrate interviewed the sergeant of the constables, who confirmed Byardil's account with a great deal of accuracy.

One of the jurors raised a hand. The magistrate nodded. The juror asked her question.

"What was the victim doing at a school? He is a mature man and obviously an Imperial citizen."

The magistrate was cool. "Byardil has accepted his one year of service by becoming a teacher. He teaches Imperial language and culture at a local primary school. I spoke to the head teacher yesterday and she stated for the record that Byardil is an excellent teacher, a friendly and well-liked member of staff and a decent man. His kudos level is amongst the highest of any Imperial person in Byekvoranp. Do you need any more information?"

The juror shook her head, but Byardil could see that his credibility had risen sharply.

The magistrate continued. "I spoke to the perpetrators, who are here today the defendants. Each one admitted the attack. The arresting officers were at the scene and witnessed the latter part of the attack. I have no doubt or hesitation in recommending to the jury that these men assaulted this individual and caused the injuries that I have described. Does any member of the jury have any questions?"

Nobody spoke and the magistrate sat down. Now the lone man on the judges' panel stood up. He was a tall, commanding figure with white hair and a slight stoop. He had a rugged face tanned by years of harsh weather. "I represent the farmers and I am the Second of Five. I will speak to the defendants directly: so tell me, young fellows, now that you've been caught red-handed beating up an innocent man and I see it's your fifth offence, why we should not send you straight into banishment?"

The ringleader of the gang stood up quickly. His face was flushed and he spoke in a rush of words. Byardil struggled to follow his appalling diction.

"'Snot fair is it, right? We's just bashed a fucking Imperial yeah and a bent one an all so whats alla fuss about? He's teachin kids yeah and why is we allowin that because them Imperials they comes ere and takes us slaves but we's not even tryin to get back at em cos we's afeart of em I dunno like for why. Oh no, we gives em high-kudos jobs, jobs a

Byekiy coulda done. I say we's alright to give im a kickin he's not Byekiy so it don't count yeah? So why am I here? I done nothin wrong cos he's not us, so not our law, right?"

He sat down, terrified by his own eloquence.

The Second of Five stood up again. "Jurors, the defendants argue that Byardil of House Bdescu is not subject to Byekiy law. They argue that he is our enemy. If we had met him on the field of battle we would have killed him. He represents a slaver culture. He is therefore beyond our laws and they are entitled to beat him, to treat him as an enemy."

He turned to the defendants, looking at the spokesman. "Have I correctly stated your views?"

He looked relieved. "Yeah. What he said is right."

A buzz went around the room. The Five conferred. The jurors talked amongst themselves and the audience murmured.

Another judge stood up. She was a tiny lady of very advanced years. She looked around the court room with myopic eyes. But her voice was clear and steady. "Jurors. There is no point of law here. Byekiy justice applies to everyone who is within its jurisdiction. Byardil is under our laws as if he had been born here. He enjoys the same protection as every citizen. You MAY consider that the defendants did not realise this when they attacked him. If this were their first offence, you might be swayed by that and vote mercy. However. This is the ninth time they have appeared in court and have been convicted every time. They have stolen. They have forged kudos books. They have performed violent acts, including an attempted rape. This is not a singular event but a pattern of behaviour spanning several years." She sat down.

The jurors conferred for a few moments in low voices. One of them stood up and called a unanimous guilty verdict.

The First stood up and looked at the guilty ones. "You are a menace. You are young but are already criminals who prey upon ordinary folk. I recommend banishment. Does any person in this room know of any reason why these men should not be sent into exile to starve in the woods and freeze in the winter snows?"

There was a long silence. The First took a breath to say the sentence that would condemn the lads to certain death. Before she could say a word, Byardil interrupted.

"May I speak?" The First nodded.

Byardil looked at Renketh, who smiled and nodded.

"Friends; Byekiy people who have made me so welcome. I am no slaver. I was a slave, a victim of Imperial cruelty not a perpetrator of it. I came here a slave. We were defeated and I became a prisoner. So my status remained the same, or so I thought. But as your prisoner I have enjoyed more freedom than I had ever had before in the whole of my life. The Byekiy do not have money. They do not believe in ownership. They believe in freedom, mutual help and the social value of people. I love Byekvoranp. I have found happiness, acceptance and fulfilment here. I have a favour to ask you. Please, do not banish these young men."

The court broke out into a dozen conversations, as everyone talked about this bizarre development in what had looked a routine case.

The First of Five judge looked at Byardil and smiled. "What do you propose as an alternative?"

Byardil took a deep breath and looked back at her. "I have been given a large house and a plot of land. I can manage a house easily, but I have no skills on the land. I am expected to grow food and am willing to try but I cannot do it alone. The people I lived with have now all left the household and taken higher-kudos positions amongst our Byekiy neighbours. I am struggling to manage. I could try to find a smaller place but there are none in the village and I love working at the school so I do not want to move. Give these young men into my care. I will be responsible for them, they can live in my house, have their own rooms and be like a family. They can help me grow some food and earn back their lost places in Byekiy society." At this point, he ran out of breath.

The judges conferred in murmurs. The court held its breath. Another judge had questions. "Mr Descu, what happens if these young men steal from you, or decide they can dominate you, rule over you?"

Byardil looked at the three defendants. "They caught me unawares when they beat me up. This was lucky for them. They think because I am a gay man that I am weak. Fools. The last man who attacked me had a knife. I killed him with a kitchen spit. That's one reason. Then there's my friends. If anything happens to me there are people who care about me. A few Byekiys and a couple of Imperial soldiers. One in particular, my Lord's former freeman-sergeant, would hunt them down and strangle them. That's two reasons. But the third and most relevant reason is that they'll be OK with me. I'll help them to express themselves better. I'll teach them stuff. They'll get to like life with old Byardil and they'll get over this bad attitude. Let me try, anyway." His breath had failed him again. He looked at Renketh, who was sitting back in his chair smiling broadly. Intense relief suffused his whole body.

One of the jurors stood up. The First nodded. The juror, a darkly-tanned woman in her thirties, spoke nervously. "The facts seemed to indicate banishment. I for one was minded to vote for it. But Mr Descu has shown me the value of compassion. If he, who suffered injury by these young men, can give them another chance, then may I humbly suggest that we cannot ignore his plea? We'd be uncharitable indeed if we vented more anger on them than he does." She sat down, flushed. The other jurors seemed to be nodding.

The First stood up. "Jurors, do you all feel the same? Raise your right hand for agreement, left for denial." She sat back down while they voted.

All fifteen voted with the dark-skinned woman. Byardil sighed and slumped in his seat. Renketh was shaking his head, but still smiling.

The First conferred with the four judges. There seemed to be agreement. The First stood up. "Defendants please stand up." The miscreants got to their feet, looking confused.

"By vote of jury and by order of these judges I sentence you. You are guilty of the charge of assault on Mr Byardil Descu. You are released into Mr Byardil Descu's custody subject to these conditions: one, that you remain in his care for as long as he deems necessary; two, that if he makes a single complaint to the constables about any of you, that individual will be banished at once without further trial; three, that you follow his instructions in all matters; and four, that you respect his person, guard him from harm and care for him as if he were your father. Any questions?"

The lads looked blank and said nothing. "So ordered. Case ended. Court adjourned."

The clerk of the court had drawn up a document listing the boys' names. Apparently he now had three "sons" called Dancle, Brindah and Vutch. He'd worry about which was which when they all got home.

Byardil, Renketh and the boys tried to leave the court but were besieged by their grateful mothers, all three of whom wept on Byardil's shoulder and called him a merciful, wonderful man. He smiled uncertainly as Renketh eased them out of the room.

"Right you lot, let's get over to your houses, pick up your things and get you moved into House Bdescu! Look lively, there's a lot to do before dark!" The lads smiled uncertainly and they set off into the village at a brisk walk. Renketh, as village policeman, knew exactly where the miscreants lived. He took the shortest route to Vutch's family home.

Byardil smiled gratefully and thanked God for this forceful, kindly man.

Baby Bond

Cvelthan had started to get used to his hosts' inability to pronounce Imperial dual-consonants. His name seemed to have become Kelthan and he'd decided to accept it. The old couple were called Prelvo and Sivale, his wife. The old lady had cooked a simple evening meal, then they had all gone off to bed. Cvethan had fallen almost instantly asleep, exhausted by the day's fighting. He suspected that his hosts had shed many tears in a long night. He slept in their daughter's room, a bright and sunny place with a high double bed that was utterly comfortable and white painted furniture that made it cheerful.

In the morning after a good breakfast, the old couple had gone off to make arrangements for the burial of their son and his wife. The children were lodged with an uncle and would come to the house later. Cvelthan was sorry for their loss. It had been hard, watching them be so brave.

After breakfast and with the house to himself, Cvelthan washed himself in a basin on the porch. The house was stone with a green slate roof. Around three sides of the house was the porch. Two steps off the ground it was a planked wooden deck supported on timber posts set on stone blocks buried in the ground. It allowed shade on hot days and one could sit outside when it rained, which it seemed to do a lot in these hills. It gave a soldier privacy to strip to his breechcloth and have a proper wash. He dried himself on a towel and turned to squint into the morning sun. He could vaguely see a womanly figure getting off a coach at the corner of the street. He watched as the person started running flat-out towards him. The figure ran up the street towards the house, moving fast and breathing heavily. As it drew nearer, he noticed a bouncing motion in the person's upper body and realised he was looking at a very curvaceous woman. She reached the gate, ran up the garden path and up the two steps onto the porch. Her hair was red. He saw it was Pelva. She jumped into his arms, wrapping her legs around his waist. He whirled her around and said "what are you doing here?"

She kissed him a dozen times on the face and babbled. "You saved my parents, my nephew and niece and my whole village! I love you, Cvelthan. Will you make a baby bond with me?"

He laughed. "Yes. Will you marry me?"

"Yes." Tears were streaming down her face. Her brother was dead. Her sister-in-law too. She looked anguished, trapped between the joy of seeing him and the desolation of her loss. She sobbed into his shoulder and he held her tightly. But with Bdescu dead and no surviving nobility at hand, who the hell was going to marry them? Not today's problem.

He dressed in kilt, shirt and boots. She went into the kitchen and fetched water for the both. They sat on the porch steps, her head resting on his shoulder.

"I have thought about you every hour from the moment I met you. I know nothing of women because I refused to use whores and I never asked my master to buy me a slave for a wife. You are the only woman I have ever loved and I want you to know that I will be true. I have waited a lifetime for you. For me, this is all I ever wanted." She stroked his hair, which was black, short and glossy. She was puzzled.

"But you're a freeman. So why can't you just marry a free woman?"

"No such thing. Only male slaves are freed. Woman are either nobles or slaves when they're born. Slave women're never freed by their masters. They can only become free by marrying a freeman who can afford to buy them off their master."

"Wow. Women have it pretty tough in your Empire, my love."

"Everyone but the fucking nobility has it tough, Pelva. But yes, women are even worse off than men. The good news is that they don't get to be miners, farm slaves or rowers on galleys. Those are the slave jobs that kill you. Few slaves live past thirty in those jobs, believe me. But of course slave women are the property of a master who can fuck them, beat them, kill them if they want to. They get pregnant and are at his mercy... I never thought there was any better way. Until I got here."

He stopped speaking because she was weeping. He held her close to him and stroked her long red hair. After a while she stopped.

"Shall we make a baby, my rugged legionary?"

"Yes love. If she's lucky, she'll have your looks, intelligence and talent. And if she gets those qualities from me, well then, she'll be a boy, eh?"

She smiled up at him. "I thought I didn't want kids. But now I do, more than anything. I know you might be killed at any time in these hard days. I do not care. That fact just makes it more urgent that I make a baby with you, right now. I don't know why or how you came to fight for my people, but I am glad you did. I will always respect you for that. I want to have your child inside me before you leave this place. That way I will always have a piece of you, beside me, always. Our baby, Cvelthan. What do you think?"

"Yes." He could say no more. He too had started weeping.

"Right. I don't know when Mum and Dad will be back, or what state they'll be in. But I have to tell them before I do anything else. Then we'll go and see the Elders, get a couple of our mates for the ceremony and get this thing arranged. What do we do about arranging an Imperial marriage?"

"Ah. Well, we need Bdescu or his heir to perform the marriage ceremony for us. That's the head of my House. Sadly my lord fell in battle so we have a problem. Can I worry about that another time? Right now I just want to be happy to see you." She nodded.

"Who will stand for you at the baby bonding, Cvelthan? You've no old friends and I know you've no family."

He smiled. "Nowadays I am not short of friends. Trouble is, who to ask? My closest man is Podge and he'd be thrilled. But the other eight trusted men will be so hacked off."

"Ask Podge to do the talking but get the other eight to stand with you. I'll ask my friends and family to do the same. That way your men will know that you love them all the same."

"Love my men? I suppose I do. It's the damndest thing, Pelva. Once you've stood in that cursed shield wall next to a man, and lived through it, you trust him more than anyone you've ever known. Just because he doesn't run away and leave your shoulder exposed. That's how my Lord Bdescu got done. The old stab under the armpit. Straight through, into the chest and half his organs pierced. He'd have been lucky to last an hour, poor bastard." A few more bitter tears ran down his tanned cheeks.

They talked for a while and her parents returned. There was an emotional reunion that made Cvelthan, a man with no family, rather sad. Pelva's young nephew and niece arrived later and a subdued meal was eaten around the family table. When the children had been put to bed, Pelva spoke up.

"Mum, Dad. I know this seems strange to you, but the man I met when I was on the road, singing, was Cvelthan here. I told you about it. Then I come home and find him washing on our stoop! He's my man. I've pined for him for weeks. I now know that he feels the same and I want to do a baby bond with him. Sorry to spring this on you both, but I've fallen in love and my man will march out of here in the next few days. He might get killed. I have no time to waste. If we manage to make a child, I'll bring it up here with my brother's kids. With luck, Cvelthan will come back and we'll make a life together. If not, well at least I won't die a sad and lonely spinster." She brushed angrily at the tears rolling down her cheeks.

Her father looked at his wife and motioned for her to speak. Sivale looked troubled. "Are you sure, Pelva? Is this what you want? Kelthan saved our lives, along with his troop. There's nobody we like better. But do you know him well enough? And you, Kelthan, you barely know Pelva. She's a fiery lass, you know. Doesn't sit and home, cooking and cleaning. She's off singing whenever she feels like it. She's not all sweetness and love, I can tell you."

Cvelthan smiled at her. "I love her. My first love. My first birthday. My first kiss. These are precious to me. I don't know what a Byekiy woman is supposed to be like, I just know I love your one." His accent and diction were poor and he used the rough words of a soldier. But his heart was open and Sivale could see that. She looked at Pelva.

"Cvelthan's right. He was a slave who won freedom under a brutal regime. He had no family, no friends, just work and killing. But he is a kind and gentle man. I gave him a few small tokens but they mean the world to him. I don't want a familiar Byekiy guy with his smooth talk and smoother skin. I want this rock hard soldier with strong hands that will never hurt me."

Her mother waved a helpless hand. "Well, if you two are that determined, I'll be there."

Her father smiled. "Lass, I never thought you'd find a man. I actually wondered if you were a lesbian for a while. But now I see you come to life. Full of light and energy. You're happy and I support that. I will be there too."

The parents came around the table and hugged them both. Pelva laughed. "Cvelthan, that went well, let's hope your troops don't mutiny when you tell them!"

In the bright morning, Cvelthan sauntered over to Podge's billet, a small cottage a few doors away alongside the village green. He found his friend picking flowers in the front garden. Podge looked up and smiled. "Hello Boss. How's the billet?"

Cvelthan looked serious. "I promise you I am not kidding. I am billeted with Pelva's parents. Last night she came home and offered me a baby bond."

Podge closed his mouth. "Wow. Somebody's having a run of luck, eh?"

Cvelthan grinned. "Yes. And I have a question... what?"

Podge was pointing over Cvelthan's shoulder. "Runner. Looks like we're wanted."

A runner was dashing across the green. He swerved by the pond and came straight at them, the message case bumping on his hip. He skidded to a halt on the dusty road, threw a fast salute and opened the message bag. He held out a scroll to Cvelthan and stood panting, hands on knees and head down.

Cvelthan read aloud in his accented Byekiy.

"To Cvelthan Bdescu, Decanus, from Janthro, Legion Commander.

Hear and carry out this direct order. Owing to severe casualties during recent street fighting, the Legion has suffered losses of officers. In accordance with standard operating procedures we are promoting high performing soldiers if they enjoy the support of their men, peers and superiors.

You have been selected on the strong recommendation of your centurion and with the endorsement of your legionnaires. I hereby appoint you Centurion of the seventh century of my legion. Select an optio as your second in command. Present yourself with your optio at our temporary HQ tomorrow at morning muster for formal brevet. Congratulations. Shoulder to Shoulder.

Signed,

Janthro, Commandant, 13th Snowhammer Legion by Order of Fifth of Five, Republic of Byekvoranp."

Podge grinned at Cvelthan's ashen face. "Cheer up, boss. Promoted and proposed to in the same day! You could be a general and a dad before the winter's out!"

"You and the lads all knew about this, I suppose?"

"We guessed. Why else would Janthro and his officers talk to a bunch of low-kudos lads like us, eh? Wanted to know if we trusted you, if we took your orders, if the story about you and Blondie in training was true, stuff like that. I guess we told 'em the good stuff, seeing as you got the job, Boss!"

Podge stepped forward and gripped his friend's wrist. "We all voted for you. All in. Nobody argued, nobody hesitated, nobody flinched. We're your men and we're shoulder to shoulder."

Cvelthan smiled. "So, you gonna be my optio, then?"

Podge looked panic stricken. "No chance, I haven't even been a decanus. If I can't manage ten men, how am I gonna help you manage a hundred? They'll never give it to me, even if you ask. So, massively flattered and all that, but no thanks!"

"OK. So I don't take the centurion job then." Cvelthan folded his arms and Podge knew the gesture only too well.

"But Boss, just think for a few beats. They're gonna have an optio already picked out. A guy they know, a guy the rest of the century know. S'obvious they won't let you pick me. I'm not qualified. What the hell will you say?"

Cvelthan hadn't stopped smiling. "I'll say this. I trust Podge. My men trust Podge. If I don't get my trusted man then I ain't doing it. Simple really."

Podge looked around, thinking furiously. "Listen to me Boss. I am really happy that you feel that way. But we need you to lead the century. We'll all feel a hell of a lot safer with you in charge. Ask any of the lads, we're all up for it. So if you turn it down over me, the lads'll kill me. You can't do it."

"I can. I will do it. And you know what? I'll get the job and so will you. Now stop being a sissy. You don't want the job because it scares you. Arseholes to that. If the good guys don't run the legion, the fools will be promoted. We can't have that. Step up, soldier. Get your shield up, your point straight and your feet planted. Now, are we shoulder to shoulder on this? Or are you going to crap out on me?"

Podge nodded and Cvelthan hugged him. Podge remembered that the Boss had a question. "Oh yeah, what did you want to ask me, before the runner came?"

"As well as being my optio, I also need you to be my man at the baby-bonding. You have to tell the Elder that I am worthy of Pelva and any child we create together. This time there's no pressure from me, son. You have to want to do this."

Podge nodded. "Yes. My honour, Sir."

"Go tell the lads they're all invited, they'll all stand up with me. Best kit, clean shaves and plenty of polish and swagger. Then you meet me at my billet at first light. Full combat uniform, armour up. Weapons belted and secured. We're going to see Janthro so let's look proper serious. Put your game face on and we'll scare the shite out of him. Dismissed!"

Podge threw a salute, smiling. He spun and marched three paces as he fell out. When he turned around, Cvelthan was marching quickly towards his own billet to tell Pelva the news.

Colonel Janthro looked up as his adjutant coughed. "Sir, Decanus Descu is here with an extremely large legionnaire."

Janthro was slightly irritated. "What do you mean, extremely large?" He stood up and walked swiftly to the door, his adjutant jumping smartly out of his path. As Janthro emerged from his office he saw two of the most soldierly men he'd ever encountered. The Imperial, Descu, was a head taller than most Byekiys and a giant by Imperial standards. Descu stood at attention, his armour and clothing immaculately presented. His dark skin shone with vitality and his forearms were interlaced with multiple combat scars.

The Byekiy soldier was even bigger, a rock of a man. His enormous arms were clenched at "parade attention", his fists the size of a woman's head. His vast chest gleamed with polished armour and his helmet gleamed. His skin was tanned but paler than Descu's. His knuckles were scabbed but his face shone with suppressed excitement.

Janthro looked them over. "So, Descu, I assume this man is your selection for Optio?"

"Yes Sir."

"Tell me why I should allow you to make the decision and not appoint one of my trusted men to watch over you?"

"Sir. Here are my reasons. One, I trust Podge. Two, the men trust Podge. Three, he is well educated so he can cover for my ignorance. Four, he's brave enough to tell me, privately, when I'm being a fuckshy stonehead. Five, he's proven in the front line and we promote on merit. Sir."

Janthro turned to Podge. "Used to be overweight, Legionnaire?"

"Yes Sir!"

"So how did Descu come to know you so well?"

"Sir, we were in Basic together. I was failing because I was fat and slow. Beast here comes over to me and he says that if I teach him Byekiy then he will turn me into a soldier. So he stayed late on the training ground and worked on me. Taught me to run. To lift weights. Even to breathe. Then we sat up late doing lessons for him. Then he starts giving me responsibility and made the other lads rally round me. 'Podge can hold the line', he says. 'Podge is steady, form on Podge', he shouts. I never had any friends, Sir. Now I do. Not just Beast. All the lads are my mates now. He changed me. And he changed them. I joined up to be a soldier and he made it happen. He's a leader of men, Sir."

Cvelthan and Janthro were both quite taken aback by this unexpected paean.

Janthro looked at Cvelthan. "I see what you mean, Descu. I have honestly never heard a soldier say anything like that about an officer before, to my shame. I knew I was right to brevet you to Centurion. And I'm right about letting you choose your optio, too. First Spear Ranjeck is now your boss, both of you. Report to him at the Centurion's mess immediately. He will sort out your new insignia. You'll be formally breveted at tomorrow's muster. Any questions?"

Cvelthan took a risk. "Ah, yes Sir. I am baby bonding tomorrow with a local woman. I wondered if you'd be kind enough to share a beer or two with us after? The lads would love it."

"So. The lovely Pelva and you are the talk of the village. Even I have heard that you're to bond up with the famous singer. So, yes, I'll happily come for a beer, I might even stand you a round. Now scarper you two, before I change my mind about all this."

Two smart salutes and a hasty exit found the two new officers outside, standing in the morning sunshine grinning at one another.

"Beast, there is never a dull moment since I met you" gasped the bewildered Podge.

"Never mind that, laddie. Get the lads lined up for the brevet ceremony, then a quick meal at the inn. Baby bonding at the village hall with the Elders at Fifth Bell. Full dress kit, no armour or weapons. Hair cuts, clean shaves, you know the format. I'll get the inn to organise food and drinks out of what's left of my kudos. Pelva's friends will be there, so tell the lads it's best behaviour or death by my hand! Clear, Optio Podge?"

Podge snapped out a parade-ground salute, grinning maniacally. "Shoulder to Shoulder, Sah!" And with that he set off down a side street at a dead run. Cvelthan noticed that he had a neat turn of speed for so big a man.

At the Inn, Cvelthan found Jinno, the cheery proprietor, loading empty beer barrels onto a wagon in the roadway. Soundlessly, Cvelthan started lifting the barrels onto the wagon bed as the older Jinno took a breath. Cvelthan swung the heavy, clumsy hogsheads with little apparent effort and no sound. The barrels were placed, not dropped, onto the cart's floor. When all were loaded, the driver clicked his tongue and the heavy drays slowly started to move the load. Cvelthan sat on the bench and put his proposition to Jinno.

"Jinno, I need a favour. I'm getting baby bonded tomorrow and I need to bring the folks here afterwards for drinks and food. Can you help? I think I have enough kudos to cover it."

Jinno grinned. "All taken care of, Beast. Now, you'll not believe this but I swear it's true. Last night, late on, I was just closing up when your Colonel Janthro shows up with a tall woman in a hood. She drops the hood and she's only the Fifth of Fucking Five! I kid you not, son. The real woman, in person. A looker, too. Not young but mature, get my drift? Fit as a runner, too. I digress... She starts by awarding me more kudos than I normally get in a whole summer. She says 'there's a mate o' mine getting bonded, day after tomorrow, and I want the best. Load up on food, ale and brandy. Clean up, polish the floors and tables. Some lasses and lads will come round first thing on the day and put up garlands and all that.' I had no idea you knew such important people, young fellow! So I've restocked the place and we've been cleaning and polishing since dawn. I've closed for today to keep it looking good." And the good innkeeper wiped his sweaty brow, as if to emphasise the point.

Cvelthan opened his mouth to protest. Then he had a moment of inspiration. He had never met the Fifth. But maybe Pelva had been to school with her, or something. Byekiy ways were still strange to him. He found silence to be the best option. So he merely smirked knowingly. "Ah, excellent. She's on top of things, as ever."

Jinno looked sideways at him. "Powerful friends for an Imperial ex-slave, eh?"

Cvelthan was taken aback by Jinno's knowledge of his past. He had never thought that the Byekiy locals were so interested in him but supposed Pelva was a local celebrity, and hence the attention.

"Yeah. Last year I was a sergeant in the Imperial Army. Now I'm a Centurion, about to be with the loveliest woman on God's earth, and who knows? Next week stabbed in the throat by an Imperial spearman. It's a funny old life, is it not?"

Jinno grinned. "With your luck, pal, I wouldn't bet a single kudos point on that Imperial soldier or his poxy spear. Where will you get your tattoo done?"

Cvelthan answered swiftly. "I thought I'd ask you. I have 'Pelva' on my left forearm, she has 'Cvelthan' on her right forearm, is that right?"

"Yep, that's right. Go see Tremplude up at Crossfork Road. He has a sign outside. He's quick, painless and we all use him for the Bonding Script because he does it so neatly."

Cvelthan nodded agreement and set off upriver towards the Crossfork neighbourhood, an area of smaller houses where single Byekiys tended to live if they either wanted to live alone, or use their house as a workshop. Once again the Byekiy network was ahead of him. Tremplude was awaiting him in a small neat house little larger than a stable. The tattooing chair was polished, his needles were boiled and his inks already mixed. With a wolfish grin he settled Cvelthan into the chair and started work "Might sting a bit." This turned out to be a major understatement, but Jinno was right about the clear, sharp-edged attractive script that appeared on Cvelthan's arm. His arm was bruised and tender. He was delighted. And Tremplude had also been paid already, but this time by Jinno's son, who had dashed here just before Cvelthan arrived.

Sons of Byardil

Dancle, Brindah and Vutch stood in the garden of Byardil's house staring dumbly at the wilderness of weeds and rank grasses. Renketh was working. Byardil had asked the boys to start clearing away the mess after breakfast. Now at mid-morning progress was negligible and the boys were surly. With these expressions they looked an ugly bunch.

"Can't you just pull them out?" asked Byardil.

"Too 'ard" was Dancle's contribution.

Byardil knew that summer was slipping away, and if they were to get any crops at all from the garden, he'd need to plant up right now. He was shocked to find that the boys were as useless at gardening as he was. He wished Renketh was home, he'd know what to say, what to do. The adrenaline rushing through his system made him nervous and angry. It also speeded up his thinking.

"OK. Here's the situation. You don't want to do this work. You don't like the idea of getting your hands dirty or your backs sore. You think that if you stand here looking stupid I will give up and stop asking you to work. That is a teenage attitude and I do not accept any crap. If you worked for me in the Imperium, I'd take a whip to your backs. You'd soon wish you hadn't given me any crap."

They looked at their feet. No eye met his. Byardil took a deep breath. "Which one of you is the oldest?"

Brindah nodded. "Me."

Byardil walked calmly up to Brindah and slapped him across the face once, hard. The blow knocked him back a pace and Byardil slapped him backhand on the other side of his face. Brindah put his hand to his face, breathing heavily. Byardil backed away.

"Get to work. See that stump? I want the weeds cleared as far as that stump before dark. You will get drinks every bell. You will get fed when I decide you've done the work I asked of you. I will say nothing to

Renketh if you do as I say. If you do not, he will hear of it. You can beg but I doubt he'll hear it. Perhaps he will slap you. Perhaps he will beat you. Maybe he'll just throw your useless lazy arses back to the court for banishment, starvation and death. There is no alternative. Either work for me and be my friends, or not. Decide while I go and get some water for us." Byardil walked into the kitchen and threw up in the sink.

Renketh got home a little late, held up by a heated border dispute out in the farmland by the forest's edge. He walked around the house, looked into the garden and whistled. He wandered into the kitchen to find Dancle lying on the table with Byardil rubbing his back. Vutch was washing his upper body at the sink while Brindah peeled root vegetables by the wood stove.

Renketh smiled broadly. "Well done, lads! That's a really good day's work out there! Cleared up to the stump already!" He walked around, clapping each boy on the shoulder.

"See lads? I told you he'd be pleased!" Byardil chortled happily.Later they sat down to dinner. As soon as they finished, the three lads hurried off upstairs to their beds. Byardil told Renketh about the morning's difficulties and how he'd dealt with them. Renketh pursed his lips. "It'll take time. They've got to adjust to a disciplined life. They'll start to enjoy it but not straight away. Tomorrow they'll be stiff and a bit sore. That might be when they turn nasty and give us grief. Luckily it's the weekend, so no work tomorrow. We'll need to ease them into it. They're young and their muscles will soon build up, but at first they'll complain. I gave them plenty of encouragement tonight and I was really pleased to see how well you'd done with them. You've some good leadership qualities my love."

For the taciturn Renketh, this was eloquence indeed, and Byardil basked in his approval. Renketh had more to say.

"News from the village. There's a baby bonding ceremony tomorrow. Big do, apparently. Some legion guy bonding up with Pelva, who's quite a celebrity around here."

"She's a singer isn't she?" asked Byardil.

"Oh yes. She's really good too. Quite well known all over the republic. Travels a lot, does shows all over. Mostly in the summer, obviously. All the straight guys fancy her. And does she want any of 'em? Nope. She wants a massive Imperial guy. Huge tough soldier type, apparently. Anyways, I've got to be on duty. On our weekend too. Sorry."

Byardil waved a hand. "No matter. Can I go and have a look? I have never seen a baby bonding. What happens?"

Renketh sat back, his hot mug of chasser in hand. "Well... I kind of get that in the Imperium people get married. Here the idea is that full-on sex has consequences for women. Pregnancy, that is. So if a man wants to do full sex with a woman, he has to persuade her that he's going to stay around long enough to help her bring up a child."

"We have that in the Empire. It's called marriage!"

"Not quite. A man can divorce a woman in your Empire. He can leave her to starve in the hedgerows. Kids run around hungry, robbing travellers and stealing food. Feral kids are a huge problem in the cities. Not so?"

Byardil nodded.

"So, we had that problem too. Then a very clever woman came up with this idea. If a man wants sex, he has to make a baby bond. What that means is that they meet in front of the community – so you can certainly go and watch because it is a public occasion – and they swear an oath. They get each other's names tattooed on their forearms. From that day, any children born to that woman belong to that man. Half of any kudos he gets are given to the child or children for their upkeep and upbringing."

"But hang on. What if she's unfaithful? The kids might not be his!" Byardil looked mystified.

"Well, then the risk is with the man. Not the woman or child. In our thinking, the least vulnerable person should always carry the risk.

Always the man, see? He'd better keep on the right side of her and be a good man. Then if she does cheat on him, somebody will tell him. If he's a scumbag, nobody will care!"

"What if they decide it isn't working? How do you get a divorce, or whatever you call it?"

"Not often, but sometimes people fall out. Bound to happen. They get a line tattooed through the names and wait nine months. Provided no baby arrives, they declare the bond closed and they are both free. Simple."

Byardil thought hard. It seemed so simple, so obvious and logical. The Byekiy were a strange people but somehow their odd ways seemed to work. He sighed.

"I wish we could have a baby bond!"

Renketh leaned back in his chair and stared at Byardil. "Really? Are you serious? We haven't known each other long."

Byardil smiled. "I know. But I love you. I want to stay with you. Plus I love kids. But it's kind of academic. We can't have kids."

Renketh sprang to his feet and paced the floor, speaking quickly. "We could. We could sign a baby bond and adopt a child. There are loads of orphans because of the war. No saying how old, but under eleven years of age. Older than that they have a different arrangement. And probably a girl. They tend to prefer that gay men adopt girls. They think it works better, I do not know why."

Byardil stood up, eyes shining. "I'm off to see the bonding tomorrow. You have a think and see if you want to do this. No, don't speak now. I will put no pressure on you. You know how I feel. Take a day or so. Please."

Renketh nodded. "Come to think of it, this legionnaire might be one of your lot. His name's Descu as well."

Byardil stopped breathing. "First name?"

"Kelthan, I think."

"Cvelthan? Cvelthan of Bdescu?"

"Yes, that's his name. Sorry about the pronunciation. I can't seem to get anybody's name right, except yours. But you obviously do know him, then?"

Byardil smiled. "Oh yes. He was one of my master's Trusted Men. Bought him as a field slave, trained him, freed him and named him. Cvelthan would give his life for my master."

"Apparently he's some kind of army star. Promoted to Decanus in training, blooded in first combat and field brevet to Centurion. A real hlant so they call him Beast, apparently."

Byardil laughed. "I can see why. He is a hlant. Big, fearless and strong. He's got a lot of experience but I always thought him a bit stupid. Now an officer? Well, men can surprise us I suppose."

Renketh smiled. "Yes."

"Yes what?"

"Yes I want to sign a baby bond with you. I want to adopt a child. I want us to be a family. I want your name on my arm. I love you, my friends all like you, my sister loves you and my Mum. My Dad died in the war so we'll never know. But I know, and I say yes."

Byardil grinned. "Will a tattoo hurt an awful lot?"

"Yes. Let's go up to his place and get them done now, before you get too scared."

Byardil sniffed. "You misjudge me. I'm a lot braver than I look."

They headed off to Tremplude's small house leaving their three charges to snore in peaceful ignorance. Byardil planned to ask Cvelthan and Mridka to stand up and vouch for him at the bonding ceremony.

Dinner for Four

Summer let go of Bdescu and held him at arm's length. "It's wonderful to see you! You look great! How are you?"

He grimaced. "Alive, thanks to your sorcery."

She grinned. "All will be explained. Mostly. But first we must eat. We have an old friend of yours joining us for dinner. Come in!" She walked briskly through the door.

He noticed as he entered that the door was as thick as his thigh and seem to be made of solid metal. It closed behind him with a hiss of trapped air. The corridor was like the Fifth's apartment, but painted an ochre colour. A door on the left took them into a vaulted dining room, the ceiling panelled with white-painted timbers. In the centre was a polished dining table big enough to seat eight or ten people. Seated facing him was a grey haired woman in a smart blue shirt. Her hair was neatly braided and decorated with gold slides. She wore strange frames on her face, holding panes of glass in front of her eyes. Her eyes were bright and clear. He looked at her blankly for a heartbeat. "Mridka!"

He walked around the table as she stood up. He took her in his arms and hugged her. "God above! It's so good to see you, old friend!"

She cried for a few moments but soon got herself under control. She spoke a clear, unaccented Byekiy that was better than his. The old, guttural Mridka seemed banished by this new, confident old woman.

"So, my lovely Gvant. Survived every hazard as usual. God, but you're a tough one, eh? And I am so very glad to see you, my Lord."

They sat down to dinner. Roasted meat in a spicy sauce, beans with spices and mashed roots. Then a pie with sharp fruits lightened by a sweet sauce. The beers were chilled. The Fifth introduced herself properly. "My name is Storm. And this is Summer. My baby sister."

Bdescu looked at them both. The likeness was obvious and striking, especially the eyes. Their tall, lean physiques were similar, although Storm had far more muscular development and looked older. He sat by Summer and inhaled her strange, wonderful scent. It made him feel dizzy and aroused. Summer tapped her beer glass with a spoon. "Gvant, now that dinner is over, to business. Mridka is here as my guest. She has some news for you."

Mridka put down her spoon and looked at him. "My Lord. I have a lot to tell you. Some of it comes from me, some from these two ladies and some from others that you know and trust. I start with you. I am sorry to tell you that your elder brother died two months ago from Blue Plague. He died hard, took a week of suffering until his lungs shut down and he choked. Would have been kinder to give him a quick end, but he didn't ask and nobody had the guts to do it, so he lingered on. That means you are now the Seventh Baron Bdescu of House Bdescu. His widow and three daughters are all now your concubines. Second, Baron Mnufort made you his Bondson. As he has no sons and no formal Will, you inherit all his lands. His widow and four daughters are now your concubines. So, as of today you have nine concubines, fourteen hundred farms with cottages and slave barracks. Three hundred vineyards, six mines, five mills, twelve thousand slaves, almost two thousand freemen and two Great Houses. I do not know how many mounts and beasts you own. I also don't know how many of the Baron-Generals levies survived the battle with the Snowhammer Legions, nor how many soldiers your brother commanded, because I never saw them, but I bet a load of slaves and freemen-sergeants are also under your banner now. I do know this: you are the second richest man in the Empire after the Emperor himself and easily the most powerful of all the Barons."

Bdescu had become pale. Storm handed him a shot glass of fruit brandy, which he absentmindedly drank down. His former slave had not yet finished. Mridka was implacable, tears running down her cheeks as she spoke.

"You have a brother. Well, a half brother actually. Hs name is Byardil."

Bdescu finally spoke. "How in God's holy name is my secretary become my brother?"

The old lady, still weeping, carried on with a visible effort. "Your father had a slave girl. She was called Mridka. She was a pretty little thing and he was fond of her. As for the slave, she worshipped him. She was honoured to be in his bed, in his arms. She thought of him as a God. Your mother was jealous, of course, but your Dad wouldn't give up his slave. The wife got pregnant again, her second. The slave a few weeks later. The wife had no milk and lovely little Gvant would have died. But Mridka had enough milk for both babies. One on each tit, you see? So the wife grew to love the little slave girl. Once Dad had sired two boys and the wife looked a little careworn, Dad decided to get a younger slave girl, so the two women were both abandoned. They became a comfort to each other. When she died, the wife made the slave girl promise to always keep the Lordling and the slave child together as brothers should be. But never to tell the Lordling the truth. The pretty young slave worked to keep the boys happy and together. She ended up as the Lordling's old cook, and happy to be that. Today I break the covenant I made with your mother. I renounce the Empire and all its cruelties. I will not lie to you, or anyone else, any longer. I am a free woman of Byekvoranp, a midwife and proud of it. My debt to that poor woman is long paid, my Lord. Now you know the truth. You and Byardil share the same father but different mothers. He is mine and I love him. As I have loved you." She put her head in her arms on the table top and cried helplessly. Bdescu walked over and put his arm around her shoulders.

"Mridka, there's no need to cry my dear. I'm glad Byardil is my brother. I've always loved him. And you too. I have always looked out for him. I was told he was alive. Is he well, and happy?"

She raised a tear-streaked face and nodded. "He's alive. He's doing well. He's teaching at a primary school. That's a Byekiy name for a school that teaches littlies. He's living with a burly policeman called Renketh. Nice man, if a bit stern. And he's sort of adopted three absolute losers. He's trying to save them, I think. You know Byardil, always taking in strays. My guess is that it will end in tears, but what does an old woman know of life, eh?"

Bdescu nodded, grateful that his scribe was flourishing.

Summer spoke. "Gvant, I'm afraid there's more. Only one other senior noble survived the battle. It was Jcluid Vrabelm, the young man you befriended before the battle. He lost an arm in the fighting. We saved him by amputating his arm and he was healing nicely until he escaped and fled into the forest. We found him three days later. Hlant attack I'm afraid. You are now the leader of what's left of the Baron-General's army. Not just his personal levies. Vrabelm and Ltencha, the other two Barons also had large levies and you now command them too, by right of the Rankings. That's in addition to being the senior noble of the entire Empire."

"The Emperor does not know any of this. I have not been ratified, so this is theoretical."

She shook her head and he noticed that her hair was shorter but more blonde. "Not so. Imperial Commissar Rbunft has briefed the Emperor that you are alive, although he thinks that you are our prisoner. The Emperor has ratified your promotions in the Order of Nobility. It suits him to do so. There is huge unrest amongst the nobility. The failure to conquer the Republic of Byekvoranp has coincided with three slave rebellions, a drought, a famine and two major plague outbreaks – including the one that killed your brother. The Emperor dare not argue against a Bdescu, the oldest and most orthodox of the noble families and a known supporter of the Imperial Family. He might lust after your lands. He might want you dead. But right now, he needs you safely home and on his side. You would stabilise the unrest and he is smart enough to know that."

"How exactly did Rbunft escape from his one-year penance in the Republic?"

She grinned. "Ah. That was my sister's idea. We told him what we wanted him to know and sent him home with a few slaves, mounts and food. He got back last week. We know what he said and how the Emperor reacted."

"You have spies in the Imperial Court?" Bdescu was stunned.

Storm took up the plot. "Yes of course. Much easier for us to spy on him, than him on us. Easy to bribe your people with gold, but they can't bribe a Byekiy 'cos we don't use money. Anyway, we Byekiy know we're at war. Most people in the Empire have no idea what's going on from one month to another. Anyway, you met my Spymaster, Lundy Brench. He liked you a lot. You look a bit peaky. Here. Have another brandy." He knocked that one straight down as well.

Mridka had recovered her composure. She wiped her eyes on a napkin. "Right. I've got to go. I can't stay out past dawn, Byardil will worry if I don't see him and everybody at breakfast. I'll just make it if I leave now." She and Storm got to their feet. Gvant and Summer walked them to the door. The old lady kissed his cheek. "Goodbye my Lord. Forgive an old friend for deceiving you. I did it out of love and I am glad you know the truth." He nodded, dumbly. Summer closed the door and they were alone.

"You look all in, Gvant. Sorry you had to hear all that in one go. Let's get to bed before you fall over." She hugged him. They walked along the corridor and through a second doorway. The bedroom was large, painted white and the floor covered in a thick rich carpet. The bed was large, with a fine timber headboard and footboard. It was covered with sheets like fresh snow. She undressed him and they lay together. He meant to think, then get some sleep. Her magic started to work on him instead. They made love as they always had, tenderly and slowly. Only then could his mind relax and let go of the day. She put out the lamps and a cool darkness filled the room. He slept with her head on his chest.

He awoke very early as was his custom. Summer was asleep on her side, breathing softly. He slipped out of bed without disturbing her. He padded along the room to where light was showing through the join in a pair of curtains. He flung the curtains back. He stepped backwards, inhaling sharply. Fear prickled in his stomach. For out of the window he could see stark rock mountaintops with trails of snow blowing off their peaks in long feathery drifts. Below these he could see the tops of clouds lying in what could be a valley. And soaring above the clouds, huge white birds. For an instant he thought the birds must be very close to his eyes, to appear so huge. As his eyes adjusted to the scale of this view, he perceived that the birds were some distance away, which meant they were larger than he. A bird bigger than a man? That defied belief. He rubbed his eyes, but the seven or eight white animals continued to soar, twisting, rising and falling in complex patterns as if showing off their flying skills. They were a solid white colour, their grey bills were hooked as a bird of prey. Their dark grey legs were held out rigidly behind them, and were tipped with huge, gnarly feet that were gripped into fists. He heard Summer pottering around, lighting the stove. She called out from the far end of the room.

"See any Snowhammers?"

To the Bonding

Word had spread around the small town. Pelva was famous and the story of her bonding to the strange Imperial turncoat was attracting gossip everywhere. The Five Elders of the town were present at the Hall during the weekend as usual, because all Byekiy ceremonies happened on this day of the week. Cvelthan had been banned from Pelva's family home until the ceremony and had spent the night at the camp with his brother Centurions, having a few drinks and getting to know them. In the morning his troop arrived, sparkling in polished kit and under Podge's best discipline. They marched smartly down to the Hall. When they arrived, dead on time, he saw Pelva and her family, all dressed in their best, gathered outside. Standing at the edge of the family group were two surprises.

"Miss Summer? Byardil?"

The two, who had been deep in conversation, walked over smiling. Byardil shook his hand and wished him well, tears in his eyes. Summer looked different. She seemed taller and more blonde. But that tall figure and those unique eyes gave her away. She was more foreign than he was, Cvelthan suspected. She took his hand.

"Centurion Cvelthan of Bdescu. I am pleased to see you."

"But... what in God's holy name are you doing here?"

"Later. Right now I'm here to stand up and vouch for Pelva, my oldest and best friend. You're in for some more surprises, Cvelthan. Look over your shoulder." As she said this, Byardil gasped.

Cvelthan looked over his shoulder and saw an upright elderly lady who was undoubtedly Mridka. And walking beside her, arm in arm, his master Bdescu. As Bdescu arrived, Cvelthan fell to his knees on the grass. He put his forehead to the ground.

"My Lord. Forgive me. I was told you were dead. I thought myself free of my bond to you. I have joined the Byekiy army and made a career for myself. What must I do? Hand me a blade, I will take my life on your word!" He raised a tear-streaked face up toward his Colonel and master. The newly-made Baron smiled. He dropped his hands, palms up, and took Cvelthan's hands in his strong dry grip.

"Stand, freeman Cvelthan of my House." He raised his head as Cvelthan rose to his feet. He spoke in High Tongue, the antiquated language of the Imperial Court.

"Byardil. Mridka. Summer. Renketh. Pelva. Bear witness to the words of the Seventh Baron Bdescu of that House. By my Position and Rank I make an award. I grant Cvelthan my House Name as a full member of Bdescu Clan and Family. He shall be Cvelthan Bdescu, no longer Cvelthan of Bdescu. He is freed of all legal obligations except those of family duty. He is free in all senses of that word. He shall inherit one-twentieth of my wealth on my death. I make this elevation not from kindness but from indebtedness. I am here because he stood over my wounded body and saved my life. I declare him my kin and give him my oath that I will come to him if he ever asks for my presence or my support."

"And, if he is to ask me, then I will perform his rites of marriage to the beautiful woman of his choice."

Cvelthan stood perfectly still, barely breathing. Bdescu clapped him on the shoulder.

"Cheer up, big fella. Could be worse. The sun's shining. Your mates are all here. The beer is paid for, full kudos, as much as your lads can drink. She's a looker, your lady. Now, get your game face on and introduce me to her." Bdescu embraced his former slave. He spoke in Cvelthan's ear. "God be with you, my brother. I am so happy to see you."

Tears rolling down his face, Cvelthan introduced everyone to everyone he knew. Then teachers arrived, police officers and dozens of others that just came for the occasion, including a class-full of chattering schoolchildren, who crowded around Byardil, yelling excitedly. A double bonding was always "a proper do" as the Byekiy say. And so it was. The two couples were bonded in Byekiy law first. Once their witnesses had vouched for them, the Elder asked the crowd if anyone knew of any relationship that might preclude the match – were they siblings or first cousins? Bonded to another? Of age to bond? The crowd yelled "no" to every question. When the short ceremony was over there was prolonged cheering and whooping from the crowd.

Bdescu had obtained a plain white shawl with which he covered his head and shoulders. Curious Byekiy clustered around to see an Imperial marriage. Bdescu raised his voice above the murmurs of the crowd. "I am of Noble Birth and Imperial Rank. I claim right to marry all and any persons affiliated to my House, which is Bdescu. Who can stand before me and claim a right of marriage?"

Cvelthan also wore a borrowed shawl. He had attended several marriages as a bearer so he knew the ritual well. "I am Cvelthan Bdescu of your House and I claim a right to be married. Will my Lord permit this?"

Bdescu said loudly "I will commit you to marriage if your chosen one agrees. Show her forward." Pelva stepped out of the crowd, stunning in a dress of her favourite green. The dress was close-fitting and showed off her curves perfectly. Her red hair was shining in thick waves around her shoulders. She wore dainty white shoes and her bare arms were flawless and pale. She stood beside Cvelthan.

"Do you, Pelva, agree to marry this man, Cvelthan of my House?"

"I do."

"Do you, Pelva, agree to join our House, to take our Name and be of our Kin?"

"I do."

Bdescu stepped forward. He lifted his white shawl and placed it over her. He arranged it neatly around her face and stepped back.

"With the colours of House Bdescu I recognise this marriage on behalf of the God Emperor and the Rector of God's Chosen, who are our temporal and spiritual masters. By their grace I declare you man and wife in the service of and under the protection of our House. May God bless and honour your union. Now swear to be faithful, be fruitful and be loyal to one another for infidelity is a sin against God. Do you both agree to this oath?"

"We do" they said in unison. And they were bonded and married that same afternoon. The crowd went wild, cheering themselves hoarse. Bdescu, grinning, kissed them both on each cheek and said a few private words of congratulations. Pelva wept openly. Cvelthan looked about as happy as a man could be.

They all walked the fifty paces to the inn. Jinna had done them proud. Tables groaned under the weight of food. The whole village had contributed cold meats, pickles, cheeses and every type of bread. There were tureens of soups, stews and roasted vegetables. The hot foods were in tureens and wrapped in plaited straw and cloths to keep the heat in. And there were barrels of beer in a chilly cellar, fresh, cool and foaming.

In the inn yard, the policemen and the legionnaires played tug of war with a stout rope. With much sliding, groaning and catcalling, they were evenly matched. Big men on both sides sweated and grunted, the crowd cheering them on. Dancle, Brindah and Vutch got very badly drunk. Vutch threw up in the street and lost kudos for unsocial behaviour. Dancle made a pass at a gorgeous young Byekiy girl, who gave him a few kisses. This surprised Byardil but he was glad that the lad had got lucky. Brindah fell asleep propped up against the inn wall and so he and Vutch were taken home on a borrowed handcart and put to bed.

The party went on until dusk. People smiled blearily and wandered away home. The reunited folk of Clan Bdescu headed for Byardil's large house for some proper catching up. Byardil and Renketh walked with Mridka and Cvelthan. Pelva chatted to Bdescu and Summer. They sat around the scrubbed table in the warm kitchen and told their stories until dawn. Bdescu edited out all mention of mountaintop eyries, Snowhammer birds and magic. Mridka told Byardil of his brother's existence, which was a very shocking experience for Byardil. Bdescu hugged him and called him brother. Cvelthan was bemused, but nothing else could surprise him today.

Bdescu discovered that Summer had known Pelva for seven years. They had become friends when they met playing the crazy game known as Bagataway. Pelva played for the local club, Summer for one in the next valley but one. Playing twice a season, home and away, they had become fast friends. Bdescu had no doubt that this was the reason that his household had all ended up here. He knew that Summer had picked out this particular place. But how Summer could know that Cvelthan would meet Pelva, and that they would become a couple, that seemed a stretch too far, even for Summer's skills of manipulation. Bdescu could see that his people were happy and settled here in Byekvoranp. He knew that nothing could uproot them from their new lives. He could never call in their oaths and make them march home to the Imperium. If he did, he doubted that they would follow, so complete was their absorption into Byekiy society.

He stood up. "Now folks, Pelva and Cvelthan have some er... consummation to perform. In an Imperial marriage the tradition is that his Lordship lends them a guest room, then everyone clears off and gives them some privacy. As I am homeless here, I have asked the Elders to help. They have found a lovely cottage near the bridge. Look for a blue front door, you can't miss it. The family are off visiting a sick relative and it's unoccupied for three days. Jinna has provisioned the place. I have given it a blessing. Summer has changed the bed linen. Now, off you go and have a relaxing time."

With much emotion, the party came to an end with Pelva and Cvelthan's departure. Mridka headed off to bed, exhausted. Summer stood up.

"Sorry everyone. I have to leave. Duty calls, I'm afraid. I need to be somewhere else and I've already stayed too long. Gvant and I have agreed that he will stay with you for a couple of days, then one of my people will stop by and pick him up. I know you've all got a lot to talk about and you don't need an ignorant foreigner cluttering up the party!"

She exchanged embraces and kisses with everyone. As she hugged Byardil they heard the sound of a troop of heavy mounts arriving outside. Summer waved, ran out of the door and vaulted effortlessly into the saddle of a free mount. The six or seven other riders were all Byekiy cavalry, which none of the Imperial folk had ever seen before. They formed a cordon around her as they whole troop moved off together at a smart canter. Once she had left, Renketh spoke from the heart.

"Now that is a real power of a woman. Am I the only one here who doesn't know who she is?"

Bdescu and Byardil started chuckling. Bdescu spoke first.

"Nope. I love her. I sleep with her. I wash and cook with her. And yet I know virtually nothing about her. I know she's not Imperial nor is she Byekiy. I think not anyhow. I do know that her sister is your Fifth of Five." That made them both widen their eyes, especially Renketh.

"Having said that, I know virtually nothing else. Sorceress? Princess? Envoy from a far-off land? Or just an ordinary woman of exceptional talents? I do not know, my friends. All I know is that she works as a secret agent and her talents saved all the Blenvan people from slavery. She contributed to my defeat in battle. She has manipulated me at every turn. She has outsmarted my every move. She should be my worst enemy. And every time I see her I feel – and act – like a fucking sixteen year old."

Byardil smiled. "You're in love, brother. Simple as that. Oh, and congratulations. No ordinary woman for you, eh? Had to pick the most complex, unfathomable creature in the world! Typical Baron Bdescu eh?"

Bdescu smiled ruefully and drank his chasser. "I'm going to get some sleep. Suggest you do the same."

"Not me, I'm working." Renketh had a shift that day and was soon washed, dressed and gone. Bdescu washed and headed for a spare room. Byardil went to his own room and was soon fast asleep.

Bdescu woke, feeling tired and muzzy. Sleeping in the daytime never suited him. The bed was comfortable though. He sat up, fixing pillows to support his back. Then he heard glass breaking and cursing. He distinctly heard a cry of pain. It was Byardil's voice. He threw back the sheets, leapt out of bed and dressed only in an undergarment, raced downstairs into the kitchen.

As he entered the door, four figures were frozen, staring at him. Byardil was bent face forward over the kitchen table. Vutch and Brindah were holding down his arms, each one threatening his face with a sharp kitchen knife. Dancle was standing behind Byardil, obviously about to rape him. Bdescu's brother was gagged with a kitchen towel, and gave a stifled scream when he saw the Baron. Bdescu gave a low growl and advanced towards Vutch who was nearest to him. Seeing he was unarmed, Vutch let go of Byardil's arm and moved towards Bdescu. Brindah followed suit. Bdescu spoke in Low Tongue, which the boys would not understand.

"Stand up quickly, brother. Butt him in the face with the back of your head." And Byardil reared, throwing his head back at furious speed. His skull landed on the bridge of Dancle's nose, and blood poured out. Bdescu saw no more, the boys were on him. Vutch arrived first because Brindah had to walk around the table. Bdescu stepped into Vutch's path. The boy stabbed at Bdescu's stomach. Bdescu swept the thrusting arm aside with his left hand and rammed the heel of his right hand up under the lad's chin. With a ten thousand hours of sword practice the arm was strong enough to break Vutch's neck. He fell to the tiled floor, twitching. Brindah hesitated. Bdescu stepped into his space and grabbed his knife wrist. He turned the wrist over, the boy flinching away with a gasp of pain. Bdescu threw his body weight against the back of Brindah's arm, snapping it at the elbow. Bdescu stepped smartly back, expecting a third attack. He scanned the room but Dancle was no threat. He had fallen to the floor. Byardil had picked up an iron trivet and dashed it across Dancle's face. The boy rolled on the floor, crying, with hands over his face and blood pouring between his fingers.

Bdescu's calm never wavered. "Well my brother, I didn't realise you were so irresistible! You lads sure know how to throw a party."

Byardil fell on his shoulder, gasping. "Are they dead? Am I in trouble? Help me!"

Bdescu smiled. "Go and get your handsome police officer. We will soon find out. But whatever happens, if any of them die, just say I did it. They like you. They'll be happy to blame me, the evil slaver. Go on, now. I'll watch 'em. Maybe even offer some first aid, if they behave."

Byardil returned in a few moments with seven officers, none of whom was Renketh. Renketh's superior, the woman that had saved Byardil from the three young men's first attack, was in charge.

Vutch was dead, killed instantly by Bdescu's mortal strike. Brindah had a broken arm. And Dancle seemed to have lost all his front teeth as well as having facial bones broken. The police took statements from Bdescu and Byardil. They were calm, solemn and quiet. The wrote down every word. At the end, the two Imperial men had to agree that their statements were true and accurate and complete. Then they signed. Three carts came to the front yard. The first took Vutch away for burial. The second took Dancle and Brindah to the cells. The third carried a doctor who would treat their wounds in the cells.

Six of the police constables left. Their senior officer stayed behind. She gratefully accepted the mug of chasser that Byardil handed her. "Well. I know you thought you could help these young men. And I applaud you for trying. But please remember that you are lucky to have a friend with military skills. If Baron Bdescu had not been here, with Renketh away on duty you'd have likely ended up dead. Apart from the rape, which must have been awful, these kind of people don't just threaten to kill, they usually do it too."

"What happens now?"

"They get banished. Right as soon as they can walk. We'll take them somewhere remote and turn them loose. Give each of them a few tools and some warm clothes and leave them out there. If they are very lucky they'll survive the winter. If not, well that's what you get for rape and attempted murder. Fuckshy shitters." She shook their hands and walked out of the front door.

Byardil started cleaning the blood off the kitchen floor. Bdescu made some fresh chasser and washed his hands.

Slaver Bane

Three days after the bonding ceremonies, Bdescu hiked up a steep woodland trail with Lundy Brench. It had been a six day ride from Byardil's village up to the high mountain hamlet where they had left their mounts and from where they had started the walk. They carried leather packs full of food and sleeping sacs. Soon the trees thinned out and their path went through a meadow dotted with small flowers of pink and gold. The air was clean and cool after the stuffiness of the woods. Brench walked easily. Bdescu knew that the young man was a lot tougher than his dandyish looks suggested. They camped in the meadow. Brench started a fire and cooked up a stew using stream water, an iron pot from his bag and dried meat and vegetables from Bdescu's pack. The food was plain but to the hungry men it tasted delicious. Bdescu made chasser in the fire's embers and washed the pots afterwards.

They stretched out, warm in their fur bags and looked up at the stars. "Who is Summer, actually?" Bdescu enquired.

Brench raised himself on one elbow and peered across the dying fire through the darkness and smoke. "I have no idea. She has never told anyone, so far as I know, where she or her sister came from. There are rumours, of course. Descended from the sky in a flaming chariot is one of the more colourful theories. But I do not believe in fairy stories. I'll tell you what I know. She speaks at least seven languages fluently. One of them she uses only with her sister and nobody else knows what it is. That suggests it's their native tongue. She swears in that language too. She's stronger than her frame suggests, so Storm is not the only warrior in the family. She has a higher tolerance of pain than anyone I have ever met."

Bdescu remembered the rape that Summer had suffered, and grimaced agreement.

"She knows more about plants and animals than seems possible to remember."

Bdescu needed to say it. "Including Snowhammers?"

Brench didn't flinch, he just nodded assent and carried on. "Plus, she can obviously fly."

Bdescu laughed. "I thought you didn't believe in fairy stories?"

Brench lay back. "I don't. But you'll soon see how hard it is to get up to the refuge. And you'll also learn that nobody can get their faster by any other route. In fact there are no other routes. But I left her in the hamlet one morning and trekked up here. When I got to the house the stove was lit, food was cooked and there was a note in her handwriting telling me to eat it. That food took an hour or more to cook, plus the time for the stove to get warm... you tell me."

Bdescu remembered his rescue from the woods when the gang of men were trying to kill him. One moment he had been helpless, the next he was at the refuge staring at a severed limb. He'd had no sense of time passing, of being unconscious or of missing an instant of what happened. Flight seemed at least an explanation. He knew that a human being cannot fly. Enough tricksters and fakirs had tried. All had crashed and many had died. He thanked Brench and went to sleep.

In the bright morning they slogged on upwards. Bdescu was finding the exercise very demanding. His legs and back ached, but he would never reveal any weakness to the younger man. The meadows were long behind them. They walked and half climbed over solid rock. Wherever the path was dangerous there were ropes hanging from cleats wedged in the rock face. They scrambled over boulders the size of houses. They edged across edges with breathtaking drops. They crawled under overhangs with just enough space for a man and his pack. Bdescu knew that no army could possibly attack this place. All defenders would need to do was remove the ropes and not a single man would make it. With the ropes in place a decent bowman could hold off a regiment until he ran out of arrows.

Finally they came to a sheer cliff. Hanging down it was a stout rope ladder and a rope. Brench tied their packs to the rope and set off up the ladder. When he climbed over the top and smiled down at

Bdescu, the Baron set off up the ladder. This was a lot harder than he had guessed. He made it to the top, praying never to see another rope ladder. He found himself in the corner of the vegetable garden of the hilltop retreat where he'd first met Brench. Brench hauled up the packs, the ladder and the rope. They were secure. He looked up at the snow covered crags looming high above and smelled the cool crisp air with its scent of wild flowers. In his language, the mountains were the Teeth of God. In Byekiy, Slaver Bane. So the Byekiy thought that their mountains would keep away the Empire? He shook his head.

"Drink?" Asked his host and Bdescu nodded gratefully.

They drank a cold beer each. Then Brench brought them some of the Byekiy snacks called janneries. He ate everything and licked the plate. The afternoon was slipping away. Bdescu was glad to rest for a while.

"Right, Baron Bdescu the Seventh. I have instructions. I am to tell you to go to the 'other place via the same route you used last time. Only this time shut the door behind you.' Does that make sense to you? I have no idea what it means but I'm supposed to stay outside and count to 500. Then I'm to spend the night alone here, then go down on my own. From this I deduce that you will not return. Now, I know this place well, so I am going to be really puzzled if that actually happens."

Bdescu sprang to his feet, shook Brench's hand and nodded. "Yep. I know what it means. Yes, I will not return today. Sorry I can't tell you. It's a secret, like so much about our mutual friend. Goodbye for now. Safe journey down the hill."

Brench took the handshake and smiled.

Bdescu walked into the house and opened the pantry door. The passage behind was open. There was a clear view of the strange, smooth-sided tunnel and again, fresh air flowed into his face. He closed the pantry door behind him and noticed a soft light in the tunnel. Enough to see by, he thought. He pressed forward until he could go no further. The disembodied voice spoke to him.

"Are you Bdescu?" He was prepared this time and simply replied.

"Yes. I wish to ascend."

Arms by your sides. Move a hand width to your right and a pace forward." Bdescu did so.

Bdescu felt the heavy pressure on all sides of his body. His arms pressed against his ribs. This time he was expecting the upward rush, and hoped to see the exact moment when he emerged through the floor of the eyrie's lobby. It happened too quickly and he was standing on the white tiles before his brain could register the transition from tunnel to lobby.

He had arrived in the lobby. Summer's door was open and he strolled through it. She was coming down the corridor, smiling. She kissed him quickly and said "follow me."

They went back into the lobby. She made some muttered sounds to one of the doors and it whispered open. Cooler air flowed into his face. She walked through the door and he followed. Light glowed from nowhere in particular. He saw an enormous storage facility. Racks of large shelving held goods whose purpose he could only guess at. She walked briskly over to a rail which hung from brackets attached to the smooth rock wall. She started lifting fur garments off the rail and throwing them to him. The garments had the fur on their inside. The outsides were rough suede.

"The pants first. Just climb in and put the straps over your shoulders." The trousers came up high, to his armpits.

"Then the boots. Put them under the trousers, not over. Overlaps are always good. Even though you're freezing, you must not sweat or you'll really suffer." Bdescu realised that they were going outside.

A heavy fur jacket with a hood next, the hood tightened around his face with thongs. Only his eyes were visible. He saw the room as if through a dark tunnel. He tightened mittens on his hands. She walked over and checked his fastenings carefully. Then she handed him a small tablet of plain white.

"Chew this. It will help you to breathe. The air is very thin up here." He chewed it slowly.

They walked further into the room. She opened another heavy door and they stepped into a small room that was freezing cold. She opened a second door and he saw the mountain. Stretching in front of them was a clear vista. The wind whipped lightly across his face and it stung like a slap. She handed him a stout wooden staff that came up to his shoulder. She took another and together they set off across the flat snowfield towards the sheer cliff face that rose opposite their position. He looked to the left. All he could see were dozens of other huge peaks. He looked right but the wind blinded him instantly, tears starting in his eyes. He huddled forward and pushed on after Summer's form. She moved confidently across the snowfield. The staff helped enormously, he needed it to stay upright. The wind speed varied from moment to moment, at one instant a niggling nuisance and the next almost taking his legs from under him.

They reached the lee of the cliff and the wind abated. He saw a cleft in the rocks. A cave. She walked through it, for it was wider than a large man. Inside it was dark and quiet now they were out of the wind. She stopped. She took a spirit lamp from a niche in the wall and fiddled with it, her body concealing her actions. Sudden light glowed from the lamp. He had heard no spark. They moved carefully forward. She spoke in a low voice.

"Do not make loud sounds. Keep your arms by your sides. When I ask you, lower your hood and show your face." Bdescu was certain that he was about to meet her people. Maybe this would explain the mystery that was Summer.

The passage opened into a large chamber. As he looked up and his eyes took in the scene, his guts tightened with fear. A bass drumming reverberated around the chamber. A huge Snowhammer reared up, thick wings outstretched. Each wing had a claw in the middle of its leading edge. A claw as long as his hand, grey and ridged with a sharp hooked tip. Its mighty feet scrabbled on the floor as it came at them. Summer spread her arms and began to drum to it. Her mouth did not move. The sound seemed to come from inside her clothing. It was as loud as the animal's own sounds. His ears hurt.

"Boom doom-doom. Boom boom."

The Snowhammer calmed down. It emitted some guttural grunts. This time Summer's mouth did move. And she talked to a giant bird in the same grunts. The only word he recognised was his own name.

Then it talked back.

She said to Bdescu, in Byekiy, "slowly raise your hands. Undo the thong and lower your hood." He complied, shaking. The bird, taller than him, taller even than Cvelthan, walked towards him. It lowered its terrifying beak towards his face and Bdescu was braver than he had ever been before. He did not move. The bird's eyes were amber with vertical, slitlike blue irises. They were three times the size of a human eye and set at the front of its face. A predator's eyes. A clear membrane flickered over its eyes, moving swiftly from side to side across the eye, as a second eyelid flicked downwards. Its head was unlike any other bird because it had a slight forehead above the beak and a ridge along the top of its head, a hand span high. Its sleek feathers were pure white, and much smaller and finer on its head and shoulders. Its smooth grey bill was as long as his forearm and sharply hooked at the end, a hook the size of his little finger. The beak looked hard as bone at the tip, but more flexible further up, as it melded into the face. Two huge nostrils opened in this part of its face. With a whistling sound it took a deep breath, sniffing Bdescu's scent. To his relief it stepped back.

Summer spoke quietly but clearly. "He likes you. Please don't be alarmed, he is my friend. It is his job to be suspicious. He is on guard duty. His name is ----------." She emitted a series of sounds that Bdescu could never have made. The Snowhammer repeated the sound. Then, to his astonishment, it distinctly said "Sunner! Descu!"

Bdescu laughed. The relief flooded through him. He was a visitor rather than prey. Summer laughed too.

There followed more conversation between Summer and the bird. It seemed long to Bdescu. After a while he looked around the cave. In a corner lay a fresh carcass. It was a domestic animal the Byekiy called a Verong. It weighed as much as a ten year old child and this bird had carried it up here. The Snowhammer's strength and flying skills must be enormous to perform such a feat. Perhaps he now knew how so many Imperial sentries had vanished during the occupation of Blenvan. So this thing could be a man-eater after all.

The Snowhammer moved aside. Summer walked past it into another tunnel. He followed Summer further into the mountain. In a second chamber they came upon a nest. Thick branches were plaited together to form a circular base. On this were laid furs. On top of those, a thick carpet of feathers. Sitting in the middle, a Snowhammer female. Slightly larger than the male, she looked placidly at them. From under her nearest wing a small head appeared. A baby Snowhammer. It looked at them with its beautiful eyes and gave a small drumming sound, its chest beating rhythmically as the sounds emerged.

Summer had a second and even longer conversation with the female. All seemed to go well and Summer turned and smiled at him. "Time to go, Gvant." They walked carefully out so as not to disturb the infant, stepped around the male as Summer called her farewells and found themselves outside in a few moments. Summer adjusted hoods and checked mittens.

"You breathing OK?"

"Yes. I feel a little breathless now though."

"We need to get back. You'll get altitude sickness quite soon. I will get you indoors as fast as possible, but we must take care out there. Call out if it gets worse. Now we move."

They managed to cross the snowfield without mishap but he could not see any door in the rock. Perhaps they had crossed to the wrong place? She knew better. A large section of what looked like raw rock opened in front of them. The rock door was lined with the same substance as the internal doors. Obviously the rock cladding on the outside was camouflage. Even up here, where a man could barely breathe, she took fanatical care of her safety. A skilled search team could not have found that opening.

Sitting in a wonderfully comfortable chair, breathing easily and sipping brandy, he gazed at his unfathomable lover.

"OK Gvant. Ask me anything. I promise to be truthful. I do not promise to answer all questions."

He sorted his questions and plunged in.

"How did you build this place?"

She looked surprised. Obviously not the question she'd been expecting, he guessed.

"Well... we used the same 'sorcery' that brought you up to the half-way house, as we call it, to lift all the tools and people up here. Then we hollowed out some natural caves. We sealed the caves, brought all the stuff inside as quickly as possible to protect it – and us – from the appalling weather and low air pressure. Then once we had air flowing up from down below and we could breathe OK, then we took our time fitting out. The water comes from snow and ice melting off the roof. Everything else comes up the same way that you did."

He looked dissatisfied. "How many of your people are here?"

"Now? Two. Me and my sister. The original group varied from fifteen to thirty-six depending on what we were doing. Once this safe house was finished, the two of us were left here to fulfil our mission."

"What is your mission?" He was remorseless.

"To protect the Snowhammers."

That answer completely stopped him. His face gave nothing away, as ever, but she could almost hear his mind racing.

"From what?"

"From you. From the Empire. From being hunted to extinction by a bunch of lazy, cruel men who take what they want and eat it or break it."

Bdescu clearly was taken aback by this new direction the conversation had taken. She knew that and grinned wickedly at him.

"You think I'm joking. You think I'm really some sort of spy, an agent trying to subvert your Imperial plans for conquest and expansion. Sadly, no. That's my sister's job. I'm here to study, learn from and teach, the Snowhammers. The only Highly Intelligent Avian Life Forms that we know of. They have the narrowest niche that nature could ever provide. Too heavy to fly unless there's a howling gale. They have to hunt in the winter. They haul whole carcasses up here and let them freeze on the glaciers. Then they bring the carcasses indoors, thaw them out and eat them all through the other three seasons. They have social events, parties even. They talk across huge distances with their drumming. They can breathe and fly in air so thin it would kill you or me in moments. Their feathers are some of the best insulation ever seen in nature. They are the highest predator in the world. Yet Imperial hunters would eliminate them in less than a generation."

Bdescu was baffled. "Where are you from, Summer?"

"That's the question I may not answer. All I may say is far away."

"Why do you favour the Republic over the Empire?"

She walked over to the sideboard and poured two glasses of brandy. She handed him one. He admired the glass, its flawless clarity and perfect symmetry. She settled back into her arm chair.

"OK. There are many ways for a civilisation to develop. They form a sort of range. Here, there are two civilisations from opposite ends of the range. The Empire is one extreme. The republic is the other. They are pretty much opposites."

"The Empire is run by one man. The Republic is run by dozens. The Empire concentrates ownership in few hands. The republic doesn't recognise ownership, it really sees a sort of custodianship. The Empire has a huge capital city, the Republic dozens of small towns. The Empire ranks people into social classes. The Republic sees individuals as all being of the same rank but widely differing abilities and needs. The Empire is about owning land, the Republic thinks that land owns us. The Empire consumes, the Republic develops more resources. The Empire has a monotheistic religion, the Republic believes in rational thinking. I could go on but you get the idea."

"And why then do you support one over the other?" Bdescu seemed genuinely puzzled, even slightly offended.

"My love, this is not easy to explain without giving away secrets. Please do not ask me how I know the things I am about to say. Just trust me that I believe them. The Empire can succeed as a civilisation. But it will cost the people and the world a great deal of pain. Forests will be felled and burned. Wars will be fought and slaves taken. Evil men will rule over good ones and women will be treated as goods rather than people. Mines will be dug for useless baubles while children starve. Women will be sold, raped, beaten and murdered with no recourse from anyone but their male relatives. Animals will be hunted to extinction. Wilderness will be replaced by cities and the land will become unfit to grow food. Plagues and pestilences, wars and starvation, racial pogroms and religious wars will become frequent and accepted as the natural way of things. Most of these evils are already happening. They will accelerate as the Imperium develops new skills and weapons. Until, perhaps two or more thousand years from now, the exhausted people decide they must change or die. Then, perhaps, change will happen and the world will be healed."

He chewed his thumb. "And none of these things will happen if the Republic is triumphant? I find that hard to believe!"

She smiled wryly. "I know. So do I, sometimes. The Byekiy are wilful, stubborn and difficult. Storm thinks we're wasting our time. She's here because she's a warrior, like you. She follows her duty, her mission. She influences events. I'm trying to influence peoples' thinking, which is harder. But basically, my answer is yes. If the Republic's belief system prevails, then peace and prosperity become more likely. A Byekiy world will be a peaceful world of small farms, small towns and local culture. Decentralised, cooperative and friendly. The Byekiy believe they only have one enemy: starvation. Their winter is so harsh that they have been forced for thousands of years to collaborate. They've become very good at it. None of this is certain, of course, because nothing is certain. Wiser heads than mine say it's highly likely. Because I believe in their sincerity and good intentions, I came here."

He stared moodily out of the window, watching swirls of snow twisting in the erratic mountain winds. She had more to say.

"Gvant, the Empire is already close to its first major collapse. Over farming starves the land of nutrients. Crops fail. Mono-cropping leads to plagues of insects that decimate harvests. Hungry slaves have revolted. Water supplies to the capital dry up and people die of thirst in the streets as the rich ride by, oblivious. The Empire needs better governance. The Emperor is a pervert and a braggart without courage or true authority. The Barons are quarrelling over who should kill him and take over. The Empire needs someone strong, someone with moral authority, martial skills and a reputation. The Empire needs Gvant, Seventh Baron Bdescu of House Bdescu, to ride to its rescue."

She drained her brandy and smiled faintly. A warm smell of bread floated over from the wood stove. She leapt up and fussed with gloves, filling the room with fragrance as she shook the bread out of its tin and onto a wire mesh rack so that it could cool and dry out.

After a simple dinner of bread, cold meats and fruit, they went to bed. Their lovemaking was slow and tender. It had a poignancy that both of them could feel.

She woke at dawn. She felt the bed with her right hand. His side was empty and still warm. She turned over, revelling in the warm smell of a shared bed. He was standing at the window, stark naked and perfectly relaxed. She loved his utter lack of body modesty. She admired his clean, lean shape, the muscles long, hard and flat across his shoulders and lower back. He turned to her. Tears ran unheeded down his face.

"Summer, I love you. I have never loved another woman as I love you. I want to stay with you. I want that very much. Yet I have twelve thousand people to look after. I have two Great Houses to run. I have nine women to protect. With the Baron-General dead and no heir, other Lords will come sniffing around his women. His widow will be a target for fortune hunters and opportunists. Knights will try to rape the daughters so that they can claim prior rights. My brother's women folk may be OK, he had a few Trusted Men that I know can be relied on. But the Baron-General took all his men with him, leaving behind only the few who were too old or infirm to fight. A determined local lordling with a few accomplices could ride in there and wipe them out in an afternoon. Lady Mnufort and her daughters need my protection."

Summer nodded, her eyes shining with unshed tears.

"I know. I've always known that our relationship was not to be. I cannot give you children. I represent a culture that competes with all you hold dear. I've loved you since the first glance. I love your smell of spicy food. I love the salt taste of your skin, the soft hair on your body running under my fingers. You've given me the privilege of love and I will always be grateful. We will not grow old together, much as I would love to imagine it. You'll sire five sons from your wife and two concubines. You'll possibly even be Emperor one day. If that happens the entire Empire will have me to thank for my sacrifice! And it is a sacrifice. I know I must do it. Even if I didn't, I am ordered so."

"You must go home, love."

He nodded. "Aye. But not soon, I fear. It is a long hard road, even after the Byekiy let me go. By my poor reckoning I've been here a half year or less. What will I find when I do get home?"

Summer shook her head. "No. You'll not serve out a year here. I have certain... powers. I will send you home."

"When?"

"Today, a bit later on. Things might happen amongst your people back in the Imperium if we delay until tomorrow. We'll go down to the safe haven. We have assembled a complete, brand new set of Imperial armour and clothing for you. The armour will protect you better than any weapon the Imperium possesses. Your sword has been replaced with some better metal. This one will outlive you. I want you to live, my love. Lundy has made drawings of all your Imperial heraldry and we've had a proper surcoat made in appropriate Baronial design and colours. You've been away a long time. It's vital that people know exactly who you are."

"What will we do today?" She smiled.

"Today we go to see off Cvelthan as he marches off to war."

A loud high bell tone sounded. Like so many mysteries of this place, to Bdescu it seemed to come from the wall behind his head. Summer jerked her head up and ran flat out into the kitchen, where she stared at a small object on the wooden counter top.

"Trouble. Pelva needs me. We go. We go now. Get dressed, Gvant."

Like any soldier, he could get dressed fast. She was ready at the same moment. She carried a leather bag. "Ready?" she asked, breathlessly.

He nodded. "Time for some sorcery, my love. Out into the lobby, down the tube to the safe house. From there we'll head out on our final mission. Ready?" He nodded and she kissed him fully on the lips. They ran into the lobby.

Honeymoon's End

Cvelthan walked into the bedroom carrying a tray. Breakfast and hot chasser for his wife. She slept, naked and uncovered, completely unselfconscious and at ease in his presence. He looked at her for a few moments, revelling in his recent luck. From field slave to centurion in a few short years. From loneliness and misery to marriage and bliss in a few months. In his mind, he owed it all to Bdescu, now his sworn brother. He shook his head and put the tray down so that he could awaken her with kisses.

After breakfast and more lovemaking they strolled around the village. His legion had awarded him a four-day leave for his bonding. Byekiy expected a bonded man to need time for consummation. The lads had ribbed him without mercy. Nothing could upset him, especially the troops' envy.

Pelva spoke as they walked along the river path. "Cvelthan, I have a favour to ask."

He smiled down at her. "Even if I could refuse you anything, I won't! Ask away."

"Don't be so keen to agree. This is a big ask. My parents are struggling to cope with my nephew and niece. My Mum has a few health problems. My Dad can't see very well. The kids are lovely but a bit too much at this stage in their lives. They are grandparents, not parents."

"And so?" he prompted.

"Can we adopt them? Start our family straight away? The Elder suggested it when I went to ask for the bonding ceremony and I've been thinking about it. But it's not viable unless you want to do it. I mean really want to, not just agreeing with me because you're lovestruck. I would rather die than manipulate you. They all think you are my big scary Hlant, but you're really a big softy underneath."

He laughed. "You think I don't have enough love to share my life with those two imps? You think I'd be jealous and prefer my own seed?

Naah. I thought about suggesting it myself, I can see your Mum struggling. After all, I saved their lives. In the Imperium that means they belong to me. No slavery here, that's not what I mean. I just think that I created a blood debt when I saved 'em. You know what Bdescu would say?"

She shook her head, the red hair waving around her face. Her eyes shone up at him.

"He'd say 'if not us, them who? If not now, then when?' What he meant was, there's no advantage in delay. Better to decide and get on with it than waste time over thinking it. If it's right then it feels right. And it does feel right. Yes?"

She hugged him. "Yes! Yes it feels right."

Cvelthan smiled. Now he knew that if the next battle cost him his life, she would never be alone. If she had conceived, that would be a bonus. But his chances of living long enough to sire more than one child were not great. Better a family than a lonely child. The former slave had firm views on family life. He only wanted the best for his wife and his children.

Their walk led them back into the village. They called at the Elders' Hall to discuss possible adoption with the Elder for Families. She was a lovely grandmother called Belsharve. She seemed to know a lot about their situation and encouraged the move, subject to Pelva's parents' approval. She promised them that the village would build them a family home on one of the plots where a house had been burned down by Imperial troops. Cvelthan liked the irony of this.

They headed back to her house and were surprised that Prelvo and Sivale agreed to the adoption with evident relief. Sivale's chest was wheezing badly which upset Pelva, who had not noticed in her own happiness that her mother had become quite ill. Cvelthan, ever practical had a suggestion.

"Your friend Summer is the best healer I ever saw. Why don't we ask her to help your Mum."

"Yes! He's right! Mum, let Summer help you. She's a wizard with herbs and stuff." Mum smiled and nodded. Leaving her parents to break the news to the children, Summer and Cvelthan set off.

"How will we contact her, though? Summer, I mean. We dunno where she lives, do we?" Cvelthan had found the flaw in his plan.

Her face was bright. Nothing would dull her happiness today.

"Come with me, handsome man. I will show you a bit of magic."

Back at the cottage, Pelva went through her bag and took out an embroidered jewellery roll. She wore only a few personal ornaments, all of which were given by family or friends. She never accepted gifts from fans, it was bad kudos.

She took out a plain gold necklace. Cvelthan was startled. It was the same one that Bdescu had worn.

She dropped the necklace in a glass of water. Then she took it out. She repeated this action twice more. After three dunkings, she dried the piece and carefully put it on.

"Is that it? That's the magic?"

She grinned. "Yes. Now we wait for it to work." And she laughed at his sceptical expression.

Cvelthan went to the privy in the yard. He washed his hands in a washbasin that they kept on a small table on the porch. He heard a polite cough behind him. He turned quickly. Summer was standing in the garden. She wore a kilt of fine tartan wool, a shirt of linen and a hide waistcoat with many pockets. Her sporran was old and worn. Her boots were polished and her socks rolled down over the boot tops. Her blonde hair hung to her shoulders, clean and fine, moving gently in the morning breeze. At her feet was a leather bag of an unusual design.

"She calls, I answer. Please ask the lovely lady to cover herself up. That perfect figure always makes me feel skinny and unattractive."

Cvelthan laughed and went inside, shaking his head.

They sat at the kitchen table. Pelva told her story and Summer agreed to help. After breakfast they walked over to Pelva's family home. Sivale was glad to see Summer. A very worried Prelvo fussed around in the kitchen making chasser with Cvelthan while Summer examined his wife. They were called in. Prelvo was shaking so Cvelthan carried the tray loaded with chasser and biscuits.

Summer sat next to Sivale, who nodded as they entered. Summer looked intently at Prelvo, addressing her remarks at him.

"Sivale has a lung infection. It's caused by a tiny fungus, so small you can't see it. Here's a pot of oil. Do not touch the oil. Do not drink it or spill it, it's not good stuff. Put a spoonful of the oil into a bowl of boiling water. Straight away put Sivale's head over the bowl and cover her head, and the bowl, with a towel. She's to take twenty deep breaths. Towel off, breathe twenty normal breaths. Then back under the towel for twenty more. That's three times a day after meals. Do not stop the treatment until all the oil is gone, even if she seems better. Use it all. In between doses of oil, she's to try deep breathing. Full breath in, hold for a five count, release slowly. Do that after every dose of oil. Once the oil is finished, keep doing the deep breathing three times a day. It will strengthen her lungs. Then the infestation probably won't come back. Also, as soon as she's feeling better, take a long walk every day. Winter and summer, unless it's actually dangerous to go out. If after all that she's not better, just call me back." Summer smiled at them, her eyes gleaming. She handed the oil pot to Prelvo.

She smiled at Pelva. "It's great to see you so happy, love. He's a good man is Cvelthan. Gvant loves him and so do I. Please do not follow me outside, I have to go right away." She kissed them all. She gave Pelva a hug and whispered in her ear, making Pelva giggle.

Summer waved from the doorway and disappeared.

They drank the chasser and left Prelvo to minister to Sivale. They wandered homeward arm in arm. They saw no sign of Summer. Cvelthan had seen yet another facet of Summer's mystery, which seemed to bother the Byekiy people not one bit. He had just two days left and a very busy agenda, mostly concerned with lovemaking. After a few hours he had stopped thinking about Summer and concentrated on Pelva. A woman that he could understand seemed a better option to the Centurion.

The next day they went to the Elder Hall and registered their intention to adopt the two children. Pelva went to see how Sivale was doing. Cvelthan called over to the main Legion camp on the outskirts of the village. He looked in on the Centurions' Mess tent and found a buzz of excitement. He was about to ask when Janthro threw back the tent flap and walked in.

"Officers of the Fifth Snowhammer Legion. Time for action. Kudos awaits us. A large hostile force is marching up Twisted Gut Valley. This time our scouts saw them coming. We've evacuated all civilians from their path. We've harvested what we can and burned the rest, so they're hungry. No captives, no leverage so they can't stop us attacking them. The Legion musters here this afternoon. We will leave tomorrow morning. Full battle kit, please."

His adjutant rushed in and spread a huge map on the dining table. Janthro scanned the map and pointed.

"We are here. They are there. At their current slow march they'll reach their target, the town of Smiling River, in four or five days. We will march over this pass and into the valley behind them. We will attack from the rear. The ground is rough. It will be hard to keep formation but even harder for them to charge in line with cavalry. Jarleh and her lassies are already coming down Twisted Gut valley from the top end. We hope to time it so that we hit them from both sides. It will be hard fighting and we will lose good men and women. But if they get to Smiling River they'll cause fucking havoc. There are nine thousand civilians in the town, we have no chance of moving so many people in time. We're it, we've got to stop them. Questions?"

Cvelthan raised a hand.

"Ah, the newlybonded! Gentlemen, please don't let this man be killed. He's only had three days with Pelva, the famous singer! And your question, Kelthan?" The men laughed. Nearby officers clapped Cvelthan on the back.

"Archers sir?"

"Just the few hundred that we have with us. We won't be able to drag artillery over the hill either. This is going to be nasty hand to hand stuff. It will test our resolve to the limit."

He held a short discussion about the terrain, assisted by a female scout from Jarleh's skirmisher regiment. The girl looked young and vulnerable, but she spoke incisively, describing the terrain well. Janthro had not exaggerated, this would be really difficult. The ground was mostly broken rock and streams, interspersed with reed marshes and bog. The valley sides were steep so at least their flanks could be anchored. Cvelthan was sure the Imperial troops would fight on foot, but had not the confidence to say so. Janthro thought differently.

"Centurion Kelthan. Will the Imperial knights fight on foot?"

"Most likely, sir. Mounts are no good on rock. They easily slip, turn an ankle, break a leg. Then they won't charge, they get too nervous. If the commander has any brains he'll use the heavy troops to hold us as the spearmen stab over our shields. Watch your face and neck if they do that." He took a deep nervous breath, embarrassed by his poor command of the language.

"Heed Kelthan's warning, men. He's an experienced soldier and he knows these people. His advice can save your lives. Ask Kelthan anything about Imperial weapons and tactics and spread the know how to your men. On the march we will do more planning. Get moving. Muster and brief your men. Pack up for forced march. Full armour and kit. Present in marching order at first light. If you've acquired a girlfriend, give her a kiss. You might not see her again so make everything right. Fifth Snowhammer Legion... dismissed!"

Cvelthan walked to Podge's billet and briefed his new Optio. Podge scrambled off to tell the rest of the century.

Cvelthan set off towards the cottage to enjoy what might well be his fourth and last night of married life. Then he realised that Pelva wouldn't yet be back. He'd need to see Byardil first.

Mopping Up

Byardil and Renketh finished cleaning up the mess in their kitchen. Byardil was subdued and Renketh left him to his own thoughts while they finished the job. After a cup of hot chasser they sat outside. There was a smell of sweat and spilled food in the kitchen, so they left the doors and windows open to air the place. Apart from a painful behind and a few bruises, Byardil was not too badly hurt. His morale was a different matter. He felt violated, fooled and stupid, all at the same time. He felt no anger, which surprised him. He felt guilty, which was ridiculous, but it would not let him be. If he hadn't failed, he might have saved the three lads from banishment and himself from all this pain.

Renketh smiled a little. "Perhaps we need something to do. No good hanging around here. It'll just depress us. Let's go over and see if Jinna has any beer left. I'm hungry too, I could murder a plate of Janneries..."

Byardil smiled bravely and nodded. Renketh was right, getting out of the house did help a little. Next day Byardil began to feel better. He went back to work and had to tell his class of bubbly children an abridged version of the last few days. When he had started teaching he decided never to lie to the little ones. He never pretended to know something he didn't. He always admitted his own ignorance, but he always found an answer from someone else, or a book in the library. For some reason this honesty seemed to work. His authenticity was obvious to the children and they all liked him. After the excitement of the last few days he found work comforting. The children were all agog at the news of the Legion marching off to war again and asked him a dozen questions. This time he had an inside track.

"Well I know a centurion in the Legion. He's my adopted brother. He'll probably come to say goodbye before he leaves. I will try to ask him when I see him and if he agrees then I'll tell you, OK?" The kids were thrilled and started asking lots of questions about armies and wars. He surprised himself by how much he'd learned over all these years with Bdescu and the levies. He answered every question until it was time for sport.

As he walked along the sunlit corridor he met the head teacher. She beamed at him. "Another excellent class, Byardil? About eight kids have been telling me all about your mastery of warfare, tactics, logistics and weaponry. Quite a session, I hear!"

Byardil smiled. "I think I was running out of material at the end. I surprised myself."

"Well you don't surprise me. I know you're an excellent teacher and so do your colleagues. You've been a grand addition to this school. I am glad you came here. Not many men are good with the younger kids. Most of the primary age teachers are women. So it's really good to have a man as a role model for some of the boys.

"Oh. Well, thanks very much." Byardil was deeply pleased by her remarks. He had started to really enjoy teaching. He knew that he'd been improving but her words confirmed his progress.

She had more to say. "Anyway, what I actually came to tell you was, you have a visitor. Biggest man I've ever seen and I can't pronounce his name."

Byardil laughed. "Was it Cvelthan Bdescu?" She nodded. Her favourite teacher sprinted down the corridor and called thanks over his shoulder.

Byardil ran into her office. Cvelthan was standing looking out of the window. He turned as Byardil entered.

"Morning Bro!" he hugged Byardil.

Byardil looked him up and down. Cvelthan was lean yet massive. His muscular arms bulged out of his linen shirt. His neck was roped with powerful tendons. He smelled of soap and leather. His dark hair was cropped very short and his deep-set eyes smiled through a network of wrinkles.

"May I just ask you a tiny favour, Cvelthan?" asked Byardil, innocently.

"Course you can. What is it?"

"Follow me. I'll explain on the way..."

A little later that morning Cvelthan stood in front of the class. He talked the kids through the enemy's plans and how the Legion meant to beat them, in simple terms and with as little reference to the violence as he could. The children listened intently. He invited questions and they were not too shy to ask. He found their questions unnervingly honest and penetrating. They asked about tactics, logistics, the morality of killing and how one cleaned up after the battle. The treatment of wounded came up too. After he had answered their questions they gave him a spontaneous cheer. Cvelthan walked out with Byardil while the children ate their snacks.

"God in all his Heaven! That was nerve-wracking. I couldn't do your job for all the kudos in Byekvoranp. How in Heaven do you do that all day?"

Byardil smiled. "I love it. I love them. Easy as that, really."

Cvelthan smiled. "Well, brother, each to his own Place, as we used to say. I'm off to fight my former friends. I can't say I'm happy about it but it's what I do best. My lads need me. I'll be off at dawn. Pelva will keep in touch with you, so if she hears news of me, so will you. Remember – no news is good news. Try not to worry." He hugged Byardil and set off home with long strides. Byardil waved and sniffed back a few tears.

"Dust in my eye." He said firmly.

In the small hours of that night, Cvelthan and Pelva sat in the kitchen drinking chasser. They had made love with an urgency they had not felt before today. Now both were fully dressed, Pelva in kilt and shirt, Cvelthan in his military kit except for body armour and weapons. Cvelthan looked steadily at her.

"Be brave, my darling girl. The march is a couple of days, the battle a couple more. If we're sent on from there, they'll bring news back to you so that you know where I am. If not and we're sent back here, I'll be back in six or seven days. You are listed as my next of kin. Because we don't yet have our own house, I gave your Mum and Dad's house as our address. Tell them I hope they don't mind. The Legion people will send any news of me there. If my luck runs out, please tell Byardil and Renketh, the Baron and Mridka that I love 'em. If I get wounded, I'll probably arrive back here before the post does. The Legion always gives wounded a high priority."

She nodded. "Just come back, big man. I'll be your nurse if you're badly hurt - and proud to do it. Nurse, wife, either is good for me. Just come back, OK?"

She quietly and efficiently helped him to armour up. She tied his fastenings swiftly and expertly, she seemed to know what to do. She buckled his sword belt and checked that his dagger was in the right spot to be drawn swiftly. He used an Imperial stiletto that Bdescu had given to him years ago. The thicker Byekiy knife was round his back, he used it for camp chores but preferred the slimmer blade for wet work. She sniffed at him.

"You don't smell like you anymore. You usually smell warm and spicy. With this stuff on, you smell of iron, leather and old sweat. Not very attractive, my man."

He grinned at her brave humour. They walked outside and he picked up his furca, the forked stick from which hung his kit: a leather bag of food with his brass plate and spoon; a bedroll that doubled as a waterproof cloak; a neat little folding spade for entrenching; and his canteen. His arming cap sat comfortably under his helmet's sprung straps. His neckerchief stopped the armour from chafing and his boots were broken in and as comfortable as old slippers. With the furca over his shoulder and his two peelums, his left hand was free to hold her hand. They walked over to the camp just as the trumpets sounded reveille. At the entrance to the camp they found Summer, Byardil, Mridka and Bdescu waiting. Cvelthan was relieved that Pelva would not be left alone as he marched away. He hugged his friends, kissed his woman and marched smartly to his unit, who were assembling by the tree.

Summer put her arm around Pelva's shoulders. With trumpet calls of various notes and tones, the ranks assembled. In what seemed no time, they were marching out. Cvelthan looked proud and grim as he led his century out for the very first time. Bdescu gave him an Imperial salute, they others waved. Cvelthan's face cracked into a broad smile and he winked at Pelva. Soon they could see nothing but dust.

"Have they gone?" The others nodded and Pelva broke down into helpless tears. "I'll never see him again!" she wailed. The five friends walked slowly back to Byardil's place. Renketh was on duty overnight. Byardil was working in a couple of hours too. But he'd laid on a breakfast, knowing that they'd all be there to see Cvelthan off on his mission. And with very mixed feelings, they wished him well.

After breakfast, Mridka had to go and see a young woman nearing the end of her pregnancy, Byardil headed off to school and the other three wandered back to Pelva's parents' house. She could not face the cottage without Cvelthan being there, so Bdescu walked over to the cottage and packed up all their stuff then in four trips, walked it all back to her home. Summer stayed with Pelva, getting her to tell all about the giant and his ways, which certainly perked Pelva up. Pelva's earthy and unflinching descriptions of her newly-found love life made Summer chuckle.

"So, are you glad you bonded with Cvelthan?"

Pelva smiled wistfully. "He's lovely. Packed with power. Can't tell you about the loving, wouldn't be fair... but I will say this. If I'm not pregnant already, it must be a miracle! He says I'm his first. In which case, he is really trying to catch up fast, know what I mean? He really is as strong as a hlant. I'm not a skinny girl but he can lift me in one hand and carry me down stairs! With a full cup of chasser in the other and not a drop spilled. With all that, he's so gentle. I haven't so much as a bruise on my body, nor a scratch. He's fanatically clean, too. Hair, nails, everything. He sweats, he washes. I quite like the sweat though, because he smells like some exotic foreign food. He's spicy. Know what I mean?"

"Yeah", breathed Summer. "Bdescu smells wonderful. Funny enough he says the same about me. Must be an 'opposites attract' sort of thing. I think we've got to admit one thing though. These Imperial men are pretty damned virile, aren't they?"

The two women were still giggling when Bdescu arrived. He grinned as if he knew exactly what they'd been discussing. Pelva actually blushed.

After yet another pot of chasser, Pelva went to bed in her own room. Sivale said she'd keep an eye on Pelva so Bdescu and Summer headed out.

Return of the Bondson

Bdescu and Summer stood in a quiet woodland glade on the outskirts of the village. She handed him a hood made of a soft dark material then backed away a couple of paces.

"You've seen the magic a couple of times now. The first time was a scramble and we accidentally maimed a man, which was very regrettable. The last one wasn't so scary, was it?" Bdescu shook his head, unable to speak.

"We cover our faces to protect us from the flash of light. We stand away from any trees, people or buildings. On my command, we jump up into the air as high as we can. Ready? Hood on."

He put on the hood and stood in perfect darkness.

"Ready? One, two, three, Jump!" Perfectly together, they jumped into the air. And vanished.

He landed. He had seen and felt nothing. He pulled off the hood. She smiled at him. He looked around the garden of the safe haven house, safely on a cliff high above the island city.

"I'm starving. Let's eat." She grinned and he followed her into the house.

After a light lunch which she served outside on the porch, he had more questions.

"How does the magic work?"

"Difficult to explain. For instance, you know how to use a sword, obviously. But can you make one?"

He shook his head.

"Well it's the same with the magic and me. I can make it work. I understand the basic idea but I could never make one, it's not my expertise. What I know is this. Up there," and she pointed vertically upwards, "is a machine. You can't see it because it's too high up. It has enormous power. When I command it, it lifts us up and puts us down. Fast."

"Is it the same sorcery that makes lumps of stone raise us thousands of heights into your fortress from here? Is there such a machine hidden in the pantry?"

She laughed. "Hell, you're a bright one, you are. Yes, sort of the same machinery."

"And not the same one that makes tunnels in castle walls when I'm not looking?"

"No. That's a whole different kind of machine."

"And this trinket around my neck, that makes me your pet, is that another machine again?"

She looked pained. " I am truly sorry Gvant. I never meant to offend your dignity. I know you hate the idea of being beholden to anyone. I was trying to protect you."

He nodded. "I know. Next time trust me? I'm old enough and ugly enough to make my own decisions about things."

She nodded. "I understand. But if ever you do need me, dunk the necklace in water three times in a few beats. It will send me a distress signal as Pelva did. Storm or I will respond at once.

She turned away and walked to a cupboard, which she opened with her back to him. She turned back towards him and bowed, her two hands holding out an object. It was a sword in a scabbard painted beautifully in the purple and silver of House Bdescu. He drew the blade smoothly from the scabbard, which held it in a precise fit. The blade was almost the same size and balance as his previous favourite, broken on the practice floor by Storm. But this one was matte black, except for a sliver of silver along its sharp edges. Instead of a point it had a sloping chisel tip. He touched it with his thumb and drew blood. It was shaving sharp, even at the tip. He made a few passes with it, marvelling at its balance, feel and weight. He slid the deadly weapon back into its scabbard without a sound. She handed him a sheathed dagger that was almost the same as the sword, in miniature. It was also viciously sharp and had the same chiselled point.

"These were made by my people. The weapons are designed to pierce armour without shattering or blunting. They replace the items you have lost. No sword or axe made anywhere in this world will break these blades and I hope that they protect you in every fight, from every enemy you meet. Take them as tokens of my love and regret." She kissed him almost shyly on the cheek.

She showed him the clothes and armour. He could feel the quality of the gear and was impressed. It looked exactly like Imperial armour. But it was much lighter. It weighed a fraction of a standard hauberk's mass and he could move easier than ever before. The gambeson that went under it was the same; light and easy to wear, flexible yet tough. Once he was dressed, she carefully put the surcoat over his head and belted his new weaponry about his waist. A strap ran from the belt and over his shoulder to spread the weight of sword and dagger, just as he'd always done. The surcoat was emblazoned with House Bdescu colours and the signifiers of baronial rank. He put on the arming cap and helmet. Mailed gauntlets protected his hands. Summer stood back.

"You look fucking magnificent." She said, in High Tongue with a little gutter coarseness thrown in. They hugged. "I will see you again, Gvant. In this life or the next. I hope that your God is kind to you. Think of me sometimes."

She could see the pain in his face.

He stepped outside and walked down the path. She fiddled with something behind her back and stayed on the porch. She waited until he had covered his head, helmet and all, with the black hood.

"One, two, three, Jump!" He jumped into the air and was gone. She sat down so that she could cry properly.

Gvant landed and whipped off the hood. He was standing on the paved forecourt of Castle Mnufort, the Baron-General's ancestral home, and his home for the years he had been bondson to the family. He could hear screaming from inside the house. He sprinted through the gateway and headed straight across the large inner yard, towards the keep where the family apartments were. As he galloped upstairs, he heard another scream. It was Lady Mnufort, the Baron's young wife. He drew sword and dagger and dashed into her suite, crossing the anterooms rooms swiftly as he headed towards her bedroom.

There were four armed men in the room. They had heard him coming and attacked as soon as he came through the door. A blade glanced off his mail, high on the chest. His sword skewered the attacker in the throat. He deflected a thrust from the left with his dagger and jumped hard to the right to avoid a downward slash by the third assailant. Yanking his sword out of the first man he parried another blow and stabbed with his dagger, catching one of them in the side of the chest. The man twisted away with a squeal, tearing the dagger out of his hand. Something clanged against his helmet. He took two fast steps back through the doorway. One man came at him head-on. A fatal mistake against Bdescu. He parried the man's thrust and in the same movement twisted his sword up and under the assailant's guard. He stabbed the attacker clean through the chest. Three down and the fourth backed away. Bdescu followed him into the room, moving fast before the man could reach the Baroness, who was lying on the bed.

As the man tried to put his knife blade against her throat, Bdescu's sword slid under his arm, alongside his chest and pierced his wrist. The man cried an oath and swung his free arm backward. Bdescu had already moved. As the arm's momentum spun the man around, Bdescu thrust forward. His blade went through the man's mail as if it had not been there, through his heart, through his shoulder blade and out through his back. He coughed once and died. Bdescu put his foot up onto the man's belly and hauled the sword out of his corpse.

He spun, expecting more men. Silence. He spoke to the Baroness without looking at her.

"My Lady Baroness. Are there any more, do you know?"

"I've only seen these four, my Lord Gvant."

He turned to her. She had been spread across the bed, her wrists and ankles tied with strong cords to the four corners. Her skirt had been pulled up around her chest. Her underwear was intact. He guessed that he had arrived in time. He cut her free, rearranged her clothing and sat beside her, rubbing her sore wrists. She was two years younger than Bdescu and one of the loveliest women he had ever seen.

"Where are the girls, my Lady?"

"They are at Bdescu Hall I hope, sir. When I started having trouble, I sent them over into the care of your sister in law. I sent my two most reliable men with them. The servants were due back last night. They did not arrive, so God knows whether they had trouble going there or coming back. I am at my wits' end. Oh God, Gvant, my Lord. We all thought you were dead. It's so good to see your face!" He hugged her gently, his mind racing.

"Dlaria. We must be strong. How did those men get in here and who is in the house that I can trust?"

"I think they are friends of my butler, Nmadler. He let them in. They've been lurking around the grounds for a few days, my maid saw them. She says she saw Nmadler talking to them. She was afraid, she thought they were bandits. I asked Dbelvio, the second butler, to see if he could raise help from the village. Next thing I know they're bursting into my room, grabbing me and demanding all my jewellery."

"I dare not leave you alone. I do not know who to trust. You must follow me, watch our backs and shout if anyone appears behind us. If I hold up my hand like this, you stop dead and stay silent. If I wave like this, we move. If I point left or right, we turn that corner... Can you do that?"

She nodded, eyes wide with fright. He checked that all four assailants were dead. His martial skills were as lethal as ever, for none lived. He retrieved the dagger and cleaned both blades on the clothing of one of his dead assailants. The rich bedroom carpet was splashed with blood, as were the bedclothes and drapes. They moved out onto the landing. He raised his hand in the halt sign and peered downstairs. Nothing moved. He waved them onward. They padded silently down, seeing nothing. He headed for the servants' quarters in the rear.

As he eased open the kitchen door, he saw two men with their backs to him. Each had one of the Baron-General's swords in his fist. The other slaves and freemen were sitting on the floor looking terrified. Before anyone could react, Bdescu's sword took one man through the back of his neck. Simultaneously his dagger sank into the neck of the other. Both men fell to the floor, choking out their final breaths. From behind him and with considerable coolness, Lady Mnufort said,

"Staff of Castle Mnufort, may I introduce the Seventh Baron Bdescu of Bdescu and Baron Mnufort of this House? I recommend that you do as he says."

There was a gasp as staff began to recognise him. The titles began to sink into their minds. The former bondson was now the Baron, the Baroness his concubine. They all remembered the grim and stern second-son of Bdescu. Standing there in his magnificent battle panoply with a blade dripping blood in each hand, he was an unforgettable sight.

"Who are these men?"

One of the kitchen maids spoke first. "Nmadler and Dbelvio, my Lord Baron."

"Are there any more people, men or women, in this house who wish harm on my Lady or her kin?"

He looked intently at Dlaria's maid. The maid's eyes looked to the right, Bdescu's left. He walked over to the man she had indicated and stared at him. His forehead had two tattoos, an old blurred slave tattoo and a very fresh Freeman mark. Bdescu did not recognise the short but muscular fellow. He must have arrived in the household after the Baron-General had left to go to war.

"Name and Rank?"

"Freeman Dboltu, my Lord."

"Dboltu, why are you hiding a dagger under your shirt?"

The man flinched. "I'm not, my Lord!" he cried.

Bdescu lifted the wet blade of his sword. With the very tip of the blade he lifted the loose hem of Dboltu's shirt. The staff saw the hilt of a long knife in a narrow sheath. Bdescu lifted the blade and placed it against the man's throat.

Before anyone could react, Dlaria stepped forward to Dboltu's side and swiftly yanked the dagger out of its sheath. She stepped back quickly. Bdescu smiled, but with only his teeth. This Lady thought quickly and had courage. She held the dagger up in front of Bdescu's face so that he would not need to take his eye off Dboltu.

"House Vrabelm dagger," Bdescu confirmed. He stepped back. Dboltu relaxed. Bdescu sprang forward and thrust the sword straight through Dboltu's chest, the fatal heart and lung thrust taught by every fencing master. The freeman gave a hard gasp, the last free air he would ever draw in. He fell to the ground. His last gasps were mainly blood. Bdescu ignored him and watched the staff. Every face showed relief and Bdescu knew that the first phase was over. Now they must come to his side.

"You two, kitchen porters. Yes, you!" Take this body outside, and those two over there by the doors. Then go to My Lady's chambers. Remove the four corpses you'll find there." The staff gave an audible gasp.

"Build a large bonfire at the far side of the front terrace. Pile the timber to the height of your heads. Plenty of kindling to be sure she burns fast. Then put all seven corpses on the bonfire. Light is as soon as it goes dark, not before. Now, repeat my instructions. Together."

The lads haltingly stammered out a fair rendition of their instructions. He dismissed them. They almost ran out of the room. Once in the hall, they really did run.

"You two house porters. Once the corpses have been taken outside, take up the rug in My Lady's bed chamber. Put it on the bonfire, go!" These men also left hastily.

"Lady's maid! Take three other maids. Once the rug is gone, clean My Lady's floor. Send any bloodstained fabrics to the bonfire. Once clean, remove all her clothing, personal effects and ornaments and move them into my suite. I hope my suite is clean and available?"

The maid nodded vigorously. "Yes Sir! My Lady said we were to act as if the Baron-General and you'd come home at any time of the day or night!"

Bdescu reeled off a long list of instructions. Dlaria listened with rapt attention. He organised a full lock down of the castle, watchmen on the walls and patrol patterns. He threatened murder to any man found sleeping at his post. Nobody doubted the sincerity of this scarred killer who was now the Master. He set cooks to producing a hot meal for the gentry, hot soup for the sentries to be provided now, and hot drinks every bell throughout the night and a hearty meal for all the staff. He forgot nothing and every person was set to work. Finally he wound down.

"Members of House Mnufort. I returned from the wars to find chaos. I have had to restore order with violence. We seem to be facing a threat from Clan Vrabelm. Pdense and Jcluid Vrabelm were both killed in the war. I do not know who owns House Vrabelm now. When their agents fail to report, because I have slain them all, Vrabelm will try to find out our status. Therefore I require vigilance from you. Look out for strangers and advise me at once, no matter how innocent or needy they might appear. Even children can be used as spies. Tell everyone you meet that Gvant, Seventh Baron Bdescu has said these words: 'I am in residence. I am in control. And I am in a killing mood.' That should check them, until they find out how few trained men we have. I will fix that as my first priority. Questions?"

The silence was complete. Bdescu spoke once more. "To work!" They set to with speed.

He led Dlaria to the fireside in the sitting room. He opened a fine bottle of Mnufort wine and poured her a glass. He raised his glass. "To the brave Lady Dlaria!" She smiled.

Sitting together on a couch, she seemed perfectly relaxed.

"So, Master, I am to move into your suite, am I?"

He laughed. "I am afraid so, My Lady. If not, the staff will gossip. Your status will not be clearly defined. Then they will think I might cast you off. 'Perhaps he has another wife?' They'll say. They will not give you proper respect. But if they think I am assuming full rights over you, then they will quickly settle. Staff need their gentry to be clear, direct and proper. Then we can expect them to behave in the same way. We keep to the Rules, we expect the same of them. I give you my word that I will never force my attentions on you. I am not a rapist. I take no pleasure from unwilling women. You may choose to sleep in whichever room you please. Just make sure the staff think you are in my bed and all will be well."

She smiled at him. Her lashes were long and fine. Her hair was dark brown, thick and curly as it fell halfway down her back. She looked young, fresh and beautiful. She spoke carefully

"Gvant, when you walked into my room I felt like a thousand weights had been taken off my back. The fear melted away. Your coming home is the best thing I could ever imagine. I have known you ever since Pdoverin bought me for a wife. You have always been a perfect Gentleman. I trust you. I am sorry that Pdoverin died and I will mourn him. I never expected to run this estate on my own and I have really struggled. We were short of Freemen so I took on Dboltu. I did not know he was an agent. I failed and I'm sorry."

Bdescu waved a hand. "You did well. Mistakes are just that, errors. So long as we learn from them, we progress. We do our best, that is all that the Rules expect of us. What God expects too, I imagine. So let's take a break and catch up with one another. I will need to show my ugly face on the battlements. They need to realise what I'm like, what I expect. Try not to be alarmed if I see to my duties at odd hours."

She nodded. "Oh, I remember you doing that. That's why the General's men were so damned good at soldiering. 'Cos the scary Bdescu was watching them!" She moved closer to him and started to tell him about life alone on Mnufort Estate. He told her a brief version of the war, leaving out far more than he told. When he looked out, it was dark.

"Now, where's my fucking bonfire?" He muttered.

Dlaria smiled. "Gvant. Go and keep us safe. I'll get ready for bed, the chambers should be ready by now."

He smiled and strode off. She hugged herself and chuckled. The bad days were over, as far as Dlaria Mnufort was concerned. Then she frowned. The girls were still missing. Perhaps the new Baron could save them.

Stragglers

Bdescu awoke at dawn. Dlaria was asleep, her hair spread across his chest. She had been in his bed when he returned from sentry inspection. She had wanted him and he had need of some comfort too. She was not Summer but he never expected to see Summer again, so he could tell himself that seeking respite in the arms of his former Bond Mother was just a nobleman doing his duty. Hypocrisy did not come naturally to Bdescu and the deed itched in his mind. She smelled wonderful, a deep scent of sex, sweat and clean woman that was tremendously arousing. Judging by her passionate responses during lovemaking, he must have learned a lot about sex from Summer. He washed and dressed silently then rang the bell and kissed her awake. The chambermaid appeared so fast that she must have been waiting outside the door. He'd put the fear of Holy God into the staff.

The chambermaid saw her mistress in her Lord's bed, tousled and sleepy. The slave beamed. "May I help you bathe and dress, My Lady?"

Dlaria nodded and smiled at Bdescu. Now all the staff would know that her status as My Lord's concubine was assured.

Bdescu had already washed and dressed so he left the ladies to the tricky business of dressing and walked off to the battlements for morning inspection. As he reached the stairs he heard a warning shout. He knew the sentries were following orders to the letter as he dashed up the stairs. "Armed men approaching! Armed men approaching!"

On that brilliant sunny dawn the sun was still behind the trees but the light was enough to see a straggling column heading up the West Drive. He squinted into the half light. The column seemed to be dressed as soldiers, right enough. Many seemed to be in carts. With sudden insight he started to laugh. He clapped a sentry on the back. "Friends! Open the gates! You, go and get the kitchens up to full speed. These men will be hungry!" He dashed down the stairs two at a time, ran out of the keep with two men at his heels and they started to crank open the gates and raise the portcullis. Bdescu was laughing aloud. His enthusiasm infected the men, who grinned too. Once all was open, Bdescu set off along the drive. They could not keep up with him.

The bearded, grizzled but youngish veteran at the head of the column looked at the man dashing towards him. His face split into a wide grin as he rushed forward too. He met the onrushing Bdescu after thirty paces and to his amazement the Lord grabbed him in a bear hug and lifted him off the ground.

"Fenjent! By the Living Breathing God Above, I am pleased to see you! How the hell did you get here?"

Fenjent explained that the Byekiy had helped the Blenvan people to reclaim their city. They had somehow cleared the hole in the city wall of all the rock that Bdescu had put there. They had once again built a bridge in apparent silence. This time they had flooded the city with legionnaires. Fenjent's men were taken by surprise and overrun with almost no loss of life. Then he described the Byekiy leader, who Bdescu could see was obviously Storm, the Fifth of Five. She had ordered Fenjent to return at once to Mnufort Estate. She had given his people wagons and food. They had marched home unmolested by the Blenvan or the Byekiy. He apologised, tears in his eyes, at his utter failure to hold the city.

By the time all this was explained they were at the castle. Dlaria greeted the column at the gate. She looked beautiful in a blue gown and white shoes, her hair caught in a complex twist.

Bdescu called to the men of the column, who were gathering in the courtyard.

"As Bond-Son of Mnufort I have inherited his lands. I am now your Lord. I have also inherited Bdescu, although I have yet to invest that property. I arrived from the wars yesterday. This lady is Dlaria Mnufort, the Baron-General's widow and now my concubine. You will afford her full courtesy of Rank at all times. My Lady."

She stepped forward. "Men of Mnufort. Ladies, lads and lasses too. Welcome home. My staff are ready to help you. First we'll get you all a decent homecoming drink. Water first, then a glass of good wine to welcome you. Fruit juices or milk for younger ones. Wounded men and those with older injuries will eat first, along with any children and wives. The able bodied should see to their carts. Hand your mounts over to my grooms in the stables under the South Walls, then get washed in the troughs. After eating, get the wounded and injured to the infirmary where my physician and nurses will care for you. Mums and Dads with kids will be found rooms. Single men to the barracks under the West Wall. If you need anything, find me, any member of the staff will bring you to me. I hand you back to the Master, My Lord Baron, now."

Fenjent led a cheer for the Lady. Then all the able-bodied men fell to their knees and swore loyal service to the New Baron and his Lady. The wounded and injured repeated the oath if able.

Bdescu and Dlaria spent a busy day helping their new garrison to eat, be treated, be briefed and billeted. In the late afternoon they brought Fenjent into their private sitting room. Fenjent, looking younger with a wash and shave, and astonished to be so singled out, was a little quiet at first. A glass of superb Mnufort wine, a snack and their encouragement worked magic on the Trusted Man. He soon opened up. He told the story in a clipped soldier's report. Bdescu knew how easily the Byekiy would have overrun the garrison, and waved aside Fenjent's apologies. Reading between the lines, Bdescu heard a story of a young man's stoic attention to duty. Their passage through Blenvan lands had been protected. But on entering Empire lands, hell had broken loose. Anarchy seemed to prevail throughout the Empire. They had endured dust storms, famines, starvation, thirst, bandit attacks, mudslides and flooding. Not one wounded man had died or been left behind. Nor had any man deserted. Fenjent passed Bdescu his list of people, which was present and correct.

Dlaria could see it too. "Freeman Fenjent, you protected the women and children perfectly. Every woman from the baggage train was praising you. The kids all love you. One of them showed me the whistle you made for him. My personal thanks for saving our people." Her eyes were brimming with tears.

Bdescu spoke suddenly. "Both of you, please follow me. They are all outside learning of their billet arrangements. This is a good time to speak to them all."

Baffled, Dlaria and Fenjent followed the Master. Once outside, all the people in the courtyard of the castle stopped speaking. In the hush, Bdescu climbed onto the back of a wagon.

"People of Mnufort. I am happy to see you all. Tell me, who led you here?"

With one voice they all called Fenjent's name.

"So it was that Fenjent followed his duty and brought you home to our care. I made him a Trusted Man. Was I right to do so?"

"Yes, My Lord!" They bellowed approval.

"Fenjent, climb up here." Fenjent complied, looking very concerned.

"On your knees, Fenjent." Bdescu drew his sword, now sparkling clean. "By Rule and by Right I call Advancement on this man. I call this for devotion to duty. I call this for self-sacrifice. I call this for recognised contribution to the welfare of this House and its people."

He placed a hand on Fenjent's head. He drew his sword and raised it vertically above his own shoulder. He spoke in his old fashioned High Tongue.

"On this day I Rank you Knight. I give you Family Name of Fenjent Bdescu of House Bdescu. I give you Position of Guard Captain, House Mnufort. In the eyes of all the Clan, I take your oath."

He led Fenjent through the oath and stood him up. He hugged him and made his own Oath of friendship and loyalty. The crowd cheered madly, waving, shouting, whistling and whooping. Fenjent followed him to the family chambers as the crowd of retainers went happily to their billets.

Dlaria sent for a Knight's uniform from stores, guessing his size with perfect accuracy. She had dressed hundreds of men for the Baron-General. Once the gear arrived, they left Fenjent to dress in private. Once he had finished, he joined Bdescu in the Briefing Room. Bdescu patted him on the back, told him he looked great in his new surcoat, and drew out maps. As they discussed the availability of skilled troops, the likely direction of threats and the best ways to counter them, Fenjent began to relax. Bdescu was not a man to make a fuss of anything, Fenjent learned. Bdescu cared about Duty. Fenjent had always admired him. Being a Knight under him would mean a new career and status. He felt breathless at the prospect and almost forgot something.

"Oh, Sir?"

Bdescu smiled "what is it, Sir Knight?"

"The Byekiy don't have any use for money, but as you recall, the Blenvan do. And we had their treasury to protect. The Blenvan searched us for the contents of their treasury, of course. They found most of it."

"Most of it?" Bdescu asked, eyes widening.

Fenjent chuckled, and led Bdescu out into the coach house. There was nobody around. Fenjent picked up a handy crowbar and levered open the bed of the longest wagon. Laid out in the low space were twenty long cloths twisted into dozens of small disc shapes. Each cloth had been pulled taught and nailed down at each end so that they would not move. Fenjent tore one free and held it up, over the cart's bed. As the cloth untwisted there came a shower of bright gold coins. Fenjent grinned. "Yes my Lord. They only found most of it."

Bdescu laughed delightedly. "My man, I think this calls for another drink. Let's get these little darlings into the Treasury. Oh, and I will record one coin in every eight as being yours. That's the Rule for treasure trove. Independent wealth and a new Rank. You're having quite a day, aren't you?"

Fenjent spoke with conviction. "The best part, My Lord, was seeing you running towards me."

Bdescu was filled with purpose now that he had invested and secured Mnufort for Dlaria and himself. His Duty now was to make sure that the Baron-General's children were safe and well. That meant tackling whatever problems had arisen at Bdescu Castle in these lawless times. Nobles preying on helpless widows was a new and unspeakable trend to Bdescu's mind. The old Emperor would never have allowed these atrocities. The young Emperor must be told of these sacrileges, and soon.

The Baron-General had four daughters. The elder two were by his first wife, now dead. She had died giving birth to a still born son. So the Baron-General had married Dlaria, still hoping to sire a boy. Two more daughters were his reward. The elder two were of marriageable age, nineteen and seventeen. The younger, Dlaria's daughters, were seven and five years of age. Bdescu knew all the children well. He worried constantly about their safety, their mother's concern and his Duty to their dead father.

He blew out a long breath. "Right, Fenjent. Once again I leave you in charge of all I have. You have proven yourself. Give me a dozen of your most reliable men at arms and we will head straight for Castle Bdescu. It will take all day so we will leave at dawn. Provisions for two days in case of delays. Bedrolls and rain cloaks, full weaponry. With luck and a benevolent God, I'll be back here in eight days. If all is well, expect a messenger by the fourth day. If you do not hear from me, lock down the castle, protect my people and wait for me to come back or send word. Send scouts if you hear nothing but proceed with caution. You know the strategy so don't follow me into disaster. Do not reinforce my failure."

Fenjent nodded. "Thanks My Lord. I will do as you instruct. On behalf of every man, woman and child in this House, I wish you success and a speedy return."

They shook hands and Bdescu left to pack his gear and find a suitable mount. He packed a grappling iron masked with strips of cloth and a strong rope long enough for the walls of his family home. He packed a back scabbard with straps to suit. Then he checked the sentries. All was in order. Fenjent's men were a close-knit community with real esprit de corps. He knew that the castle was in safe hands.

He arrived at his quarters to find a small table set with cold cuts, salads and bread. A bottle of wine and two goblets stood ready. Dlaria was still wearing her smart dress but had released her hair. This made her look younger, fresher. He smiled and sat down. She served him food and wine, then sat down and waited for him to speak first.

"I must see that your daughters are safe. We have heard nothing from Castle Bdescu so I leave at dawn with a dozen guards. We will reconnoitre the castle. If all is well I will make contact with my sister in law and see what's amiss. After that I must improvise. God knows what we'll find."

Dlaria stared at him. "Gvant, please be careful. I've already come to rely on you. I'm three quarters in love with you, too. I know you'll not pass a Duty onto another man. But that doesn't mean you can't delegate a few of the riskier jobs. These men will die for you. We all need you, so don't get yourself killed. Please?"

He nodded. The two of them retired early and their lovemaking was wilder and more uninhibited than the first time around. She held him tightly as she fell asleep. He stroked her back and wondered, for the hundredth time, what was happening in far-away Byekvoranp.

My Brother's House

In a misty autumnal morning, Bdescu and his small band saddled up and moved out. A couple of women waved sadly to their men. Dlaria stood amongst them, waving like any ordinary wife. She comforted one of the women, who wept on her shoulder. Bdescu looked back at her and called confidently.

"My Lady Dlaria. The Castle is yours. Fenjent and his men will protect you all. Look for me an eight-day from now. May God bless you all!" She blew him a kiss and he cantered off, his men waving and forming a close order behind him.

He kept to the main roads, which were in a very poor state. He suspected no maintenance had occurred since he had left. Dlaria had paid people to do the Estate's maintenance, but the thieving wastrels had not done the work. That was a problem for another day. By midday his troop had reached the edge of the Mnufort estate. They had seen, and avoided, four groups of armed men. These vagabonds were living off the forest game, poaching from Mnufort herds. Raiding farms too, he guessed. There had clearly been a major breakdown in law and order since he'd left for the war. At the edge of Bdescu land they left the main road and struck off through forest paths which Bdescu had known since boyhood. He led them unerringly towards the Castle. As the light began to fade, he motioned his troop to halt and conferred with their leader.

"Keep the men here and the mounts quiet. There's a hill ahead from which I can see the house. If you hear the opening bars of the Mnufort House Anthem, follow me. If I see anything off key, I'll come back and we'll make a plan."

"Yes My Lord." The old soldier grinned at him. "Just like old times, eh My Lord Colonel?"

Bdescu smiled back. "If anyone has harmed any one of my kin, they'll wish I had died in the fucking war." Without a rustle in the thick undergrowth, he was gone.

Bdescu made his silent way forward. After the experience at Mnufort, he was on edge. He sweated as he moved silently up the ridge. The earthy smell of leaf mould and undergrowth rose as he moved. A slight mist was arising in the autumn dusk, but Bdescu needed no vision to navigate this close to home. Close to the summit he dropped into a crawl. He raised his head between two clumps of grass. Sitting right in front of him was a sentry. The man had long grey hair caught in a braid. His tunic was dirty but his weapons were bright and laid on the beaten grass at his side. Bdescu could smell his unwashed body and clothes as well as the freshly trampled grass. The man was awake and alert. But to Bdescu's utter disdain he was facing the wrong way. He faced the south wall of the Castle instead of watching the woods. All sentries become lazy when on watch for too long. The sentry heard the sound of Bdescu's sword slicing through the air. It was too late to stop it slicing clean through his neck, severing his head in one expert blow. The head thudded to the ground and rolled obscenely down the slope. Bdescu held his breath. He heard nothing.

He dare not whistle. He regained the troop. Their Master Sergeant looked at Bdescu's dripping sword, cocked his head and whispered, "how many My Lord?"

"One. A very poor sentry. We must find all of them. Leave none alive. You look doubtful..."

"I do not want to argue with you, My Lord."

"Speak, man. Any man may speak his mind to me. If I am wrong I need to know."

"Sire, should we not take a prisoner? Then we could find out their strength. Make a better plan? Jus' an idea, Sire."

Bdescu was tempted but declined. "Killing can be silent. Capture never is. One sound and we could all get killed. No. Kill all you find as quietly as possible. We must act now, before darkness hides them. You take half the men and go left. I take the other half and go right. The forest surrounds the property on all sides. The sentry was on the edge of the forest. He was a criminal not a soldier, so with luck these are brigands. Keep under cover. Find them, kill them and meet me on the other side of the house. And God be with you and your men."

Bdescu and his six troops crept through the forest edge, eyes searching in the failing light. One of the men carried Bdescu's saddle bags, with strict instructions not to help with the killing, just to keep the bag and move silently. After a hundred paces or so, they found a pair of sentries sitting around a camp fire and chatting amiably in Low Tongue. Bdescu would have liked to listen for a while, but time was not on his side. He patted two men on their shoulders and indicated that they should take the left-hand sentry. He patted his own chest and pointed to the right. He motioned for the rest to hold station. He and his two assassins crept closer to the two sentries. His men moved first, Bdescu an instant behind. He drove forward on the balls of his feet and dived onto the sentry from the back, forcing his head down onto his chest and stifling him from screaming out. He stabbed out hard with the dagger, scraping through muscles and ribs, feeling for the heart. Once he found it he tore the dagger left and right, until the man flopped lifeless. He almost toppled over him. Regaining his balance he looked left. The two men had cut their man's throat. They had hands over his mouth while he died. Perfectly done. Fenjent had chosen well.

The next sentry died alone. Bdescu let two of the others handle it. Again they did well, with the throat cut and hold tactic. They pressed on until Bdescu judged them half way around the house. There were no further sentry posts. After a few beats the Master Sergeant led his men to them. He shook hands with the officer and nodded to the men. In a low voice me murmured the next step.

"I will go over the wall. I will open the door from inside. Get into position directly opposite the door. When I open it, walk calmly across and enter. Do not run. Do not appear stealthy. Anyone seeing movement in the dark will not know who you are. Until it is time for them to die. Questions?"

Not one man spoke. They all made the Sign of God's Blessing. He had almost forgotten the Blessing. Comforted, he made the Sign back at them, picked up his saddle bags and vanished into the gloom. Reaching the wall without any sound of an alarm, he unpacked the grapnel hook and rope. He knew exactly how to do this. He had used this method to get in and out of the castle when he was a teenager. His father had often confined him to quarters but never checked that he was actually there. He had spent many a pleasant evening in the town when his family thought him upstairs asleep. He flung the hook high into the air. It caught in the back of a castellation. He tested its hold, then hand over hand on the rope he walked up the wall. When he reached the top he caught hold of the parapet and climbed over, hardly breathing. The battlements were deserted. Not a sound, not a movement. He hauled up the rope and hid it in a storm drain. Sword sheathed on his back, he moved silently across the walkway atop the battlement. At the edge of the staircase he paused. Still no sound. He moved downstairs, dagger in hand. The stone steps were worn uneven, but he knew every step. His senses were heightened. He stopped and took a few deep breaths, testing the air for the rank smell of the unwashed bandit. Nothing but the castle's own smell of dust, stone and animal dung. He moved around the wall, keeping in shadow. A dark shape was walking across the courtyard. He froze. It was a woman. She carried a basket of bread and walked as if injured. He ghosted behind her. He put his hand over her mouth and whispered in her ear.

"Name and Rank? Speak quietly when I release my hand. Or you will surely die here."

"Slave Jclelleh. Please don't hurt me. I already did it for your leader. I can't do any more sexing, I beg you!"

He knew Jclelleh, she had been his brother's chambermaid. He drew her quietly into the shadow of the wall.

"Jclelleh, I am Bdescu, now Baron Bdescu. Gvant, of this House." She gasped. He quickly covered her mouth.

"How many brigands hold my House?"

"Twenty-one. My Lord. They raped us. Us slaves I mean. Killed all the male servants. Then they've had a party. Drank lots of wine. Sent me out for bread."

His heart sank. "And Milady Bdescu? The girls?"

"Nobody knows, My Lord. Not allowed in the Keep."

"Good lass. Keep hold of that bread but follow me to the main doors."

Unchallenged, he unlocked and opened the main gate. His men strolled across the open space from the woods. Their nonchalant walk was a masterpiece of control. These men would form his training cadre, while he built up his forces to restore law to the realm. They gathered just inside the gate, which they closed and locked behind them. He had Jclelleh describe the scene they would find inside the main hall of Castle Bdescu. She described the men, their weapons and how they had been seated when she had left the room. Bdescu asked her to deliver the bread, as she had been ordered.

She walked in her sore, awkward way up the steps to the door of the main banqueting hall. She opened the door and light flooded out. As she stepped into the room, a hairy man took a swipe at her. "You've been to fucking long, slave! I know what you need! Come he-"

His voice was cut off by a soldier's axe landing backhanded in his throat. Bdescu and his men charged into the hall. Shouting, the brigands leapt to their feet. As they drew swords, knives or clubs, the Imperial troops cut them down. Bdescu was counting in his head. Nine sentries dead. One killed on entry. Ten more men died in the hall. One was missing.

"Are any still alive?" he asked, panting.

"This one's bad, but he's breathing." Bdescu walked over to the wounded brigand.

"Where is the last man? I know there are twenty-one of you. Speak and I will ask my men to treat your wound and spare your life. Refuse and die here. Bleed to death, nice and slow. Choose once. Choose now."

The man started to gabble, desperate to live. "The Boss is in the Keep. He's fucking the Ice Queen. She don't like it so he threatens to do the little girls. He says if she does him nicely, he'll keep the young 'uns safe and sell 'em as virgins. If she doesn't please him, he'll fuck 'em all and make her watch it happen."

Bdescu looked down at the squirming man. "I keep my word. One man stay here and bandage him up. Do all you can to save his life." It mattered little. The man died a few instants later.

Bdescu jerked his head and the rest of the troop followed him outside. Once in front of the Keep, Bdescu motioned for them to wait. He started to climb up the wall of the Keep. He had done this as a boy too, for a dare of his brother's. Using footholds he had almost forgotten and hand holds he had to find by touch, the Baron inched up the sheer face of his own Keep. The soldiers watched, half enchanted and half terrified. Terror took the upper hand as he climbed higher and higher. Finally, they lost sight of him in the wall's shadow. They waited for the awful sound of his falling body. After a while they began to believe that he had made it.

Then the door of the Keep opened with a loud groaning sound. Light spilled out, illuminating a bright hall within. A man staggered out. He was covered in blood. Dozens of shallow cuts lined his body. He screamed, a ragged sound. Bdescu walked out behind him. He called to his men.

"Kill this thing. Shallow cuts, one each. Make him hurt. Let him bleed out."

Bdescu went back inside and the troops vented their recent fear on the bleeding villain. He died slowly and in great pain.

Bdescu appeared at the door and waved them all inside. The staff were all in the main hall of the keep. They were all female and in poor shape after seven days of brutal treatment. Rapes, beatings and worse had been happening to all of them, old and young alike. His troops moved in to assist. Wounds were washed and bandaged. Bdescu went into a room at the back. He emerged leading a woman. She was around the same age as Bdescu. She had been badly abused. Her face was covered in contusions. Her hair had been hacked off in chunks. She had suffered a bite on her upper arm and walked stiffly. All the men knew why she walked that way.

But Milady Bdescu of House Bdescu was an aristocrat. She stood upright and smiled at her rescuers with dignity. She spoke High Tongue with native grace, hissing slightly through her swollen lips.

"The Houses of Bdescu and Mnufort have been friends and allies since our great-grandfathers' day. On our day of greatest need we are proud and grateful that you came to free us. My Lord and Father-in-Law gave his second son in Bond to Mnufort. Now that son is Baron of both our Houses. Once we were friends. Now we are one family. As members of this family I bid you welcome. To house, hearth, home I bid you welcome. Those of my staff who are fit to work will prepare a meal for us all. We will eat together, safe here in the Keep. Now please excuse me as a poor hostess. I must confer with my new Lord Baron."

The soldiers murmured their thanks and Lady Bdescu walked steadily out with the Baron. Once alone in a small sitting room she started to cry. Bdescu put his arm around her. He said nothing. What can a man say to his sister in law when she has been so abused? He resorted to direct action, his default.

"My lady, where are your daughters?"

She shook her lovely bruised head sadly. "Dead. I am sure they killed them. Oh, they threatened me that they'd rape them in front of me. But they never once produced a single girl. No. I think they killed them in the first horrible day."

Bdescu jumped up. "My Lady. I will search the castle first. Just to make sure. For your sake. For those we have both lost, such as husbands. Brothers. Friends." He charged out, leaving the poor woman sobbing.

Bdescu stopped in the hall. A dozen people clamoured for his attention. He shook them off gently, ordering them to form a line and get his Master Sergeant to make these decisions. He headed towards the cellar stairs. Castle Bdescu had no cells. If he'd wanted someone kept against their will, he'd put them in the wine cellars. He unlocked the door under the main staircase. The ancient hardwood groaned as he forced it open. Inside it was cold and pitch dark. He groped for a torch in the sconce on the wall just inside the door. He lit it from a burning candle in the hallway and returned to the cellar door. Holding the torch in his left hand and his naked sword in his right, he carefully made his way down the steep stone steps until he was firmly standing on the rammed earth floor, deep below the Keep.

He moved slowly. There was always a chance that Jclelleh had miscounted or just not seen one or more of the brigands. He painstakingly searched the cellars. Right at the back there was a heavy door that led to the best wines. It was always kept locked to prevent pilfering. He had no keys, but the large old-fashioned key was in the lock. He turned it slowly but it squeaked loudly. He yanked the door open and barged into the room, torch high, sword low ready to gut an opponent. He was met by terrified screaming from seven scared girls.

He stepped back and sheathed sword. He bowed low.

"Young Ladies. I am Baron Gvant Bdescu. My nieces and Bond-Sisters, I salute you. I have retaken the castles that are your homes. Your mothers are alive. My Lady Bdescu has been sorely abused but is alive and desperate to see you all. My Lady Mnufort is unharmed. I have cleared both castles of invaders. All those men are now with God. We will let Him show them mercy, for we had none."

He spoke slowly and clearly, giving them time to adjust and to recognise him as their relative. He watched them. They all seemed unharmed, he could see no evidence of violence. Had the brigands been saving them for virgin sales? Or had someone else organised this mess with an even darker purpose? They started peppering him with questions, but he smiled and shook his head.

"No, my Ladies I beg of you. First we pay our respects to Lady Bdescu, who fears that you are dead. Now, have any of you been interfered with?" To his immense relief, they all said no. His heart soared. He led them upstairs to a rapturous reunion with Lady Bdescu. She hugged him, relief all over her face.

"Gvant, Gvant. You are a prince of men. Your brother was a good man and I loved him. But I swear he could never have dealt with this frightful situation. That took a true Lord. You are the Baron in every way. If I were not soiled goods I would be proud to be your concubine. I cannot ask you to share a bed with this poor ruined woman!"

He looked her squarely in the eye.

"My Lady. You are mine if you wish it. Not out of pity or Duty. But by right and by my will. You must remain the Lady of this House. We will rebuild it. All I ask is that you are by my side. I too am soiled goods, in a way. For instead of the wife I always envisioned, fate has granted me two concubines and their fair daughters. I cannot marry both so I can marry neither. I must own and run two households, sleep in two beds, bring up seven daughters, care for two households... I cannot do these things if you resent Dlaria, or she resent you. How say you? Will you be on my left hand?"

She nodded. "So you will treat the girls as daughters, as your children, not concubines? By rights you are perfectly entitled to fuck all nine of us, singly or collectively, if you so wish."

He grimaced. "These girls are either kin or bond kin to me. I do not want anyone to hate me, nor am I a child molester. They will be as my daughters. You may be my concubine in name only, if you do not wish my bed. I seek no unwilling bed mates, Nvuldera. If you wish it, we shall be as husband and wife. It is up to you. But in the name of God, please trust me with the safety and well being of your family and House. Now, I must attend to many duties before I sleep. Try to get the girls fed and off to bed. We have much to do tomorrow."

He rushed around arranging the household. First a huge bonfire was built downwind of the house, to burn more than twenty corpses. In autumn's humid warmth, the dead would soon rot and he feared the plague that would follow. He made sure that the injured were treated, the rape victims put amongst friends to support them and the bereaved comforted. He checked that all were fed, then he opened a case of good wine and ensured that all were given a goblet. He toasted their courage, fortitude and loyalty. He thanked them all for being House Bdescu through these hard times. He could feel the mood improving. He marvelled at his new skills in managing a household. Nvuldera stood at his side. She muttered in his ear.

"You were born to it, Gvant. And I thank God for that."

In the small hours, with his men fed and the servants made comfortable, Bdescu grabbed a couple of hours' sleep. He slept in his former bedroom, in the small bed that he'd left as a teenager to join Mnufort House. He found its familiarity oddly comforting. Nvuldera slept in her huge Baronial suite with all seven girls in her gigantic bed. Sentries paced the walls. Brigands burned on a funeral pyre. Bdescu was home at last.

Baronial Rule

Dlaria walked up the stairs and stood on the front watch area of the Keep as she had every day since the Baron had left her side. She could hardly credit how much she missed him after so short an acquaintance. She ached for him. Her belly turned like a leaping fish when she thought of him. She thought of him all the time. The sensation had become familiar. She dreamed of bearing him a son, a lovely hardy boy with his father's pride and strength. She hugged herself to think of it. Then her thoughts turned to her missing daughters and her heart sank.

She could see miles down the main road from here. She saw a rider coming. She ran down the stairs, heart pounding. Whatever had happened to the Baron, she must be the very first to know. Her saddled mount was held at the gate by a groom. She jumped onto a mounting stone and climbed onto her favourite mount. In seconds she was racing towards the messenger, hair flying out behind her. She gritted her teeth and muttered through them, "he's alive and well, my girls are alive and well..."

She pulled up as the messenger did. She recognised one of Fenjent's troop. He snapped a salute.

"Baron's greetings, My Lady!" She almost fainted, holding tightly to the wooden pommel of her saddle. He was alive.

"Baron says to tell you Castle Bdescu is took. Villains killed and bodies burned. Young ladies unharmed, all. Lady Bdescu not so good but alive and healing. Male servants all dead and females all abused criminally. Baron says lots to be done. He'll clear out any bandits, poachers or other ruffians from the lands first so the ladies can travel safely. Then he'll bring them here, My Lady. We are to expect him in three days. I'm to instruct Knight Fenjent to take half the soldiers, selected few male Freemen staff and male Slave staff to House Bdescu. That's to help Her Ladyship get the place back on its feet, Sire says. Fenjent will be Steward there in the Baron's absence. That ends my report, My Lady."

She could have kissed him. All her wishes had come true. The girls were well, her new man was coming home and her friend and neighbour, Nvuldera, would soon be here, also with unmolested daughters. She suspected that the home invasion had gone very badly for Nvuldera. Perhaps she could help. She felt a pang of jealousy at having to share Bdescu with the older woman. Maybe Nvuldera would never want sex with the Baron. Knowing his strong male attractiveness, she strongly doubted that it would work out that way. Nvuldera was a beautiful, elegant creature. Bdescu was bound to find her attractive. Dlaria shook her head. Enough of worry. She'd find a way to make it work. He'd find a way. She headed back, the messenger riding half a head behind her.

Fenjent and a large troop left at dawn the next day. She had selected a picked band of her steadiest serving men to help Lady Bdescu at the castle. She supervised their leaving and bade her newly-Advanced and devoted knight every success in this, his latest challenge. Fenjent was quiet and respectful as ever. He was still learning that he could speak freely in his new Rank.

"My Lady. Thank you. I know that the Baron gave me the Advancement. But I also know that he asked you first. Everyone says you spoke up for me. I am delighted to be a knight in this House, House Bdescu or anywhere else that you go. God bless you, My Lady."

His bow was clumsy but heartfelt. She patted his arm.

"Go, true man Knight. I know you love the Master as I do. Protect my liege lord and all his people. May God bless you too." She kissed his cheek. He blushed to the roots of his hair. But he rode away glowing with pride.

In the late afternoon of the third day, as promised, Bdescu and his troop rode up to the castle. Dlaria waited patiently outside. As soon as they came into sight she ran up the road. Her daughters and her older stepdaughters ran to her and mobbed her excitedly. She greeted Nvuldera with a hug and a kiss. She ran to Bdescu, who was dismounted and jumped into his arms, wrapping her legs around his body with a squeal. He hugged her and smiled.

"Pleased to see me, then?"

Dlaria spent a happy evening with her girls. They told her of the home invasion by the brigands and the awful things that had happened to the staff and Nvuldera. They ate in with her in the Baronial suite, to excited to sleep, too tired to do much except sit and chat. The eldest, her step-daughter Cberia, asked a slightly awkward question about her relationship with Bdescu. Dlaria decided to be frank.

"Well, he gave me the option. Separate quarters if I wanted. He's a gentleman, for all his apparent ferocity. He's only brutal to people who want to harm us. He was lovely to me, always kind and attentive. I was lonely. I hadn't seen your father in over a year. So I decided to move straight in with him. And I haven't regretted that decision, not for one instant. And now, after almost no time at all, I find myself completely in love with him. I never expected to feel this way again, but there you go. A lucky woman."

The younger girls were giggling at Mum for being soppy. The elder two smiled knowingly.

"Come on you lot! Bed time now!" She shepherded the girls off to their rooms, which were down the landing near her former suite. She'd talk to Gvant about them all being a little closer together. Tonight he had enough to be doing.

When he came to bed she asked him about the mission. He frowned.

"Dlaria, I am sick to my God-given bones of killing men. Why can't they leave us alone? Why must I defend my family every day? I have no desire to kill anybody. They invade my homes, violate my loved ones, kill my servants, try to steal what little gold I have left. How long has this lawlessness been going on? What in the world has happened while I was away?"

She looked pensive. "When you and Pdoverin went to war in the spring, the old Emperor passed away almost immediately. The young Prince became Emperor. The people say he's evil and that God hates him. As if to prove them right, there was a famine almost immediately. It had been a bad harvest the year before. The rich people's agents had bought all the grain during the winter. Come spring there was nothing to plant. Farm slaves and freemen were turned out and roamed around seeking work, dragging their whole families. The towns and villages turned newcomers away. People turned to robbery. Then the slave rebellions started and the Emperor had his soldiers roam the countryside. They took food without payment, raped girls and wives, caused havoc. I did alright here. We rationed food. I supervised it and my factors did the distribution. I kept enough grain to replant so our people were all well. I know Nvuldera did the same. We visited one another's Houses often, we supported one another. She is my best friend, really."

His look became even darker. "This is appalling. In hard times the nobility must keep order. Grain and dried fruits must be rationed, stores guarded. People being turned off the land just causes criminality. Why have they forgotten the very basics of Rule and Order?"

Still frowning, he motioned for her to continue.

"Well, as I said, we were doing well. The farms came through and the vineyards made enough cash to feed our folk. We all worked hard. Then one day I got a message from one of the Vrabelm clan. On the same day, Nvuldera did too. The letter said in so many words that things were going to get very dangerous for single women, especially widows, who owned land. So we'd better get married to one of their three sons or we'd be sorry. I wrote back saying I thanked them for the kind offer but I'd fulfil my mourning first and then make a decision. Nvuldera did something similar. Then they started raiding villages, burning farms and trying to drive our people off their land. I put out patrols with the few men I had. I relocated the burned-out villagers and sent money to rebuild houses. Then they ambushed the patrols and invaded our home. The rest you know." She smiled wanly.

"Are you completely sure that this is the work of Vrabelm House?"

"Yes. Their men boasted of it in every village. Their land adjoins both Mnufort and Bdescu Estates. They stand the most to gain by taking us over. I am sure of it, yes."

He nodded, his face distant. "God's thanks to you, we still have our Estates. I will never forget what you did for our people, My Lady. You behaved with true Nobility. You are perfectly fitted to your Rank. The whole estate could have been lost if you and Nvuldera had not been so determined and so brave. Thanks also to my newest knight, Sir Fenjent, we have a little spending money. They were too quick to rape and too slow to rob, so both treasuries are intact, although the famine and trouble has depleted our finances. The extra cash restores us to good health, thanks be to God. I must think on this. Our borders are too long to defend, even if we had plenty of men, which we do not. Vrabelm has few too. His knights were annihilated in Byekvoranp, and his freemen and slave soldiers are still there. That's why he's using criminals as agents of his filthy plans. That is also his stupidity. He might intimidate a few villagers and servants but he'll crumple in the face of proper military action. Who rules House Vrabelm?"

Still beaming from his compliments, she replied swiftly. "Gtarclu. He was Jcluid's younger brother. He's supposed to be a greedy, selfish sort of man."

Bdescu had briefly met Gtarclu, some years previously. He ground his teeth. "D'you see what I mean? We have a rich, powerful fool on our borders. Put there by the death of his brother, Pdense. Who I killed, by the way. This is why I am sick of it all. I kill a monster and his brother gets busy despoiling my lands behind my back. That's why there is no solution in killing. We need to get back to the rule of law. That's the Emperor's job. And if he's on Vrabelm's side, we really do have a problem. I will need to go and see His Majesty. I need to know where we stand in the wider picture. But I can't leave you alone with so much threat out there. I will not put you at risk again. For the very first time in my life, I don't know what to do!"

Dlaria took his hand. She led him over to the bed and stripped off his clothes. She motioned for him to lay face down. She fetched some oil, warmed it in her hands and knelt beside him. She rubbed his neck and back. She worked her way down his arms. She stood at his side and massaged his hands and fingers, down his legs and finally his feet. When he was completely relaxed, she blew out the candles, pulled the covers over him and slid into bed beside him. She cuddled up to him and whispered in his ear.

"Tomorrow is for problems. Tonight is for sleeping. Rest, Gvant. You're not a killer. You're not a machine. You're just a good man doing very well at a really tough job. You'll figure it out. We all love you. Especially me."

She kissed his cheek. He slept, soundlessly, until dawn.

He awoke early, as ever. He looked at Dlaria as she slept. Her face was serene, half smiling in her sleep. He realised that he had known her for years, ever since she had arrived as a teenage bride for Pdoverin Mnufort, his Bond-father. In all that time he had never seen her smile until these past few days. Life with Pdoverin had made her look worried and afraid. Now she bloomed. She shone with a radiant life that cheered his soul. His mind raced.

He remembered the staff at Castle Bdescu and how they had reacted to him. He remembered the relief and joy that Fenjent had shown when seeing him again. He recollected the fear and unhappiness he had felt in both Houses when he had retaken them and compared it to the jollity he could hear now. The kitchens bustled with happy clamour. The grooms whistled as they groomed the mounts. The soldiers told dirty jokes as they kept watch. They flirted with the maids who brought them hot drinks. That was a Bdescu innovation as well: a hot drink for sentries at every bell. The girls seemed not to mind, the soldiers loved it and he had stopped worrying about men being awake on watch.

In a few days he had made hundreds of people happy. Their happiness derived from the sense of safety that he had brought back into their daily lives. He lay on his back and thought hard. It was his role to do this. Not to slay enemies but to protect his people. His days of slaughter were over because now he had inherited his birthright. From this day on, he would build a peace for them all.

Dlaria came awake next to him. "Morning Gvant! Are you feeling better today? You were a bit down last night, you had me quite worried."

He grabbed her and rolled her up onto his chest. "Yes! I know what I have to do now. Thanks to you, I've realised what my mission is. Hah!"

She wriggled on his chest and smiled in his face. "See? Magic Massage, courtesy of Lady Dlaria Mnufort. Works like a charm."

He became serious. "By the way. I love you too. Will you marry me?"

She blinked away a few tears without noticing and hugged him. She nodded vigorously. "Yes. Yes. And yes again. We'll make a happy home here, Gvant. Just you see. The bad men won't stand a chance once you get organised. You've been here a few weeks and changed all our lives for the better. Holy God knows what you'll achieve in a whole year!"

It took them a long time to get out of bed. When they made it down for breakfast, still in their nightclothes, the maids giggled in the corridors. Sir and Lady were at it again, the gossip ran through the castle. The Head Cook summed up the feeling.

"Well, she's a lovely woman and God knows, he's a virile one, our Master. If I was in his bed, I'd never get up!"

Her assistant had a point of view, too. "If you ask me, we'll have a little Master running around before year end. The Mistress is young enough and healthy too. If he keeps up this bedroom action, she'll miss her next moon, sure as God's Mercy!"

Even the Head Cook, famous for arguing, could not dispute that one. She just wished she'd said it first.

The Seventh Baron Bdescu started on his plans immediately. Thanks to Byardil, Bdescu could read pretty well, but he'd never really bothered to learn to write, especially Noble High Cursive Script, which baffled many a scribe. He had seen Dlaria write many a letter for the Baron-General, so she became his scribe. He started with a set of objectives.

"These, my love, are the reasons for the plan. They answer the question 'why are we doing this particular action?' Then, when we plan an action, we test it. We ask if it actually helps us achieve an objective. If it does, we do it. If not... OK. Here's my list."

He dictated these:

1. Clear any brigands from the woods and fields of the two Estates;
2. Set up a warning system to protect homes in case of further incursions;
3. Arrange a way to respond to the warning system;
4. Repair, replace or repaint all the Estate's Boundary Marks; and
5. Secure supplies for winter, namely animals and crops.

"Five objectives is about right, is it?" Asked Dlaria.

"Yes. Three to five is best. More than five and you end up dropping a few through lack of resources."

"What resources?"

He laughed. "Damned good question, My Lady! Well, there's replenishable resources, like food, water or manpower. Then there are fixed resources, like time. Lose time and it's gone forever, as we both know. That's what happens if we try and do too many things, we'll run out of time, the winter will come and the roads will be too muddy to move fast. We'll bog down. So, we have around six weeks before that happens."

"Next, My Lord?"

"Action plan. That's got the following: what we will do; who will do it; what they'll need to do it; what might stop them; how we avoid or overcome that obstacle; and by when it needs to be finished."

"Gvant, where in God's Kingdom did you learn all this?" She seemed genuinely interested.

"Some I made up while I was soldiering. You get a hell of a lot of time doing nothing on campaign. I got bored, so I started making plans. Oh, they often don't work out. I just find it helps me to think things through before I try and do them, that's all. As I moved around I met other officers. Some of them had ideas too, so I stole them, quite shamelessly. Sometimes I'd spend days planning an advance or a campaign. Other times I'd make up a strategy whilst riding up to an opponent, based on the few things I could see before he lunged at me."

He thought hard. "Some officers laugh at the idea. They think that it's futile, because once you meet your enemy he will never act as you planned, so all plans have to be changed due to circumstances. That's all true. But the men still need to be fed. Mounts need grazing and watering. Weapons must be readied, armour serviced and latrines dug. So apart from the moment of battle, everything else does respond to planning, actually. Men rely on their officers. How can I expect a man to stand next to me, risk his life for me, if I forget to feed him?"

Dlaria nodded. "You know what? It makes me feel better too. Not because I have a plan. Because you are designing a better future. You make it up in your handsome head, then you go out and make it happen. I never once met a man who thinks like this or acts like this. That's why all your troops and staff love you. Because you create order. You have an iron self-control and you constantly try to impose that same control on the chaos that surrounds us."

"And, pretty Lady, is that why you love me?"

"Oh no." She grinned. "I just fancy your big muscular body, really."

Bdescu, smiling, got back to his planning and reflected on how relaxed he felt with her. Summer had made him feel aroused to an astonishing level. Not once had he felt a kinship with her. She had made him feel stimulated, challenged, but never relaxed. Dlaria cooled his temper, cleared his mind of the daily dross and made him feel at home. And, unlike Summer, she could give him babies too.

The very next morning he started work. Soldiers were mounted and sent out with messages to Castle Bdescu. He explained the plans to Fenjent and asked him bring the Lady and a troop of his best men, to meet him at a village on the edge of the Bdescu Estate in twenty days. Then he set off with a small troop of his own best men and Dlaria. He visited the villages. He met their headmen and gave gifts of wine and cured meats. He asked farmers to present their biggest, strongest field slaves to him. He asked each farm-slave if he wanted to become a slave-soldier. This alarmed the headmen until Bdescu showed them a gold coin, which brought back their smiles. Most of the field slaves, whose lives were very harsh, immediately took up his offer. He paid the farmers fair prices and handed his new recruits over to his Freeman-Sergeants for training.

He heard the villagers' grumbles, took census of their people, animals and grain stores. He set men to update the maps. He set others to fixing all the boundary marks, so that no man could enter his lands without seeing the Mnufort arms and a warning sign; a blooded sword. He judged disputes with honesty and fairness. His awards were fair and his judgments tended to leniency.

He judged a few criminal cases too. One he thought was nonsense and had to have a private word with the headman. The headman agreed to quash the case, release the prisoner and stop wasting Baronial time. The other was a ghastly murder case. A man had slaughtered a family by burning down their house. Six dead children and a father. The mother had escaped by pure luck, but had then been badly burned trying to rescue her loved ones. Her testimony was very moving and the crowd in the headman's hall were braying for vengeance against the young man who was accused. Bdescu spent a long, harrowing day hearing the evidence. He adjourned in the early evening.

Bdescu never imposed himself on his tenants. He brought tents for himself and his men. He slept on the ground, as his soldiers did. He had not wanted Dlaria to sleep on the cold hard ground, but she had insisted on coming. She packed a slim rolled-up mattress made of coarse linen packed with wool and cross-stitched to keep its shape. She had stitched together several warm soft blankets to make a kind of envelope that was closed on three sides and open at the top. She spread this out in his tent, slid inside and Bdescu followed her in. She rubbed up against him and asked what he thought of her arrangements.

"Dlaria, I swear I have never been so comfortable or so warm on a campaign. The sewn-up blankets are pure genius! No drafts, they don't slide off, they're amazing! And the thin mattress works too. Could we get the staff to make these for all our men? A man who sleeps well is always a better soldier, that's for sure. We'll call them the Dlaria Dozers!"

She was thrilled. "I know you're kidding about the name. But if you think these are a good idea, then I'll get the staff working on it, yes. I'm so flattered you like it. I only did it for my own comfort."

He nodded. "That's how we'll win them over, my darling. What's good for us is good for them. When people see that, they begin to trust us. We are rulers but we must not take advantage. We must BE their advantage!"

After some very quiet lovemaking so as not to disturb the sentries, they slept. She found this newly-motivated Baron quite breathtaking. And her moon was three days overdue.

In the morning he decided that the culprit was in fact guilty. In the middle of the village green he had a vicar say the Prayer for the End of This Life over the man's bowed head. Once the prayer was over, Bdescu cut off the man's head with a single swipe of a borrowed war axe. He would not soil his sword on a criminal. That would dishonour the noble fighting men that had faced his blade in real combat. By Custom the axe was burned with the criminal's body. They did not stay for that part. Somehow Dlaria knew that Bdescu felt the need to dispense this final justice himself. He did not discuss it.

It took twenty days to tour the villages. He renewed acquaintances, took oaths and dispensed justice. News of the tour was now well ahead of them. Their small band was met by lines of children, waving and cheering. Boys scampered amongst their mounts and small girls threw posies to them. Everyone wanted to see the new Baron and his beautiful concubine. When they met Fenjents's detachment at the first Bdescu-Estate village, he sent his troops back to Castle Mnufort with sixty big strong recruits, along with detailed instructions for their training. Fenjent's eyes lit up when he saw the new troops.

"Hail, My Lord! I see you've been busy these last days! They look like good brawny lads!"

Bdescu slapped his knight's shoulder. "Aye. I hope they scare our enemies. They certainly scare me! And thanks to you bringing that gold, we'll double our forces before the rains come."

Bdescu dismounted, walked over to the Lady Nvuldera and bowed. "My Lady, welcome. Our plan is to inspect the villages, buy some new troops and carry out Baronial justice. Are you happy to accompany me on this?"

"My dear Baron," she smiled, "more than happy."

Nvuldera was dressed in a fine robe of russet brown. Her light brown hair whipped around her clear, aristocratic features in a smoky cloud. She looked healthy, her skin had healed and looked rosy and clear. She rode on his right, with Dlaria on his left. Fenjent took station slightly behind his Lady Nvuldera, who he guarded with near-religious fervour. Bdescu glanced at the knight and saw the utter devotion burning in his eyes whenever he looked at Her Ladyship Nvuldera of House Bdescu.

After their visit to the first village they had set up camp, eaten a meal around their camp fire and were seated on camp stools, talking in low voices. The men cleared up and went off to their own tents. Bdescu was left alone with the two Ladies. This was a moment that he had been dreading. He had absolutely no desire for Nvuldera. He liked and admired his sister-in-law but he loved Dlaria. He did not know how to manage two concubines. His simple soldier's heart was in deep conflict over the whole matter.

Nvuldera poked the fire with a stick. The flames licked up a little higher and the fine smell of burning jeltwood reached their noses. She shrugged and looked up at him.

"Dlaria and I have been talking. We often talked of you before you arrived. Not had much time together since you got back. When Rbunft, the Imperial Agent, called to tell us that Pdoverin was dead and that you'd died too, she and I mourned together. When you returned, she wanted to be your concubine. I had suffered a rape and wanted no man near me so I was glad for you both to go forward. You were patient and kind, as you've always been. Now I am recovered and I will submit to whatever fate My Lord has in mind for me. Gvant, you look troubled. Please do not be so on my account."

Dlaria kept silent and avoided his eye. He had never felt so awkward. Soldiering was much easier than this.

"My Lady, I am a simple soldier. I love Dlaria. I do not know if I can manage to love two women. I want to do what's best for both of you. I have always loved you, but as a sister. I have never desired any more than that. I admire your beauty and your courage, your nobility and grace. But I feel no physical desire for you. Tell me your mind. Speak freely, I beg you. Between us, surely we can make arrangements that allow peace and happiness for us all?"

Nvuldera smiled. "Be easy, my Lord. We are in the same mind. I feel exactly the same about you. You are my brother-in-law. I hope Dlaria is my sister, now and forever. I am more than happy to keep it that way. But how can we manage the Estates as two households without your presence to hold it all together? You cannot pretend to be my Master, especially once Dlaria starts giving you children, surely? You'll want to be with your woman and your children, not chasing over to House Bdescu all the time?"

He laughed in sheer relief. This was a problem he could resolve. "My Lady. I thank God that my feelings are in line with yours. The issue of managing the Estates is a problem, but your happiness is far more important to me than that. I could solve it, given time..."

Nvuldera was ahead of him. "I have a proposal for you, My Lord. The whole things is perfectly clear to me. Are you both ready for a truly shocking idea?"

He and Dlaria looked at one another. She beamed at him and they nodded together.

"Amalgamate the two Houses into one unified estate. Bdescu Mnufort Estate will be the grandest House in the entire Empire." He took a breath but she held up a palm.

"No, Gvant. Please hear me out." He subsided, nodding.

"Here we go, then. Believe me, My Lord, I tried running an Estate as a woman alone. It was impossible. I hate the idea of being alone at Castle Bdescu. Allow me to marry Fenjent. He loves me. It shines from his eyes like the morning sun. He is kind and gentle, like you. In fact he has learned everything from you and worships you. I have come to trust him, to be easy with him and lately, as I recovered I have started to find him attractive. Make Fenjent your Steward of Estates. He's a knight so it will be appropriate Role for his Rank. I'll be taking a step down in becoming a steward's wife but my status will be formalised. I will be married to your vassal, with your authority. With your iron man Fenjent in charge, not a coin will go missing or a field unploughed. The villagers already respect him. We had a bandit attack eight days ago. Fenjent got the message, armed up and was gone before I could count to a hundred. The raiders were dead inside the day..."

She ran out of words. In the silence the two women stared at Bdescu. He looked into the smoking embers, lost in thought. Neither woman took a breath.

"Yes. I agree. Fenjent does love you, I can see that. He is my Trusted Man. You are my kin. If he wants it as you do, then I will marry the two of you. I will do this thing, not because it solves a problem for me, but because you both wish it. I will go and speak to him now."

He stood up, still thinking furiously, and walked over to the soldiers' tents further up the field. Dlaria hugged her friend, who seemed to be weeping. Not from sorrow, she judged.

Bdescu found Fenjent standing at a camp fire briefing his group of Master Sergeants on tomorrow's plan. As he saw the Master approaching he shouted out: "Master on the Field!" The men sprang to their feet.

"Master Sergeants, I need to brief Sir Fenjent of Bdescu. Take a short break, grab a cup of wine at my tent. Tell Lady Dlaria the code word is 'Concord' and she will know you have my permission. Relax. You've done good work protecting our lands. You'll find out soon that good things happen to loyal Bdescu men. Go now."

When the men had left he asked Fenjent "My noble Knight, is it your wish to be married to the Lady Nvuldera? And for God's sake, speak honestly, Sir!"

Fenjent looked aghast. "I am truly sorry, My Lord. I know she is your concubine. I know that I may not love her. I swear by God's Holy Law that I have said nothing to her that might offend your Grace or hers..." he noticed that Bdescu was laughing and came to a halt.

"Ah, how complicated all this is! It's so much easier to kill a man than manage these affairs. Fenjent, I do not love Nvuldera. Nor she me, except as a brother. She does not want to be my wife, nor my concubine. I love Dlaria and want her as my own. I cannot marry them both but I do want to take Dlaria as wife so that her children become my heirs. Two women is one too many for a simple warrior. So, the proposition is that I make you my Steward of Estates, you marry Nvuldera and you look after my property. She suggested it. That means she loves you enough to take a big step down in Rank. Not many women love a man, or trust a man, enough to take such a long step down. So, old friend, what do you say? Do you want to give up your carefree knight's life and take on three daughters, a posh wife and the job from Holy Hell, working for the World's Worst Taskmaster?"

"You're not kidding, are you Master?"

"No lad, I'm not kidding. Look me in the eye and tell me the truth. Do you want this?"

"Yes. Ah yes, My Lord. I do. I do want this. All of this. Ah if it please you, Master..."

Bdescu hugged him. "You must now come with me and get on your knees before Her Ladyship. When she has accepted your proposal in a formal way we can go ahead and tell your men."

Dlaria cried as Fenjent proposed and Nvuldera accepted.

In the morning, they assembled all the troops, all the villagers and farmers in a field outside the village. Bdescu, standing on a cart, announced his forthcoming marriage to Dlaria, the betrothal of his beloved sister-in-law to his Trusted Man Fenjent and a public holiday for the weddings. Free drinks and food, all persons invited to Castle Mnufort for the party.

When the cheering subsided, he held up his hands and motioned for silence.

"By my Rank and Position, I make field promotion in God's Holy Name this day. Sir Fenjent of House Bdescu is Advanced to Earl-Colonel and Master of the Guard, Steward of my Estates. His wife to be will therefore keep her Rank and Position as Lady. The Earl Fenjent will announce his own Advancements from the Trusted Men of his choosing, subject to my approval. We will arrange Freeman Sergeant Advancements later. May all men know that the Earl and his Lady rule with my authority. Sir Fenjent, to me!"

The bemused Fenjent knelt at his feet on the cart bed. Bdescu carried out the Advancement under his drawn sword.

"Arise, Earl of Bdescu and Mnufort! Take your Rank and Position in the service of the God-Emperor!"

The cheering was wilder, as Fenjent's men reacted to the astonishing largesse handed out by their grim Lord. Advancement had meant nothing under Mnufort or Bdescu before. Now they'd seen a humble, decent man elevated to Lordship in a few years of loyal service. The implications of that worked their way into everyone's conscious.

There were parties in the camp that night. Fenjent and Lady Nvuldera were the centre of attention, with people clamouring questions and congratulations. Bdescu slipped away. He had business with Dlaria under a very warm blanket.

Call to Fall

Winter had come and gone. The Estates had survived a very wet, unusually cold winter and were flourishing in the hot summer sun. Fields were filled with grains, animals fattened and orchards and vineyards were hung with fruit. Bdescu was married and contented. Dlaria had recently borne him a son. The birth had been trouble-free, although Bdescu had worried himself into a state of near collapse. The boy was a large, lusty baby and they had named him Byardil. Bdescu thought that the girls would spoil him but he was healthy. Her milk ensured a well-fed baby, she was radiant with pride and he was delighted.

Nvuldera, over at Bdescu Castle, was heavily pregnant. Fenjent had told him that if she gave them a boy, they'd name him Cvelthan after their old mate and if a girl, Nvuldera insisted on Dlaria. Both choices delighted Bdescu and his happy wife.

They had bought and trained soldiers. Freemen had flocked to join them over the winter and Bdescu and his Earl had chosen wisely, hand picking men by testing, detailed questioning and physical challenges. They now commanded four hundred armed, trained men. The Estate's single boundary was thoroughly patrolled. Bandits kept away now that so many of them had been killed or driven off. Vrabelm had sent gifts for the Baron's wedding and Bdescu had held out an olive branch and had invited them. None had come, pleading ill-health. He'd been glad. He'd never been good at playing politics.

On a sunny morning Bdescu was on the terrace behind the castle with Fenjent and his four newly-Advanced Knights. All were proven Trusted Men. Three of them had been with Bdescu as he had re-taken Castle Bdescu from the brigands. Fenjent chose men of his own stripe: decent, brave and loyal. Bdescu was increasingly relaxed about his subordinate, who was growing well into his role under the Baron's tutelage.

Bdescu now had detailed maps of all his lands. A large-scale map was spread on a trestle table under a Fredil tree that was heavy with bright pink fruits.

"Now, here's where we share a border with Vrabelm. At first the raiders came across there. Vrabelm thought he had nothing to fear from two helpless women and a few aged retainers. Now he sends them around to here – and here – to come at us unexpected." He pointed at the map.

Fenjent had questions. "My Lord, we've had no incursions for a season now. Perhaps he's learned his lesson? Or is he planning something new? The old methods ain't working for him, are they?"

Bdescu smiled grimly. "No. Bvarinu, your report, please."

Bvarinu was one of their crippled ex-soldiers. With his missing leg and a wooden peg in its place, nobody thought him a threat. But he had sharp eyes, a good memory and a natural cunning. Bdescu had made him a spy. He roamed the villages outside their lands, selling toys from a cart full of children's puppets, picking up gossip. His mission was to find out more about Clan Vrabelm.

Bvarinu was the only one seated. He had permission to speak thus. "My Lords. Knights. The factors from Clan Vrabelm have paid good coin for mercenaries. I've seen a column of around eighty men joining their banner. A man I trust in one of their villages claims they have almost two hundred mercenaries under arms. Which looks about right to me. It matches the numbers of mounts that their grooms are tending and the food their factors are stocking in. So I think two hundred is correct. Sirs."

Fenjent spoke first. "Excellent job, Bvarinu! And My Lord Bdescu and Mnufort for putting you out there as our spotter. Two hundred men? Are they planning a full-scale invasion? Is it war?"

Bdescu shook his head. "I doubt it. They're probably as aware of our strength as we are of theirs. They have no war experience. They must know we'd crush them on an open field. It must be something more underhand and we must be on guard. Double the patrols. Warn the men. Arm up. Sharpen blades, ramp up training. How's the segmented armour coming along?"

Fenjent had over a hundred of the Byekiy-style cuirasses back from the smithies and ready for deployment. "Good. Issue at once, starting with us. Then one man in ten chosen randomly throughout the ranks. Train the men to fit it and service it. Then get them training in it. Now, the new bows. How are we doing with archery?"

Fenjent grinned. "It's much harder to use the war-bow than our hunting bows. Drawing the heavy bow back as far as your ear plays hell with sighting. It's more instinct than eye-line. But the men are getting used to it. The butts are packed every fine morning and we're coming along fast."

Bdescu looked seriously around his assembled officers. "Look at the site of this castle. There's a clear open space all around the building so that we can see an enemy. Yet the trees are not too far away. The trees are big, mature ones that take a deal of cutting down. The roads enter the trees then turn sharply away. Please explain why I want it like that." He folded his arms and looked around the men.

Bvarinu looked uncertain but spoke up clearly. "My Lord. I think the trees are there so that an enemy cannot use trebuchets or catapults without coming into arrow range. Same applies to a straight road; they could build siege engines of any kind out of bowshot, then walk 'em up to us and give us a lot of pain. But the narrow roads, sharp bends and big trees stop 'em from doing that...Sir."

Bvarinu saw the slow smile on the master's face and knew he was right. "Well done, lad! So, what this means is that we don't need pinpoint accuracy yet. We need heavy arrows, shot from embrasures or off battlements, at a hell of a rate, to stop an enemy from escalade or battering ram. Because knocking our walls down is not so easy, boys. Come up nice and close and we'll kill you where you stand! Castle Bdescu is built the same way. My granddads knew their tactics."

The knights laughed. All fighting men seek a leader who knows the game of war. They trusted their Baron. He had one more item, his usual question. "Any questions or suggestions?"

One knight thought they should test the early warning system against a whole village being taken over. "Good thinking, Sir Knight! See to it yourself. Report results to Fenjent. Anyone else? No, then you're dismissed, gentlemen. Wine and food in the dining hall at the next bell. See you there."

They walked away, joking and laughing together. Fenjent stayed behind. "Morale report, Sire. I believe we are at combat readiness. Training is complete. We have to adapt to the new armour but it's easily done. Stocks of arrows are at full. Spears also. All inventory is complete at both Houses. I have zero desertions, zero sick or injured, all men battle ready. Spirits are high. I stand by my last report, we could fight a full battle today if need be."

Bdescu grinned evilly. "Good lad. Now let's go find a way to fuck these Vrabelms right in the arse! As the Baron-General used to say, hit 'em back first!"

The knights followed their captains into the hall, chuckling.

Bdescu ate heartily, with Dlaria at his left side and Fenjent at his right side. As he raised his glass in the Loyal Toast to the God-Emperor, a soldier came into the hall. Fenjent called, "Report!"

"Sire, my Lords and Ladies. There's a delegation outside from Sire Flantr, the Rector of God's Chosen. He asks that my lord Baron comes immediately to see him on a matter of State. Sirs."

Bdescu was puzzled. Why in the name of Holy God would the Empire's most senior clergyman want to see a Baron? What matter of State?

He turned to Dlaria. "I must go. This man is senior to me. Plus he has the ear of the Emperor and he's friendly with Rbunft, Head of Commissary, the Emperor's finance manager. Everyone stays here until I get back."

He looked hungrily into her eyes. "My love, I hate to leave you. You must defend the hearth and family. You know the plans. Fenjent will run the evacuations and patrols. Please concentrate on getting our people inside, settled and safe. You have my trust, along with my love."

She smiled up at him and nodded once. He hugged her hard, then kissed her swiftly.

"Fenjent, to me!"

In the lobby he whispered urgently to his second in command. "Lock down. Get every farm's family into one of the castles. Tell them to bring only cash, bedding and food. We are good for water, both castles have deep wells and full cisterns. Strip everyone off the land so my people cannot come to harm. If we are attacked, they will never be hostages. The headmen are all briefed. We have practised for this day. Initiate full emergency patrol protocols. Arm up and be ready. Leave three of our four new knights here. My Lady will direct the defence. You get off home, to direct forces for Nvuldera. Your wife is in a delicate state. She won't sleep unless you are there. She will give you a copy of the defence plans and show you some tricks that I put in place a long time ago. A few small surprises for when an enemy knocks on our doors." Bdescu grinned, a savage humour.

"Four bells after I leave, send scouts to watch the city. If they see a force heading this way, then you'll be ready."

"If I'm not back in three days, do NOT reinforce failure by riding to His Holiness' palace with half the troops and trying to get me the hell out. Take a small group, civilian clothes and hidden weapons. Scout the town, pick up intelligence, plan and act. Just as I've taught you. Oh, and listen to My Lady. She's not just gorgeous, she knows all my plans. Clear?"

Fenjent let out a breath. "Clear, My Lord. How much trouble are we in?"

"A lot. Fucking bound to be. Smells like rotten fish to me. But no armed men are allowed in the Holy Palace, so I can't take a guard. Not so much as a sword. I have to spring it, if it's a trap. Watch over my girls – and my boy."

"With my life, Sire."

Bdescu stripped off his sword belt that held Summer's witch-blade and handed it to Fenjent. He took off his knife too. He grabbed a smaller dagger from the rack and concealed it under his clothes with a wry grin. He shook Fenjent's hand and strode out of the castle to his waiting mount. The palace messenger waited impatiently alongside.

Bdescu mounted and rode off with the Holy Palace's messenger. Dlaria waved to him from the top of the keep. He looked back and saw her, holding his baby on her hip and waving with her free hand. He waved back once and disappeared around the bend.

The messenger said little. He had no idea what this business was about and Bdescu soon tired of asking him. They rode hard. After a bell or so they reached the cross roads and there stood a couple of other retainers holding fresh mounts. They changed mounts and kept up the killing pace. Bdescu had no inkling of why this forced pace was required but it must be an emergency. Perhaps the Emperor was ill? At dusk they changed mounts again and kept up their pounding rhythm in starlight until they finally reached Gvorbia, the city that housed the Vicar of God's Chosen and his palace. It was late and the streets were quiet. A few drunks and beggars were all they saw as they rode through the streets.

Suddenly, the streets of this unremarkable town widened dramatically into a broad, tree-lined boulevard. At its end, the sprawling baroque edifice that was the Palace of God on Earth. Its white walls reached to Heaven. The walls were surrounded by a wide and reputedly deep moat, tapped off the nearby river by an underground culvert. Four towers reared above the walls at its four cardinal corners and two lesser towers flanked its main gates. The bronze-clad gates were thrice the height of a man. Bdescu had been thrilled to visit here as a child. He had not returned since. This visit gave him no such thrill, just an abiding sense of unease. He was bone-tired after the long ride. He longed for his hot bath with Dlaria soaping his back and giggling as she slipped and slid around him. He felt a deep desire for his dark-haired wife. He shook his head angrily and tried to concentrate.

At the open Palace gates they dismounted and handed their mounts to waiting grooms. The messenger led him into a lobby and bade him wait. It was a squarish room with a door in each wall. The exterior door was behind him, one ahead and one each to his left and right. It was lit by many candles, their perfume sweet but cloying on the warm evening air. The lobby was extraordinarily ornate. Every surface was etched, relieved, gilded or adorned. Model angels flew from plaster mouldings inset into the walls. Paintings of God and holy men were hung in profusion on almost every wall, above doors even. The doors themselves were carved with scenes from holy books. The effect was impressive but to his view, a little gaudy. He preferred his religion more austere, with its emphasis on Duty.

The exterior door slammed shut behind him. Instinct made him draw the concealed dagger. The three other doors flew open and men poured through. The men were huge muscular types, their bulky torsos naked and glistening with oil. They wore breeches of rough fabric. These were the legendary Soldiers of God. Men so terrifying, so fearless that mothers used them to frighten naughty children. The nearest man threw himself at Bdescu and impaled himself on Bdescu's dagger. Another crashed into Bdescu from the side and the weight threw him to the smooth tiled floor. His wrist, still holding the dagger, was pinned under the weight as bodies piled on top of him. With agonising slowness, his wrist bent. And bent. And broke. He screamed. Something foul-smelling was clamped over his face. He held his breath for as long as he could, but the foul smell crept into his nostrils. In a few beats the excruciating pain in his wrist forced him to gasp in air. The foul stuff passed into his lungs and he lost consciousness at once.

Tearing pain brought him around. He was lying on a cold floor of expensive polished stone. He could see an extensive room, well-lit and ornate as all were in this decadent place. Hands spun him around, rotating his body easily on the smooth surface. He looked up and saw a dais with two very comfortable chairs. In one sat the Rector of God's Chosen, Flantr. He was a fat man with pouches under his eyes. He wore beautiful robes of the finest fabrics. He wore gold rings with stones as large as birds' eggs. His eyes were small and bright.

On the other chair sat the tall, lean figure of Rbunft, the Imperial Commissar. He stared at Bdescu.

"Oh dear. Baron Fucking Bdescu AND Mnufort? Who in the name of God do you think you are, eh? When people say a man is dead, I want him fucking dead! First you lose the battle, you pathetic arse. And you get stabbed. A fatal wound, they tell me. Under the armpit and right through the chest. Heart and lungs, one hundred fucking percent fatal. But are you dead? Nope. Here you are, large as life and ten times more inconvenient. Not dead, so I've been misinformed and somebody will die for that. Now you're running around killing my friend's agents, rescuing women that I have just given to somebody else. On top of that, you're promoting fucking commoners! Making knights, in the name of the Holy Arsehole. Have you lost the tiny amount of brains that God granted you? What did I tell you? We need TREES, Bdescu. Wood. Timber, you stupid barn-bred yokel fucker. You were supposed to beat the Byekiy and cut down trees. Float them down the pissing river. Not too hard, was it? Apparently it was. An army lost. The Baron-General dead and without issue. And you playing Baron of Every Fucking Thing in the Realm!"

Bdescu had a gestalt flash of pure insight. He looked up at the Commissar. "Rbunft, did you order the murder of my brother?"

Both men looked startled. Bdescu's eyes watched them closely.

Flantr spoke. "Nobody murdered your brother, cretin. He died of the plague. I wish to God you'd been with him."

Bdescu laughed bitterly. "So it was you, not Rbunft. The so-called man of God killed my brother. My brother was a God-fearing man. You were often at his House. His wife didn't like you, nor did she trust you. But he did, and he died for it. I knew it was you, shit spawn."

Flantr looked confused. "Why ask Rbunft then?"

Bdescu shook his head. "It doesn't pay to teach criminals the secrets of interrogation."

Rbunft and Flantr laughed but in a hesitant, off-key way. Flantr spoke in a melodious bass rumble. "Oh, very good, Baron. Keep guessing. You are a fine soldier, I believe. Not good enough to beat the Byekiy rabble, of course. Oh dear. But really, you've no fucking idea, have you? You think the Emperors run the Empire? Let me enlighten you. The Emperor is a halfwit inbred. He likes playing with dolls and molesting little boys. He's just stupid enough to do as we tell him, just as his idiot father did before him. He'll sire a child, a boy successor. It won't actually be his. He couldn't impregnate a woman if his life depended on it. The child will be ours. Mine, Rbunft's, it doesn't matter. He'll do as he's told too, and we can rule with more direction."

Bdescu was shaken to his heart. He felt sick. His brother had been murdered to gain control of the family Name and lands. His world felt like it had punctured, the air rushing out of it like a bladder in a child's game. The ache in his wrist was forgotten. But even the murder was nothing compared to this monstrous duplicity, the betrayal of everything he'd been brought up to believe.

"So, our esteemed celibate Vicar of God's Chosen has a family, eh? An oath breaker, an apostate, a murderer and a thief." Bdescu spat the words.

Rbunft ignored him and spoke directly to Flantr. "What's the plan, Your Holiness?"

"The Barons all know he's back. The name Bdescu carries weight. He's the only one of his Rank who has escaped from the Byekiy. Minstrels are singing about him in taverns and village greens. He's rapidly becoming a fucking folk-hero!"

Bdescu caught this. "All your other armies got beaten too, did they? Not just Mnufort and me, was it? You lied to us. You knew all about the Byekiy, didn't you? You sent men to needless deaths with dreams of Advancement and wealth. Why? Because you're so steeped in lies that you couldn't bear to be honest, could you? You manipulate people out of reflex."

"You've no idea how to beat the mountain men, have you? Easy to be brave with other men's lives, you cowards. But not so easy to beat a bunch of hillbillies, eh? There're coming, My Lords. The Fifth of Five is coming for you. You think you can mock her, that she's just a weak woman. Oh dear me... I have the advantage over you. I've faced her on a practice floor. I've felt the hammer of her forces. You've lost Mnufort and you intend to kill Bdescu. And when Bdescu's gone, who will protect you from the beaks of the Snowhammers, then? The other Barons? Weak, divided and squabbling, thanks to you. The only two Barons who knew how to beat the Snowhammer Legions will be gone. And you two limp-dick useless criminals will face her wrath all alone, you sad, sad men."

Flantr made a gesture. Bdescu felt a sharp pain as one of the Soldiers of God kicked him in the spine.

"Be quiet, little man. We're not impressed by your mythical birds. Since you were beaten by the "hillbillies" you're obviously not the man to protect us, the Empire or anything else. On the plains, on our ground, the cavalry will crush them. Meanwhile, shut your yapping mouth and let the grown-ups discuss your death." Rbunft grinned at him as he writhed in pain.

Flantr continued. "We must keep our hands clean. First of all, I cannot spill blood in the Palace of God, you know that. I can get away with almost anything, but if that got out, the game would be up. Politically, we have a problem too. The Barons like this worm - as they liked his infuriating father and his intransigent brother. Bdescu's married the Baron-General's wife instead of just keeping her as a concubine. The other Barons like that, it's tradition. But he didn't cut the other concubine off, his sister-in-law, like a normal man would. Nope, he married her to his vassal. Then he promoted the vassal so she wouldn't lose Rank and be humiliated. The damned Barons love this tradition shit. He's got a fucking admirers club. They're dining out on stories about his fucking exploits. Basically, they all wish they were him. He could unite the Barons against us. We must be able to face them and tell them our hands are clean."

Rbunft looked baffled. "But how?"

Flantr gloated. "The Church knows how, my Lord. We drown him. Then we stand up and swear on God's Breath that we drew not one drop of his blood, harmed not one hair of his head, and we did not see him die... see? Easy."

Rbunft laughed with sheer relief. "Flantr, you are always wise. No wonder God loves you! We'll drown him, then. But it must be done quickly. I insult this oaf for his political ineptitude, but he's still a damned fine soldier. By my guess, he'll have a contingency plan. Intuition tells me there's a rescue team somewhere. So, if we delay there'll be a troop of his crack freeman-sergeants baying at your gates within a day or two. We'll wait until the small hours and fling him into the moat. Simple as that?"

"Simple as that", confirmed Flantr.

Rbunft gazed down at Bdescu. "Bdescu, I am sorry in a way. I think you're a man who could have been a real asset, if only you'd seen the world for what it really is. Here's where you've gone wrong, my friend... Commoners do not respect people like you. They think you're weak. They'll talk about you behind your back and smile in your face. Fear is the only coin that makes them work. Slaves, freemen, knights, they're all the fucking same. They need the lash. They need rich, clever men to tell them what to do. You live in a fool's world. You half-kill yourself for Mnufort and what does he leave you, eh? A pretty little tart that he's already ploughed. A run-down castle with no soldiers to guard it. Pillaged lands full of lazy serfs. A life of hard graft. I make more money than you while I am sleeping! So does Flantr! My friend, you're so stupid, you'll be better off dead. Obviously we'll wipe out your whole tribe soon. Once you're dead we'll move on your castles. With all your family dead I can install a more... tractable Baron."

Rbunft stood up, kissed the sleeve of the Vicar's robe and swept towards the door.

Before he reached the door, Bdescu made his oath, speaking in his archaic but flawless High Tongue. "Rbunft. Flantr. You owe me and my House a blood debt. You think I have no friends, leave no legacy? Sleep lightly, traitors, because the vengeance of House Bdescu will burst into your halls. I swear that one day soon, one of mine will cut you open and leave you to bleed out like barnyard animals. I swear this on the Breath of God."

Rbunft waved a negligent hand and left the room. Flantr heaved his bulk upright and waddled out of another door. Bdescu was left on the floor, chained at wrist and ankle and watched by six of the massive bodyguards.

Bdescu tried to move his hands within the bonds. He looked down at his fetters. There was a steel hoop around each wrist, secured by a metal hook that had been bent over with pliers. Each hoop had a large ring on it. A short length of chain joined the two hoops together. The same arrangement held his ankles. Looking around the room, he was certain that he could loosen his bonds if left unattended for half a bell. One on one, he knew he could overcome a single opponent, even one of these wrestler types. No bodyguard is a match for a trained, blooded killer. These guards are used to subduing people, not fights to the death. The chains would be effective weapons for striking or strangling. But the short stride necessitated by the ankle chains was a real handicap. If all six bodyguards set on him at once, he knew that he'd end up in the moat. But he'd faced death before. His concern was Dlaria and little Byardil, the girls, Nvuldera and Fenjent... his people.

He was stiffening from the enforced position and his back and broken wrist ached abominably. As the candles shortened, slaves brought new ones. The room remained bright. From the floor he could see three bodyguards. He knew there were more behind him. He could hear them breathing. He tried to relax, to ready his muscles for his final attempt at freedom. He suspected it was futile but it was not in his nature to give up.

They surprised him.

He heard no signal, no command. There was a very quick shuffling of feet. He felt an awful weight fall on his legs and chest. A bag was pulled over his head. It smelled of old leather. He could hardly breath. Powerful hands held his arms and legs. He was turned face down on the floor. He heard more men entering the room. Without a word being said, they all took hold of an arm or a leg and lifted him bodily from the floor. He tried to struggle but there were too many strong grips resisting his muscles. All this happened without a word being uttered. It dawned on him that every single one of these huge men was a mute. Tongues cut out, probably. They walked effortlessly up stairs. Turning, up more stairs. This was repeated six times, until he was dizzy from counting the turns. Finally, he felt fresh air on his body and knew that he had reached his final destination, the top of the Palace wall. His last chance to die in action came and went. He could not move. Two strong men held each of his limbs. Without a word, they lifted him. He felt the cold hard stone of the battlement wall scrape against his chest as they hoisted him over the wall. One of them yanked the bag off his head. In his last seconds, he wondered why. Probably so that he could be truly terrified as he fell to his death. He stared down at the blackness below him. In perfect unison, they let go of his body.

Bdescu fell towards the stinking waters of the Palace moat.

Bdescu twisted as he fell, desperate to enter the water feet-first. He knew that if he landed on his head he'd be knocked unconscious. If he landed on his face or flat on his back he'd be winded or possibly break some ribs. He kicked down and hit the water at an angle, but thankfully his feet did strike first. The impact slid him under the water. He opened his eyes and tried to see which way was up, but clouds of bubbles and near-complete darkness made this impossible. He clamped his mouth shut and kicked. He pushed down with his hands, a frantic paddling motion. He seemed not to move at all. What he felt was the excruciating, lancing pain of paddling with a broken wrist.

His head broke water and he gasped in a lungful of the stinking air that hung heavily above the polluted water of the moat. Paddling frantically to stay upright, he looked up the wall and saw a row of faces staring down at him. He realised that the bodyguards had been told to watch him to make sure that he drowned.

He relaxed for an instant and sank beneath the fetid water again. For a couple of beats his exhausted body could not find the energy to rise again. Then a wave of panic surged through him and he lunged frantically back to the surface, ignoring the searing hurt in his wrist. This time he surfaced facing the opposite way, out towards the town. A silent line of implacable, oiled bodies lined the bank of the moat. One of them made an obscene gesture towards him. He sank again. This time it was even more difficult to rise. His clothing was now saturated, adding to the deadweight of the steel fetters. Yet his head broke the surface for a third time. He took a long, shuddering breath and yelled out.

"Flantr is a traitor!"

The effort startled the watching guards, which gave him an odd sense of satisfaction. He was exhausted. The moment he stopped his manic paddling, he sank for the fourth and final time. The pain in his wrist was now matched by agony in his forearms and shoulders. Wrists and ankles were rubbed raw by cold steel. He held his breath, no longer thinking, just clinging to this life for a few more beats, mentally cursing Rbunft and Flantr for their deceits.

His feet hit the bottom of the moat. He tried to wade ashore, but the thick ooze trapped his feet as he sank into it. He could no longer move. Nothing stood now between him and God. His lungs burned. He was out of time, out of life itself. He let go of all hatred and fear. He thought of Summer and her eyrie at the roof of the world. He thought of Dlaria, smiling in her sleep and little Byardil gurgling in his cot. He saw Nvuldera's joyful face at her wedding to Fenjent. He imagined Byardil, happy with his police constable. He wondered if Cvelthan had survived the wars. He wished them all a long and happy life and commended himself to his God.

With a shrug, he opened his mouth and took a deep lungful of water.

No water flowed into his mouth. He breathed a long gasp of air, Stinking and rather rank air, to be sure, but a lot better than drowning. He guessed that he had died and made a swift transition to the afterlife, whatever that entailed. He opened his eyes. Baffled, he glanced around. He blinked water out of his eyes but all he could see was the black water of the moat. He became more aware as he calmed himself. His clothes were still waving around in water but from the neck up he seemed to be in a sort of helmet of air. Water dripped off his eyebrows and into his gaping mouth. It was foul and he spat it out. It flew forward and hit something in front of him.

Someone took a firm hold on his left shoulder from behind. Immediately afterwards his right shoulder was gripped too. He would have jumped, except he was completely immobile in the mud. A calm and familiar voice spoke into his ear from behind.

"Bdescu, hold still. Stop gasping, please? We don't have that much air and we need to stay down here until those dumb bastards think you're dead. Slow, even breaths please. Oh, and congratulations. Forcing your head and shoulders out of the water three times was really smart thinking."

It was the Fifth of Five, Storm herself.

His shoulders moved under her hands but she could not tell if the Baron was laughing or weeping.

Printed in Great Britain
by Amazon